FALLOUT

Thrillers by Peter Hain

The Rhino Conspiracy (2020)
The Elephant Conspiracy (2022)
The Lion Conspiracy (2024)

FALLOUT

Beijing, London, Harare, Pretoria

Peter Hain

MUSWELL
PRESS

First published by Muswell Press in 2025
Copyright © Peter Hain 2025

Typeset in Bembo by M Rules
Printed by CPI Group (UK) Ltd, Croydon CR0 4YY

A CIP record for this book
is available from the British Library

ISBN: 9781068684470
eISBN: 9781068684487

Peter Hain has asserted his right
to be identified as the author of this work in accordance
with the Copyright, Designs and Patents Act 1988.

*This book is a work of fiction and,
except in the case of historical fact, any resemblance
to actual persons, living or dead is purely coincidental.*

Apart from any use permitted under UK copyright law,
this publication may not be reproduced, stored or transmitted,
in any form, or by any means without prior permission
in writing from the publisher.

Our authorised representative in the EU for product
safety is Easy Access System Europe, Mustamäe tee 50,
10621 Tallinn, Estonia. gpsr.requests@easproject.com

Muswell Press, London N6 5HQ
www.muswell-press.co.uk

MIX
Paper | Supporting
responsible forestry
FSC® C013604

For those who bravely waged freedom struggles against apartheid South Africa and racist Rhodesia – and the equally brave human rights activists in modern China.

Also, for those who have not betrayed the inspiring values of such struggles.

CHARACTERS

Amir Bhajee – ANC official in Harare
Ruth Brown – Jenny's radical aunt
Jannie Craven – young South African activist
Florence Dube – deputy Zimbabwe security chief
Jim Evans – British nuclear physics professor
Jonathan Fletcher – Green Planet headquarters official
André Geffen – Captain in Zimbabwe Air Force
Simon Jeffries – British 'Noted Person Delegation' member
George Kasinga – ANC chief in London
Thabo Kumalo – South African miners' leader
Oliver Magano – ANC's man in Lusaka
Major Keith Makuyana – Zimbabwe security chief
Selby Mngadi – senior in ANC's military wing, MK
Stan Moyo – Zimbabwe President's security chief
Moses Msimang – ANC official in Harare
Ed Mugadza – deputy Zimbabwe security chief
Wang Bi Nan – senior Chinese ministerial aide
George Petersen – ANC official in Harare
Shu Li Ping – official interpreter
Hu Shao Ping – Chinese student
Dick Sewell – Green Planet activist

Jenny Stuart – British political activist
Captain Mauritz Swanepoel – veteran apartheid assassin
Lesley Stapleton – Jenny's activist friend
Robert Temba – ANC chief in Harare
Venter and Coetzee – apartheid assassins
Jan Viljoen – apartheid agent
Harold Williams – member of 'Noted Persons' delegation
Jimmy Wentzel – South African human rights lawyer
General KJ van der Walt – head of apartheid intelligence and security

PROLOGUE

The cold, cruel wind had howled unremittingly all night across the lowveld, penetrating everything.

Finally, a sliver of sun peeked over the horizon, seemed to think better of it, and settled back.

A *dassie* surfaced, sniffed, twitched, then scampered down its burrow.

An owl, beacon-like eyes swivelling, watched and waited, knowing its hunting time would be over when darkness ended.

But inside, the prisoner had lost all sense of night and day.

The relentless bright light had seen to that. Whichever way he turned, or however tightly he closed his eyes, the glare pierced through, blurring him into semiconsciousness.

'We'll leave the light on to keep you company – so you don't get lonely.' The thick accent made the sneer more biting, the mirthless laughter more sinister.

They had gone with a promise to 'come and talk again', the door banging shut, then firmly bolted.

The prisoner was enveloped by utter loneliness – and numbing fear.

Fear of being forced again to stand at an angle to the wall, his feet a metre from it, fingers resting against its whitewashed surface taking his bodyweight. Simple yet devastating. Any slump, and a strategic kick sent him back into position.

At first, he needed complete concentration just to stop screaming. Later, his senses were so deadened he could barely produce a grunt in answer to the endless questions – eventually sliding down the wall, collapsing on the concrete floor, too exhausted even to groan.

As their voices died away, he tried to get a grip. The room was bare, save for some old sacks in a corner. The bitter cold disorientated him. Surely this was supposed to be a warm country? Well, not this time of year. Not at night anyway. Not here in this remote building.

Painful memories returned. Feeling groggy on the car's back seat; being lifted into a helicopter, half conscious, aware only of deafening noise.

Minutes later, bundled out again in the dusk and deliberately allowed to glimpse the total isolation: no chance of help.

Ever since his abduction he had implored them to explain. What did they want? Where were they going? Who *were* they? But no answers. Instead, more questions, more accusations.

'You're making a terrible mistake. Don't know what you are talking about. Don't know anything. Anything ...'

Even now, hours later, denials bounced round his aching head, seeming to echo away into the cold – only to be thrown back by the dazzle of light.

Then, through the silence, broken only by the unfamiliar screech of a hadeda, came a sudden, even more bewildering, thought.

They wouldn't go to all this trouble for nothing.

Perhaps I *am* guilty after all?

If only they would tell me what on earth I'm supposed to have *done*.

1

Bound for the Great Wall, the minibus assigned to the so-called 'Noted Persons Delegation' pulled out of the hotel parking area and threaded through a swarm of bicycles into Beijing's East Chang'an Avenue.

Professor Jim Evans, bookishly earnest, was fascinated by the cyclists' dexterity: weaving, dodging, avoiding buses and cars, their bells ringing incessantly – the din intensified by continuous instructions to passengers from loudspeakers on trolleybuses.

Even louder were constant exhortations from speakers attached to patrolling vans. Political propaganda? No, Evans realised: traffic control.

The 50-kilometre journey northward to the tourist section of the Great Wall took longer than expected. Although cars were conspicuously absent, the roads were filled with packed buses, lorries, handcarts, even more cyclists and bullock carts – some piled high with produce or live chickens in bamboo baskets. Also, families on foot: some leading goats, or driving pigs and cows.

Vast fields stretched into the distance, framed by trees lining the roads. Despite the sense of great space, the countryside was too full of life to be desolate. There were clusters of commune buildings, and peasants in their production brigades tended fields of grain and vegetables.

'What's that?' Jenny Stuart – charismatic, exuding warmth – pointed along the edge of the road where winnowed grain was spread thinly in bands several feet wide.

'It's laid out to dry,' Evans explained, 'the roadside's the only free land available.'

He knew that just one-tenth of China's land was cultivable. Other statistics almost defied comprehension – like the 35 million people employed simply to spread sewage on fields. For at least 4,000 years it had been the law that all excreta should be used as fertiliser, and collectors still called daily at every house with their barrows.

The driver revved his engine impatiently as they slowed behind a long queue of traffic in the foothills.

Wang Bi Nan, the interpreter assigned to them for the day, looked embarrassed. 'Sorry for the delay. We have chosen to visit our Great Wall on a Chinese holiday.'

Wang, a thin balding man with horn-rimmed glasses, had joined the minibus just as it departed, unexpectedly replacing the official interpreter assigned to the delegation since their arrival.

The minibus wheezed up a steep hill alongside a sparkling stream, which disappeared between neatly cultivated terraces towards the fields below.

Excitedly, Evans caught his first sight of the Wall. Built of great stone slabs 2,000 years before, when China was divided into warring kingdoms, it stretched more than 4,000 kilometres from the eastern seaboard to the north-west. It was the only human-built landmark visible from space: perched high, straddling hill tops, winding its way through distant misty mountains.

Wang singled out Evans as the bus eased into the crowded parking area. 'How about a photo? For your friends back home.'

You can tell them President Nixon stood on the same spot during his historic visit in 1972.'

'Will your reputation survive *that*?' muttered Jenny Stuart, sarcastically.

Wang took Evans by the arm and led him firmly up the wide steps onto the Wall itself. About ten metres wide and up to 40 metres high, the pedestrian section on top was paved and had parapet walls on either side where sightseers could lean.

Wang indicated key sights and trotted out historical facts and figures.

Then, pointing to the south-west, he said sharply: 'There! That is where you were yesterday at the Atomic Energy Authority Institute. Did you enjoy the visit?'

He swung round suddenly. 'I hear you were rude to one of our scientists.' No longer smiling, his eyes were hard, watchful.

Evans was at a loss for words. What could the interpreter mean?

Sensing his uncertainty, Wang continued: 'The scientist you sat next to at lunch was most insulted. Told us he had met many Western visitors, but none had ever questioned his professional integrity.'

'What? I don't know what you're on about!' Evans was bewildered.

Wang continued regardless. 'As you know, he is one of our leading researchers in nuclear energy. That is why we agreed to your request to visit the Institute. But our scientists are dedicated to peace. They are most upset that you might think otherwise.'

'But I *don't* think otherwise!' Evans' initial confusion turned to anger in response to Wang's manner.

Collecting himself, he said stiffly: 'There has obviously been a misunderstanding. Please apologise to my hosts on my behalf.'

Better to offer a straight apology. No point explaining his interest in the conversion from nuclear energy technology to weaponry.

'Have you been photographed for posterity yet?' Jenny called as the rest of the group joined them, clutching onto the handrail for the sharp climb.

'Let me take one,' she said as Evans nodded absently, his mind churning. He posed uncomfortably, hunching his tall frame, feeling embarrassed as the rest of the group watched.

'Damn it! I'll have to take another shot. Wang walked behind you that time and blocked the view. Smile please!'

They all took pictures of each other and when Wang firmly refused to pose with them, persuaded him to take snaps of the whole group using each of their cameras in turn. The light-hearted banter lifted Evans' unease.

Wang struggled awkwardly with the different cameras. He was so different from their official interpreter, with her friendly proficiency. Again, Evans wondered why she had been replaced.

A group of Chinese teenagers passed by chattering excitedly. One, wearing a digital watch, posed by the side of the Wall as another took his photo. Then he passed the watch around so each of them could have their picture taken, sleeves ostentatiously rolled up to show it off.

Another sign of creeping consumerism, Evans thought. He recalled the car parked outside the main gate of the ancient Forbidden City which they had visited on their first day. The queue of Chinese waiting to be photographed by the car's open door, their hands resting nonchalantly on the steering wheel, feigning ownership.

'I'll pass on your apologies.' Wang had approached quietly, making Evans jump and jerk his gaze back from the sheer drop to the rocks below.

'But if you want to meet other scientists during your stay you must avoid insults.'

With that, Wang nodded stiffly and strode back to the minibus, brooding in stony silence throughout the return journey.

Evans pulled out his notebook. At 33, he was one of the

youngest professors in the field of nuclear radiation. He'd made copious notes the previous day while visiting the Institute.

The place had intrigued him.

Not just the old equipment left by the Russians when they suddenly withdrew their technicians in 1960 after the Sino-Soviet split. Not the appallingly rudimentary safety measures on the main reactor. Not even their hosts, who couldn't have been more hospitable – the canteen at Aldermaston would never have turned out a twelve-course lunch of such delicacy.

No. It had been the scientist in green overalls who had spouted out facts in a machine-like monologue: an impressive feat, since his English was otherwise limited.

But some of the information didn't add up, and Evans had put question marks in the margins of his notes. Now, he flicked idly through the pages – then suddenly stopped, shaken.

The relevant notes had been neatly removed.

Captain Mauritz Swanepoel was sweating profusely.

Despite the cold weather, the tension got to him every time he set the mechanism.

His colleagues said he sweated because he was unfit and pot-bellied; his wife said his diet was so bad his kidneys didn't function properly.

He had a simpler explanation: fear. An odd emotion for a man whose trade was terror.

Earlier in his long career he'd been a member of the notorious Z-squad: part of BOSS, the South African Bureau for State Security. Named after the final letter in the alphabet, the squad specialised in 'final solutions' – the assassination of apartheid's enemies.

Swanepoel had become expert in making and sending letter bombs. First victim: Eduardo Mondlane, leader of FRELIMO, the Mozambican liberation movement, killed in Tanzania. Next, exiled South African student leader Abraham Tiro, murdered in Botswana.

Also, the device which killed writer and leading ANC activist Ruth First in Maputo – and the one which failed to detonate at the London family home of a British anti-apartheid leader.

When BOSS officially ceased to exist in August 1978, Swanepoel transferred to DONS: the Department of National Security. Then he joined the National Intelligence Service (NIS), where his expertise was much in demand. He dispatched letter bombs all over Africa, targeting organisers of the South African resistance movement: the African National Congress.

Currently he was an undercover agent in Harare, capital of Zimbabwe. He rented a house in Avondale, once a whites-only suburb but racially mixed since the early days of independence. Here, Swanepoel was inconspicuous, easily passing as a retired member of the old Rhodesian civil service.

Over 160,000 whites – about two-thirds of the white population – had emigrated to South Africa when Zimbabwe achieved majority rule in 1980. But some had returned, realising they could still enjoy a life of swimming pools and servants.

Swanepoel had stolen the identity of one such man: Paul Herson, a former civil servant who had actually died soon after moving to Johannesburg. Armed with Herson's documents, Swanepoel was sent to Harare to coordinate covert activity against ANC leaders based in the city.

Now, he crouched under a spotlight making final adjustments to the device clamped to his bench. Consisting of metal cylinders and wires protruding from a balsa wood base, it was slim enough to slip into an A4 jiffy bag, and could pass as a large book.

The trickiest bit was setting the gap between the contacts. The device exploded when pulled out by the unsuspecting recipient, leaving behind a small plastic disc attached to the inside of the envelope and positioned between the contacts. If they were set too close, the disc could not be inserted. If they were set too far apart, it didn't go off.

This one was destined for Robert Temba, the Harare-based ANC commander. South African intelligence believed he was training black resistance fighters in sabotage techniques and infiltrating them into the country. They also suspected he was behind recent bombings of South African defence installations.

Swanepoel gingerly fitted the disc between the contacts, tested it to his satisfaction and ran a final check on the letter bomb. Then he carefully inserted the device into a large envelope he had acquired from Harare's Grassroots bookshop. Its label would not invite suspicion.

Exhausted and stressed, he reached for a new bottle of his favourite South African brandy, KWV. Tomorrow he would drop off his package at a post office in the city centre amidst the lunchtime crowds.

Two days later it should reach its destination.

It was three years since the first limpet mine had exploded in the harbour.

Dick Sewell was thrown half-asleep from his bunk bed in the stern of the eco-activism ship. He hardly heard the shouts and screams of the eleven other members of the crew. The shock of the explosion battered his eardrums almost senseless.

Sewell dragged himself off the floor and made for the deck, hardly conscious of an ugly gash on his left leg, or his bruised back. Seconds later the converted 40-metre fishing vessel, belonging to the international environmentalist organisation Green Planet, started to list.

Numb and disorientated, he caught a glimpse of the Green Planet flag fluttering in the harbour breeze. Then a second limpet mine exploded through the hull and the boat began sinking.

Quick, get into the dinghy!
Move!
Where are the others? Yes – some already climbing in, some

jumping into the water. Shouts. Let's check – is everyone alright?

Wait ... where's Maria?

Sewell struggled back down to the bows where the young medic had been sleeping. Water was pouring in, the darkness was menacing. He thrust his way forward, desperately calling. Maria *must* be there!

Come on, come on, where are you? The mess was terrible: documents, bedding, food, personal possessions everywhere – and a smell of oil.

Through the gloom he spotted the medic's bunk. Or what was left of it. Maria's body, torn by the explosion, was sinking in the rising water.

Sewell shook her frantically, uselessly. Christ, no!

A shout from the deck: 'Dick, what the hell are you doing? Get out! It's going under!'

Sewell woke up with a start. His heart still pounded, and his mind raced as he lived it all again. His own horrific, recurring nightmare. He took a few deep breaths. Tried to compose himself.

Now he was on another anti-nuclear mission in a very different part of the world. He stretched out, arms behind his head. It was only 3 a.m. but he knew he wouldn't get back to sleep.

Muscular and fit, Dick Sewell was still haunted and hardened by the might of the explosion. Soon afterwards, he gave up his job as a PE teacher to work fulltime for Green Planet. He'd never regretted the decision. He felt privileged to have found his life's mission.

But his personal relationships suffered. He moved out of the small flat he had bought with his girlfriend in a working-class area of East London, rapidly being gentrified. She was fed up with him. He was increasingly obsessed with his political activism, and never around. Married to Green Planet – not to her, as she'd once hoped.

Sewell moved into a bedsit. He joined Green Planet's non-violent, direct-action group. He protested against the hunting of seals in Canada, and the dumping at sea of nuclear waste. He volunteered for an expedition to disrupt the annual massacre of thousands of pilot whales in the Faroe Islands. Such carnage. The hunters claimed they were killing for food, but it was really just for sport.

Was he a driven man? Boringly, exclusively, dedicated to his mission? Sure, he wasn't like other blokes. He didn't have time for women or drinking, but that didn't make him better or worse – just different. He could be content with that. Though sometimes he felt wistful for what he might be missing.

He was jolted back to the present by the snores and grunts of other passengers on the train. Soon it would be dawn. Out there was another country to add to his list: a new challenge in a strange place. He felt the usual excitement and fear.

But this might be his most dangerous assignment yet ...

Normally, Green Planet operated openly, but this time his instructions were to contact an underground group in China: a nation known for its intolerance towards dissidents. He'd need cover, of course. That's why he'd been told to join an official tour group so he could blend in.

Stomach tightening, he wondered about his task in Beijing, still hours away, on this long train journey from Shanghai.

Chung Kuo: the Chinese name for their country. Literal translation, 'Middle Kingdom': the centre of world civilisation, containing one-sixth of the human race.

Jenny Stuart remembered this as the minibus drove through the gates of the English Language Institute, not far from their hotel. She'd been asked to give a current affairs lecture to the students, and was feeling rather nervous.

'I've no idea how much English they'll understand,' she had confided to Evans. 'It's difficult to know how to pitch it.'

'I'll join you. Should be worth it – an English socialist lecturing the Chinese on socialism!' he'd teased.

They were accompanied by their official interpreter, Shu Li Ping. She was delighted to return to the Institute where she had learned English. Unusually, she had also studied in Britain for two years. She wore Western style skirts and blouses and quizzed Jenny keenly on the latest London fashions and pop groups.

But she was evasive when Evans asked about her absence earlier in the day. 'I was needed for other duties,' she replied, quickly changing the subject.

The chatter in the packed lecture hall hushed as they entered. Evans took a seat at the back while Jenny walked to the platform, watched curiously by 200 mostly male students. He could imagine how she was feeling: those nagging nerves whenever one was about to address an unknown audience.

'I don't like it when people speak in a self-indulgent way,' she had told him on the way to the Institute. 'It's important to make the effort to *relate*. You won't communicate anything of value unless you do. That's something we emphasise in the women's movement.'

As Jenny took her place at the podium, her tension seemed to vanish. She began by greeting the students. Then, with an air of authority, she quipped: 'I know I have blonde hair, but I am not Margaret Thatcher!'

The students burst out laughing as Jenny had hoped. She'd heard of the impact made by the British Prime Minister on a visit to China. She relaxed – and so did Evans, realising how anxious he had been on her behalf. He found himself studying her closely.

Aged 25, she was a South London social worker. She'd become active in student politics while studying history at Sussex University. Her tutor had been on the committee of the Society for Anglo-Chinese Understanding, and had put forward her name for the delegation.

Jenny had an enthusiastic manner and was good

company – though her penchant for straight talking sometimes caused offence.

Now she was forcefully defending her membership of the Campaign for Nuclear Disarmament. She questioned China's possession of nuclear weapons, and asked why it was reluctant to criticise America's escalation of the arms race when it condemned Russia's. She also challenged China's foreign policy: particularly its indirect support for extreme right-wing movements, and regimes like the Chilean junta.

'It is wrong to adopt a certain stance simply because it is the opposite of Russian policy towards a particular country. In the case of South Africa, how can China possibly justify its refusal to back Nelson Mandela's ANC, just because it received Soviet aid? Apartheid is an evil. Our two nations, China and Britain, should adopt a principled foreign policy not aligned to either of the Cold War superpowers.'

Jenny Stuart was a charismatic speaker: a quality Evans found intriguing in people who were not pushy or egotistical. He observed how her swirling white skirt and close-fitting jumper accentuated her provocative figure, in contrast to her usual jeans and shirt. But then he felt guilty. Was he objectifying her by indulging in such thoughts?

Jenny sat down to an enthusiastic ovation. He wasn't surprised. It was always a sign of success when the audience laughed naturally at jokes. Though sometimes, exactly the same jokes went down like a lead balloon.

Nevertheless, Evans was struck by how well the students responded to Jenny's ironic humour. And they had obviously followed her arguments closely because they were now vying with each other to fire questions: mostly about foreign policy and disarmament.

'Don't you understand,' one addressed her earnestly, 'the Soviets have been aggressors throughout our history. They even failed to support us against the fascists at a critical time in the

1930s. Now their missiles are pointing at us all along our border. Remember Czechoslovakia. Remember Afghanistan. Never mind Gorbachev – the Soviets are expansionary imperialists!'

Jenny responded to each point carefully and patiently, impressing Evans with her calmness and the way she treated every questioner with respect. The students were lively and articulate, making their points openly, often disagreeing amongst themselves.

There was none of the rigidity or uniformity Evans had anticipated. Nor were there any taboos. They applauded again at the end, and a small group gathered round Jenny, chatting excitedly, asking more questions.

She beckoned him over. 'Some of them want to talk to us back at their hostel. We can't meet them tonight because of the banquet. What about tomorrow?'

Evans was surprised, but nodded in agreement. He'd heard that Chinese people were wary of foreigners and didn't tolerate open discussion. Yet these arrangements were being made easily and spontaneously.

'You will be coming too?' A bespectacled youth with an intense expression addressed him anxiously. 'She told us you are an expert in nuclear technology. Please give her this.' He pressed a piece of paper furtively into Evans' hand and slipped away.

'A lively bunch.' The familiar voice of Harold Williams – another member of the delegation – startled him.

'They certainly are,' said Evans, instinctively pushing the paper into his pocket. 'I didn't realise you were here. Are the rest of the delegation with you?'

Williams shook his head. 'I was a little late. Thought I'd come and listen to Jenny. Polished performer, isn't she?'

With his heavy jowls, Williams had the slightly pompous air of a government official, which was what he had been. Something in the Foreign Office before his retirement the previous year? Evans couldn't recall exactly what he had said.

The interpreter Shu shepherded them outside to a blue-grey

Shanghai sedan, based on a 1950s Mercedes design. The most common kind of official transport.

Cars of different sizes and colours were allocated strictly according to rank: blue-grey for the lower orders, large, shiny black ones for senior Party cadres. As with all official cars, the rear window was curtained off – for reasons of privacy, Shu said.

'So ordinary people can't see who's being chauffeured about!' Jenny whispered sceptically to Evans.

Their driver banged his horn incessantly, hooting to announce presence, not to give a warning.

Back at the hotel, Evans drew Jenny aside as they walked with Harold Williams to the lift. 'Could you come to my room? Got something to show you.'

She looked at him warily, wondering if he was making a pass at her. But, intrigued, she nodded.

Inside his room, he showed her the scruffy bit of paper.

'Thought I should wait until we were alone. One of the students asked me to give this to you,' he explained, sheepishly.

She stared at it, perplexed: CHINA FOREIGN POLICY SINCE 1978. DISCUSS IN DETAIL.

'What is that supposed to mean?'

'No idea – looks rather like an essay title. We'll have to ask him tomorrow when we meet again at the hostel.'

As she closed the door, he looked again at the paper.

Another strange incident.

Should he tell her about the notebook, and the weird exchange with Wang?

Or was it simply too trivial?

The newsflash interrupted a music programme on Swanepoel's car radio.

'There was an explosion an hour ago at the Harare home of African National Congress organiser Robert Temba. Several people are feared dead, but no further details are available.'

Swanepoel let out a whoop of delight and speeded back to his house to contact his 'handler'. Almost immediately he began to think about the next stage of their plan: codename NOSLEN – the first name of the imprisoned ANC leader Nelson Mandela, in reverse.

His letter bomb had been delivered as scheduled. Scrutinised and scanned by the team who guarded Robert Temba's home 24 hours a day, it was passed to his twelve-year-old daughter, Nomsa.

'Can I open it, Dad? It's a package from Grassroots. Looks exciting!'

Temba had a lot on his mind that morning. He was in a 'Dad's daze', as his three children fondly called it: registering family life going on around him, but not engaging properly with it. Most of the time, he could only really focus on the challenges of coordinating ANC resistance activities.

The pressure had been intensifying relentlessly. Following Mozambique's non-aggression pact with Pretoria, most Frontline States no longer allowed ANC bases to operate from their territory. So, the ANC devised a new strategy: to ferment military action at home, in South Africa's black townships. Temba played a key role in this task.

Now, he glanced at the package, vaguely registering the bookshop label, and nodded to his daughter. Then he took the rest of the mail to his study, at the rear of the bungalow.

There was a deafening roar.

Temba instantly grasped the enormity of his error. In desperation, he tried to run towards his daughter – only to be knocked over by falling masonry and buried under rubble.

There was nothing left to identify Nomsa. No corpse. Her small body was torn apart: lumps of flesh and bone fragments, scattered through the pile of bricks and wood which had once been the family living room.

Some patches of dust were darker and damper than others.

Redder, too. A foot, torn from the child's leg, stuck incongruously out of a still-shiny shoe.

The ANC security guard was trapped under a collapsed door arch. He peered half-conscious at the gaping hole in his stomach and closed his eyes in horror. They never would reopen.

A grim silence descended, broken only by water gushing from broken pipes.

The Shanghai express pulled slowly into Beijing station as Dick Sewell leaned out of the window for his first view of the city.

Swarms of people filled the station concourse.

The overnight journey had been comfortable enough. As arranged with his Green Planet colleagues he was travelling incognito, with a regular tour party of holiday makers. They travelled 'soft class': in compartments with four berths, the thick mattresses and lace curtains signifying foreigners, senior officials, or army officers.

Locals travelled 'hard class', jammed together in wooden triple-decker bunk beds with no mattresses, exposed to the smoke-filled corridors.

Led out by a guide from the station towards a coach, Sewell was weary after the long trip, hours of sleep lost after his nightmare.

It was early evening, and he was looking forward to a shower. Then maybe a cold beer and a walk to suss out the bar where he was due to collect a package from an unknown contact the following evening.

Despite the city's humidity he shivered with apprehension.

The buzzer sounded at 9.16 a.m. in Major Keith Makuyana's office in security headquarters.

He picked up the phone immediately, listening intently, writing down details, asking questions, thanking the caller for his trouble: an old friend on duty at Harare police headquarters.

The two had been active in ZANLA, military wing of the Zimbabwe African National Union (ZANU), whose successful liberation struggle had propelled it to power in 1980. Now, they had an understanding: Makuyana would be tipped off about any politically sensitive incident. This would enable him to troubleshoot potential rivalry and jealousy between the police and his own intelligence organisation.

Makuyana's brief was to maintain links with the South African resistance – also to monitor the apartheid government's attempts to disrupt such resistance, or to interfere in Zimbabwean politics.

A tall, lean man, he always wore dark prescription glasses. This gave him an air of menace, though his staff worshipped him for his loyalty and kindness. Now he was on the phone to them, issuing precise, clipped instructions.

Exactly two minutes later, an unmarked Nissan estate car was waiting in the underground car park. He strode out of the lift and climbed in, with two of his officers.

Immediately behind was a grey Volkswagen Transporter, also unmarked. It looked rather dilapidated. Nobody would have guessed it was armour plated and contained a folding bed, medical equipment, a range of arms and sophisticated electronic gadgetry.

Makuyana reached his destination just ten minutes after his buzzer had sounded. Police and soldiers were milling about, cordoning off the bystanders, who had gathered in shock outside what had been Robert Temba's house.

The VW van had pulled up 100 metres away, parking discreetly as Makuyana's car arrived.

He quickly took control, flashing his ID with a word of explanation.

The house had been sealed off and was being searched. Makuyana restrained himself from a feverish urge to tear into the rubble in case there was still some life. He was close to the

Temba family and had enjoyed many hours of hospitality in the now unrecognisable bungalow.

Makuyana forced himself to search methodically. Obviously, the explosion had occurred near the entrance, where the corpse of the security guard now lay. No chance anyone else would have survived in that part of the house. He moved to the rear.

A shout from his sergeant: two bodies, then another. Two children and their mother, all dead, crushed under the building, covered in dust. The younger girl still clutched her doll – its severed head was lying beside her.

He turned, his dark glasses hiding his pain. Where was Robert? Had his old friend been out of the house? He felt a glimmer of hope – then he stumbled over another body.

The ANC organiser was lying flat on the floor, holding some brown envelopes, his head in a pool of blood. Makuyana stooped to turn the body over, preparing himself for the inevitable.

But then ... something unexpected. Years of experience had taught him that dead bodies felt different. He reached for Temba's pulse. Yes! A few flickering signs of life.

God, let it be so, he willed desperately.

Keith Makuyana had a reputation for being cool and professional under pressure – and for making decisions quickly. Sometimes that got him into trouble: especially when navigating internal office politics. But he didn't care. He was not a desk man. He came into his own in the field.

Now – as he considered the options – he fought to overcome the emotions of a close friendship lost. The ambulance would be here soon. So would the other emergency services and police reinforcements. He called his officers over.

'Cover this man up. I don't want anything showing. But treat him very gently. He may still be alive. Then get the other bodies and lay them out in the front garden. Leave a mark where you found them.'

Grabbing a radio handset, he spoke urgently to colleagues in the grey VW van. It was 9.36 a.m. – barely ten minutes after he had arrived on the scene.

Apparently, a fire had broken out at the National Sports Stadium over the hill along the Bulawayo Road, and there was still no ambulance. It gave him the opening he wanted, and he went over to the police guarding the crowd.

'Six dead, the whole family and one security guard: no survivors. Get those bodies on the lawn covered. I want them out quickly. There's going to be one hell of a political row, and we don't want anyone getting in the way while we investigate.

'One body is in a really bad state. My men have covered it up. We can't wait for an ambulance, so they will take it now. Then the forensic boys can come in and get a clear look at the house. They must leave no stone unturned. I want a full report. We *must* get to the bottom of this – and quickly!'

As he was talking, the grey VW van slipped down the drive, its sliding side door opening out of sight of the spectators. Temba's battered body was lifted gingerly onto the mattress inside the vehicle.

Makuyana climbed in the front and the driver radioed ahead. Not to the main hospital, but to special premises whose existence was known only by a chosen few.

On the way the VW passed an ambulance tearing towards the scene, siren blaring. Meanwhile Makuyana's remaining officers performed a rapid, systematic search, gathering up any legible documents. They had almost finished when the local police superintendent arrived to take charge.

Beijing was pitch dark when Evans and Jenny were dropped outside the imposing gates of the student hostel, where eight young men waited expectantly.

They looked like any group of students thought Evans, except for their shiny dark hair in neat crewcuts, open-necked shirts and cotton trousers – so different from the jeans and sweatshirts of their British counterparts.

'We were not sure you would come,' said a lanky youth, as he courteously led the way towards one of several drab concrete buildings.

No lift, so they climbed to the fifth floor. The meeting was in a room about 10 metres square – typical, they were told. Bunk beds on either side, desk at the end: lodgings for six students.

The students crowded into the small room, some sitting on the floor, others on the bunk beds and even the desk, their visitors given the only two available chairs.

As they were about to begin there was a late arrival – Hu Shao Ping, the student who had secretly passed Jim the note yesterday.

Short and slightly built, Hu looked older than the others. His eyes anxiously peered from behind round thin-rimmed spectacles, and he seemed to carry a heavy burden on his slim shoulders. Apologising for his lateness, he said he had been delayed at home: unlike the others he lived with his parents.

Soon a lively discussion developed about China's foreign policy, as tea was handed round in an ill-matched assortment of mugs.

The students argued, cracked jokes and told stories. Each was openly cynical about the ruling Communist Party, blaming it for betraying the revolution's ideals.

'Is anyone a member of the Party?' Jenny asked, surprised at their candid opinions.

Only one youth embarrassedly raised his hand, and was ribbed by his friends. Several volunteered that they had demonstrated against Party authoritarianism and the lack of democracy.

Others explained that, although the Party was all-powerful and seemed huge with its 42 million members, this figure was actually less than 4 per cent of the population.

'What do you remember of the Cultural Revolution?' asked Jenny.

She'd read of the tumultuous years after 1966 when Chairman Mao's young Red Guards had acted as vanguards of revolutionary purity, fighting for political and social renewal.

'You would have been small children then. Could we have had this sort of meeting?'

'Never! We would have denounced you as foreign imperialists and chanted at you with our little red books!' They all burst out laughing: thrusting up their hands, clutching imaginary booklets, punching the air in imitation of the Red Guards.

All, that is, except Hu Shao Ping, who had barely participated. He merely listened studiously, studying the two foreigners.

Evans, remembering Hu's request the day before, tried to draw him in.

'What do you think? Are they correct?'

'My father was very badly treated then,' he answered carefully.

A silence descended on the room as the laughter ceased and the others turned to him respectfully.

Evans sensed his diffidence: 'What happened?'

Hu slowly told his story in the clear, clipped English they had all mastered, encouraged by his friends whenever he faltered.

'My father is a scientist – a nuclear physicist,' he bowed to Evans.

'He studied first in America, but after Liberation in 1949 he came back to help build a new China. When Mao launched his cultural revolution with his famous swim in the Yellow River in 1966, my father was a respected member of his profession.

'Then some local Red Guards found out he had been a student in the USA, and denounced him as a "rightist" and an "imperialist", even though he had always been a communist.

'He was taken away one night by a mob and beaten. They imprisoned him in a basement room at his work for several months before he was dispatched to a remote village in the mountains.'

Tears welled up and were impatiently blinked away. 'My father had so much knowledge. But they made him work all day with a pickaxe in a quarry. Our family were all denounced as "rightists".

'My mother is a nurse – she was forced to clean floors and toilets of the hospital ward where she had once been supervisor. My older brother and sister were both expelled from their junior high school and assigned to street cleaning. I was still an infant, but we all suffered by being children of a "reactionary". They destroyed our family.'

'What a terrible waste,' Jenny murmured.

Hu sighed, nodding. 'The Cultural Revolution *was* a waste. A disaster. Over a hundred million people were persecuted. The tragedy is that Mao started the Cultural Revolution to rid the country of complacency, corruption and bureaucracy. He wanted to recreate the socialist momentum which followed Liberation. But it became a nightmare.

'Only after Mao's death and the overthrow of the Gang of Four – which had been running the country in his name – did things begin to improve.

'My father was brought back to work again as a scientist, though at a lower grade. My mother also got her nursing job back, and we children tried to make up for lost years. But my father never fully recovered his health. He is now retired.'

Hu paused, looking intently at Jenny: 'I told my father about your lecture. He wants to meet you both. Can you come to my home?'

As Jenny and Evans looked doubtfully at each other, he added quickly: 'Please do not refuse. I will accompany you on the bus later, and we can talk more.'

The discussion continued for a while longer, and then the students escorted their guests to the hostel gates.

'I've learned more tonight than from all the delegation briefings,' Evans remarked, shaking hands with each of them.

As they walked with Hu to the bus stop on the main road, Evans noticed how badly lit the streets were. Yet he felt safe – quite different from London, where he felt increasingly insecure out at night.

'By the way,' he remembered to ask as they reached the bus stop, 'What did that message mean: on the paper you gave me?'

'My father will explain. It is something important that he found when he worked at the Atomic Energy Institute. As I said, he retired only two months ago.'

'You mean the Institute at Nankow?'

'Yes.'

'I visited it earlier this week.'

'You *did*? Even better,' Hu smiled – for the first time that evening. 'When I told him of Miss Stuart's lecture and of her criticisms of China's foreign policy, and that you are a nuclear physicist, he immediately wanted to see you. You *will* come, won't you?'

The trolleybus arrived and they all climbed aboard. 'Can't you tell us more?' Jenny asked.

The bus pulled away, its doors swishing closed, and then stopped almost immediately to let on a tardy passenger. Panting, the man brushed past, taking a seat at the back as the bus jerked off again.

'I am sorry, I do not know all the details. My father was insistent on talking to you personally. He is worried about China's nuclear programme and its foreign policy. He also supports your strong opposition to the apartheid regime. '

'South Africa! What's that got to do with it?' Jenny asked.

Hu shrugged; he didn't know.

'I suppose we could squeeze in a visit tomorrow afternoon,' she said, and Evans nodded. The mention of the Institute had reminded him of the missing page in his notebook.

Hu smiled again. 'I will come myself to collect you. Your hotel is not very far away. And we can easily take a bus to the place where I live.'

'What is your home like?' Jenny asked.

'It is in a *hutong* – a traditional alley in the old part of the city. It's a small house with four rooms built around a courtyard compound. We share our toilet and kitchen with neighbours. It used to belong to my grandparents.'

He glanced out of the window. 'Look down the next street. If it is light enough, you will see our house sticking out from the first *hutong* on the left. I will meet you tomorrow at 5 p.m. on the pavement outside your hotel gates.'

'Why not wait in reception, in case we're late?'

Hu laughed, shaking his head. 'As an ordinary Chinese, I may not enter the hotel without special permission.'

Then he pointed: 'Look! There is my home. The one with the chimney sticking out above the street wall.'

The bus stopped and Hu got out, waiting formally by the kerbside until the doors closed and it moved off.

As his slight figure faded into the darkness, there was a shout from the rear of the bus. The driver answered, obviously angry. The passenger shouted back, and the bus screeched to a halt.

The back doors opened and a man climbed out. The same man who had boarded at the last minute, outside the hostel.

The lead story on Voice of Zimbabwe's news programme was brutally direct: ANC official Robert Temba and his entire family were dead after an explosion at his house.

There was a brief obituary praising Temba's commitment to the 'heroic struggle for liberation', and a statement from an ANC spokesman, angrily denouncing 'South African terrorism'.

In the safe house near the city centre, Keith Makuyana switched off the radio. So far so good.

But his immediate anxiety was whether Temba would pull through: he was still unconscious. They had taken him to a purpose-built medical centre at the back of the building, acquired several years before under a Presidential directive.

Very few knew of its existence. Not even the President's coterie of security and military advisers, who were rapidly becoming a ruling junta as the values of the freedom struggle faded fast.

Makuyana felt increasingly estranged from the corruption and authoritarianism spreading throughout the system. He was also unhappy about the fusion of the state and ruling party. The intelligence service would soon be a tool of Presidential fiefdom, instead of the guardian of national security.

But this was not the time to worry about the future. He had work to do.

The safe house resembled an old-style Rhodesian family home, now sandwiched between rows of office blocks: a relic of a colonial age in an area which had been extensively redeveloped. The spacious back garden was long gone – replaced by another set of buildings which could not be seen from the road.

The grey VW van was parked in a covered garage, next to several other vehicles. Beyond, was a central corridor with rooms on either side.

Down a flight of stairs, through a security door, was a central control room. It boasted a sophisticated communication system, which linked to the medical centre – and every part of the country.

A skeleton staff maintained its facilities all year round and monitored events 24/7. Now they were joined by others, who brought a sense of urgency to the usual calmness.

'Still no leads?' Makuyana was getting impatient. His officers recognised the mood only too well. They exchanged glances, as he paced round the bank of monitors, telephones and printers.

Despite a thorough search of Temba's ruined house, they had uncovered no evidence to trace the source of the bomb. All they knew was that the time of the explosion coincided with the mail delivery. The postman remembered an A4-sized package addressed to the 'special' Temba household, but it wasn't large enough to arouse suspicion.

Makuyana's team had interviewed staff at the mail sorting office, where the atmosphere was tense. They always took great care when handling bulky packages addressed to 'special' households. Letter bombs were a real nightmare: any rough handling or a small fault, and they could explode at any stage of their passage through the postal network.

But somehow, the Grassroots envelope had passed through the system, undetected.

'Run another check on suspected South African agents in the country,' Makuyana instructed. 'And ask for a priority monitor on any irregular communications to South Africa since this morning: phone calls, radio signals, the lot. Whoever was responsible must have reported back.'

A very long shot: his staff could spend hours fruitlessly combing surveillance records and double-checking intelligence reports – but there was little else to go on.

Makuyana strode through to the medical unit. He peered anxiously at the screen displaying Temba's erratic heartbeat, and listened to his comrade's fitful breathing.

'Will he pull through?' It was mid-afternoon and he needed to know. Perhaps the ANC man could remember something important.

'An outside chance,' the young doctor replied. She looked at Makuyana, sensing his anxiety. 'He's important – yes?'

'Very.'

She knew, and sympathised. 'I may be able to bring him round so you can have a few words. But the trauma could finish him off. He shouldn't really be forced prematurely into consciousness. My professional advice is to let him rest. But ...?' She held his gaze: questioning, not judging.

Makuyana looked away. 'Bring him round as soon as you can.'

His words ricocheted harshly off the stone floor, as he abruptly left the room.

2

Evans spent the day meeting more scientists, and being briefed by officials from the Chinese energy ministry. He also had time to think and update his notes.

He had slept badly. His mind kept racing all night: the confusion over the notebook, Wang's menace – the coming visit to meet Hu's father.

Now, with a free half hour, he forced himself to relax. He sat down on the steps of the Great Hall of the People, a short walk from his hotel, trying to imagine what it must have felt like to witness one of Mao's famous addresses to the cheering masses assembled below.

Tiananmen Square stretched out before him, the towering Martyrs Memorial honouring revolutionary heroes on one side, a vast area which had held over a million people in its time.

Now it was calm in the afternoon sun, as people went about their business, some pausing to stare at him. As a white foreigner, he was an object of curiosity, but their stares were respectful, not intrusive.

Evans found this place deeply compelling – even though he was wary of behaving like latter-day colonialists who patronisingly 'fell in love' with developing countries.

But he couldn't help being captivated by the straightforward dignity of the Chinese people, and the way their courtesy and old-fashioned formality contrasted with the informality of their attire. Even on official visits, open necked shirts and slacks were the norm, and he had been happy to jettison his own tie and suit for more casual attire.

Paradoxically, the more he discovered, the more questions he had: especially about the use of power, and how ordinary people lived and thought.

The influence of global brands took him aback. The minibus assigned to the group was a Mitsubishi, and the first thing he had noticed on the drive from Beijing's futuristic new airport was a giant billboard advertising the Japanese vehicle firm. Coca-Cola signs were also ubiquitous at tourist attractions.

Evans admired the way the Chinese had rebuilt after their liberation in 1949. Gone were the days when carts went round the streets of cities like Shanghai every morning at dawn, picking up scores of bodies of homeless paupers who had died in the night. Gone were the days when landowners used private armies to control and maintain peasants in a state of near starvation. But who was benefiting from all this consumerism? Certainly not the women pulling handcarts piled high with surplus produce from their communes to sell privately in street markets, their faces prematurely aged with fatigue.

The hourly chime sounded on his digital watch, which had half a dozen knobs and carried as many different functions: from a miniature calculator to an alarm. Better get back to the hotel, have a shower and freshen up before the sticky humidity of the evening and his important appointment.

But there was a note in his room from Jenny. She couldn't make it, so he would have to see the student Hu and his father alone. Disappointing – and disconcerting. He would have felt more secure with her: she was the politico; he just a scientist.

Evans poured himself a cup of jasmine tea from the thermos

flask which seemed always to be topped up. Every hotel room had one, together with a set of cups with elegant lids. Checking that his notebook was in his jacket pocket, he looked out of the window.

It was ten minutes before Hu was due. But the young man was already there, standing unobtrusively several metres from the gates, apparently studying the traffic, deliberately not looking at the hotel.

Then, Evans froze.

One minute Hu was there, the next he was surrounded by three men, hustled towards a black saloon in the hotel car park and bundled in. Evans saw him struggling, caught a last glimpse of his gaunt face: his expression of despair vanishing behind the car's curtains as the door was slammed, and the saloon roared away.

Despite the warmth of the afternoon, Evans shivered. He recalled Hu's haunted look; the furtive arrangements to meet his father – now so cruelly aborted.

Nobody seemed to notice, still less to care. Not the cyclists, not the pedestrians, not the tourists hanging around the hotel. Only *him*. And who on earth could he trust?

He felt a surge of disbelief, remembering the notebook incident and the confrontation with Wang. Then resentment. All he had wanted was to visit China. Just as an observer – not a bloody activist.

Evans sat down to pour a fresh cup of tea, nervously spilling it onto the table. An image of the stranger jumping belatedly on and off last night's bus flashed through his mind.

Robert Temba's eyes took an age to open. He stared dully at the two figures bending over him: one clad in white, the other wearing dark glasses.

He didn't want to wake up. Better just to lie there – but the dark glasses triggered something deep down in his numbed mind.

The glasses were signalling to him ... what? Couldn't get his thoughts together – and his body told him not to. Much easier to close his eyes and rest again. But the glasses kept shining, recognising him. Or was *he* recognising them?

Then a voice, also far away. 'Robert – can you hear me? It's Keith.'

Temba tried to bring the voice nearer, to get hold of it. But it kept slipping away.

He closed his eyes. Bliss. Leave me alone.

'Robert! Please wake up! It's important.'

Suddenly, it all came tumbling back. The face behind the glasses – that familiar voice ...

The instant he recognised his old friend Keith Makuyana, he remembered the searing, terrible roar of the explosion. Then the pain flooded back.

'My fault.' The words stuttered out of his dry, caked lips.

'What was?' Makuyana's voice: gentle, encouraging.

'The bomb. Should have checked. Must have been the Grassroots envelope.'

'Grassroots? Are you sure?' Makuyana sounded disbelieving.

'Yes. Sure.'

'What did it look like?'

His voice felt alien, like a machine. 'Large. Brown envelope. Grassroots label. My daughter ... No! Nomsa ... my fault ...'

He couldn't continue, didn't want to.

'Leave me alone ...'

His eyes were shutting. Didn't want to open them again – ever.

The doctor motioned Makuyana away and smoothed the blanket. Grimly, she checked Temba's pulse and temperature, focusing only on her patient.

Makuyana headed straight back to the control room, barking instructions to check out the Grassroots bookshop.

'It was a local job. Bastard could be based here in Harare!'

*

While Makuyana's staff combed the intelligence reports, Swanepoel was gazing at the evening ZTV news bulletin.

The broadcast led with his handiwork. Images of a shattered family home, bodies being taken away in canvas bags. Even he had to admit: it was not a pretty sight.

The bulletin highlighted the children's deaths. He sneered. How predictable. He had grandchildren himself, but black kids weren't worth his sympathy.

The Zimbabwean authorities were blaming 'South African backed terrorists'. That didn't surprise or worry him. They'd probably be looking for an outside group, and would focus their attention on the border.

He drove to a hotel where it was safer to make phone calls. Public call boxes were rare in Harare.

First, he called the mortuary, pretending to be a friend, and received the welcome confirmation that the entire family had died. Next, he tried to contact his handler – a businessman based in the city centre – but the man was unavailable, so he had no alternative but to make direct contact with Pretoria.

Direct dialling between Harare and the South African capital wasn't too risky. But as soon as he had given the codename NOSLEN, he was careful to disguise the conversation as a family matter.

There was a chance that the Zimbabweans could monitor calls to Pretoria and Johannesburg: direct dialling to the Transvaal area was via a satellite link, and they had the technology to listen in.

He'd been warned that computerised eavesdropping could be programmed to identify key words and phrases. They could 'suck' suspicious phone calls out of the jumble of routine ones, and record them.

After buying some hamburgers and beer, Swanepoel returned home to eat and relax. He missed the familiar tones of the state-controlled South African Broadcasting Corporation and avoided local television, preferring to listen to Afrikaner folk songs on his cassette player.

Reaching for a fresh bottle of KWV brandy, he filled and swilled his favourite shaped glass, the aroma drifting pleasingly up to his nostrils. People said KWV wasn't up to fine European brandies, but he didn't agree: no better companion to fend off the loneliness of an agent in the field.

These days he felt the need for such consolation. The job was no longer what it had been. His thought nostalgically of his youth: the discipline, the crusading spirit, the certainty. Crisp brown shorts, with neat turn-ups. Toe-capped shoes, always polished by servants. Summer evenings with friends.

Above all, the burning pride of Afrikaner nationalism, rousing a generation sick of the arrogance and paternalism of English-speaking whites. Those *Engelse* were so smug, behaving as if the British Empire would always be nanny.

How good it had been to join the clandestine Afrikaner nationalist group, *Ossewabrandwag* (Ox wagon Guard). An honour to be chosen by the elite *Stormjaers* (Stormtroopers) – a wing of *Ossewabrandwag* which supported the Nazis and carried out sabotage against the Allies.

His first experience of explosives was when he planted dynamite on a railway line, damaging a train carrying British troops. The man who would later become South Africa's prime minister, Balthazar Johannes Vorster, was a senior colleague.

Those were the days! A man really felt like a man, fighting for the cause. But the cause had become stale now: everybody was getting soft, including himself. He was well into the brandy when the phone rang.

'Long-distance call from South Africa,' the operator said, mechanically. 'Please hold.'

It was his wife Noeline, crackling down the line from their daughter's home in the small town of Port Alfred on the Eastern Cape coast. Unusual for her to phone.

'Is that you? Have you been drinking again?' she asked.

'Only a bit,' he slurred.

'We have another grandchild. Isn't it marvellous! Can you take some time off and join us? The family is coming down next weekend to welcome our new one. They'd love to see you.'

Swanepoel thought for a moment. He would have to lie low anyway after the letter bomb. A good time to return for a holiday.

'*Ja*, why not? I'm due a break. I'll make arrangements.'

He said goodbye and topped up his glass. An hour later he was fast asleep, oblivious to the significance of his wife's call.

'Still nothing, sir.' Makuyana's deputy, Ed Mugadza, looked apprehensively at his boss.

Dawn, the day after the bombing, and his staff had been working non-stop. No unusual movements on the border: extra vigilance at crossing points like Beitbridge hadn't turned up anything. Harare security reports were also unhelpful – and the Grassroots bookshop was still closed at this early hour.

'Alright, send the team home to sleep, but I want everyone back in five hours. Will you stay here? You can take a rest on a camp bed. I don't want to lose momentum. There's something out there waiting to be spotted.'

Mugadza returned after a few minutes. He needed a whisky, but his boss never touched spirits. Makuyana offered him orange juice instead.

'Unless the bomb was brought into the city to post, the equipment to make it must still be here,' he said. 'They wouldn't shift that about and risk getting caught. Put yourself in their position, Ed. If *you* had sent that bomb . . .' – Makuyana paused briefly – 'you'd have made contact afterwards with your superiors, wouldn't you? By phone – yes?'

Mugadza nodded. Radio contact would have been too risky.

'Right. Talk to our people at telecom HQ. See if their

eavesdropping system has picked up anything and ask for a print-out of every operator call made between Harare and South Africa in the last 24 hours. Outgoing and incoming. A long shot, but until we talk to the Grassroots staff, there's nothing else to go on.'

He motioned Mugadza away. 'That's all for now. Get some sleep. I'm going to check on Robert.'

He made his way to the medical centre. A nurse was at Temba's bedside, checking his heartbeat and adjusting his drip.

She looked up. 'He's not recovering. May not last much longer.'

Makuyana looked at his friend. He knew it was all over – as surely as he had earlier sensed life in the battered body amidst the rubble.

He found himself reaching for Temba's hand. Holding it, he gently locked their thumbs together, in the traditional handshake of the African National Congress.

'*Amandla*,' he said quietly.

'*Awethu*,' the nurse behind him replied.

Makuyana turned around, surprised by her response to the ANC's freedom struggle chant.

Then he murmured: 'This man is special – look after him, please.'

Earlier, Dick Sewell had sussed out the bar in downtown Beijing where he was due to rendezvous that evening.

Now he headed back, having avoided a group trip to a concert.

He was the only non-Chinese, and the place was packed with young people. Tables and chairs spilled out onto the pavement in the warm evening. No proper counter – just a little platform across which beer and a thin fruit juice were served.

'Do you speak English?' A girl in a grey tunic and matching trousers stopped politely in front of him.

'Yes,' he replied hesitantly.

'We are students studying English,' she said, pointing to a group watching them from a nearby table. 'Can we practise on you?'

Surely this wasn't the contact? Sewell looked at his watch: 20:20 – ten minutes too early – but he'd had been told English-speaking tourists could be politely accosted in this way.

'Yes, why not,' he smiled, 'but first, how do I ask for a beer?'

The girl giggled, ordered, helped him select the necessary yuan, and they returned to her friends.

'Are you married?' she asked.

What was this? A pick-up? Sewell resented the intrusion. He had an aversion to discussing personal things, and prided himself on being self-contained.

'No. How about you?' A characteristic change of tack: always ask a question to fend off talking about yourself.

She smiled. 'I am too young. We have a marriage bar of 28 years for men and 25 years for women. But some of my friends live together in their parents' home. The government disapproves, but still it happens.'

'Can I buy everyone another drink?' It was now 20:40 and he glanced around, worried. He was attracting mild curiosity, but nobody seemed to be taking a close interest.

The girl in grey reappeared to help him order again. 'When you return to your table you will see a large brown envelope leaning against the chair,' she said quietly. 'Please pick it up when you go – as if you brought it with you. It is very important. Good luck.'

The conversation continued for a while, then Sewell bid farewell, leaving them chatting. With the envelope tucked under his arm, he hurried back to the hotel, tense but relieved.

An hour later, when the students went their separate ways, a bespectacled youth lingered behind. Then he headed on his own towards an anonymous building occupied by the Ministry of State Security.

There he asked at reception for a Mr Wang Bi Nan. The two had an animated conversation, during which Wang reprimanded his informant for not discovering the identity of the Englishman.

An hour after the student Hu had been snatched, Evans was still in turmoil.

Christ, if only Jenny had been there! He'd looked for her without success. What would she have done? He was feeling increasingly guilty – but knew it was self-indulgent to panic. He had to pull himself together and do something.

He had to go to Hu's house and find the young man's father.

Evans grabbed his coat and scribbled a quick note, which he pushed under Jenny's door.

A trolleybus came almost immediately and he climbed apprehensively aboard. He was conscious of being scrutinised by the rest of the passengers. Most foreigners went about in cars or tourist coaches.

Hu's house was only a couple of kilometres away and Evans recognised the road leading to it. He disembarked and stood deliberately still, apparently consulting his street map, while other passengers hurried away. He waited, checking that none had lingered, then crossed the road as soon as a gap appeared in the stream of cyclists.

Nobody seemed to be taking any real interest in him. Not, he supposed, that he would necessarily have spotted a professional watcher.

Who *were* these watchers, anyway? He felt exposed, as he considered his next move.

Hu's house was just a hundred metres away, at the end of a network of *hutongs*. It was one of many small houses positioned in a web of winding alleys leading off the main road. It wasn't always clear where the boundaries of one compound ended and another began. The walls were mostly made of bricks and large stones set on each other without any mortar. Piles of rubble seemed to merge into the buildings.

The *hutong* was quiet in the evening sunshine, in contrast to the noisy main street, but Evans was unable to shake off his nervousness. Nobody else was about. Perhaps Hu would be there after all? He dismissed the thought as absurd.

Instinctively he walked on past the house, checking if he had been followed, then turned quickly into another alley, his heart pounding. Each minute seemed like an hour. He felt embarrassed, hoping nobody would notice his strange behaviour.

He peered carefully back down towards the main street. Still nobody in sight. He had a sudden memory of crouching behind a rubbish bin as a ten-year-old, hiding from his friends on the way back from school, and then jumping out to surprise them.

Evans slipped through an arch into the compound where Hu's home was situated. He knocked on the battered old door, and waited.

Knocked again. Still no response. He hadn't known what to expect, had come against his better judgement. Hadn't thought what to do if nobody was at home. He began to consider the alternatives. He could leave a note and return with Jenny later; but perhaps it would be unwise. Or he could wait – but for how long?

'Psst!' He swung round, startled. A young woman at the doorway of a house across the courtyard was motioning urgently to him.

He walked tentatively over. The woman was in her early twenties, obviously nervous. That makes two of us Evans thought glumly. Maybe he had knocked on the wrong house by mistake?

He was shown into a small room, clearly the living quarters. A table and chairs stood in the middle, and at the back was a large bed which doubled as a settee and had a fireplace built into its base for warmth on bitter winter nights. The ceiling was so low that he had to stoop.

The woman looked terrified. 'Hu's family gone. Nobody there. Empty! Empty! Go!'

Evans' fear surged, and he longed for the security of his hotel. He walked swiftly away, down a dark alley. Smells of cooking mingled with the tang of sewage, as the sun disappeared behind the houses.

A group of students walked by on the pavement, chatting. A mother pushed a pram made from bamboo. Life went on as if nothing untoward was happening. He had a sudden urge to shout out the truth – but then what *was* the truth exactly?

Sudden relief: a trolleybus pulled up across the opening to the alley. Evans, feeling absurdly conspicuous, jumped aboard.

Safely back in the hotel, he went straight to Jenny's room, and knocked.

'Who is it? I'm in the shower?' Her voice was muffled.

'Me. Jim. I need to talk, urgently'.

'Okay – come in. I'm nearly done.'

As was customary in Chinese hotels, the door was unlocked. He pushed it open and entered the room. A minute later Jenny came out, wrapped in a towel. Her blonde hair was dark from the shower, water dripped off her bare legs.

'Sorry to disturb you,' he said.

She brushed aside his obvious embarrassment, noticing he seemed pale and drawn. 'What happened? Are you alright?'

She stared at him intently, seemingly unaware of how disturbingly attractive he found her. Evans had to force himself to concentrate. When he had finished his story, she pulled the towel closer, staring at the floor. She seemed oblivious to his presence.

'S-shouldn't we inform our delegation leader?' he stammered.

Jenny shook her head emphatically.

'No! We're official guests. They would feel obliged to notify the authorities, who may be behind all this. And what exactly would we report? A missing notebook page? A student's story? An empty house?

'We'd better sit tight, Jim.'

Wang Bi Nan requested an urgent appointment with the Old Man. His office was at the end of a long corridor on the tenth floor of the state security building.

Wang knocked and entered, relieved the Old Man was alone. Normally, someone as lowly as himself would never get to see such an important government minister without being summoned.

The Old Man looked up from a pile of documents. 'Any progress?'

Wang stood in awe, having to restrain himself from saluting. The Old Man did not suffer fools gladly, and Wang spoke in clipped, formal terms, summarising events as precisely as he could.

'So – you intercepted the student Hu and his father before they could get to the English visitors? Very efficient.'

A flush slipped across Wang's sallow complexion. 'Yes, sir.'

The Old Man cut in sharply. 'But we still have another problem, do we not?'

Wang pursed his lips. 'Yes, sir. My student informer insists the Englishman took away an envelope. Although he did not see it passed over, he's sure the foreigner arrived at the bar without it. He didn't know the Englishman's name, but we must assume it is our friend Evans again.'

'I am surprised this Evans was not vetted for the Noted Persons Delegation.' The Old Man drummed his fingers in exasperation, swinging his chair around with his back to Wang.

Silence. Wang staring at the giant revolutionary paintings on the wall, their bold simplicity expressing confidence in the triumph of communism. Peasants, strong and handsome, striding confidently into the future with workers at their side.

Wang longed for the resurrection of that conviction, that mission. He still worshipped the Old Man, who alone remained uncorrupted whilst lesser leaders veered towards the market economy and the capitalist West.

Although China's one-party state seemed monolithic, Wang knew that there were many internal divisions and jealousies, some about ideology or policy, others about access to personal enrichment.

Periodically, prominent leaders found themselves 'disgraced': one day the fount of all wisdom, the next 'revisionists' or 'counter-revolutionaries', their rise and fall symbolic of factional battles teeming underneath the inscrutable surface of the state edifice.

Wang's eyes swivelled to fix on the frail shoulders sunk in the deep padding of the leather chair. He waited.

The Old Man turned abruptly. 'The Englishman presents us with a dilemma. We must be careful. We cannot afford to arouse the suspicions of our colleagues in the Public Security Bureau or create a diplomatic incident. He must meet with an accident. And keep an eye on the girl. Find out if she knows anything. Also try to recover the envelope handed over by the students at the bar. And the students themselves ...' – he paused, hesitating – 'no, leave them for now. They can be dealt with in due course.'

Makuyana woke with a start as his assistant Mugadza shook him hard.

He jerked awake and looked at his watch. 'God – ten in the morning! Why the hell did you let me sleep so long?'

'Bad news, I'm afraid.'

Mugadza's face told him everything. No clarification needed. Robert Temba had not made it through the night.

Makuyana dressed quickly, then hurried to the medical centre.

Neither the doctor nor the nurse looked at him directly. Just as well. Was there a hint of reproach in the way they silently washed the body?

'Thank you for all you have done,' he said quietly, as arrangements were made for his friend to be taken to the mortuary.

'We have some other news,' said Mugadza, following him out to the control room.

'There were 211 phone calls logged to and from South Africa in the period you specified. We are going through them systematically – though it could take days, even weeks, for a complete check. But one of the Grassroots staff said a man came to the shop three days ago. He bought a solidarity poster and some cards, and asked for a large jiffy bag to post them to relatives. She remembered him because he had a heavy accent and she wondered if he was South African.'

Makuyana didn't respond. His mind was elsewhere.

'We have a description,' continued Mugadza. 'A balding, overweight man, elderly: probably in his sixties. I'm having a photofit made up.'

Mugadza stopped. He had never seen his boss so distracted.

But Makuyana *had* heard – and understood – even though his thoughts were far away.

He was remembering an incident in the bush, many years ago. He and Robert Temba were tracking a group of South African soldiers who were on a sabotage raid deep into independent Mozambique. Suddenly they walked into an ambush.

Temba had saved them. Makuyana could see him now behind a boulder in the gulley, firing at the attackers, with his AK-47 fixed on automatic. Then lobbing three RGD-5 fragmentation grenades, just to be sure.

The four South Africans didn't stand a chance. How could they have known they were taking on the ANC's finest field combatant?

No wonder Pretoria had targeted Robert. Yes, they had got

42

their revenge – but they wouldn't have the last word. He was determined about that.

'Get hold of the ANC. I must talk to them,' he told Mugadza, softly.

It was late before Sewell was able to open the envelope.

Arriving back at the hotel, he had bumped into some people from his tour group, buzzing with excitement about the concert they'd attended. They insisted he join them for a drink.

He felt obliged to accept. He needed to blend in and not be seen as a morose misfit, for that might invite suspicion.

Now, he was finally back in his room. He spread out the contents of the envelope on the table, staring in amazement: copies of official documents, a couple of maps and several sheets with writing in English, meticulously neat, almost childlike. A map of the Gobi Desert marked a spot about 150 kilometres north of the town of Hongor. Another map indicated an area in the Gulf of Chihli to the north of the Yellow Sea: near the small islands of Tachin, midway between Penglai and Lushun.

As the documentation made clear, these were secret Chinese dumping sites for nuclear waste – unprocessed and stored in sealed containers for burial under the desert, or lowered onto the seabed.

To boost much needed foreign exchange earnings, China had been accepting foreign nuclear waste for storage. But alarmingly there'd been leakages – which the authorities had covered up.

Sewell was familiar with the technicalities. He knew that 'high level' waste was extremely dangerous, that it contained unused enriched uranium and fission products such as plutonium. He studied the details, absorbing the terrifying implications.

His responsibility was clear: it was vital to alert the world before a major international disaster occurred. Taking a deep breath, he carefully inserted the documents into a special compartment built into the bottom of his suitcase.

There was nothing more he could do until he got home. To avoid suspicion, he must stay with the group for the remainder of the two-week tour: a few more days in Beijing, followed by a trip on a steamer down the Yangtze River.

3

Evans felt like an agent living a double life in enemy territory.

But agents were trained to appear normal – even under the constant threat of exposure. Some married and had families: neither their partners nor their children had any idea of their real identity. They had active social lives, followed football teams, had favourite TV programmes.

Some, maybe all, were dedicated to an ideal that made them despise the values and lifestyles of their 'friends', or even their 'loved ones'. They could turn emotions on and off, express false enthusiasms, argue fiercely for things they didn't believe in.

Did that make it hard to distinguish between right and wrong, between reality and unreality?

Evans was finding it hard to avoid looking over his shoulder – though he was unsure what he was seeking. Even the tranquillity of the Summer Palace failed to soothe his nerves. He felt claustrophobic in the humidity, as if there was a cloud hanging over him. He shuddered involuntarily.

'Are you alright?' Jenny asked quizzically. They'd hardly had a moment together since their discussion after Hu's abduction; even now they were in a crowd.

He shrugged, embarrassed. For a moment he wondered if

the events of the previous evening had actually happened. It all seemed unbelievable: especially here, with such serenity before him.

The Summer Palace had belonged to the last of the Qing empresses, its splendour epitomising an imperial retreat. A covered walkway linked one set of pagodas to another, its ceiling decorated with intricate scenes of colour and shade. According to Chinese legend, if a pair of lovers passed through, their futures would be entwined forever.

Ornamental bridges stood among water lilies. Temples towered on Longevity Hill over Kunming Lake, where a huge marble paddle-steamer was permanently moored to a quay. The Empress had built the Palace from funds earmarked for the Chinese navy: the outlandish steamer a defiant gesture at navy commanders who'd jibbed at her decadence.

Boats drifted languidly in the late afternoon, but something seemed to stir in the shadow of the marble steamer. Evans peered closer. Reflected in the water were two pairs of staring eyes protruding from the pale, haggard faces of Hu and his father, grotesquely shimmering together.

Christ!

He narrowed his eyes against the sun hanging low across the water.

Then the vision passed. What was true and what was false? He was relieved that nobody had noticed his panic.

Keith Makuyana's ANC appointment was in a discreetly guarded safe house in the suburbs of Harare, where he and Mugadza were searched before being let in to meet Selby Mngadi, a top man in the ANC's military wing, *uMkhonto weSizwe* (MK).

In his late forties, Mngadi was a veteran of MK's first abortive attempt in 1967 to infiltrate guerrillas into South Africa through the old white-run state of Rhodesia. High on South African security's wanted list, he had survived a number of assassination attempts. A slight, wiry figure with a small beard, he had a ready laugh and an easy manner which contrasted with the Zimbabwean's gravitas.

Makuyana was all too aware that relations between the main South African liberation force and the ruling Zimbabwe African National Union (ZANU) had been tense prior to independence in 1980, with rocky moments since.

During the liberation struggle, the ANC had worked closely with the rival Zimbabwe African Peoples Union (ZAPU). Both had enjoyed the patronage of the Soviets and had been courted by the West. ZANU had a lower international profile, its chief supporter being China.

Makuyana laid all his cards on the table. 'Robert Temba and I had an understanding which overcame any tension between our organisations. It was built on trust, based on years of friendship. That's why I'm asking you to give me a direct link to the ANC.'

Mngadi did not seem over-impressed. He was wary of Zimbabwe security – too often they seemed to obstruct the ANC just when Mngadi and his comrades most needed assistance.

But Makuyana carried on: 'We know there has been a recent spate of attacks on ANC people in Zimbabwe.' He paused, weighing his next words carefully. 'I gather you suspect Pretoria has infiltrated the ANC at a high level. Their targeting has been very precise, and Robert's murder convinces me they have a cell based here in Harare. I cannot tell you why, but we strongly suspect the letter bomb was local.'

'Really?' The ANC man leaned forward, alert where he had previously been non-committal.

'If we can crack this cell, it could be very important,' Makuyana continued, 'not only in neutralising their activity here, but in getting to the source of their ANC infiltration. Trouble is, we've drawn a blank with our investigations.'

Now he had the MK man's close attention: 'So, that's why I need your help,' he concluded.

Mngadi leaned back in his chair and stared at the ceiling. Help, huh? Why didn't *he* get any when he most needed it? He turned to a colleague, lounging in the doorway: 'Leave us alone for a minute, please.'

The man looked surprised but left the room. Mugadza, taking the hint, excused himself too.

Makuyana continued: 'Let's keep it between us from now on. Please, no intermediaries. Just the two of us. And whatever we tell each other goes no further without joint agreement.'

'Sounds fine to me,' Mngadi paused. 'We've just had a breakthrough. Our people lifted an inspector in the security services in Pretoria. You saw the news?'

Makuyana nodded. Images of white officials running around like headless chickens trying to trace the inspector who had disappeared from his house in the old Afrikaner capital, Pretoria. It was still causing a minor panic in the comfortable white suburbs. The war was coming home.

'Well, he talked – like nobody's business. About infiltration and disruption of the ANC. Also, about a Harare cell. Apparently, Pretoria thinks it is now too risky to launch assassinations from home. Has to be organised locally. Didn't get any names unfortunately, but we do have the codename for the operation: NOSLEN.'

'How do you spell that?' Makuyana made a note. 'You didn't ask him about Robert's death by any chance?'

'No, we lifted him the day afterwards – too soon to brief our people. Communications with the comrades inside are difficult. Could be easier if we had more help from our friends.'

Makuyana ignored the jibe. He was known to stay cool, never rising to the bait. Instead, he bade his farewell and they exchanged direct line phone numbers.

As he and Mugadza drove off, Mngadi's colleague noted their car registration number and then went back inside. 'Any joy?' he asked.

'What? That lot? Only the usual fishing expedition. I sometimes think our days are numbered here – we're just an embarrassment to them.'

Mngadi's colleague hid his disappointment. Didn't believe a word his chief had just told him. That car number could be more important than he'd imagined.

'Purpose of your journey, Mr Herson?' The young border guard glanced sharply at Mauritz Swanepoel.

'Holiday – to see grandchildren in the Cape,' he replied easily – wasn't going to be bothered by someone the age of his children, and a black guy to boot.

'How long?'

'Two weeks. Maybe three. I'm retired now. Don't have to rush back.'

The guard disappeared inside an office to run a computer check, leaving Swanepoel unbothered. His cover was watertight.

He stared down into the muddy waters of the Limpopo swirling 40 metres below, thinking back to the days when he used to bring his kids in the other direction across Beitbridge to holiday in what was then Rhodesia. Never any delay. The white customs and passport officers had been friendly in those days, waving them through with only cursory checks.

'You can go now Mr Herson.' Swanepoel looked up as the young guard handed back his passport. He felt contemptuous: the kid didn't have a clue he was on his way to security headquarters in Pretoria before travelling southward to the Cape by plane.

But as Swanepoel drove off through the lowveld, Ed Mugadza was knocking on his front door back in Harare. Mugadza was just going through the motions. The name Paul Herson was number 194 on the long list supplied by Zimbabwe telecommunications and he had no reason to suppose it would yield any more information than the previous ones.

No answer. He knocked again. Still no reply. He walked round the bungalow. Looked deserted, nobody about, back garden unkempt – perhaps the owner had been away some time?

He turned back to his car, almost bumping into a small boy on a BMX bike.

'Uncle has gone on holiday,' said the boy.

'Your uncle?'

'No – I just call him that. Don't know his name.'

'Nice bike you've got there. I bet you can race fast on it,' Mugadza smiled. 'When did Uncle go?'

'Early this morning. I was out on my bike before breakfast.' The boy grinned confidentially, as if sharing treasured information.

'What does Uncle look like?'

The boy shrugged his shoulders. 'Bit fat. Old. Has a moustache.' He got back onto his bike and rode off.

Mugadza put a routine tick against Herson's name on the list and scribbled: 'Gone on holiday today. Old, fat.'

Then he paused. Old? The Grassroots description had mentioned an elderly man. On holiday. Just a coincidence? *Where* on holiday? On impulse, he called for a check on people crossing the border to South Africa that day. Maybe a waste of time. But then the whole laborious exercise seemed a waste of time.

Ed Mugadza drove off to check the next address, idly wondering if he would be too exhausted for his five-a-side football match that evening.

Across the other side of the world, another old man was also on the mind of someone younger.

Wang Bi Nan was troubled about his mentor. The Chinese Communist Party Congress had just ended, and most of the older champions of Marxist orthodoxy, veterans of the 1934–5 Long March, had been pushed out by Deng Xiaoping's younger modernisers.

Now everything depended upon Wang's boss, the Old Man. Aged 85, his mind was as sharp as ever. He had joined a peasant uprising in 1927, was a captain in the Long March, then joined the Politburo in 1956 and had remained a member through the shifting alliances of the next 30 years.

His colleagues saw him as a pragmatist, perhaps a little weak, but an efficient minister who always upheld the Party line. They never realised how fiercely his anger welled inside, as he witnessed the principles of Chinese communism crumble all around him.

'They are corrupt. All corrupt, these modernisers!' he had ranted at Wang in a moment when his usual control had uncharacteristically snapped.

The reformist circle never imagined that the Old Man had the backing of leading officials in the State security ministry or that he still had considerable support within the People's Liberation Army.

Wang stared out of his sombre office, hardly noticing dusk closing in, or the dancing shadows of homeward cyclists, silhouetted against the orange-red sky.

His immediate task was to deal with that nuisance Evans. Could be tricky because it had to be done through unofficial channels. Any mistake and Wang could find *himself* under investigation from China's ubiquitous security services.

He sighed in disgust. It showed how deeply the rot had set in when a revolutionary patriot like himself could become the target of his own Party's apparatus.

Makuyana was buried under a pile of paper.

Days of inquiries and still no progress on the Temba case. His staff were exhausted, losing their drive. No breaks and now mutterings from his superiors about wasted hours, as they clamoured for results in the wake of another raid across the border.

The South African helicopters had come in at dawn. They flew low to avoid radar, skimming above the bare landscape, blending into the blue-grey sky, hardly arriving before they were gone, leaving a wreckage of terror and devastation.

Almost nothing was left of the village they hit. The first choppers had come in slowly, confident there were no defences, dropping scores of metal eggs which burst upon impact, filling the atmosphere with a silver, shining cloud which drifted – seemingly innocuous – over the thatched huts.

Alerted by the thunderous sound of the engines, the sleepy villagers stared up, bewildered as the damp, clammy, mist enveloped them. They cowered as one of the choppers turned back and hovered briefly. But all it did was drop a small burning object before banking sharply away.

Suddenly the mist ignited and napalm ate the villagers alive. Screaming children ran out of their beds with skins on fire, only to fall, writhing in agony, until becoming terribly still.

Parents could not heed their desperate cries because they too were on fire, tormented by an attack that had come out of nowhere: no machine guns, no bombs – just the deadly rain, soaking through everything.

The village was not an ANC base – but that didn't bother the South Africans. Putting the frighteners on Zimbabwe was what mattered.

Makuyana looked up from his desk as his deputy knocked. Ed Mugadza sank onto a chair, speaking mechanically.

'May have something, not absolutely sure. Paul Johann Herson. Retired civil servant, aged 67 years. I went to his home on a routine check earlier today. Seems to fit the description from Grassroots.

'I found out he just left to go on holiday. So, I checked with the border. He crossed into South Africa at midday. Said he was visiting relatives. Nothing suspicious. He was let through without a search. I contacted the pensions department and they confirmed he worked in agriculture for 20 years before retiring. No blemishes on his record. Nothing special.'

'So? An old man who goes on holiday?'

Mugadza looked sheepish. 'Yeah, not much, but it's more than any of the other names. They've produced bugger all.'

'Okay. Put out a special alert so we hear when he returns.' Makuyana didn't sound enthusiastic. 'Now, check our dossiers on every senior ANC person in the country. Our team needs a rest, I know. But this is a priority.'

Mugadza nodded woodenly. His shoulders seemed to sag. All that effort after the Temba killing, and now he was being switched to another job. He made quickly for the door.

'Ed,' Makuyana called him back. 'Sorry, should have explained. I'm not taking you off the Temba inquiry. This is another part of it. Sit down.'

The two men remained closeted for an hour before Mugadza got up again, this time with a spring in his step.

More than three million people lived in the city of Chengdu in the east of China. But to Evans it had a small-town atmosphere compared to Beijing's bustle.

It felt older, too, as if transported back in time. The people were evidently less used to foreigners and congregated to stare at members of the delegation whenever they ventured forth from the imposing Jinjiang Hotel, situated alongside a muddy river. The vegetation surrounding the city was abundant, and the climate in the province of Sichuan much wetter and more humid than Beijing's.

Half the city seemed to be a sprawling series of gaunt factories and blocks of flats; the other half, traditional brick homes with courtyards, cramming the twisting side streets. Huge markets sprawled along the roadsides, makeshift trestle tables groaning under the weight of fruit and vegetables.

53

Their hotel was again a concrete block, each bedroom with a Hitachi air conditioner, the grounds full of vegetable patches.

Early one morning, a guest in a third-floor room with a view of the main entrance, picked up the handset of the old-fashioned black phone and asked the operator for a number.

Thirty seconds later a phone rang at the other end, and Wang picked it up immediately.

'He's leaving now,' the Noted Person said.

Evans jogged past a middle-aged woman brushing her teeth, hunched over a stream of water snaking its way alongside one of the main roads through Chengdu.

'Come on! You're slacking!' His fellow 'Noted Person', Simon Jeffries, called to him.

The two men ran on, often passing small groups of people doing their early morning exercises. Old women practised *tai chi* in a slow-motion, hypnotic world of their own, oblivious to the foreigners.

Evans felt unfit, but over drinks the previous night Jeffries had cajoled him into going for a run. At least the surroundings here were fascinating. At home, even a fifteen-minute jog could seem like an hour if you had nothing else to think about.

Now he was starting to sweat, as the morning traffic became heavier. 'Can't wait for a shower,' he muttered to Jeffries, 'I've become pretty sluggish this trip. Too much eating and sitting around.'

'Watch out!' Jeffries screamed.

Evans, half stumbling, saw a car veering onto the pavement towards him. He managed to jerk to avoid its front bumper before it hit him sideways on, flinging his body away.

He caught a glimpse of a familiar curtain drawn across the back window before he hit the ground and passed out.

*

Apartheid security agent Mauritz Swanepoel whistled to himself as he drove down the long, straight road to Pretoria on a crisp, cloudless winter's day. This was *his* country – the wide expanse on either side bounded by rolling hills, the seemingly endless stretch of road ahead to the horizon. Monotonous to others, but not to him: the immense space giving him a sense of power and destiny.

Stopping briefly for petrol, he bought some biltong to help pass the time, loving the salty taste of the dried meat.

Swanepoel had mixed feelings about holidaying. His job was his whole life. He was a workaholic, with little time for family matters. The thought of retirement had filled him with dread. That's why he had pleaded with his superiors to stay on after his sixty-fifth birthday.

Most agents were happy to accept their pension and relax after years of stress and disruption. But Swanepoel was different. In his darkest moments, alone with his bottle of KWV after rather too many refills of the aroma-enhancing brandy glass, he would contemplate the utter emptiness of his future when they finally gave him the push and put him out to grass.

Mauritz Swanepoel had never forgotten, never for one moment, his *oupa's* stories. Drinking in the anger – the lasting bitterness which poured out like a torrent from the old man, as he sat on his favourite rocking chair on their *stoep*, while the teenager squatted barefoot at his feet. For Swanepoel, *Oupa* had always been a legend.

At his home on the riverbank, fishing on winter nights, *Oupa* used to cast out a line over the *stoep* and then pull his fishing rod back through the living room window. He'd put on the ratchet and lean the rod against the sill so he could feel the warmth of the fire, while smoking his favourite Springbok cigarettes and sipping a brandy: neat, never diluted with ice.

When he felt a bite he would go outside, loosen the rod and reel in a fish.

In his later years, he'd become something of a mentor to the teenager, explaining how the Afrikaner people – descendants of the Dutch, German and French Huguenot settlers from the seventeenth century – had occupied the Western Cape until the conquering British arrived, annexing it in 1806 and driving into the hinterland in search of minerals, markets, territory and power.

'The Brits were cold blooded and ruthless, arrogantly superior,' *Oupa* had explained. They had intensified conflicts between indigenous African communities and long-established Afrikaans-speaking whites.

As British settlements expanded remorselessly, eastward along the Cape coast and northward, their armies plundering and pillaging to the sound of gunfire, Afrikaners including his *oupa's* parents, began 'the great *trek*' north from the Cape into the Orange Free State and the Transvaal.

Known as the *voortrekkers* ('pioneers'), they drove their livestock into the heart of South Africa in search of more land and independence, in turn displacing and subjugating African communities, just as they had been displaced and subjugated by Britain.

These violent conflicts with the British, explained *Oupa*, spawned a fierce Afrikaner nationalism and led to an enduring resentment of their English-speaking colonial cousins from Europe.

Then, after fabulous gold and diamond reserves had been discovered in what became the Johannesburg area on the highveld to the north of the country, British forces moved up from the Cape and Natal to the west to assert themselves over that territory too.

There were two bloody 'Anglo-Boer Wars' in 1880–1881 and 1899–1902. Oupa bitterly described how his young wife had been captured and raped. She was amongst tens of thousands of Afrikaner women and children incarcerated in British concentration camps, where 26,000 died in primitive, insanitary conditions. 'It wasn't the Nazis but the Brits who invented concentration camps,' said *Oupa*, grimacing at the memory of his wife: seized, never to be seen again.

'Your *ouma* ... that's why you never met her, why you never had an *oumie* of your own. That's what they did to her, that's what the Brits did to us all. Never forget that, my boy.'

And Swanepoel never had, his Afrikaner nationalism burning strong and deep inside.

Although his Nissan saloon cruised comfortably at 140 kilometres per hour, it was late before he reached Pretoria and headed down Arcadia Street to the small hotel near security headquarters where he intended to spend the night.

The following day he would pay a visit to the office, then drive to Jan Smuts Airport and catch a plane. He had a quick steak, washed down with a bottle of ruby red wine, before turning in, exhausted after the day-long drive, but feeling great at being home again.

In the early hours he woke briefly, half conscious of a roaring noise, then slipped quickly back into a deep sleep. Next morning's news bulletins reported that a powerful bomb planted underneath a pick-up truck had exploded next to the military barracks in central Pretoria, killing five soldiers and injuring 67 other people: the majority of them whites. It was the biggest attack on a military installation for several years, since a car bomb had killed 19 people near Air Force headquarters in Pretoria.

The blast gouged a crater in the road and shattered windows in offices for several blocks around. Wreckage was hurled more than 100 metres, and the glass-fronted emergency ward of a nearby hospital was blown in, adding to chaos for the wounded.

The previous day, a black police constable had been killed in a hand-grenade attack in the township of Mamelodi to the east of the city. The day before that, a car bomb had killed four white policemen outside the city magistrate's court, and a mine had exploded in a hotel frequented by foreign businessmen.

The old certainties seemed gone for Swanepoel as he strolled to the office, spoiling his enjoyment of the familiar sounds and sights of his beloved Pretoria. He had always thought of it as *the* capital city of South Africa.

Why they had conceded co-capital status to Cape Town, he could never comprehend. What a ridiculous business, shifting all the paraphernalia of government between the two cities every six months. Afrikanerdom had been in total control for four decades: no need to pander to the bloody English anymore.

Still, his old home town seemed much the same, though he noticed black pedestrians had shed some of their obedient deference. Imagine, a black youth had just bumped into him without the usual grovelling apology!

Thoughtfully, Swanepoel turned the corner towards the precinct of security headquarters, then pulled up in shock. Although the imposing modern building was still the same, the ground floor was surrounded by sandbags.

A barbed wire corridor stretched from the entrance down to the pavement where a temporary construction acted as a security and surveillance point to guard the building. From a platform on top, machine guns poked out of slits in the fortifications and two pairs of eyes scrutinised him carefully as he walked up to a heavily guarded wooden hut.

After showing his identification, he was taken by lift to the tenth floor to meet his chief, General KJ van der Walt, known as 'KJ' to colleagues. Over six foot tall, balding with a paunch, he had dominated the security services since the military moved in to push aside the old leadership of BOSS in the late 1970s.

'Ah, Mauritz, good to see you. Are you well?'

'I was – until I saw all the changes around here.'

'You mean the extra protection? Don't you worry about that,

man,' KJ waved his hand airily. 'ANC getting cheekier, that's all. We don't want to take any chances.'

Never one for chitchat, the General got straight to the point.

'I want a favour of you, Mauritz. I know you are here to see your family, and you haven't had a break for over a year. But my men are being stretched all ways, lots of retirements recently, too many young guys. There's a special operation coming up and we need your experience. Will you stay here for a while to take charge?'

Swanepoel paused. He did not want to appear enthusiastic: would never let on they were doing *him* a favour, when he would otherwise have been bored, lounging about with his family and drinking too much.

'What do you want me to do?' he asked, noncommittally.

Jenny was too worried to enjoy the visit to the commune outside Chengdu.

Evans had insisted to everyone, Chinese state and medical officials included, that his injury had been an accident: his fault for running too near the road. He was badly bruised and shaken, though remarkably nothing was broken, and he could still walk.

But Simon Jeffries had been equally insistent that they'd been jogging well inside the boundary of the wide pavement, and he was certain the car had veered directly towards Evans.

Feigning a headache, Jenny returned early from the group excursion. She headed immediately to the hotel, and knocked on Evans' door.

No reply. Grateful for the first time on the visit that no hotel rooms were locked, she eased his door open, finding him breathing fitfully, tossing and turning in bed.

She sat down next to him and held his hand gently.

Evans jerked bolt upright, eyes wide open. 'You frightened me!'

He looked awful, she thought, haunted. Not his usual phlegmatic self.

'Can't sleep, feel drained. Mind keeps racing ... glad you came.' Evans smiled weakly, gripping her hand.

Then he grimaced. 'My room was searched during the jog.'

'*What?* Are you sure?'

'Yes. Don't think anything was taken but need to double-check. Someone turned over my files and searched my luggage. Someone who must have known I was out jogging.'

'Perhaps they wanted to search in case you didn't come back. Was it really an accident, Jim?'

'No. I told them it was because I can't prove otherwise. But the pavement was very wide. People were everywhere, doing their early morning exercises, and we were running well away from the traffic. They're trying to kill me.'

Evans slumped back, the sudden impact of the car flashing through his mind. Feeling himself being hit and thrown. Disorientated, panicking, as he looked up at the concerned Chinese faces, seemingly friendly, even sympathetic. But out there, one of their number had tried to injure, maybe even kill him.

He drifted back into sleep.

It was dark when he awoke to find Jenny reading under a lampshade, a shadow falling across her hair. She came over and sat on his bed. 'How are you?'

'Much better. Just stiff and a bit sore, that's all.'

'Good.' She leaned over to kiss him lightly on the cheek and held his hand as if he were her patient.

Then she frowned. 'I've been thinking. If they tried to kill you once, they will try again. It must be very important to them. So, don't be caught alone outside the hotel. We ought to stick together, and if I'm not around, stay with the others.'

Evans didn't need persuading, but said: 'I don't feel comfortable with our fellow Noted Person from the Foreign Office ... Harold Williams. The guy gives me the creeps.'

'Me too. Remember his sudden appearance at my student

lecture? Appearing out of nowhere, just when Hu passed that surreptitious note?'

Jenny thought for a moment, then continued. 'But the authorities haven't detained you or warned you. So, perhaps we're dealing with an unofficial group. In which case, safety in numbers may be more effective than anything.'

She frowned. 'Something else. Shu is being withdrawn as our interpreter again. She's flying back to Beijing in the morning. Her replacement is your "mate" Wang Bi Nan.'

Makuyana crouched in the shadow of a hedge alongside the driveway of the house, which was tucked discreetly back from the road.

It was pitch black and for once he was grateful for the power cut – habitual under the President's deteriorating rule – knocking out the northern part of Harare an hour earlier.

His knees were aching. It was some time since he had been on active surveillance, his responsibilities invariably keeping him at arm's length from field action. He'd been in the same position for two hours and the waiting brought back memories. Hated vigils like this. Might come to something, might not.

By temperament impatient, he had to be doing something all the time or he got frustrated. Like now.

'Where are you, bastards,' he muttered to himself.

Across the road, Ed Mugadza was hiding and watching too, with the others on call when their target appeared, ready to follow him in relays, nobody trailing long enough to be clocked.

They had been tipped off about an ANC gathering in the house. Selby Mngadi had phoned him, sounding agitated and preoccupied. Not much to go on, but he'd got wind of a meeting. Important to find out who attended. Could someone get up there right away?

After hastily briefing his team, Makuyana had been driven up in Mugadza's car, leaving it down the road. Two similarly unmarked vehicles had followed them. He hoped these would be sufficient for the task.

Makuyana wondered who was inside and what lay behind Mngadi's concern. Did he fear another assassination? He didn't like untidy missions like this. Mngadi had been insistent, but Makuyana was dubious. The targets might be on foot or emerge from the driveway in a car. He assumed there'd be more than one person, but didn't even know that.

Not for the first time during his lonely sojourn, he felt distinctly uneasy.

Then he tensed. A light shone from the side of the house as a door opened, two figures moving swiftly out and into a garage nearby. Makuyana spoke into his walkie talkie: 'Ed, they're coming out.'

The car roared past him, lights out, veering leftwards into the road. Seconds later, the familiar sound of Mugadza's engine started up. Makuyana was relieved they were both wearing special night glasses.

Then the whole road exploded, darkness turning bright then orange with blinding ferocity. One split second Mugadza's car was accelerating past him, the next it was engulfed in an inferno, pieces of metal shooting everywhere.

The heat swept past Makuyana, singeing his eyebrows. Pellets of glass dug into his face as he fell back. Then another unlit car swept past him down the drive and roared off.

For the second time in little over a week Makuyana had to steel himself. He had to suppress his emotions, summon all his willpower to focus on staying professional. He would soon be investigating the death of a close comrade.

Virtually nothing was left of Mugadza in the wreckage. The eight-kilogram bomb had been attached under the rear wheel arch, next to the boot of his Nissan saloon, activated by radio signal.

It had exploded with clinical efficiency, sending parts of the car into nearby trees and front gardens. Now, neighbours were pouring out of their homes to see Makuyana transfixed before the smoking remains.

After some time, his officers returned. They'd pursued the target vehicles – but lost them. Searches of the premises also produced nothing. One room had been used – warm cigarette ash left behind – but it was completely wiped of evidence. No leads.

Professionals, Makuyana reflected. The bomb highly sophisticated, radio-controlled, no need to link it to the engine, or another moving part, could be attached quickly – ideal for the job. Everything had been expertly planned.

Evans stared at the butcher, the man's small moustache twitching as he talked flat-out, cajoling a customer into making a purchase. Standing in the dark shuttered doorway of his shop, the butcher grabbed a pig's carcass, dangling it enticingly across the pavement. Despite the meat hanging out in the open, there weren't any flies – Evans hadn't seen any since he arrived in China – but the scene highlighted how raw life was in Chengdu.

He and Jenny strolled through the backstreets. Though still unsteady, stiff and bruised, he felt relieved to be out: surrounded by shops on all sides, small workshops with people crouching over ancient machines, cyclists dodging market stalls bulging with fresh produce.

They wandered into a park, where Jenny took him by the arm, answering his clumsy question about her private life.

'I was involved with someone until last year – but he couldn't stand the pace! Said I was too much like hard work.' She smiled. 'And you?'

'Oh, I've been too busy for a relationship.' He didn't like talking about himself, but couldn't now avoid it.

They gazed, fascinated, before a row of alcoves housing a dozen statues about five metres high. All brightly coloured, all enormously fat men with thin handlebar moustaches and pointed caps. In a London park these would have looked garish, here they were simply part of the scene: monuments to local rulers from past dynasties.

Spits of rain, as a fresh breeze drew them closer. Evans put his arm around her, feeling the warmth under her thin white blouse which became damp and transparent as it clung to her skin.

Perhaps Chengdu wasn't too bad after all.

In another part of the city, Wang replaced the receiver in its cradle, his conversation with Beijing hurried, and his instructions icy.

On no account must Evans leave the country alive. But on no account must there be any more risky attacks in public.

Wang clenched his fists in frustration. Why was he surrounded by such incompetent fools? How he longed to have the full resources of the state at his disposal.

One day that would be the case. Then *he* could pull all the necessary strings.

Swanepoel peered out from the Casspir, feeling uncomfortable but secure in the armoured personnel carrier. It was some years since he had been into Mamelodi township outside Pretoria.

He'd made a special request to join a routine patrol, wanting to soak it all in again. The smog, hanging like a permanent cloud over the shacks and small square homes with their corrugated roofs. Babies with streaming noses, crying continuously. Women washing household goods in bowls under standpipes. Bitterness directed defiantly at the Casspir.

Swanepoel didn't like to admit it, but God, the kids frightened him. Wasn't bothered by the adults, had seen too many of them bruised and bleeding, cowering under interrogation.

But their *children*? Getting more militant all the time. In Soweto in 1976 when hundreds revolted against being taught in Afrikaans and sparked off countrywide conflict, the leaders were in their mid-to-late teens.

Now the leaders were eleven, twelve, thirteen – and the younger they were, the harder they seemed. There was something reckless about them: they didn't seem to care for themselves, didn't seem to have much to lose.

Why didn't they realise how bloody lucky they were, when their black brethren to the north were trapped in countries run by communists like Mugabe?

The Casspir slid round a corner. People were gathering: screams and discordant chants as a terrified young black man burst out of the crowd, running for his life. Teenagers led the chase, as he ducked into what was apparently his home.

They battered down walls, broke windows; axes and hammers swirling in a frenzy, knives glinting.

'God, they're going to demolish the house with their bare hands!' Swanepoel exclaimed to the Casspir driver.

But he was wrong. The young man's relatives pushed him sacrificially out of the front door, and he was immediately set upon, knives jabbing, fists flying as he tried to flee, blood spurting from his back. The crowd seemed possessed: unaware of the Casspir. Swanepoel had never seen such brutality close-up: his violence was calculated, clinical – usually orchestrated remotely.

Finally, the young man shuddered to the ground. Swanepoel knew the instant he died. His eyes finally glazed over, his body went rigid. The crowd drew back, ecstatic, then fell silent as they noticed the Casspir. It revved and then pulled away quickly: no point looking for trouble.

'Another informer eliminated,' the driver muttered laconically. 'Your sources will be drying up soon.'

Little love was lost between the soldiers who took all the flak, and the security officers who manipulated from behind.

Fourteen years had passed, but the memory was still painfully fresh.

A camouflaged ZANLA camp deep in Mozambique.

Makuyana's wife, pregnant with their second child, was watching her husband clown around with their three-year-old son.

She enjoyed pregnancy, looked radiant. Her bulge was sexy, he told her. Ridiculous, she retorted! Men hadn't the faintest notion how damned uncomfortable it was carrying a baby.

He had been thrilled to cup his hands over her belly and feel the kicks inside – especially at night, when they made love gently, almost until the day her contractions began.

As the years rolled by, he had torn himself away from those memories. Could not wallow in nostalgia: it would have consumed him. Instead, he buried himself in his work. Anyhow, he rationalised, it was safer not having a family. He was relieved Ed Mugadza had been single.

But the memory still haunted him. The steaming-hot day when a Rhodesian army killer squad attacked their camp and destroyed it in minutes: barracks, school, temporary hospital, make-do homes, people.

He had been spared but not his wife and son.

Leaders like him didn't openly shed tears, but for weeks he wept inwardly. Was it wrong to bottle up emotions? Maybe. He knew that people often thought him cold and aloof...

Now, it was late. Makuyana sat in his office, a lamp lighting up the file on his desk. Most of his staff had gone hours before, traumatised by Mugadza's murder, though the hardened agents concealed it better than others.

The subject of Makuyana's attention was the MK commander, Selby Mngadi. There was nothing in the file to suggest the man was suspect. True, he was a Zulu – but he had not joined Chief Buthelezi's anti-ANC Inkatha movement. Instead he'd become one of the ANC's most trusted officials.

Mngadi's father had been a leading ANC man, too: in the Ladysmith area of Natal. Jailed, placed under house arrest and later murdered after a reported clash between Inkatha activists and ANC supporters of the United Democratic Front.

Mngadi himself had been responsible for some of the most successful ANC incursions deep inside the country, notably the sabotage raid at Sasolburg – the town in the Transvaal so dominated by South Africa's indigenous Sasol oil refinery that local car number plates bore the prefix 'OIL'. The raid had stopped production for three weeks and caused a slide on the Johannesburg stock exchange and a devaluation of the rand.

But could Mngadi really be trusted?

4

The sweaty smell of tension always appealed to Swanepoel. He was back in action again, going in early to catch the residents of Mamelodi unawares before they rose at 4 a.m. to catch trains and buses to serve whites in Pretoria city.

His wife Noeline had been none too happy at news of his delay, suspecting correctly that he was actually delighted.

The unmarked car crept slowly down the dusty track that passed for the township's main street. Having visited with the Casspir the day before, Swanepoel didn't feel he was coming in cold – nevertheless he sensed the once omnipotent security apparatus was losing control. So different from the old days.

Outbreaks of anarchy were more frequent. Also 'necklacing' where victims' arms were broken, heads pushed through old car tyres, drenched with petrol and set alight – or sexual torture, where women were violated with fragments of broken glass. Such black-on-black violence signalled a grisly deterrent to would-be collaborators.

Things were indeed getting messy in the townships. It was a piece of cake in the old days to hit a suspected ANC safe house, but now – as an added complication – the residents were more militant, and the white police state carefully fostered such divide and rule splits in the black community.

There was sharp conflict between the 'comrades' and the 'vigilantes'. The comrades: young and highly political – brooking no compromise, treating elected black councillors as quislings, attacking their houses and businesses. The vigilantes: more willing to cooperate – especially those secretly being paid by the security forces as informers, or agents provocateurs.

When the comrades attacked a 'collaborator', the vigilantes retaliated: mercilessly harming any ordinary people who got between them.

A clever ploy, Swanepoel thought. Encouraging civil war *within* the black community. But risky too, for the communal violence had started spilling over into neighbouring white areas.

Meanwhile, the government was trying to build a black 'middle ground' which could be coopted politically – to give the appearance of self-government in townships on the brink of anarchy.

At the same time, real power was being exercised by a network of township joint management committees, under the control of the military and the police, not elected and only barely publicised. A soft outside and a rock-hard inside to run the show. This appealed to Swanepoel.

The local police and army knew he was going in and maintained a discreet distance, but were on immediate call if needed. The house they were about to hit had been used by those who had kidnapped a Special Branch inspector. The bastards: he would teach them a lesson.

They went through both the front and back simultaneously, crashing in the flimsy doors as if they weren't there, to shrieks from children and screams from women asleep on mats across the bare floor.

'The *men*! Where are the *men*?' Swanepoel shouted at one of the women, probably in her early thirties but prematurely aged.

Bursting in when they were still half-asleep and disorientated could achieve more than physical assault.

She sobbed, terrified. 'Away. At the mines.'

'Don't lie, you bitch.' He shook her, turning to a colleague: 'Take that kid out and stick it in the car.' It always helped to grab a child if parents were obstructive.

But none of the women had anything to tell them.

By now the home had been turned upside down, precious possessions thrown outside, blankets trodden on, food ground under boots.

Swanepoel bellowed in frustration. All his experience told him this wasn't a safe house after all. They had turned over the wrong place. Without so much as a backward glance he ordered his men out. He was seemingly unaware, and certainly uncaring, of the sobbing chaos behind him.

Across the road two men stared out of a small window where the inspector had spilled the beans and spoken his last words. A narrow escape. Time to move on.

'Noted Persons Delegation'? Sounded a right bunch of wallies. Dick Sewell frowned upon hearing that his party was to join another group, also on a visit from England, at Chongqing for the trip down the Yangtze River.

Sewell disdained people he considered posers: people who seemed not to accept their responsibilities; who lived their lives expecting others – people like him? – to sort things out.

He'd made the most of his holiday – first proper one for years, a real treat, and a bonus that Green Planet was funding it.

But there were student uprisings all over the country. In Beijing, 100,000 demonstrators gathered at Mao's mausoleum, the Great Hall of the People and the gates of the Forbidden City. In Shanghai, several thousand surrounded the Party headquarters demanding democracy and freedom of speech. In other cities, students were joined by workers carrying banners demanding reform.

Sewell learned of unprecedented riots involving not only the young, but peasants, workers and even football fans.

Exciting, and in a different context he would be urging them on. But he was flying home in a week's time – with the precious documents from the student safely hidden in the false bottom of his suitcase.

'My room was searched again this morning,' Evans told Jenny, matter-of-factly. 'Nothing taken, no idea what they wanted.'

The delegation was touring a local primary school, noticing how obedient the children seemed: sitting in disciplined rows before their teachers, or playing table tennis outside on concrete tables.

Jenny seemed remote. Did she find him irritating? Out of place in her political world? The thought bothered him.

But later she asked him to come to her room for a chat.

'I've been trying to make sense of the last few days,' she said. 'It's all so intangible, but perhaps there's one aspect we could pin down: China's nuclear policy. Do you know much about it?'

It felt odd to be treated as an authority: up till now he'd followed *her* lead. He considered her question.

'Not much is known. China wouldn't sign the Nuclear Non-Proliferation Treaty. Nor join the International Atomic Energy Agency. After the Sino-Soviet split in 1960, the government made a big push to develop an independent nuclear weapons capability, and a major civil nuclear programme.'

'But I thought China had a good supply of alternative energy sources?' Jenny interjected.

'True, probably the biggest fossil fuel reserves in the world and huge untapped hydropower resources. I think they're obsessed with nuclear energy because it's so bound up with developing and sustaining their nuclear weapons programme. That's why I questioned the scientist at the Institute.'

'Ah – your question that caused all the fuss! But, is their

sensitivity really about nuclear weapons?' Jenny thought for a moment, recalling Hu's comments. 'What about links to other countries?'

'I remember China selling unsafeguarded heavy water to Argentina. And supplying nuclear fuels to Pakistan. Also enriching uranium for apartheid South Africa.'

'South Africa? Really? Now *that's* interesting. Didn't Hu say his father had some information about that very thing?'

They both fell silent, remembering Hu's abduction. If only they had been able to meet his father . . .

Jenny yawned and glanced at her watch. 'Well, all we know for sure is that somebody here is pretty damn sensitive about matters nuclear.'

Suddenly she heard a rustle at the door. Then the sound of footsteps receding quickly. She rushed out to the corridor. To her left, a door banged shut – the one leading to the central stairway.

Heart pounding, she ran towards it. Down the stairs. One flight. The sound of another door shutting. She swiftly followed: through the second door and into the corridor below.

Nobody to be seen. Just the click of another door closing, quietly this time: a bedroom door. She couldn't tell which – only that someone on the third floor had taken a good deal of trouble to avoid being identified.

Jenny started to walk back up the stairs, the stillness of the sleeping hotel all around her. Then on impulse she took the lift down to reception and asked to check which guests were staying on the third floor.

She recognised only one name: Harold Williams.

Makuyana was unusual for a ZANU man.

Almost without exception his comrades were from the majority Shona people. He was too. But he also had relatives from the minority Ndebele who were concentrated in the south-west of the country around Bulawayo, and he was fluent in three languages: Ndebele, Shona and English.

As he waited for the MK commander Mngadi, he reflected that he couldn't help liking the man. His own Ndebele heritage gave him a special affinity with the South African, because Ndebele people were descendants of the Nguni who formed the majority of blacks in South Africa. Culturally, they were close relatives of Mngadi's Zulu people.

Makuyana bitterly resented the way the West, the British especially, referred disparagingly to 'tribalism'. The word 'tribe' had become pejorative – yet what were the Scots, the Welsh, the Cornish, if they weren't 'tribes'?

He felt proud of the cultural traditions of his people, and frustrated at the way these traditions were denied or suppressed by European settlers.

There was a knock on his door and Mngadi was shown in – alone, as requested.

The atmosphere was thick with tension and Makuyana wasted no time on formalities. 'You know what happened last night at that house you sent me to?'

'Yes – and I blame myself entirely.'

No response from Makuyana. Deliberately no response.

Mngadi changed tack. 'I need some help.'

'*You* need help! My deputy was killed on a wild goose chase *you* started! I can't get a single damn lead on the culprits – and my department has been thrown into chaos!'

Makuyana reigned himself in, otherwise he would explode. But his outburst seemed to break the ice.

'Apologies,' Mngadi said, 'should have made myself clearer, but I feel so guilty, and I need some help.'

He sat back in his chair, choosing his words carefully. 'At the moment I am not certain who I can trust. I told you when we first met that I suspected infiltration. This was confirmed when we lifted that security agent in Pretoria. When I was tipped off about the meeting in that house, I asked you to go there because I thought that would be the most secure and effective method of surveillance. I'd been informed there were ANC men there. Now we know it was a set-up.'

'Where did the tip-off come from?'

'Phone call. Anonymous. The caller sounded frightened. But when I asked him for proof that he was genuine, he gave several facts which could only be known by someone deep inside the ANC's Harare network. He also knew where to reach me: significant in itself.'

'Why should I trust you?' It was a good question to ask, as Makuyana had learnt through years of experience as an interrogator. Put people on the spot. A professional might be able to dodge around it, but most of the genuine ones reacted in one of three ways. They might accept being misunderstood, show hurt at their integrity being challenged – or just get plain angry.

Mngadi got angry, his white teeth flashing.

'Why should you trust me? Bloody good question! Any idea what it's like to be plagued with doubts about your closest comrades? How it feels when you can't risk telling them things, and yet you have to in order to get anything done?

'Do you know what it does to your spirit when you can sense the cancer of corruption and betrayal in a movement for which people are willing to sacrifice everything: their home comforts, their careers, their families, their lives?'

His clenched fist smashed down on the desk.

There was a knock on the door. 'Coffee, sir.' A teenage boy entered, put two cups down on the desk, then retreated swiftly from the unpromising atmosphere.

The coffee relaxed them. Makuyana drank his black, and had a habit of gulping it straight down, however hot. He peered upwards at the bare light bulb hanging from the ceiling.

All his human instincts, all his professional know-how, told him that this man was to be trusted. Makuyana had reached a senior level in Zimbabwe security because he could take decisions quickly – and he took one now.

'Okay Comrade Selby, what help do you need? Where do we begin?'

Makuyana leant forward, making notes as Mngadi talked.

'It pains me to admit it, but MK and the ANC are seriously penetrated. I've already told you about the information coughed up by the Special Branch inspector when we lifted him in Pretoria . . .

'Now we think there may be a problem in London. It was impossible to vet everyone who came out and joined us after the Soweto uprising in 1976: it was a logistical nightmare just to place and disperse them. Would have been easy to infiltrate sleepers or agents at that time.'

Makuyana pushed his chair back and stood up to stretch his legs.

'So, what do we do about it? How can we help?'

'I want you to work directly with us.' Mngadi paused, plucking at his beard, as was his habit.

'It's hard to give concrete reasons, but I believe we are entering a crucial time. Something important must be on the boil. Otherwise, they would not take so many chances: killing Mugadza, for example – so very risky.

'We have to get to them before the cancer spreads. We must expose and smash operation NOSLEN before it smashes us.'

When Swanepoel reached the scene, he immediately spotted the tell-tale signs of a professional job.

The assassination had been clinical. No hiccups. No clues left behind. Getting better all the time, these terrorists. Clean job, the only mess being the flesh, bone and blood that had once been the Minister's head.

He'd been shot through the temple by two rounds from a heavy calibre pistol: the force was enough to throw him backwards for two meters. The gunman must have been quite close: perhaps within ten metres, Swanepoel surmised, staring down at the body of Chris Kruger.

The man had been tipped as a future prime minister. But Swanepoel now found it difficult to recall the charismatic politician who could captivate smalltown audiences in the Free State just as he could charm television viewers abroad.

Perfect all-rounder: Doctor of Philosophy from Oxford University, and a Springbok fly-half who would have been internationally famous amongst rugby followers had South Africa not been boycotted.

A man who, two hours ago, had been in his prime: those rugged, handsome features and blonde hair which had led the local press to dub him the 'Afrikaner Robert Redford'.

Swanepoel smashed his fist against the palm of his other hand. Would these bloody politicians never learn? Why did each one always think *he* would be the exception and never get caught having an affair?

Kruger's personal assistant was in a state of deep shock. A sophisticated young woman with dark hair falling over her bronzed skin, she confirmed they had come many times to this spot in the hills overlooking Pretoria. *Their* spot, she sobbed. Somewhere they could be together in the sunshine at weekends, when he had an hour or two to spare from his family or professional duties.

She didn't remember anything significant about the assassin. She had been lying face down in the sun on a blanket propped up on her elbows, sipping a glass of cold wine, when Kruger had got up.

He didn't seem particularly bothered so she hadn't realised there was anything amiss until the double roar of the gun had hurled him, dead and bleeding, on top of her.

She couldn't believe that bullets had enough power to throw a 75-kilogram man into the air like that – and she was too hysterical to concentrate on anything except the mess of his body draped grotesquely over her. She just had a vague memory of running footsteps and a car screeching away.

Swanepoel pondered, rubbing his belly as he looked out over the city in the distance. They were getting good. *Too* bloody good. No point chasing after them, hoping they would make a mistake or leave a calling card. Let the police do that. His team had more important priorities.

Outnumbered six to one, whites couldn't survive forever by force of arms, they had to destabilise the black majority. Had to Balkanise the country and create conflict and division amongst the blacks through forcing them into the 'homelands' most had never seen, but from which their community ancestrally hailed. Nurture a black middle class. Sponsor black businesses. Coopt some of their politicians.

They had to finance rival political groups, rival trade unions and rival community networks. Pit Zulu against Xhosa; sponsor Buthelezi to rival Mandela. Encourage the Inkatha Zulus to knock the hell out of the United Democratic Front. Set comrade against vigilante. Invade hostile neighbouring states.

Above all, through operation NOSLEN, penetrate the resistance movements, break them from within.

A total strategy. Beautiful. As beautiful as the hillside around him: a pity it had been temporarily disfigured by this dreadful stain.

In his room on the fifth floor of the Chengdu Hotel, Wang was on the phone to Beijing again.

More information for the Old Man. He knew it was important enough to risk talking on an open line.

'Evans may be onto more than we think. He was overheard talking to the girl last night.'

'*What*? Another suspect? Is the whole delegation full of subversives? The Old Man sounded highly irritated.

Wang summarised the overheard conversation between Evans and Jenny. There was a long pause. He knew the Old Man would sometimes stay silent for a full minute during a telephone conversation as he considered one option after another.

Finally, his boss spoke.

'Keep your ear to the ground. But don't get him in Chengdu. The rumours going around security circles here are bad enough already. We don't want another incident or the Sichuan police will start getting even more suspicious. Just get him as soon as possible afterwards.'

The Old Man put down the phone, wondering whether his protégé was up to the job. In the old days he could have moved in someone fresh. Not anymore: he no longer had the reach. Still, Wang was conscientious and loyal – and that counted for a great deal, especially in this dark period.

He settled back to digest the brief on his desk. The Party Leader was postponing major reforms for two years because of the economic crisis. Good. Another sign things were falling apart. He turned to a second memo. There was an acute aluminium shortage, and an edict would shortly be issued forbidding anyone to use aluminium window frames.

What a joke, the Old Man mused, shaking his head.

The Noted Persons were now well into the second half of their trip.

Chengdu was 160 kilometres distant. Evans pulled the blanket more closely around him, and listened to the regular beat of the carriage wheels on the track underneath. They would be in Chongqing by early morning.

To really see China, he'd been told, travel by train. He tried to visualise what the countryside might be like as it flashed by anonymously in the darkness. Would he fall asleep again? More likely that he'd drift through to the morning half awake, his mind alive. By dawn, he wouldn't be sure if he had slept or not.

Eventually, the train pulled in. It was 6.50 a.m. exactly. Chinese trains had a reputation for punctuality.

During the Second World War, Chongqing had been the capital of the nationalist government headed by Chiang Kai-shek's anti-communist Kuomintang Party. Now it was a heaving industrial city perched spectacularly on cliffs and hillsides with the Yangtze and Jialing rivers converging around it.

The whole population of six million seemed to be teeming through the streets as Evans watched from the minibus which had collected them from the station. It pulled up outside the most extraordinary hotel he had ever seen, standing in spacious gardens, almost palace-like, with domes and spires, reflecting a tatty decadence. Such a contrast to what lay outside, where toiling women pulled handcarts along hilly city streets.

Time passed quickly. They visited the hot springs, the university, the Working People's Palace of Culture and – as a highlight – the Red Crag village. This had once been a communist base in the city during the Second World War, when Mao's party was in an uneasy alliance with Chiang Kai-shek's Kuomintang nationalists against the Japanese.

Evans stood in the bedroom where Mao had slept when he came to negotiate with the Kuomintang in the autumn of 1945. He touched the desk where Mao had written thousands of his famous words. A guerrilla for all those long years, until the triumphant liberation in 1949. A hero of the peasant masses and yet a womaniser and an autocrat. What sort of a person was he really?

A touch on the shoulder interrupted his day-dream. It was Jenny, looking around to make sure they were alone.

'I've been asking around the delegation about Harold Williams' background,' she said. 'It seems he's just taken early retirement from the Foreign Office – but apparently he gets very edgy if you ask him about his old job. My guess is he was in British Intelligence.'

Before Evans could react, the room filled. They stared out at the control post across the small valley, 200 metres from the Red Crag Revolutionary Commemoration Centre.

Deserted and innocuous, the control post had been positioned perfectly for the supervisory role assigned to the Kuomintang soldiers, who monitored the comrades' comings and goings, night and day.

Not exactly the relationship of trusted partners in a united war front, Evans mused. How had the comrades slept, or carried out their daily tasks, when guns and binoculars from the control post were permanently trained upon them? They must have known the united front would fracture at some point, and that the order could come to open fire.

They must have lived in a constant state of tension, he thought. The way *he* was feeling now.

Callous wasn't a description Swanepoel would have applied to himself.

Ruthless, yes. Calculating, too. Hard, of course.

But the terrorists were the callous ones – vile specimens out to destroy Afrikanerdom. Killing a top Afrikaner politician in the sunshine, leaving his body in a bloody pool alongside a hysterical girl.

Revenge was another of his watchwords. Not blind, lashing-out revenge: but the calculating kind. Meted out according to an iron law that justified retaliation whenever your side was hit.

Always strike back. Teach them they can't mess about.

He had been summoned from Pretoria to John Vorster Square, the security headquarters at the centre of the sprawling city of Johannesburg.

With bright blue panels and plate glass windows, John Vorster Square was where scores of detainees went in and never came out. They 'fell in the showers', 'slipped on the stairs' or 'hanged themselves'. Those who didn't die were terrified of the interrogation rooms deep inside.

Swanepoel's brief was simple. But the logistics needed the care and attention of a professional. He was to take out an ANC leader in London – and a top black trade unionist in Joburg. To him, both targets were legitimate.

He despised the exiles living comfortably in the big cities of the world, and was disgusted at the way they were courted diplomatically and politically, their leaders familiar figures on the embassy cocktail circuits. All of them were vermin, wreaking havoc by pressing buttons and pulling levers from safety, thousands of kilometres away.

But black trade unionists – that was another matter. Those he feared, more than despised. The growing industrial power of the black workforce was now a serious threat to continued white dominance. He relished the opportunity of striking a blow against their unions.

Swanepoel prepared methodically for the two operations. He rang the registry and asked for the file on Dulcie September, the 45-year-old ANC representative in Paris who'd been killed by South African National Intelligence Service agents, hit by five bullets fired at close range.

Neat job, he thought. Two NIS Z-squad agents had flown in several days before, their arrival noted by the French internal secret service, the DST, according to a report in the newspaper *Le Monde*.

Only weeks before the assassination, the French had refused a request from Dulcie September for police protection: perhaps influenced by French-South African arms dealers, who wanted her eliminated.

The killers had got away unscathed and went to ground until the fuss had died down. Swanepoel liked their clean professionalism, as described in the cryptic notes on file. Maybe they could be activated again.

London wouldn't be a problem. MI5 and MI6 would turn a blind eye in practice, even if political pressure forced them to go through the motions of an investigation. They saw everything through a Cold War prism, and the apartheid government had adroitly positioned itself as a 'bulwark against communism in Southern Africa', every opponent labelled a 'communist'.

Next, he turned to the file on Thabo Kumalo, who had become internationally known for his astute handling of the last major strike in the gold mines. The file on the 41-year-old miners' leader was thick with detail.

He would have merited security service attention because of his position alone: a key figure at the top of the growing 2.5 million strong black trade union movement, which accounted for a third of the economically active black population. The previous year, nine million days had been lost to strikes by black workers. The year before it was one million. Militancy was rising.

But there was another reason for targeting Kumalo. He was suspected of helping to organise community-based street committees in Alexandra township and plotting to make the township ungovernable.

He was also said to be behind successful consumer boycotts and campaigns against black collaborators, especially black policemen who were disparagingly referred to as 'green beans' – the colour of their uniforms.

Township comrades had forced scores of 'green beans' to move out of their homes in Alexandra into tents erected in the neighbouring white suburb of Kew.

Swanepoel sat back and stretched in his chair, noting for the first time how late it was: long after midnight. The hours had rushed by since he had first opened the files. Although he felt like a drink, he knew it would be difficult to find one this late, so he decided to go back to the hotel, get a snack and a decent drink from room service.

He was tired, but content – adrenaline pumping through him. Much better than socialising with the wife and relatives. After a sleep, he would start work early in the morning on the operational details of taking out the two targets.

Dick Sewell's tour group and the Noted Persons delegation found themselves aboard the same steamer on the Yangtze River from Chongqing to Wuhan.

Both parties had been booked into first class cabins, and Sewell couldn't help feeling uncomfortable as he noticed the scores of people sleeping rough in the gangways outside, or staring through the restaurant windows, while he and his companions ate in relative luxury.

Didn't seem right, and he determined to keep his distance from the 'Noted Persons'. He disapproved of people on freebies, and their fatuous title was the final straw.

But the only spare space at lunch was at a table occupied by Jim Evans and Jenny Stuart, so he sat down reluctantly and quickly made up his mind: she was quite a girl, he a bit of a wimp.

The three grappled with their chopsticks as the dusty brown water of the Yangtze spread around their steamer. The vessel swept past villages and towns, its backwash gently rocking continuous lines of smaller boats.

There were signs of the devastation left by fierce spring storms, some with hail stones the size of eggs, driven by winds of up to Force Eleven. Several river barges had been sunk, and hundreds of nearby factories stopped production. Houses had collapsed and crops were badly damaged.

Jenny broke the awkward silence at the table. 'I know you guys usually introduce yourselves through your jobs, so I'm a social worker and Jim's a nuclear physicist. What about *you*?'

Her directness was startling, but engaging. 'Bits and pieces. Used to be in physical education.' He turned to Evans.

'Nuclear physics, hey? A practical man or an academic?' Sewell's tone wasn't hostile, but each syllable of '*a–ca–de–mic*' sounded spiky.

'A professor, actually,' Evans said, evenly.

'But not too nutty!' Jenny interjected, provoking laughter. She looked at Sewell. 'What *exactly* is your job now?'

'As I said, bits and pieces. Odd jobs here and there.' He lounged back, nonchalantly. The steamer's horn blared as it passed a large village, and a Chinese junk drifted lazily in the afternoon sun.

'Don't think I've had the pleasure of meeting your friend.' The heavily jowled Harold Williams had again appeared out of nowhere, smiling.

'Sewell. Dick Sewell. I'm with the other party on holiday.' He stood up, politely.

They shook hands.

'Old friends, are you?' asked Williams.

'No. We've just met.'

'Ah. Well, don't let me interrupt. See you all later, maybe.'

'Then again, maybe not,' Jenny muttered as Williams departed. She caught Sewell's puzzled glance. 'He's not exactly a bosom pal,' she explained.

Venter and Coetzee checked through Heathrow without difficulty, arriving overnight on a South African Airways jumbo with an open return: ostensibly to give them as much time in England as their holiday money would allow.

In their late twenties, squash rackets under their arms, they typified bronzed white South African males, and the passport officer let them through with only perfunctory queries. Might have probed further had he known they had hand luggage only, but nobody noticed or cared that they walked straight out through customs without collecting any suitcases.

From Heathrow they caught the Piccadilly line tube and

headed for an address off Earls Court Road where a self-catering flat had been booked: a week paid in advance by a middle-aged secretary in the embassy who wanted accommodation for her 'nephews'. Nobody noticed them arrive and nobody noticed them leave hours later after a sleep and a shower.

A man from the embassy was waiting for them in the pizza house off Oxford Street and they spent a pleasant hour chatting sport, each consuming several glasses of German lager before he paid the bill and they all departed. Nobody noticed that Venter was carrying a sports hold-all, left underneath the table, which had been retrieved from the diplomatic bag sent from Pretoria the previous day.

When they returned to their flat, Venter and Coetzee checked through its contents. Two air tickets via Gatwick for Berlin the following day. Details of the hotel off the Kurfürstendamm where they'd been booked to stay for a week. A new set of passports in different names. A couple of Walther pistols with optional silencers and several rounds of ammunition.

They had already memorised everything else. Name of the target. His face, from pictures studied in John Vorster Square. Images from video recordings showing the target going to and from his home. Family details, daily routines, address. Route to get there.

Venter and Coetzee had been chosen as much for their discipline as their ability. A couple of unattached young men could have a good time in London, but if Venter and Coetzee were tempted, they didn't show it – there'd be enough time to enjoy themselves in Berlin.

They spent the evening watching TV, popping out only to bring in a snack, some orange juice and food for a good breakfast from one of the late-opening stores on Earls Court Road.

Nobody noticed the lights in their flat going out at 10 p.m. as they turned in for the night. Or the lights coming back on at 5 a.m. next morning, nor the two leaving an hour later for the local tube station where they caught a Wimbledon bound train on the District Line.

Looking beyond the retreating figure of Harold Williams, Evans noticed that the banks of the Yangtze were extensively cultivated in terraces which disappeared in the mist, hardly a square metre wasted.

'You know about the nuclear industry, so can you say how much plutonium Britain exports?' Dick Sewell asked him pointedly.

'Quite a bit. Nearly four tonnes of pre-1969 plutonium produced from the civil nuclear programme were exported, mainly to America. Between 1969 and 1985 the figure was about three tonnes. All of it for the express purpose of making nuclear weapons, as the Americans at least have publicly admitted.'

In response to Jenny's quizzical glance, Evans elaborated: 'Nuclear energy and weapons are Siamese twins. Britain's nuclear energy capacity largely grew out of our weapons programme. Our military reactors at Calder Hall, Sellafield and Chapelcross all produce weapons grade plutonium for the Ministry of Defence. In the early history of the nuclear industry, enrichment plants were developed as part of the weapons programme. Only later were they adapted for civilian purposes.'

Sewell nodded, impressed. Maybe the guy wasn't such a wimp.

'So, our civil nuclear plants virtually became bomb factories for the Americans?'

'That's an overstatement, I think,' Evans replied cautiously.

'Come on!' Sewell's sarcasm was clear. Bloody academics, he thought, always qualifying in triplicate, up their own arses with their footnotes as the real world passed them by.

'Okay. The relationship is more complex than that, but I suppose you're broadly correct.' Evans frowned. 'You seem well informed.'

'I'm a member of Green Planet.' Sewell looked embarrassed, kicking himself. 'But please keep that to yourselves. You never know who's listening – especially out here.'

The target's security had been pathetic, thought Venter.

A couple of hours earlier, he and Coetzee had walked from the underground station to a large house in a leafy road in the south-west London suburb of Putney. Coetzee had slipped into the garden to wait.

The house was divided into spacious flats: one occupied by George Kasinga, his wife and two teenage sons. For such an important person in the ANC, Kasinga hardly seemed to be protected. Just one security man in the car which came to collect him.

Piece of cake.

It had all happened so fast. Everything according to plan.

The security guard rang the bell and spoke into the entryphone. Then Coetzee jumped him, breaking his neck textbook style. He grabbed the keys and climbed into the driver's seat.

The front door opened and Kasinga walked out as usual, his mind on the day ahead. Heavy calibre bullets tore into his head and through his heart as Venter pumped out six shots to make sure.

Then into the car.

Coetzee pulled away and dropped Venter near Putney railway station, where he caught the next train to Clapham Junction, five minutes away.

Coetzee abandoned the car in a quiet side street in Fulham, and joined the rush-hour commuters from Putney Bridge station to Victoria. At a Victoria Station coffee bar, he met the man from the embassy. He unobtrusively handed back the hold-all with the guns, the gloves they'd worn to avoid leaving fingerprints, and their old passports, before catching the next train to Gatwick.

With new passports, Coetzee and Venter were now flying over the manicured fields of Sussex. Meanwhile, the world's media descended on what had once been such a nice quiet road, in such a nice quiet part of London.

It was during the morning rush hour that Thabo Kumalo simply disappeared.

The charismatic trade union leader was on his way from home, near Soweto, to his office in a building owned by the local council of churches.

Nobody seemed to spot an unmarked car pulling up alongside him as he walked down Plein Street in downtown Johannesburg. Nobody witnessed the last public view of the man who had stirred up such bitterness and hatred in government circles.

Exactly what happened was never confirmed. Kumalo joined a long list of black radicals who disappeared or were mysteriously murdered. The government Home Affairs Minister officially denied any police involvement, also scorning the notion of a right-wing death squad.

But a leading black theologian warned that Kumalo's disappearance, coming on top of all the others, was causing the church to question its attitude to violence: 'It is becoming more and more difficult for us in the church to criticise people who use violence to defend themselves against the violence of the apartheid regime.'

Reading this statement in the morning newspapers, Swanepoel grimaced and entered the churchman's name in his personal notebook.

'If you want a war to the death, we'll give it to you,' he muttered to himself.

5

The Old Man sat back in the padded swivel chair behind his large wooden desk, sipping tepid tea and gazing down at the rooftops of Beijing which stretched away into the distance.

His office was high up, and the view used to excite him; now he found it depressing, the smog hanging heavily. An official memo had confirmed Beijing to be one of the world's most polluted capitals, its air thirty-five times dirtier than London's and sixteen times more contaminated than even crowded Tokyo's.

He longed for the past – for the fresh, clean air of the mountains and the beauty of the valleys which they had conquered in his youth, more than 50 years ago during the Long March.

More than 6,000 miles on foot during a year's marching to escape the pursuing Kuomintang forces of nationalist leader Chiang Kai-shek, and to join their comrades in Yan'an. Crossing mountains, glaciers and rivers, marching through swamps and snow. Raising the revolutionary spirit and consciousness of the marchers. Educating the peasants along the way. Spreading optimism.

Of the 90,000 who started, only 7,000 finished. Some dropped out, others died from wounds, hunger, disease or cold. But through this extraordinary feat of willpower and imagination they demonstrated an authority that would one day emancipate the long-suffering people of China.

He had never since experienced that same exhilaration. True, liberation had been exciting; so too had the years of progress afterwards. But now it was all going sour. Even the massive Revolutionary Museum at Yan'an was almost deserted. Once, millions had flocked to the town each year like pilgrims to Mecca, but now it was quiet, the hotels empty.

After the Long March, he had sheltered there with Mao for ten years to plan the revolution. But there was no belief anymore. The principles of the communist revolution were being abandoned to competition and market forces.

Only he could change that destructive course. It was all down to him: one of the last surviving veterans from Mao's closest circle, still in good health, the product of a careful diet and regular exercise. Not many like him in their late eighties who could retain the authority of leadership and stay the pace in the punishing cycle of ministerial responsibilities.

He was unique. Now he had to fulfil his destiny – one last task for the sake of the masses.

Evans leant over the steamer's railing, inhaling the sharpness of the night.

They'd entered the Gorges five hours before. A spectacular sunset of orange and red had been shrouded in the mist rolling down from the cliffs. Now, high above him, the mist hung heavy in the dark. Below, the swirling currents of the Yangtze stirred viciously. Powerful waters, capable of colossal destruction.

Needing some exercise after another delicious meal, he walked around the deck, picking his way carefully between passengers travelling cheaply, slumped on the deck or a bench.

Sometimes, eyes opened and faces stared up blankly, before the passengers tucked themselves back into overcoats.

Evans shivered in the cold air. He pulled open the heavy steel door, seeking the warmth inside.

Suddenly he was hit hard on the head. He reeled back, stunned. Two pairs of hands grabbed him. In the confusion, he thought they were helping. But then he was heaved up, and shoved over the railing.

No, surely not?

No! No!

Evans tried to shout, but his voice wouldn't come out. Terror spread, his legs scraping, knees scratching against the metal.

Then he was falling clumsily, half crouching, the tip of his shoe catching on something jutting out from the side of the vessel. An age before his head hit the icy, rock-hard river.

Then he was under, twisting, the current pulling him down.

Major Keith Makuyana was officially covered, with clearance from the highest political level.

He was on 'special leave', and his office was occupied by Florence Dube – his new deputy. Only she, and two others he trusted, knew the truth.

As far as the ANC was concerned, he was now a 'political liaison officer', whose role was to improve communications between them and the Zimbabwean government.

This gave Makuyana a perfect excuse to set up meetings and visits throughout the ANC network: not just in Zimbabwe, but in Zambia and Tanzania too.

And it brought back memories: the limbo life of exile in a big city; the tension of relationships, even with sympathetic governments; problems of security, whether in clandestine armed struggle or open political campaigning. The desperate vulnerability of bush camps where young guerillas debriefed and recovered after missions into enemy territory.

Makuyana watched and listened. Somewhere in the undergrowth of his talks and travels were the clues he needed. By nature, he was impatient. But this time, he told himself, patience was of the essence.

Patience and perseverance.

He had an instinctive confidence in his new deputy. Florence was the first woman to occupy the job, and her appointment had raised a few eyebrows: not least because she was Ndebele in a Shona, male-dominated profession.

She wasn't as experienced as her predecessor Ed Mugadza, but she was still a cool customer. Practical, determined and efficient. She had a good sense of humour, and she was also tough – a necessity in their trade.

Now, Makuyana was parked in a layby on the main road south, about fifteen minutes from Harare. As he leant out of the window for some fresh air, heat leapt up at him amidst a buzz of flies from the dry, dusty brown earth. It was still hot for late autumn.

A dark blue Toyota pulled up behind him. In his driving mirror he could see Florence at the wheel. They each sat still for several minutes, listening and watching: standard routine for a meet like this. A couple of lorries drove past, then a Volkswagen Golf. But their drivers took no notice of the two parked vehicles.

Makuyana started his engine and drove back along the way they had come, eyes alert for any waiting pursuers. None. He wasn't taking any chances. Not after Ed Mugadza's death. Next time someone died, he'd vowed it wouldn't be a member of *his* department.

Florence followed him. When he pulled off the main road again she parked and joined him in his car.

'*Unjani!*' she greeted him with a grin. 'How's the holiday going?'

He couldn't help grinning back. Here they were, in a serious meeting to discuss mutual progress, but she had eased the tension by teasing him.

'Not too bad. Lots of travel. But no time for boozing or socialising, I'm afraid.'

'Ah, what a shame.' She stared at her boss. He could be good company when relaxing, but she couldn't imagine him boozing. Too self-contained, too disciplined to let himself go.

'Any happenings in the department?'

'Not much. Mostly routine. Still no lead on the Temba letter bomb. As far as we know, the suspect hasn't come back into the country. But there *is* one thing. I was called in by the President's office. Apparently, there's a high-level delegation from China arriving next month.'

'Oh?' Makuyana sounded indifferent, another bunch of VIPs needing to be fussed over.

'The President's office was concerned about something unusual. As you know, we've good relations with the Chinese, thanks to their support for ZANU in the struggle. It's nothing specific. All quite hush-hush and vague. But it seems Beijing is worried about Pretoria. They suspect the South Africans are planning something.'

Crunch! The impact and freezing wetness jerked Evans back into consciousness. He felt as if he was in a whirlpool, looking down at himself in the brown water, twisting and turning in its multitudinous eddies as the river thrust its way down though the Gorges to the Yellow Sea, more than 1,600 kilometres away.

Couldn't help swallowing the stuff, his arms were heavy and useless, fighting the force thrusting at him from every direction: crushing, suffocating.

Time seemed to pause, as his emotions cascaded. Guilt. Regret. He wished he'd posted that card to his parents. Wished he'd told Jenny how he felt about her. Wished he'd left clearer guidelines on his latest research project so it wouldn't be wasted. Wished he'd made a will.

Then guilt turned to anger. Why *him*? Too young. Too much still to do.

He started to hallucinate, feeling his inner self lifting up and out of his body, which wallowed uselessly underneath, as he was summoned towards a seductive pathway of light and peace: relief from pain and struggle.

Sewell heard a scuffle on the deck, and caught a glimpse of a body tumbling over the side in the darkness. He knew it must be Evans who'd left their table earlier, and whom he'd followed out for some fresh air.

Rushing past a slammed door, he saw the body splash into the water, the fast-flowing current carrying it along in the same direction as the boat.

He was trained not to panic, so he scanned the deck hurriedly, grabbed two lifebelts and some rope which he tied onto a rail. Every second was precious: nobody could survive for long in those currents.

Tearing off his jacket and shoes, he banged on the restaurant windows, gesticulating back at the river. A wild figure startling the diners, hoping to Christ someone realised the deadly seriousness.

Sewell ran to the stern, clambered onto the deck rail, looked desperately at the water, and thought he could see a body now bobbing behind the steamer. He acted instinctively.

Clutching onto the lifebelts, he jumped – vaguely aware of shouts behind him. He hit the surface feet first, clinging onto the lifebelts as his arms almost jerked out of their sockets.

Wavelets broke over him. It was bitterly cold, he couldn't see properly, tried to paddle back, straining against the powerful current. Wasn't making much progress, but figured that even if could slow the speed at which he was being dragged back, the body stood a chance of catching him up.

The body. Christ! It *was* Evans!

If it hadn't been for a slight movement on the surface, moonlight glancing off a sodden white shirt, Sewell might never have spotted him.

Paddling furiously, frantic with worry, he reached out to grab the still form. Evans was drifting lifelessly, sinking.

Sewell would never have believed a slightly built man could be so heavy. He'd been trained to save drowning people, knew all the techniques and tricks. But training didn't cover real life – or real death.

He tugged in frustration, heaving Evans onto the spare lifebelt, managing at least to get his head out of the water. Evans' eyes were staring blankly. Was he still breathing?

Now what?

Sewell hadn't planned the next stage, and suddenly felt helpless.

The steamer's horn sounded. Was it slowing down? Was that a lifeboat being lowered down over the side?

Perhaps...

Yes! The lifeboat splashed down, rocking crazily as the steamer swung away. Sewell screamed desperately: every second meant the difference between recovery and death.

At long last, the boat was alongside. To a jabbering of Chinese voices, Evans' limp body was pulled on board, his crumpled figure prone, face a ghostly grey-blue under the boat's lamp. Then Sewell was hoisted on board too.

Sewell grabbed Evans' legs, gesticulating for help, somehow managing to communicate with the boatmen as they rolled Evans onto his back, head resting on the bottom, water dribbling out of his mouth.

Seconds ticked away, each one shortening Evans' life. They had to get the water out of his stomach.

Sewell sat him upright. Nothing. They turned him over, and Sewell pushed hard on his back, repeating the pressure until at last water and vomit gushed out of his mouth.

Quick. Get him onto his back again. Support his head. Give him the kiss of life. Shivering with tension and cold, Sewell knelt over Evans. Nothing had ever been so vital. Deep breath.

Then out. He cupped his lips over Evans' mouth. Pumped his chest hard, trying frantically to get his breathing going. Four times. Five times. Six. Seven. Wasn't working. But it had to! Mustn't fail now.

Sewell was in a frenzy, exhausted, but Evan still had no heartbeat. He roughly massaged his sternum. Evans' face contorted. A response at bloody last!

Finally, Evans stirred and spluttered. Slowly, his breathing grew steadier, though still precarious. Sewell saw that the boat had bumped into the side of the steamer. He caught sight of Jenny staring down, her eyes terrified.

'He's alive!' Sewell screamed. 'Get some blankets! Quick!'

The languid seductive brightness was ebbing. Evans felt as if he was an object hurtling backwards.

He opened his eyes, aware of a confused blur of faces. He seemed to be hooked up to an intravenous drip and a cardiac monitor. He closed his eyes again.

What the hell had happened? He was naked underneath the blanket. Where were his clothes? He felt so cold: numb, battered. As if he didn't fit properly into his body anymore.

Slowly, he began to remember. The terror returned. Fight it!

Sewell started to cry. Couldn't stop himself. He felt a surge of shame. He'd never cried in public since childhood. Stoicism was his mantra.

But then he had never pulled anyone back from the dead.

Captain Mauritz Swanepoel was reminiscing, loving his captive audience – three young security service agents, who were happy to let him talk of old times, as the beers and wine flowed.

They sat in a secluded cubicle of a restaurant in Johannesburg's Houghton suburb: a venue Swanepoel had chosen deliberately. It appealed to his wry sense of humour to celebrate the success of his two missions in this rich English-speaking suburb which had, for so many years, elected the renowned opposition MP, Helen Suzman.

'The early sixties. Good years. Less bureaucracy. Could just *do* things. Sometimes an outcry, but – what the hell – nobody could touch us. They still can't, I suppose, but there's more red tape, more desk men pushing forms.

'Things were more clearcut then.' He chuckled. 'We had some real coups. Caught Mandela's ANC cronies at Rivonia where their *uMkhonto weSizwe* group was planning sabotage. They had become too casual with security and we rumbled them.

'Then there was the John Harris business. A young teacher. Member of the old Alan Paton Liberal party – one of those Young Turks who couldn't accept the party's non-violence policy. Harris joined a group called ARM – African Resistance Movement. They were *amateurs*.' He spat the word out.

'We had the ARM sussed almost from the beginning. I remember when the call came through – July 1964, I think – that there was a bomb in a suitcase on the concourse of Joburg railway station.

'It was due to go off in fifteen minutes. The caller said he was ARM. He said something like: "This is a symbolic protest against apartheid. Nobody must get hurt. Please clear the concourse. Do not try to defuse the bomb. The suitcase is triggered to explode if it is opened."

'He wanted to have his cake and eat it. To make an impact without hurting anyone.'

Swanepoel paused, enjoying the moment, his audience expectant as he savoured his wine. 'Now what would *you* have done in a situation like that?' he asked.

'Let it go off,' the young sergeant spoke quietly. He had a reputation for toughness in the interrogation room. Some of the others looked shocked.

'Exactly! That's what we did – let it explode.' Swanepoel gave the young man an approving glance. 'Could have cleared the concourse – but we didn't.

'The ARM did us a bloody big favour. It was an awkward time. Lots of trouble, lots of resistance. But after that bomb – 22 whites injured, and an old white grandmother killed – there was fear of more terrorism, and that gave us a free hand to launch a massive crackdown. We picked up hundreds of activists. No messing – we beat the shit out of everyone. Those who had something to say talked. The others we just let go.

'When we detained John Harris, one of my colleagues interrogated him and somehow Harris' jaw got broken – don't know how!' Swanepoel winked, as laughter broke out around the table.

'Harris' close friend and co-conspirator was John Lloyd who turned state witness against him. We'd detained Lloyd several hours before the bomb was planted. Because of that some said we knew about the bomb plan in advance. Maybe.

'Anyway, Lloyd gave us the key evidence – the *only* evidence – that it was pre-meditated murder. In other words, his friend had committed a capital crime. So we hanged Harris by the neck the following year. He was the only white we executed for a political crime. I'll always remember the date: 1 April 1965 – April Fool's Day.'

Makuyana huddled with Selby Mngadi in the Harare MK commander's home, studying a list of names. Three of them, Makuyana noted, were present when he and Ed Mugadza met Mngadi after Robert Temba's letter bomb attack.

'Can you also get me a list of the people who knew your confidential number – the one they phoned with the tip-off about the house we were watching when Ed was killed?' Makuyana asked.

Mngadi nodded, getting up. 'I'm thirsty. A beer?'

'Yes, please.' He waited for the ANC man to return with a couple of bottles of cold lager. 'There's another matter. Why would the Chinese government be worried about South Africa?'

Mngadi's lips tightened, as did the permanent creases on his forehead. He paused, pensively sipped his beer, then shrugged. 'No idea, I'm afraid.'

The Gorges were behind them now, and the banks of the Yangtze resumed their muddy appearance.

The steamer had stopped for half a day while Evans was rushed to hospital and resuscitated, pulling through remarkably well to the immense relief of the delegation.

He was still deeply asleep in his cabin when Wang called the delegation together. The interpreter looked worried, even a little haggard, Jenny noted. She was feeling that way herself.

'I must ask you to be extra careful during the remainder of the journey. I will have to report the accident to my superiors in the Peoples Friendship Association in Beijing. They were most concerned when Mr Evans was nearly hit by the car in Chengdu. We cannot allow anything to happen to our foreign guests. This latest accident puts in jeopardy future invitations for delegations like yours.'

'"Accident"? A fit man falling over the side? Pushed, wasn't he?' Jenny's outburst was spontaneous. She'd not had a chance to talk to Evans or Sewell.

'No. It was an *accident*,' Wang dwelt on the word pointedly.

Later, from the radio telephone behind the bridge, he phoned two Beijing numbers: one official, the other not. The unofficial call was to the Old Man. Wang felt awkward to be reporting another failure, asking for further guidance.

Afterwards, Harold Williams made a call of his own: to a small bare office in Curzon Street. It belonged to F7: the section within MI5 which monitored 'domestic subversion' – radical groups like anti-apartheid activists, feminists, pacifists, nuclear disarmers and ecologists.

'Gerald? Good to hear your voice. Harold here. Sorry about the open line. I'm in the middle of the Yangtze.'

He smiled at the exclamation from the other end, then continued.

'Need a hand, old boy. A lead on a name. Sewell. Dick Sewell. Maybe Richard Sewell. Probably in his mid-thirties. Nothing else known. If you have anything on him, could you call me? I'll be in a hotel in Wuhan in thirty-six hours' time.' He gave the hotel number.

'Oh – and check another name too, please. Dr Jim Evans, a nuclear physicist.'

Evans' dreams had come thick and fast.

He was climbing a mountain but couldn't get any higher. He was trying to fly by flapping his arms, willing himself upward and onward, but to no avail.

Finally, he jerked awake, his heart pounding. What had happened? Where was he? Slowly, he opened his eyes and was aware of two figures. Jenny, sitting close by – and Wang, hovering.

'How are you feeling?' Jenny tucked the blanket more comfortably around him.

'Not sure,' he stammered, glancing apprehensively at Wang.

'Mr Evans. I must apologise for speaking so bluntly. But this is the *second* time in a few days you have come close to death.'

Wang paused, like headteacher reprimanding an errant pupil. 'You are causing us great worry. I must insist you are more careful. No more accidents please.'

Evans closed his eyes, trying to order his jumbled thoughts. He remembered falling over the side. Cold water. Drowning. Death. But he was no *longer* dead. And now Wang. Always Wang, reprimanding, threatening.

'Just leave me alone,' he pleaded, reaching out for Jenny's hand, signalling her to stay, then – as if escaping – he slipped back into sleep.

He awoke with a caked dry mouth, knotted stomach, splitting head, aching limbs. No idea how much time had gone by. Again, two figures, talking quietly in the corner of the cabin. He relaxed when he realised Sewell was now with Jenny: not Wang.

But the horror kept returning. The bizarre feeling that he was leaving his body . . .

What the hell had happened?

Over the next two hours the three pieced together the story. By the end, Evans was at a loss for words. Sewell had saved his life. Saying thanks seemed grossly inadequate.

But Sewell, though sympathetic, had already moved on to more urgent concerns. 'Someone on board tried to kill you Jim – why?'

An awkward silence.

'It's time we levelled with each other,' Jenny startled them both. 'Dick put his life on the line for you. Now he deserves to know everything *we* know.'

After they'd put Sewell in the picture, he looked grim, pondering his own predicament. Would he still be seen as a gallant rescuer? Or might he come under suspicion – maybe putting at risk his vital Green Planet mission? Was he compromised by his inadvertent involvement?

Yet, the nuclear link was clear. Sewell leaned forward suddenly, his broad shoulders filling his shirt. Evans felt envious of the other man's physical prowess.

But Sewell seemed indifferent. An austere man, quietly confident.

'There is something I have to tell you,' he began, 'but you must swear it goes no further.'

The other two nodded. Jenny sipped her tea, Evans pulled himself up on his pillow. As Sewell began to talk, they both fell silent – and felt even more afraid.

'For good or ill, we're now in this together,' Sewell said, not revealing the extent of his concern.

He continued: 'And now, if you don't mind Jim, I think I'll join you here in the spare bunk. They may try again – whoever they are. We have another fourteen hours before we disembark at Yichang. Jenny, could you guard him while I grab my things?'

Jenny locked the door behind Sewell, and kissed Jim on the cheek, her eyes suddenly moist. She didn't have to say she thought she'd lost him.

He didn't have to tell her how, in those last deathly moments in the river, he'd wanted to shout out how much he cared for her. No words were needed. They both knew. Her soft mouth found his cracked lips. Their tongues explored each other lightly, gently.

Jim began to feel alive again.

Selby Mngadi was in a dilemma over Makuyana's question about a possible Beijing-Pretoria connection.

Consulting ANC intermediaries in Dar es Salaam, Lusaka or even London could jeopardise their essential security network. Still, he had no choice.

He called in his three closest aides. According to Makuyana one of them was a potential traitor. But, who?

Amir Bhajee was thin and wiry: the son of a veteran Indian activist who had been driven into exile. George Petersen was a Cape Coloured, curly haired, a little overweight. Moses Msimang was tall and brooding, his skin ebony-black.

A good team, Mngadi reflected. Bhajee intense and serious, Petersen high-spirited and garrulous, Msimang driven and brisk.

Could one of *these* men – his most trusted comrades – really be a traitor? It was hard to imagine, even harder to accept.

They listened to his briefing about the China issue in silence, all showing the sort of scepticism Mngadi shared.

'Check it out for me, would you? But don't set any hares running. Be discreet,' he told them.

'A Beijing connection with the apartheid regime? Really? What's the source?' Bhajee asked, suspiciously.

'Can't say, I'm afraid. Privileged information.'

Mngadi's answer didn't surprise or give offence. They were accustomed to their boss working strictly on a need-to-know basis. Although his aides sometimes found this frustrating, Mngadi insisted the less people knew, the less they could give away.

But one of the trio was now fearful. One of them guessed who the source might be.

Agent Swanepoel had been called by his chief, General KJ van der Walt, to meet him at John Vorster Square. That morning, the city centre was abnormally still.

Nearly two million black workers had stayed at home, marking the start of a three-day protest against government restrictions on trade unions, and fresh bans on anti-apartheid groups. Early trains coming in from the townships, usually jam-packed, were virtually empty.

The biggest strike in the country's history.

The recent disappearance of Thabo Kumalo had only inflamed the situation. Protesters in Soweto carried posters with his name and picture. Two limpet mines went off on the main railway line to Pretoria, knocking it out for the rest of the day. There were petrol bomb attacks on buses. Shots were fired at patrolling armoured vehicles, and two black policemen were stoned to death.

Still, life went on, Swanepoel reflected. They won't humiliate us, he thought. His wife had given up trying to persuade him to join the family. She wasn't really missing him anyway. No physical bond between them. For years they'd slept in separate beds, growing further apart in his long absences away from home on various missions.

They had very little in common anymore, except for their children and grandchildren. As long as Noeline stayed busy looking after them, she was almost happier without him.

Swanepoel waited outside the General's office, making small

talk to a secretary about the grandchildren whose names he hardly remembered. Had to keep up appearances.

The door opened and the tall figure of KJ ushered him in. There were two other men in the room: business types, Swanepoel thought, smart suits, coloured handkerchiefs protruding from their top pockets, expensive leather briefcases and a superior air.

'Captain Swanepoel, gentleman.' The three shook hands, as KJ paused. 'Mauritz, you won't mind if I don't introduce our two friends. They prefer to remain anonymous.'

Swanepoel shrugged. Not bothered in the slightest about the identity of these two jumped-up yuppies.

'Good. Now, a whisky for everyone?' KJ's timely offer broke the tension. As he poured, he started to talk.

'Mauritz,' he began, deliberately signalling familiarity and trust, 'we have a problem, potentially very serious.'

He paused, gulping at his whisky, the sun shining through the plate glass window highlighting his features, which Swanepoel noticed seemed suddenly haggard. So, the boss was worried?

'Our friends are experts in – let us say – nuclear matters. For some years now we have been extending relationships with foreign elements to assist with our independent nuclear capability – a project crucial to our survival. We need to improve our technical know-how, and we need to import reprocessed material, and modern equipment. Launchers, that sort of thing.

'Fortunately, other countries also need this kind of cooperation. You scratch my back, I'll scratch yours! So, we have found friends in unlikely places. Israel for example – that should appeal to your sense of historic irony, Mauritz!'

KJ chuckled at his own joke as the others smiled weakly. Then his eyes narrowed.

'All this is Section 4 classified.' He turned to the two visitors, 'That means top secret. It's why I need a trusted colleague like Mauritz to help.'

He's building me up the whole time, putting on a show, but *why*? Swanepoel was perplexed, the others silent.

'There's been a leak. We've had a message from Harare. The ANC has been tipped off about the Beijing connection.'

'*Beijing* connection?' Swanepoel's surprised exclamation seemed to relax the other two, who exchanged significant glances.

One of them spoke. 'We have had secret contacts with friendly elements in China. They have been of considerable assistance. Unless that assistance continues, we may not be able to achieve our objective of becoming the dominant nuclear power in Africa.'

KJ leant forward. 'So, we must discover the source of the leak – assess its importance, to find out how to plug it.'

'Can you rubbish it as a rumour?' The younger of the two leant forward, his forehead furrowed.

A streak of annoyance passed across KJ's face. The two guests might not have noticed but Swanepoel did, recognising the telltale tapping of KJ's fingernails on the side of the whisky glass.

'Many things are possible,' KJ said. 'Leave that to us. But is there anything more we need to know? Any names? Any leads on possible sources of the leak?'

'Not that we know of.' The two seemed deflated, even depressed – and Swanepoel couldn't help being pleased.

KJ poured out another whisky, signalling Swanepoel to remain. As the two visitors left, he gestured towards the door closing behind them.

'Smart-arses. Makes you wonder why we are still fighting, Mauritz. Protecting our country's future for boot-lickers like that. They couldn't fight their way out of a paper bag. Our people have become soft, Mauritz, damned soft. One day they'll find this out to their cost.'

Swanepoel nodded in sympathy. He and KJ were kindred spirits. He supposed that was why KJ kept him for special missions. The General didn't relate well to his younger staff anymore. The generation gap was widening.

KJ handed him a refilled glass, grimacing as he paced about the room.

'That's all we're breeding these days. People who don't know what real fighting is. Not like us, eh, Mauritz! Not like us. The rate of psychiatric problems among our young soldiers on the border is now three times higher than that of the Rhodesian Army in the sixties and seventies – *three* times! I tell you, the Rhodesians were tough, man. Tough. They were reared in the bush. Ours are just townies, soft as butter.'

He sat down, breathing heavily. He's looking old, Swanepoel thought. Christ, he *is* old – and so am I.

'Anyway, Mauritz. Down to business. That leak about the nuclear connection. I want you to follow it up. Go back to our ANC source. The one on your patch in Harare. Lie low. Remember there's been lots of bother up there recently. Most of it created by us. So don't attract attention. Just fish about. See what you can catch. Okay?'

Swanepoel nodded. 'No problem.'

If he didn't sound enthusiastic, he wasn't. He'd enjoyed his spell of action in the old country and it was lonely across the border.

'There's a second matter,' KJ continued. 'The military are getting restless. Years bogged down in Angola and South West, chasing around Mozambique, and all the time the bloody ANC slipping through the *fokken* net. *Ja*, the bosses are pissed off.

'And now our youngsters are trying to dodge the draft. Their parents are worried they'll come home in wooden boxes.'

Swanepoel nodded, remembering how America's Vietnam War effort had suddenly collapsed in the late 1960s.

His whisky glass was empty again, and KJ topped it up.

'Rumour has it, the military want to teach everyone a lesson.'

He paused.

'A *big* lesson.'

Swanepoel leaned forward in his chair. KJ took a deep breath and continued.

'We've developed a new battlefield nuclear weapon. A warhead inside a special shell that can be launched from our new Olifant tank – you remember, the tank we converted from the British-made Centurion.

'The rumour is we might just try it out in Zimbabwe – to frighten off the ANC, and stop them crossing the Limpopo. Only problem is the range. It's too short to prevent our own troops being harmed – if not from the explosion itself, then from the fall-out.

'So, we're now trying to get another battlefield weapon with a longer range. Something like NATO's Lance missile which is deployed in Western Europe and has a range of 120 kilometres. It sits astride a trailer-type truck, so it's pretty mobile.

'But we're at a critical stage, and time is pressing. We lack the know-how. And that's where the Chinese come in. We may even have to import the warheads from our friends in Beijing.'

He hunched over his desk, glass empty again.

'So, there you have it Mauritz. Grade A info. If it doesn't scare the shit out of *you*, it sure does me. Be careful, Mauritz. This one is big. Bloody big.'

The Old Man asked his chauffeur to pull in, so that he could get a better view.

Rowdy students were filling Tiananmen Square, which had been closed off by police as patrol cars drove up and down trying to clear the crowds. The students were sitting on the steps of the Museum of Revolution, protesting about lack of democracy, their demands coinciding with simmering public discontent over rising food prices and public corruption.

Although the anarchy offended his sense of discipline and order, the Old Man smiled. Perhaps this latest wave of protests might trigger a new round of destabilisation and torpedo the reform programme instituted by the Party Leader. And if that happened, the Old Man could move.

Even the People's Liberation Army, the world's largest and most secretive armed force, was growing restive. Morale was flagging. The defence budget was cut again, pay and status were low – and there was a shortage of good quality recruits.

The army had been instructed to become more self-financing, by selling arms abroad and by transforming its supply factories into commercial enterprises. Deals with foreigners were no longer enmeshed in bureaucracy.

The Old Man knew these opportunities would probably be exploited by the unscrupulous for corrupt personal gain. This offended his puritanical instincts. But he had to acknowledge the irony that this 'capitalist road' had given him the opening he needed to regroup – and acquire the technology and military strength to succeed.

The Old Man hated the Leader's Western airs and graces, hated the way his wife walked the international stage alongside him, flaunting her expensive silk dresses like a celebrity. But he'd have to be on his best behaviour when he accompanied them on their official visit to Africa in two months' time: Kenya, Tanzania and Zimbabwe.

He would be a model of courtesy and deference – at least in public.

'We always aim at military or police targets, never innocent by-standers.'

Amir Bhajee gave a standard ANC reply to Makuyana's question: 'how do you distinguish between legitimate and illegitimate targets inside South Africa?'

Like Mngadi's other two aides, Bhajee looked bored. Didn't really know what they were doing in this bare room, at the back of an empty community hall in a Harare township. Except they'd been invited – instructed actually.

'But who is innocent?' Makuyana pressed. 'Surely *every* white benefits from apartheid? Even white liberals do nicely out of it, don't they?'

'Yes, of course – but we can't afford to be equated with terrorist groups like the Red Brigade.' Fellow aide, Moses Msimang sounded irritated.

'So, it's just tactical?'

'No! A matter of principle. Our fight is not with ordinary white people. It's with the system of apartheid, and the police-military power system propping it up.' Bhajee was arguing passionately now.

'We will have to – we *want* to – live peacefully with whites after we have secured liberation. We'll need their skills to help run the country. We don't deny their right to live as equals. We always try to avoid violence against civilians.'

'But sometimes you can't.'

'Yes – I accept that. There'll always be a risk of innocent casualties. A fact of war. Millions of innocents were killed in the war against the Nazis. People who weren't in uniform. Sometimes people were caught in the crossfire. I compare us to the French resistance or Tito's partisans. *Guerrilla* struggle – not *terrorism*.'

'What's the difference?'

George Petersen interjected. 'You should know. You were part of Zimbabwe's liberation struggle. Was it all clean? Was it all neat and tidy?'

'No,' replied Makuyana. 'But our roots were much more firmly based within the country. The ANC's armed action is largely organised from outside. You have to rely on hit-and-run tactics, rather than continuous attrition.'

Bhajee picked up the argument.

'Terrorism is indiscriminate, deliberately aimed at innocent by-standers: hi-jacking aircraft, putting a bomb in a crowded shopping centre. Guerrilla action may provoke casualties but that is not the purpose. The objective is to damage the state.'

'Why are you raising this question?' Moses Msimang spoke quietly. He hadn't said much, never did.

'I'm just interested in how the ANC sees things,' Makuyana replied evenly. 'What if the casualties are black? The fact is, most ANC action has resulted in more black than white casualties. What if your own relatives, your own friends were killed? Not deliberately, but as a consequence of some armed action?'

Msimang exploded. 'The trouble with you ZANU people is that you're running the country now! Stability is suddenly important for you – your jobs, your lifestyles. You want everything nice and orderly. You've forgotten what it's really like. My family are Zulus. At home in Natal they're targets for Buthelezi's Inkatha forces because they back the ANC and the United Democratic Front. We can have pretty little conversations all night. But for me it's life and death.'

He stormed out of the room.

'Don't worry about Moses,' said Bhajee, soothingly. 'He's just lost his father and two brothers. Murdered: he thinks by Inkatha, though maybe the security services.'

'What about your own families?' Makuyana asked.

Bhajee answered first. 'My sister served two long periods in detention without trial, then was banned. The family is regularly harassed by the Special Branch.'

'My family always kept their heads low,' Petersen explained. 'Just got on with their lives. It's a bit easier if you're a coloured.'

'The life of an exile isn't easy, is it?' Makuyana asked sympathetically. 'Everyone needs a home. You're marooned up here. I know what it's like. And you worry about your relatives or family left behind. Does the South African government try to get at you by intimidating those closest to you?'

'Yes, that's always a concern,' Bhajee nodded.

'Well – not so much,' said Petersen.

'Really?' Bhajee looked at him in surprise.

Makuyana had mentioned the issue almost casually, trying to

switch the conversation to a more relaxed level after his probing about the ethics of guerrilla warfare. But he had succeeded in provoking reactions from two of the three. When their families were raised, Msimang had stormed out and Petersen had given an odd answer.

Why?

Had he stumbled onto something, Makuyana wondered? What would turn an ANC cadre into a traitor? Money? Possibly – though you couldn't easily spend it.

But pressure on the family? Now *that* was an interesting thought.

Evans was slowly recovering.

Jenny had somehow managed to find some dietary supplements: zinc pills to rebuild his strength, vitamins C and D to improve his immunity.

She also tried to keep him to a strict diet: no milk products, no wheat, little meat, and no added sugar or salt. Coffee and tea with caffeine were out. Her ministrations provoked much teasing.

Evans hadn't seen much more of the Yangtze. Nor had Sewell, who stayed with him in the cabin until they docked at Yichang, where the two groups had been driven to a special entrance at the main railway station. There they waited in a room with plush rugs and deep sofas reserved for 'soft class' passengers, before boarding the overnight train to Wuhan. The two parties of foreigners were to remain together for the final leg of the tour.

Sewell stuck close to Evans, and switched accommodation to share the same twin-bedded room in their hotel in Wuhan. But he felt torn. His Green Planet mission tugged him into secrecy; his innate humanity pulled him quite the other way.

He also felt rather jealous. Evans was obviously besotted with Jenny, and it reminded him of how *he* had once felt. He had a sudden flashback to buying the one-bedroom flat with his girlfriend. It had signified their love and shared future: maybe they'd have kids one day. But that was all history now. Because *he* had made it history, and she couldn't accept his long absences.

Meanwhile, the phone rang in Harold Williams' hotel room. A call from the man in Curzon Street, who chose his words carefully on the open line.

'Hullo – Harold?'

'Yes.'

'Gerald here. Got some feedback for you. The Professor seems clean. Good professional record, no sign of extra-mural interests.'

'Oh? That's a surprise.'

'But the other laddie, quite a goer! Seen lots of action. An eco-freak. His file's pretty bulky. Of the two, he's the one to keep an eye on, I'd say.'

When Swanepoel drove up to the Beitbridge border post, he was thinking about the next anti-apartheid activist to be eliminated.

The car bomb would probably be activated about now, he thought, looking at his watch. The target was a 50-year-old lawyer, Hugh Goldberg, and the bomb had been primed to explode as he turned the key to the door of his Honda, parked outside the block of flats where he lived in Maputo.

An ANC member, Goldberg had been detained without trial under the 90-day law for his anti-apartheid activities in Cape Town in the 1960s. He was now working on a new constitution for South Africa, so he was a desk man not a combatant. But he'd still been selected by Swanepoel, following the pledge by General Magnus Malan, South Africa's Minister of Defence: 'Wherever the ANC is we will eliminate it.'

'Good holiday?' The border guard glanced casually at his passport.

'Fine, thanks. But always nice to be home.'

'Just need to run you through the computer, won't be long.'

The guard went back into his kiosk. Swanepoel was unworried – just the normal routine when re-entering Zimbabwe. He was thinking of the bomb: another blow struck against the enemy.

'Excuse me, Mr Herson. Please step inside. We need this filled out.' The border guard handed Swanepoel a lengthy form. 'Just a random check. A new procedure when we're not too busy.' He gestured at the empty road. 'We have to get some other details. Also, I must search your car.'

Swanepoel felt like moaning but was anxious to seem cooperative. 'Ah, well, us pensioners – got all the time in the world!'

He was shown into a bare office. It was suddenly chilly – even here in the lowveld.

Outside, two men made a perfunctory search of the car, then unobtrusively fixed a small transmitter under the offside rear wheel arch. Swanepoel didn't notice. He'd gone for a pee. Needed to do that more frequently these days. Inwardly he cursed officialdom. Outwardly he remained polite.

A few minutes later the man behind the glass partition accepted his form and gave it a cursory glance. 'All questions completed?'

Swanepoel nodded, imagining the buzzer positioned discreetly above the official's right knee. The buzzer which, if pressed, would produce a lot of hassle he could well do without.

'Okay, all in order. Here's your passport.'

Swanepoel returned to his car, looking around. Nobody seemed to be taking any notice.

God, he could do with a slug of brandy. The delay at the border had rattled him. Perhaps he was getting too long in the tooth for the tension of field action.

Still, not to worry, on his way now. He would stop en route to collect some booze and a bite to eat – then go home and relax.

*

As Swanepoel pulled away, Florence Dube's phone rang.

'Beitbridge here. Temba bomb subject just crossed the border. We attached the transmitter as instructed. You should pick up the signal when he gets near Harare.'

'Any bother?' she asked.

'No, the old guy wasn't too happy, but he cooperated. We swept the car. Clean. No electronic gadgets, no contraband.'

'Thanks.'

'Pleasure. Any time.' The border official tried to visualise the woman at the other end, thinking she sounded attractive.

Florence spent an hour thoroughly reading the Temba file, noting Ed Mugadza's instructions to the team at Beitbridge and his scribbled comments.

Although Herson didn't outwardly seem that suspicious, she had every confidence in Mugadza. He'd been an experienced and thorough intelligence officer. Also, there was no other lead. Just days of wasted effort: trudging round the city on pointless visits to innocuous people.

Details of Herson's background were on a separate sheet, together with a print-out from the vehicle licensing centre giving his car registration number, type and colour.

She decided to drive south on the main Harare road and look out for him. The transmitter would be a godsend. She could tail him at a distance, and check him out.

This was her chance to prove herself – as a woman, as a young person, as an Ndebele. She was an outsider who'd found herself on the inside, having to work doubly hard, never making a mistake.

She would give it her all.

When Hugh Goldberg opened his car door, there was a deafening explosion which threw him across the road. A child, playing nearby, and a passing motorist were badly injured.

The blast reduced his Honda to a pile of tangled metal, shattering windows upstairs in his block of flats.

Miraculously, Goldberg was still conscious. His right arm was shattered and his body drenched in blood, but he struggled into a sitting position and called out for help. He would soon be fighting for his life in intensive care.

The previous year a white Angolan paratrooper with a South African passport had been arrested in Maputo with a suitcase bomb, so this time KJ had insisted the agent must leave no trace.

Swanepoel, always to be relied upon, had ensured that.

Wang Bi Nan was confused by the information from London. Evans in the clear, and Sewell suspect? Didn't make sense.

Why did the British not have something on *Evans*?

Sure, Sewell had also been in Beijing when Evans had picked up the information from the students, but . . .

Wait.

Maybe *that* was it? Maybe Sewell was running errands for Evans? Maybe *he* had collected the documents?

Wang smacked the table in frustration – he should have got his man to identify the foreigner who had collected that envelope from the students at the bar. If it was indeed Sewell, it would explain why they'd never found the documents when searching Evans' room and belongings.

Wang's mind raced, not just one, but two targets now: he would have to brief his team on this latest complication.

Evans wondered if he was having some sort of breakdown.

He'd felt secure recuperating on the boat with his friends and had slept throughout the train journey, but now in the Wuhan hotel he felt vulnerable again. His concentration was shot, he couldn't follow the morning briefing at the city's university, and had asked to be excused from the rest of the day's itinerary. He tried to relax in his room, but couldn't read or sleep. Was living on his nerves.

The rat-a-tat-tat on his door jerked him bolt upright. Sewell was out for the day, Evans on his own. And the door wasn't even locked! He cursed the Chinese habit of leaving hotel rooms accessible.

'Who is it?' His voice had a note of desperation.

'Security officers.'

Hell, not more bloody officials. He'd answered enough questions already, first on the boat, then waiting for the train at Yichang while the others visited the giant hydro-electric complex which fed off the mighty waters of the Yangtze.

He opened the door tentatively to three Chinese, their stiff formality making him shiver uncontrollably.

'Professor Evans,' the senior man began, 'we work for the Public Security Bureau. We have had reports about you. First the collision with the car, then your near drowning. *Accidents*? Is that what they were, Professor?'

Evans felt he was being put on the spot: 'I can't be sure.'

'But you are doubtful – yes?'

'Yes.'

'So, who would want to harm you, Professor Evans?'

'No idea, haven't done anything wrong, have I?'

'Not that we know of.' The security man sounded chilly. 'But we cannot afford to risk anything else happening to you. It would not be good for our reputation. If you agree, from now on you will be placed under official surveillance and protection. You will not go anywhere without informing one of my staff.' He pointed at the other two.

'My men will keep your hotel room under observation and follow you wherever you go. Until you cross the border into Hong Kong, you will stay within their sight please. Is that acceptable?'

The question was rhetorical, as Evans knew.

'Thank you,' he heard himself stuttering.

6

Florence Dube was parked in an empty yard alongside a petrol station on the outskirts of the city, her car receiver able to pick up Swanepoel's vehicle. It was still nearly 50 kilometres away, its signal displayed on a small screen fixed to her dashboard.

She'd arrived early, partly to avoid the Harare rush hour and partly to read a report which her office had prepared. It documented the history of attacks on ANC personnel, including the assassination of the ANC representative in Zimbabwe, Joe Gqabi, some years before.

In another episode, a ring of six men, five whites and one black, had been arrested following a bomb attack on an ANC house in Bulawayo, and later convicted of murder and conspiracy.

The whites were all ex-soldiers in the old white Rhodesian army and evidence in court proved that the ring was being run from Pretoria. They had organised the bombing of the Inkomo army barracks armoury outside Bulawayo, destroying £20 million worth of weapons.

Later, ZANU's Harare headquarters had been ripped apart by a bomb and two ANC houses damaged: one by explosives in a television set, the other by mortar fire.

Recently a series of car bombings and other attacks had begun – even more explicitly targeting ANC officials. But unlike the Temba incident, where his whole family had died, only specific targets had been killed. Pretoria's intelligence was becoming uncannily accurate.

Florence stared out of the window, not noticing the rush of cars, unaware of the cold creeping up as the sun went down. Her mind was elsewhere.

Just how much danger was her boss facing? Any traitors in the ANC would quickly suspect the purpose of his investigations. They had tried to eliminate him once already – but had killed her predecessor, Ed Mugadza, instead. She pushed her fingers through her braids, thoughts racing.

A faint sound from the monitor startled her. Now, what was in Mr Paul Herson's file again? She flicked through it, noting the background details, all unexceptional. Then the reasons for surveillance: also, rather shaky.

But the blipping from the monitor was stronger now, the sound increasingly sharp.

Swanepoel was making good time and would soon be approaching Harare. A cassette of American country music was playing: Willy Nelson, his favourite. Helped to pass the time on a long drive.

But the petrol gauge was low. He must top up. A filling station came into view and he pulled in, unaware that he was now under close surveillance from a young woman parked 20 metres away.

If he'd been expecting a tail he might have noticed her pull out after him, several cars behind. He also didn't see that she stopped when he stopped, first at a supermarket, and then a liquor store – and he didn't notice her driving past his house when he reached it.

She'd got a very good look at him. Just an old gent, arriving home to a musty house with alcohol for companionship? Or part of an assassins' ring?

But the description from the Grassroots bookshop fitted him perfectly.

Florence decided to put a tap on his phone and order permanent surveillance. She would also tell her boss the next time he made contact.

Evans was waiting in the bar for Jenny and Sewell, his Chinese minder sitting ten metres away, reading a paper. The omnipresent security – initially unsettling – had become oddly reassuring.

'Can I buy you a drink?' Harold Williams was at his shoulder, smiling.

'Oh – that's kind of you. But I'm waiting for someone.'

'Never mind. I'll buy them a drink too.' He wasn't taking no for an answer, already at the bar.

Where were Jenny and Sewell? Evans felt exposed.

'We don't know each other that well, so I thought it was time I introduced myself properly,' said Williams.

What's coming next? Evans wondered.

'You've had a rough time.'

'Suppose so.' Evans smiled sheepishly.

'It occurred to me,' Williams paused as if searching for the correct words, 'that once is coincidence, twice is conspiracy.'

Evans shrugged, sipping his beer. 'Perhaps I've been unlucky. Could have happened to anyone.'

Williams raised his bushy eyebrows. 'It's a complicated country. Thought I might be of some help.'

'Oh?' Evans was nonplussed.

'You see, I have intelligence connections.'

'Really?' Evans feigned surprise. 'Thought you were a retired civil servant.'

'I am – but I used to work for both MI5 and MI6, so I could be of assistance.'

Evans paused. 'Very good of you, but I don't think that'll be necessary.'

Williams made as if he hadn't heard. 'Is there any reason why you might be in danger? Are you in some sort of trouble?'

'Not that I know of!' Evans felt more in control now.

Williams looked sceptical, perhaps disappointed. 'Well, if there is anything I can do, please tell me. We don't want any harm to come to you, do we?'

'Thanks, I'll let you know.' Evans almost believed his lie.

'Jim!' Jenny's voice called him from the other side of the bar.

Williams leered. 'More attractive company, I suppose? Anyway, call on me if you change your mind.'

Like hell, Evans muttered to himself. Like hell.

He joined Jenny and Sewell.

'What did Williams want?' she asked.

After buying a round of drinks, Evans explained.

'Interesting,' Jenny mused. 'They must be in a fix. He was obviously trying to pump you for information – maybe because they can't get to you so easily with Chinese security around.'

'Maybe it's because they're onto *me*,' Sewell interjected. 'Someone searched my room today. Very professionally. I might not have noticed if I hadn't taken precautions to detect tampering.'

They sat down, Evans feeling deflated again. 'What on earth are we up against?' he asked. 'Something really big?'

'Seems so,' Sewell replied, 'but what I can't understand is Williams' role.'

Jenny sipped her mango juice. 'I'm beginning to think it could be quite significant. He's now confirmed that he worked for British Intelligence.' She turned to Sewell. 'Did you read that book about the right wing faction in MI5?'

He nodded. 'Peter Wright's *Spycatcher*. He talks about a right-wing faction in MI5 which plotted against the 1974–76 Labour government. Colin Wallace, a British intelligence officer who served in Northern Ireland, gave much the same account.'

Evans felt excluded. 'I vaguely recall that stuff, but nothing much came of it, surely?'

'No,' Jenny replied, squeezing him on the knee, sensing his insecurity. 'Because they covered it up. By the mid-1970s, the establishment was really getting rattled. There was the conflict in Northern Ireland. Trade union victories against the Tories. And remember the three-day week? All those power cuts, and the miners' strikes? The petrol shortages? Many people on the right thought it was the end of British civilisation!'

'Yes,' said Sewell. 'And a senior Conservative warned publicly about the country being plunged into a state of chaos – not so far removed from a mini nuclear attack!'

Jenny smiled wryly. 'There was so much establishment paranoia. All those rumours of a military coup, with retired army officers setting up "citizen armies" – aided and abetted by right-wing intelligence officers. The links with far-right pressure groups, and the South African security agency: BOSS, I think it was called.'

'What's all this got to do with Harold Williams and our current predicament?' Evans sounded irritated. Jenny and Dick seemed to be inside a political bubble of their own.

'Be patient!' she scolded affectionately. 'The point is that many of those right-wing officers who were active in MI5 in the 1970s are still around. Maybe Harold Williams is one of them.'

Major Keith Makuyana never allowed himself the luxury of living in the past.

When his comrades started to talk about their guerrilla days in the bush, he invariably stayed silent or made an excuse and left. Never go back was his motto. He preferred to focus on current challenges.

George Orwell's novel *Coming up for Air* had made a big impact upon him – especially the main character, George Bowling, who escaped briefly from his middle-aged, middle-class life to revisit the place where he'd fished as a boy. Bowling had vivid memories of happy hours in the sun catching huge fish from an idyllic stream. But when he returned, the fish had gone, the stream was polluted, and the neighbourhood urbanised.

Nevertheless, Makuyana had to admit that he did have a pang of nostalgia now that he was back in the Zimbabwean bush. The ground was hard, the brown grass baked dry. The flat terrain was sprinkled with thorn bushes. In the distance small hills, or *kopjes*, framed the horizon. No sign of life.

Except, as he drove along the dusty track, he noticed an elderly man – tatty clothes, stubby grey beard – sheltering from the midday sun under the shade of a *musasa* tree.

A typical African image: the man curled up on the ground, battered hat tipped over his eyes, asleep.

Or was he? Makuyana craned to look, then switched to his rear-view mirror. But the dust was billowing up behind the car, obscuring his vision. He didn't spot the elderly man roll over and reach for a portable handset, speaking into it briefly.

A kilometre up the track should be the farmhouse where Makuyana would rendezvous with the man from Lusaka; the man who might have something important to tell him.

It was a remote spot, 80 kilometres north of Harare. They weren't taking any chances – not after the Mugadza affair, where another meeting set up by the ANC had gone so sour.

A Kalashnikov automatic rifle sat on the passenger seat. Inside Makuyana's slim briefcase were three grenades and plenty of spare ammunition. Under his jacket a shoulder pistol.

His eyes scanned the scene, concentrating, looking for anything unusual, deploying all the training and skills from his guerrilla days. He still felt worried, but was reassured by the fact that Florence and her team were approaching from the other side of the farmhouse. By the time he arrived, they should be in position immediately to its rear.

His briefcase also contained a radio console through which he could contact his deputy if necessary, though they had maintained strict silence during the approach to the farmhouse.

He knew that Florence would do her job quietly and with total dedication. If she drew attention to herself within Zimbabwe security circles, it was not because she was pushy, but because she was admired for her tenacity – and her willingness to court danger when necessary.

He was aware that some of the younger male officers had made advances to her, but she had politely rebuffed them. She was her own woman: she had plenty of friends but none came close enough to threaten her fierce independence.

As the farmhouse came into view Makuyana slowed down, searching the layout, assessing where any attack might come from. The farm was modern, its white-washed walls standing out from the brown of the surrounding land, flecked by sand swept in by rain. A series of outhouses and barns stood in a U-shape behind it, with several cars parked between the house and the other buildings.

If he parked there too, he would be surrounded by buildings. Or trapped. Gunmen could be hiding inside, preventing him from escaping the way he'd come.

Makuyana decided to pull off the approach road and park in front of the house, alongside a low, wooden-slatted fence. Too bad if the owners weren't happy with that.

His car rolled to a halt across the bumpy ground as he avoided several large stones and parked to face the way he had come, only too aware that there might be no return.

Makuyana waited, eyes scrutinising the front door and windows. No movement, no sound, but he couldn't see the buildings behind the house.

There was an eerie silence as he picked up the Kalash and briefcase, climbed out, and opened the gate.

*

The front door swung open and a short, stocky man stepped out.

'Comrade Makuyana? Welcome! Been expecting you.' Oliver Magano – the ANC's man in Lusaka – spread out his arms. 'Come in. Can I get you a glass of water? Not much else here, I'm afraid.'

Makuyana nodded, his eyes adjusting to the gloom. He surveyed the main living room with its large stone fireplace flanked by two men, both armed with AK47s.

'Sorry about the venue,' said Magano, 'must be inconvenient for you, but we can't be too careful. Harare is such a hothouse. Nobody can move without being seen, or even whisper without being heard.' He waved Makuyana to an armchair, ushering his men outside so that they were alone.

Makuyana listened impassively, forcing the other man to do all the talking, assessing him, thinking about logistics: size of the room, its position in the house, distance from his car. Then he refocused his attention on the man from Lusaka.

'Over the past year we've had persistent reports of political contacts between Pretoria and Beijing,' Magano was saying. 'Also, unexplained business visits – comings and goings which don't add up. Though nothing we could put our fingers on. Now the pace of activity is stepping up, but we don't know why.'

'What do you think is behind it?' Makuyana glanced at his car, just visible through the front window. The two men with the AK47s were standing idly by the low fence.

'You could help us find out.'

'Me?'

'Yes,' Magano leant forward, white pupils prominent in his dark brown eyes. 'We want you to go across the border.'

Makuyana shook his head. 'No way. My people would never sanction it. It's not worth the risk of jeopardising diplomatic relations with Pretoria. Why not use a team of your own?'

'Because this one needs total security,' Magano almost whispered. 'No leaks. No danger of betrayals. I deployed one of my most trusted men to try and make sense of the Beijing connection. The week after I briefed him, he was shot.

'The Zambian police said it was a random murder, the sort that's unfortunately all too frequent in Lusaka these days. But the killing took place in the early hours outside a nightclub. My man was teetotal, a strict disciplinarian – he wouldn't have been seen dead at a place like that. Except of course that he was.'

Makuyana ignored the sarcasm. 'Are you absolutely certain it wasn't an accident?'

'Yes. Otherwise I wouldn't have travelled all this way. My guts tell me something big is happening. But I don't know what. We need you to find out.'

'But the risk—'

'The risk! For Chrissake!' Magano exclaimed. 'Don't you think it's risky sending a team of *our* people over the border? Many never come back.' He thumped the small wicker table between them in frustration, and it almost collapsed under the impact.

'Sorry,' he muttered, 'this thing has been getting to me.' He suddenly looked desperate, like a hunted animal.

Makuyana didn't respond, just stared. The room was still. Magano started to resent the man's coolness. Didn't these ZANU people realise what the score was, now they were desk-bound?

More silence.

'Look,' Magano said awkwardly, feeling the need to say something. 'Can I make a suggestion?'

Makuyana shrugged his shoulders. 'I'm listening.'

'How about going into South Africa legit? As a diplomat or businessman. That way you could fish about with less risk – and you would be more in control. We can get you out if needs be.'

'I'm still listening.'

They talked for another hour. Then Makuyana asked for the toilet and was directed to the rear of the house. Needed a pee, but also needed to have a quick look outside the back.

It was so quiet in the courtyard. A couple of tractors, but no sign of movement. The large double door to the barn was open, but the blackness inside made it impossible to see anything. He stood on tiptoe, peering through the toilet window, hoping Florence and her team were now in place.

Magano was pacing about the room when Makuyana returned. 'Well?'

'Okay. I'll examine the feasibility. When? Who do I contact inside?'

Magano passed him a piece of paper, with a name, address, phone number and date. 'Memorise all that now and destroy it before you leave, please.'

Makuyana recognised the name – a prominent white lawyer. But the date startled him. 'That soon?'

Magano nodded, glancing outside where his men were restlessly pacing around Makuyana's car.

'Time to go. I'll leave first. Give me ten minutes. There's only one way out.'

'Which way are you travelling when you reach the main road?' Makuyana asked.

'South. Why?' Magano looked surprised.

Makuyana thought for a moment. 'There's a petrol station a few miles along in that direction. A few houses and a café, too, I think. You take my car. I'll take yours. We'll meet there to swap.'

'Why?' Magano asked again, suspicious now.

'Who set up this meeting?'

'Mngadi's men.'

'Which ones?'

'I don't know. The message came from one of his aides.'

'Even more reason to be careful. I trust Mngadi, but I'm worried about his aides. Send your men round the back to collect your car. Then we'll swap. The three of you will stand a better chance if anyone tries to attack.'

'Attack?' Magano looked baffled.

'I'm taking no chances. The last time Mngadi's office sent me to meet someone, my number two was murdered.'

'Heard about that. Alright. I'll tell my men.' Looking worried, Magano went outside.

Makuyana opened his briefcase and switched on his console so that Florence could contact him. After memorising the name, address and phone, he burnt the paper.

The two minders drove round to the front of the house in a Volkswagen Passat. Looking moody and irritated, they got out and climbed into Makuyana's car: one in the front passenger seat, the other in the back, AK47s cradled on their laps.

Magano jumped in behind the wheel. 'See you shortly.'

As the Nissan saloon pulled away, a cloud of dust rising up behind it, Makuyana walked through to the kitchen at the rear, holding his Kalash and briefcase.

He was just in time to see a jeep roar out of the barn, tyres clinging desperately to the loose surface, as it twisted through the courtyard. A man sat upright alongside the driver, with something balanced on his shoulder, protruding out of the window.

Christ! It was a hand-held, anti-tank missile! But what sort? He rushed round to the living room as the jeep screeched to a halt. The man steadied himself, then fired.

Makuyana watched, helpless, as if the scene was frozen in time. The missile rapidly closed in on his dusty car, seeming to dip down, then exploded under the boot, blowing a huge crater in the dirt track, throwing the car sideways as it juddered to a halt.

The jeep's engine screamed, its tyres spinning, as it took off in a cloud of dust towards the stricken Nissan.

There was a crash at the rear of the house. Makuyana spun around, pulling out his pistol as a man burst through the connecting door.

Makuyana shot him between the eyes. An expression of astonishment froze upon the man's face, as his weapon clattered to the floor.

He was white, the men in the jeep black. Makuyana picked up the gun: South African-made, an RI assault rifle.

He heard a shout from the courtyard: the familiar sound of an AK47. Maybe Magano's boys weren't dead?

Makuyana grabbed an RG-42 high explosive grenade from his briefcase and crept into the kitchen. A volley of bullets shattered the window and another volley poured through the open door. In the confined space the noise was deafening.

They're panicking, he thought, flattening himself on the floor.

The anti-tank missile must have been directed at *him* and likely the attackers believed Magano and his two associates were still in the house. If there were enough of them, they would probably have encircled it by now.

Makuyana withdrew along the corridor to the toilet.

No sound.

He cautiously stood on tiptoe by the window and peered out, just catching a glimpse of two men creeping beside the wall towards the back door, guns at the ready. Nobody else was in view, but others could be round the front.

Makuyana reached for his grenade and pulled out the pin, steeling himself to wait as the seconds ticked away. Then he stuck his hand out the window, lobbing the grenade sideways.

The two didn't stand a chance. They were blown apart, along with most of the kitchen wall, leaving an ugly mess of blood, flesh and bones stuck to the rubble. Dust was everywhere.

Makuyana reached for his console, tugging out the aerial, pointing it through the window. 'Florence, can you hear me?'

A crackle, then her voice came through faintly. 'Yeah, but we can also hear shots. Are you okay?'

'All in one piece. I'm inside the house, but in danger. I've taken out some of the attackers, but I think there are others round the front. Also, there's a jeep nearby with a missile. Maybe some gunmen too.'

'Right, we're coming in. Give us a couple of minutes.'

That might be too long, Makuyana thought, sliding back along the corridor towards the living room.

He noticed an empty cardboard box. Putting down his guns and briefcase, he picked it up. As if throwing a discus, he swung it around, through the doorway into the living room.

A fusillade of bullets ripped into it. So, the front was blocked. The house was indeed a trap. He had to get out through the rear.

He was pulled up short by the roar of the jeep returning. It seemed to be coming up to the front.

Christ! Under missile fire the house wouldn't last long. Nor would he.

A sudden *whoosh*, then a massive explosion rocked the whole structure, shaking the other end of the corridor in which he was crouching. They had fired directly into the living room.

He dragged his equipment towards what remained of the kitchen, catching the sound of the jeep starting up again.

It roared into the courtyard.

Knowing he was cornered, Makuyana fired a burst from his Kalash at the jeep, hoping to take out the man with the missile. Instead, the bullets shattered the windscreen. Screams from the driver suggested he'd been hit.

Suddenly Makuyana heard the squeal of tyres. They were driving back round to the front. The bazooka-like weapon was swinging round, steadying, pointing right at him.

This is it, he thought, ducking sideways along the corridor, no escaping a bastard like that in such a confined space.

Makuyana backed into what looked like a bedroom at the end of the corridor. Then a face and a gun appeared through the living room door. He fired immediately and both disappeared.

They must know he was on his own now. There was another

explosion and the kitchen seemed to collapse into the corridor, as water gushed through the debris.

Again, the jeep's engine screamed. He could see it through the bedroom window. Didn't need to check what they were up to. It was plain bloody obvious: they'd blow up every wall until they got him.

As if paralysed, he watched another missile being loaded, the ugly cylinder heaved up and swung slowly, relentlessly, in his direction.

But then ... yes!

The front of the weapon suddenly heaved upwards, as its operator was thrown bodily out of the jeep by the impact of automatic fire ripping into his chest.

Florence!

Thank Christ for Florence ...

Now he could see figures flitting across the window. Bullets were crashing everywhere.

He swung round as someone lurched into the corridor, obviously wounded, half raising a gun. Makuyana shot him in the knee, and a scream of agony pierced the din outside.

Then, save for the moaning man in the corridor, there was near silence. Makuyana stayed still, listening.

A sudden crackle through his radio.

'Are you receiving me?' Florence's voice quivered, as if expecting no answer.

'You took your bloody time!'

She roared with laughter. 'Don't be so cheeky!' Her relief was obvious.

'We've got rid of the ones outside. Is it safe to come into the house?'

Ludicrous to 'come into' a pile of rubble, he thought.

'Yes. There's one guy here, but he's in a bad way.'

Florence and her team surveyed the scene in disbelief. Makuyana took command. 'Drive the Passat up the track to my car and check for any survivors. It was attacked. The ANC men were using it.'

He went over to the man, who was curled up in agony, and shook his shoulder aggressively. 'Talk, you bastard! Talk! Or you'll get another one.' He pointed his pistol at the man's other knee.

'Don't!' The man screeched in terror.

'Who are you? Who sent you here?' Makuyana felt no pity, remembering the car bomb that killed his deputy Ed Mugadza.

Florence watched her boss. She didn't like to see him so brutal and brutalised, but there was no alternative.

The man's eyes glazed. 'RENAMO,' he muttered, 'RENAMO.'

Makuyana looked at Florence, raising his eyebrows. RENAMO: the South African-backed Mozambique National Resistance, set up by the Rhodesians in 1970 to spy on guerrilla groups then based in Mozambique.

On Zimbabwe's independence, South Africa had taken over stewardship, and RENAMO became increasingly hostile to the new Harare government.

'Who sent you?' Makuyana shook the RENAMO man once more, banging his pistol on the mess of his knee.

He screamed again, sobbing in terror. 'Pretoria!' he shouted, 'Pretoria. One of them . . . he is with us.'

The white man whom Makuyana had shot. Pity dead bodies didn't talk. 'Yes, I know *that*,' he replied sarcastically, 'but who told you where to come?'

Through his pain the man seemed almost to be smiling mirthlessly. 'Your people.'

'Which one? Which one?' Makuyana barked out the questions. He had to keep him terrified.

'Não sei . . . not know his name! Honest. Not know.'

Florence spoke quietly. 'Magano's two bodyguards are dead, but he's still alive. Just. We must rush him to hospital.'

'Okay. The other two can drive him in the Passat. We'll

follow later.' He paused, and looked at the wounded man. 'Do you want to go to hospital too?' The man nodded, hope springing in his eyes. 'Then can you identify the guy who told you we would be here?'

The man nodded, 'Yes.'

At last. Makuyana felt he might be getting somewhere.

Mauritz Swanepoel hadn't done much since his return to Harare. He'd pottered about, slept a lot. Drunk even more.

But, from a phone kiosk in a local shopping arcade, he had called a businessman in the city centre to say he was back again.

As KJ had insisted, he lay low. It was pretty boring. Little did he know the Zimbabwe security officers watching him were bored too.

They reported in regularly to Florence Dube, and she began to doubt the wisdom of allocating hard-pressed resources to the task. She would keep the watchers on for another day, or at most two, and then rely on long distance surveillance by tracking the target's movements through the transmitter on his car, tapping his phone and intercepting his mail.

Swanepoel remained nostalgic about his visit back home to South Africa. He missed the adrenaline of action, of hitting the enemy directly.

His role in Harare was more frustrating – particularly when he read reports like the one on the front page of the Zimbabwe *Herald*. Ten whites had been killed in a lunch-hour explosion at a Johannesburg amusement centre.

Swanepoel resented the restrained glee with which the *Herald* also reported on the End Conscription Campaign (ECC): a small group seeking to persuade an estimated 64,000 young whites to resist the 'unjust war against apartheid'.

Amongst the ECC's leaders were former soldiers who told how they had shot women and children in cold blood, sexually harassed women to degrade and intimidate them, driven army vehicles over flimsy huts to destroy homes, and collected ears and fingers as souvenirs.

Apparently the ECC's influence was growing, along with the number of draft dodgers.

Swanepoel threw down the newspaper. His own young *volk* were bottling out. Disgusting. Meanwhile, he was powerless, marooned in Harare.

Makuyana had sent Oliver Magano straight to hospital, but despatched the badly injured RENAMO man in secret to the medical centre where Robert Temba had been treated before dying.

He then met Mngadi and his three aides to brief them on events at the farm, but told them only Magano had survived.

'It was another set-up!' Makuyana did not hide his contempt.

As Mngadi started to apologise, Makuyana brushed him aside. 'I will be reporting straight to the President. We may decide to close down your ANC operations here in Harare.'

He was determined to maintain pressure, hoping somebody would crack or spot a discrepancy in a colleague's behaviour.

As the ANC men left the room, he called Mngadi back and closed the door. 'I want full details on the family backgrounds of Msimang and Petersen – something wasn't quite right about their reactions when I probed them the other day.'

Mngadi looked even more troubled. 'That won't be easy. Nor will it be quick. We'll have to contact our people in Natal and the Cape. That could take several days. Then a week or two for the necessary checks and replies.'

'It must still be done, but make sure neither knows they're under investigation.'

Wuhan's airport had a small-town feel, the terminal modest, air traffic light. The sense of casualness surprised Jim, who expected it to be crawling with security.

Even the military planes parked to one side were exposed to the world, and there was an air of informality in the way the pilots clambered into the old Mig fighters, pulled on their helmets and took straight off.

By contrast, Guangzhou's airport was modern, as befitted a city on the border with Hong Kong, China's gateway to the West. The 800-kilometre flight had gone smoothly, the old twin-prop Tupolev flying low so they had a spectacular view of the scenery.

Guangzhou's prestigious White Swan hotel boasted a marble lobby with birds in a gilded cage, and an artificial three-storey waterfall. It offered the visitors a panoramic view of the Pearl River, crawling with wooden junks.

The couple of days spent in the city passed without incident. But Jim was feeling increasingly claustrophobic with his friends and his Chinese minders keeping a constant eye on him. His anxiety to get back home saddened him: souring the end to a trip which had promised so much.

The three-hour train journey to Hong Kong was like being in a capsule. They were ushered on, after papers were checked and passports stamped. At the end of each carriage stood uniformed young women with suspicious eyes: they acted both as guards and hostesses.

The train didn't stop, reminding Jim of a trip he'd taken through East Germany to West Berlin. Now, as they swept across the border, past the high security fencing which separated the mainland from the Hong Kong Territories, he wondered what it would be like in the old British colony after three weeks virtually sealed off from the West.

Hong Kong's main train station was teeming with humanity: a hubbub of voices, shouting, greeting, cajoling, directing. The din was incredible, as travellers hailed porters and people pushed through the throng.

Jim felt disorientated, longing suddenly for the orderly

dignity of the mainland Chinese, and beginning to feel resentful of their pushy cousins.

As they made their way through the sunshine to the chartered bus, he saw his first beggar for three weeks, scuttling through the crowd.

Dozens of trinket-sellers hassled for trade, and it was a relief to take refuge from the throng on the air-conditioned bus. The soft beauty of the countryside had surprised him, starkly contrasting with the rampant materialism of Hong Kong city: a collage of neon lights, garish signs and dwarfing concrete buildings.

Two hotel rooms had been reserved for the group for luggage storage during their ten-hour sight-seeing tour, before they caught the overnight flight to London.

Time to shop, relax, and enjoy each other's company before the group broke up. He felt oddly sad at leaving China, but decided to make the most of the day: free from minders and the tension of the past few weeks.

Jenny slipped away from the rest of the group, as they wandered through the maze of tourist shops.

Following Sewell's request, she found a photocopy shop and quickly duplicated the secret documents. She placed them in a large, stamped envelope, which she addressed to her aunt who lived in a Dorset seaside village. She also included a note, asking her aunt to lock the envelope away until she got in touch.

Ruth Brown would understand. A veteran campaigner against nuclear weapons, she had been one of the early CND marchers to the nuclear site at Aldermaston in the late 1950s and was later arrested at Trafalgar Square during a famous sit-down demonstration led by Bertrand Russell in 1961.

Aged 63, she had joined the Women's Peace Camp established outside the cruise missile base at Greenham Common, living there for nearly a year, come rain, mud, snow or heat. Her tent was torn down ten times and her possessions scattered as the authorities made persistent but futile attempts to clear the campers.

Jenny trusted Aunt Ruth more than anyone else in the world.

Now, after checking that nobody was watching, she popped the envelope into a letter box. Then she walked back to the hotel and let herself into the room where their luggage was stored. She found Sewell's suitcase, located the false compartment, and carefully inserted the original documents back where they belonged.

Several hours later, Wang – horrified – sat studying the documents in his hands. They gave a detailed account of massive nuclear contamination in the South China Sea: utterly explosive in more ways than one!

After bidding the group farewell at Guangzhou's station and discreetly travelling in a different carriage, he'd ordered their luggage to be searched. Not at all difficult. He had sufficient agents of his own and resources in Hong Kong for almost any undercover operation – ironic that he could operate with greater freedom here than inside mainland China.

So, Harold Williams' MI5 tip-off had been corroborated: Sewell was the culprit after all. The evidence in the scruffy Chinese envelope recovered from the Englishman's suitcase was incontrovertible. But it also presented a dilemma. Had they been after the wrong target? Had Evans innocently stumbled across some unconnected information by accident? Or were Sewell and Evans acting together?

Should he risk going for both men in the few remaining hours before they flew out of his reach?

Wang weighed up the matrix of factors and the odds of success, then made his decision. It had to be *his* decision. The Old Man could not be contacted in time for guidance. He was on his own.

*

'How is he doing?' Florence Dube spoke softly, as the doctor bent over her unconscious patient.

'So-so,' the doctor shrugged. 'The operation on his chest went smoothly. We extracted the bullets and patched up his knee-cap, but he'll be crippled for life. I suppose it was just unavoidable, shooting someone in the knee?'

The question was rhetorical. There was a hint of reproach in the doctor's eyes, but no response was expected – and none given.

'How soon can I talk to him?'

'Tomorrow perhaps. Is it very important?'

'Very. He's a RENAMO man. He must talk, otherwise he's dispensable.'

Neat word, 'dispensable': so clinical. The doctor had thought this young woman might be a kindred spirit: more caring than Makuyana. Yet they were all similar, these security people. The doctor worked for them, so she understood. But she still felt sad.

Hong Kong's Kai Tak airport seemed too cramped to cope with the 74,000 flights which came in and out of the territory every year.

The main runway thrust out from the land like a giant seaside pier, squatting flat in the water. As many passengers flew into the densely populated territory as flew into China, whose population was two hundred times greater.

Jim's initial relief at leaving the unknown dangers of mainland China had given way to a realisation that anything was possible in Hong Kong's congested hustle and bustle.

Although the day's sight-seeing had been enjoyable, the tension had returned as the hours passed, but he didn't need to share his anxiety with Jenny and Dick. They all felt the same.

Jim had ensured he didn't stand near the edge of any viewing point, and he'd tried to avoid being alone. Laughable precautions when he thought about it. A sniper could be anywhere, and could easily disappear into the frenetic swirl of traffic and people.

But now at last they were at the airport, which was uncomfortably humid despite the late hour. They'd checked in smoothly, and their passports were routinely inspected.

Their Cathay Pacific jumbo jet glistened against the darkness of the mountain towering behind Kai Tak. Jim felt his tension ease as he made polite conversation.

Their flight to Heathrow was called. He picked up his hand luggage, catching a quick smile from Jenny, checked for his boarding card, and headed with her into the queue. They'd booked seats next to each other, while Dick would sit further back with his own party.

The jumbo's engines whined as it filled up. Prim stewardesses checked that seatbelts were fastened and luggage safely stowed.

Jim always marvelled at how quickly these great planes landed, were serviced, and then flew off again: almost in perpetual motion. They'd be in use for twenty years or more, covering over 20,000 flights and millions of kilometres. Extraordinary that mishaps were so few and far between.

Mishaps? He squeezed Jenny's hand as the jumbo was towed out of the loading bay, and looked over his shoulder to check on Dick Sewell. Seat 61C wasn't it? He couldn't spot him amidst the tense passengers, waiting for take-off.

As Sewell queued, waiting for the final stub to be torn off his boarding card, he caught sight of Jim walking down the gangway behind Jenny.

'Ah, Mr Sewell, a message for you.' The Cathay Pacific check-in attendant beckoned to him from behind her desk. 'Please step this way.'

She led him to a door in the boarding lounge, knocked, and ushered him inside. It looked like a staff restroom. Empty paper cups littered the low table, and a corridor led off to the rear.

'Someone will come. Don't worry, there is enough time. I will collect you in a minute.'

As she shut the door, a smartly dressed man – probably European – entered via the corridor.

'Sorry to have kept you, sir,' he said, in a voice that came straight from Eton. 'Little problem with your suitcase. It split open while loading. Just want you to check everything's still there before we strap it up. We've had lots of thefts recently. Can't take too many precautions. This way please.'

Irritated, Sewell stepped into the corridor. But then his anxiety mounted: had the documents been discovered? Was his vital mission, so close to fruition, compromised?

Suddenly he was hit on the head. Lost consciousness. Was carried down some steps, bundled into a metal skip on wheels, and pushed out across the tarmac, passing almost underneath the jumbo as the chocks on its fat rubber tyres were pulled away.

Ten minutes later the aircraft took off and climbed steeply, banking away from the mountainside and the teeming city below. The cabin staff had been informed of a very late cancellation.

Meanwhile, the man who should have been sitting in seat 61C was disappearing into the night.

MK commander Selby Mngadi was sitting with Makuyana at an outside café in Harare's beautiful park, near the five-star Monomatapa hotel.

Makuyana often arranged meetings there because it was central and discreet. Safer than a city bar frequented by security people.

Their conversation was to the point. Of course, all three of Mngadi's close aides had known of the rendezvous on the farm with his Lusaka colleague, Oliver Magano – but there was no evidence as to who might have set up the ambush.

Makuyana told him that Magano was in hospital, emphasising that the man from Lusaka knew nothing about the source of the attack. 'Make sure you mention that to your people. I don't want any heavies descending on his hospital bed.'

But he made no mention of the RENAMO survivor who could possibly point the finger.

They downed the last of their beers, the froth curling up inside the empty glasses. Makuyana left, and Mngadi made his move five minutes later.

But their separate departures didn't fool the driver of the cab across the road, who seemed reluctant to take a fare. He watched – and wondered what the meeting had been about.

When Sewell came to, he had a splitting headache. His neck was numb and cricked.

It was dark: he appeared to be in a cellar of some sort. He pressed the light on his digital watch. Well past midnight. He began to panic, realising with horror that the plane would have long taken off.

A sudden click and a blinding light. Several men crowded round, two looked familiar. Who were they? Ah, the Englishman from the restroom and ... could it be ... Wang?

It was the former interpreter who spoke first. Sneering, arrogant – his feigned deference gone.

'We have the documents. Don't waste time with denials. They were found in your suitcase.'

Sewell nodded. Everything was blown: all the planning, the effort, the courage of the student contacts. He felt old, finished. No way back.

Then, a faint spark of hope. Jenny had copied the documents and she'd got away with Jim. He was sure he had seen them walking down the boarding tunnel to the plane. He *had* to protect them – it was his only chance of rescuing the mission.

'You collected the documents from the students at the bar in Beijing.' An assertion rather than a question.

'Yes.'

'Good,' Wang looked satisfied. 'Don't waste my time with lies. We had an informer amongst the students. He reported to me that same night.'

But why then had they not acted earlier against him? Why had Evans been the target? Sewell was confused.

'Who planned it?'

'I did.'

'Don't lie!' As Wang screamed, the Englishman smashed his fist into Sewell's jaw, dislocating some teeth. Blood spurted into his mouth, the shock bouncing through his brain.

'We know all about you. You weren't acting alone, were you?'

Sewell, in excruciating pain, tried to stick to his strategy. To reveal just enough to satisfy, but not sufficient to inform. Even as he wrestled with the pain in his jaw and the horror of being at the mercy of these thugs, he knew how treacherous it would be to volunteer only partial information. Didn't know how *much* they knew, and how much was informed speculation, but he had to steer them away from his two friends.

'Okay. It was planned by my colleagues in Green Planet. I was sent in to make contact and collect the documents. We failed.' He didn't have to try too hard to sound utterly dispirited and deflated.

'Tell us all about it.' Wang sounded almost conciliatory now.

Sewell told them. How Green Planet had been contacted by radical sources within China concerned about the dangers of nuclear pollution. His role as the courier. The arrangements to make contact.

Wang exchanged significant – perhaps satisfied? – glances with his colleagues.

Then his manner changed abruptly. 'What about your two friends?'

'What about them?'

'Don't be insolent! I want the truth! Do you want me to turn my colleagues loose on you?'

Sewell's jaw was shot through with agony, a warm taste of blood in his mouth.

'They knew nothing. I swear it.'

This time the blow was to his groin. The searing shock pulsated upward through his body. He doubled up, as an incongruous memory flashed into his mind: the adolescent taunts of schoolfriends when he'd been hit in the groin by a cricket ball. 'Be careful or it'll ruin your future.'

He had no future now. Of that he was certain.

'Stop hurting yourself. You can't protect your friends. We can check with them if we need to. Save yourself.' Wang sounded almost sympathetic.

It would have been easier simply to spill the beans. But Sewell was determined to keep fighting. Otherwise his mission, indeed his own life – everything – would be futile.

'Look,' he pleaded, 'I know Evans had some story about the Chinese nuclear energy programme he picked up in Beijing. To be honest, it was all too confusing. I don't know if he could make sense of it himself. But I'd never met him before the Yangtze trip.'

'You saved his life.'

'Yes – would have done so for anybody. I was trained in that sort of thing. We only became friends afterwards.'

'Exactly.' Wang smirked, knowingly.

Sewell found himself exploding in frustration. 'He's an *amateur*.' He spat out the word. 'So is the girl. I am a *professional*. My whole mission was based upon the tightest security. Do you think I would risk that by involving strangers? Of course not. They knew nothing.'

Then, as if it was an afterthought, Sewell asked: 'Why did you search Evans' room? Why did you try to kill him?'

Wang's reply was involuntary. 'We thought it was Evans who had made contact with the students.'

Momentarily, Sewell was the interrogator. 'So, you only got

onto me after I had saved Evans' life? How ironic. If I'd let him drown, you would never have spotted me.'

Wang was unsettled; Sewell's replies made a certain kind of sense. Evans and the girl *were* amateurs. They could be watched back in Britain – and eliminated if necessary. He had decided to let them board the plane, worried, that if all three were taken out, there might be a fuss.

Wang was reassured by Sewell's replies. His decision had been justified. He *had* to believe Sewell – otherwise he'd have to answer for his own misjudgement.

A trapdoor led up from the cellar. Sewell spotted it in the gloom after they left him, locking the door at the top of the narrow concrete steps as they went.

He hadn't a clue where he was, could hardly think straight for the pain and fear. He felt desolate: an utter failure. More exhausted than he could remember, he collapsed and slept fitfully.

When he abruptly woke, he still felt dreadful.

A sliver of light framed the trapdoor but it was heavy, and he couldn't shift it. Then he noticed a large rusty bolt. Managed to slide it back – but the intense effort made his injuries pulsate with pain.

Standing on a packing case, he eased the door up and peered out into an alley, seemingly deserted.

Really? A deserted spot in congested Hong Kong? Unlikely. He waited for a couple of minutes, the moon bright, a street light almost overhead. His watch showed it was just after five in the morning.

Sewell hauled himself painfully out through the trapdoor. The alley led to a narrow road running down to the waterfront. He walked quickly, his body aching. Then the rising sound of voices: fishermen, clustered by their junks, silhouetted against the moon.

He made his way towards them, drawn to the security of the

crowd. Must be on the outskirts of the main city, in one of the poorer areas where street markets thrived. Little children ran about barefoot. Boats were moored haphazardly along the shore, water lapping against their hulls.

Market traders were beginning to set up their stalls, and he mingled with them. Exhilarated at escaping the terror of his captors, he started to plan how he could get out of the colony unnoticed.

'Coffee?' A man stood in front of him, smiling, with a steaming paper cup.

Sewell nodded, desperate for the boost of caffeine. He felt in his pocket for some coins as the man pressed the cup forward, tipping it. Sewell reached out with a steadying hand. Then he glanced up, noticing the man's eyes staring over his shoulder. He wasn't smiling anymore.

As Sewell turned to follow his gaze a hand thrust against his back.

A knife glinted as it cut deep into his larynx.

Then he understood.

How clever to let him escape into the bustling anonymity of a crowd, instead of murdering him in a place full of incriminating clues.

As Sewell collapsed, he had a sense of macabre elation. Yes, they had got him, but a copy of his precious documents was safely with Jim and Jenny.

When the local police arrived, they shook their heads – bewildered by the grotesque contrast between a grisly murder and the corpse's twisted smile.

7

Makuyana had made all the arrangements himself: false identity, complete with passport and visa, tailor-made story, and air tickets – none of which could be left to a subordinate. His deputy, Florence Dube, was his only confidante.

He hadn't sought official clearance, because he knew he wouldn't get it for such a high-risk operation. So, all responsibility rested on his shoulders: if his cover was blown, the authorities would deny everything. He'd be completely on his own.

Why was he doing it? Instinct, he supposed. But, even more importantly, he had something to prove.

Nobody was going to get the better of him. Nobody. Just because he had his own office and secretary, didn't mean he'd gone soft.

Although tense – and uncomfortable in the suit which was part of his new identity – he was looking forward to the challenge. To achieving his goal, and to finding out what apartheid South Africa felt like from the inside. That familiar buzz before a field operation: something he'd not felt since his guerrilla days.

Johannesburg's Jan Smuts airport was named after the old wartime leader defeated by Malan's Afrikaner Nationalists in

1948 – a defeat just as unexpected as Churchill's in the British general election three years before.

Makuyana was not impressed by General Smuts' reputation. Ostensibly more liberal than the Nats, Smuts had been just as dedicated to apartheid. A racist with a human face. More than that, a puppet of British imperialism.

Makuyana smiled wryly at his own inner sloganeering. Actually, he detested such rhetoric, preferring cool, rational language to lazy ZANU propaganda. His duty was to his country: not to a ruling party that had betrayed its ideals.

Jan Smuts airport was even less attractive than the man for whom it had been named. Security everywhere: white men in cubicles, watching and checking with steely suspicion.

Would his passport and new identity clear the system? He queued up, his tension growing.

'Sydney K Nkala,' the immigration official grunted the name as he paged through the passport, looking up to stare at Makuyana. 'Your visa's stamped for a trade visit. Who will you be visiting, Mr Nkala?' He spat the name out carefully, as if distancing himself from the black man before him.

Makuyana rattled off institutions and places, but the man wasn't that interested. By now he was used to blacks in sharp suits carrying briefcases and talking business. It all fitted in with his government's policy of forging economic ties with other African countries, making it less likely for them to turn on the apartheid fortress in the south. Mind you, he didn't like them any the better for it. To him, blacks were still blacks: in suits or not.

The official waited for Special Branch clearance to appear on his screen. Up it flashed.

Makuyana felt relieved at being waved through, but knew this was the easy part. From now onwards, the slightest slip and he'd be finished.

He'd remain a target for the ubiquitous eyes and ears of the police state simply because he wasn't white. Would he return here in two days' time as planned? Or would they have rumbled him?

Carrying only hand luggage – fresh shirts and underwear pressed into his large briefcase – he headed out through the bustle of passengers into the unknown.

Florence Dube made her decision. Mr Herson was just an old man, enjoying the mundane routines of his retirement.

Down to the shops and back. Walk round the garden. Cup of mid-morning coffee, then back into the garden to read the paper. A drink before lunch, and an afternoon nap. Cup of tea, walk to the local park. A crossword. A sundowner. Evening meal, with lots more to drink. Falling asleep in front of the TV.

She had the car bleeper, the telephone tap, and the mail intercept. So, she decided to call off the watchers. Easy to redeploy them if needed.

There was a more pressing matter: the RENAMO man, still in a coma in the medical centre. The doctor wanted to move him into a proper hospital with superior facilities. But Florence had refused. No chances could be taken: she had to assume the eyes of the enemy were everywhere – especially with such a serious threat to their security.

Swanepoel hated this period of dormancy which his masters had imposed. It felt like he was vegetating.

In a way he enjoyed living a double life in Harare, but couldn't cope with inactivity. At the same time he knew that frustration was dangerous, could corrode your defences, expose you. Just one careless mistake could blow your cover.

He swilled the KWV in his glass, sniffing the aroma wafting upward, the liquid shining golden in the setting sun. Soon the warmth that had drenched the veranda would be gone. Winter was looming.

His garden was looking unkempt, with grass straggling across the path. He hated gardening: women's work – if you couldn't get a reliable servant to do it for you.

True, they'd given him instructions to keep his property tidy, to play the role of a houseproud pensioner. But bugger them. They didn't know what it was like, wasting away in the field. Cut off from your roots, your drinking partners, the men with whom you could swap stories about old times.

How much longer would they keep him hanging about here? Could be days, but might be weeks, or even months. Apart from the brandy, there was just one consolation: he hadn't been rumbled over the letter bomb.

That had been his trickiest mission yet in Harare. Unusually, he'd carried out the operation himself, instead of just coordinating it. Luckily, there was still no sign that anyone suspected him.

Meanwhile, life in his little suburban street continued as normal: kids playing, people going to and from work, cars driving past, music from teenagers' ghetto-blasters.

He stood up rather unsteadily. Time for a bite to eat.

Then the phone rang. Startled, he almost knocked it over as he picked up the receiver. Apart from his wife, nobody ever phoned him here – unless it was urgent.

'Mr Herson?'

'*Ja*,' he recognised the voice.

'Sorry I didn't phone earlier. We finally got the part for your camera and the repair is done. Can you pick it up tomorrow morning? About ten if you want to catch me. Otherwise, my assistant will be there.'

The instruction was clear. Be there at ten. On the dot. No messing.

The young man in the monitoring centre at security HQ in Harare was struggling to concentrate.

Nothing much had happened since he clocked on for the late

afternoon shift. He scrolled through the text on the screen in front of him. The surveillance system hadn't logged any significant activity.

Suddenly the cursor flashed, grabbing his attention. An incoming phone call to a target. But who? He checked the system.

Name: Herson, Paul.

Address: a house in Avondale.

He noted the code number, and gave it to a middle-aged woman in the phone-tapping section.

'Can you play this back for me?'

'Sure.' She smiled, handing him a pair of earphones.

He listened attentively.

'Some message about collecting a repaired camera. Track the caller's number, please.'

Five minutes later she came over to his desk, frowning. 'Strange, this number of yours. It's a private house, not a shop.'

'Really?' He looked puzzled. 'Perhaps the guy forgot to call the customer during business hours?'

'Well, maybe ...' she sounded sceptical.

He smiled ruefully. She was so conscientious. Everything was important to her – no loose ends when she was around.

'What the hell. I'll write a note for the boss.'

She returned his smile. Good boy. He was coming along nicely.

The Old Man looked doubtfully at his itinerary.

A decade or two ago the prospect of a foreign visit would have excited him. New places to see, maybe new heights to conquer. Now he viewed the whole idea with resigned weariness.

First Nairobi, in the grip of the capitalist West. Then Dar es Salaam: at least he had some friends there, from the days when his technicians had helped develop Tanzania's infrastructure.

Finally, Zimbabwe.

They would land in Harare at nightfall, and the next five

days would be packed with receptions, visits and meetings: some superficial, others very important. His printed schedule showed that everything had been organised with the usual attention to detail.

He scanned the list of his aides. Good – they had accepted all his handpicked nominees.

Wang and the others were *his* people. True believers. Their loyalty and dedication could not be faulted. Yes, the Party Secretary's office had queried the unusually large number, but the Old Man had insisted he would need each of them.

Wang and a colleague would go on ahead to Zimbabwe. There, they would secretly prepare for the operation. He compared the official itinerary for Harare with the *unofficial* one. They fitted together perfectly.

His secretary was surprised to find him smiling. That hadn't happened for years, she thought.

Florence strained to hear what the RENAMO man was saying. His speech was slurred, and he responded only intermittently to her questions – sometimes in Portuguese. She sensed the disapproval of the doctor, who hovered behind her.

'Why did you go to the farm?'

'*Eliminar* . . . eliminate.'

'Eliminate who?'

'Makuyana. *Bastardo* . . . he shoot me.'

'How did you know he would be there?'

'*Informação* . . .'

'Information? From who?'

He shook his head. 'Don't know.'

'Crap. Don't piss me about!' She stood up angrily, turning to the doctor. 'He's no use to us. Move him to the main hospital.'

A shout from the RENAMO man. 'No! They kill me!'

'Who will kill you?' She sneered at him, feigning disbelief.

'ANC.'

'Why should ANC kill you? You're more use to them alive.'

'No. Inside ANC. Inside.'

'Who inside?'

'*Não sei* . . .' he slumped back, mumbling.

She pounced. 'Don't *know*? What do you mean you don't *know*?'

'Not know name. Only face.'

The doctor intervened. 'You must leave him to rest now. Otherwise he might not survive.'

Swanepoel was early for his appointment. He waited in his car, having checked and re-checked the car park for anything unusual, any surveillance.

Right on time a familiar figure appeared and climbed into the passenger seat. After the usual exchange of passwords, Swanepoel was given his instructions.

He was to re-activate his Harare network and keep it on hold. Two new operatives were being shipped in to give assistance: assassination specialists who would make direct contact themselves.

Target was a VIP. At the appropriate time he would be given the target's name and details of the plan. He should expect an approach from a foreigner with the necessary passwords.

Meanwhile another matter. Something delicate.

His controller paused and coughed. Swanepoel caught his face outlined in the gloom. The face of a wealthy entrepreneur who had thrown his lot in with black nationalism the moment he'd seen the writing on the wall for white minority rule. Publicly loyal to the Zimbabwean government, privately playing both ends off to protect his investments and the ever-rising profits they generated on both sides of the Limpopo.

'KJ briefed you on the foreign connection and the nukes. We think it's time to rattle a few cages. The attacks on Makuyana's mob have not yet achieved their objective. He seems to have gone to ground. We think he may be getting closer. So, you need to find out what the score is from our friends. Also, they have one of our field combatants.'

'One of *ours*?' Swanepoel was surprised he hadn't heard this news from his own sources.

'A combatant. Deniable. Seems he's badly injured – though reports from the scene were confused. We think they're spreading disinformation. Find him and eliminate.'

Florence Dube scrolled through the messages on Makuyana's computer, only half concentrating.

What should she do with the RENAMO man? Confront him with Mngadi's three aides? The ones Makuyana had been trying to check out? Risky, to say the least.

A message from the monitoring centre flashed up on the screen, but she didn't notice.

How could she organise a surprise showdown with the ANC guys?

The message stared up at her.

Makuyana's absence was frustrating. She enjoyed the responsibility but needed his guidance now.

Still the message hung on the screen.

Florence picked up the phone and dialled the medical centre.

The doctor's response was cool. 'He can't be moved for at least a day – probably longer.'

'But I need him in the main hospital.'

'Alive, presumably?' A rhetorical question, tinged with sarcasm.

'What do you think!' Florence snapped, then recovered herself. 'Look, I'm sorry. This isn't simple.'

'I know,' the doctor softened a little. 'I'll do what I can. As soon as he can be moved, I'll book a bed.'

Florence put down the receiver. Something was nagging her brain.

The unread message.

She scanned it quickly, snatching a glance at her watch. It was now an hour since the scheduled pick-up – and a full sixteen hours since the message had been sent. Perhaps it was as innocent as it sounded, but she couldn't afford to chance it.

She typed a note to the monitoring centre. Step up surveillance on Herson – especially his phone and movements.

Contact her immediately if anything came up.

The newspapers ran the story, but it didn't make the front pages. English tourist murdered in Hong Kong: no apparent motive, no trace of the killer. There was a brief mention of Sewell's background as a physical education teacher, but no reference to his activism.

In the London office of Green Planet there was deep gloom and shock, but no public acknowledgement.

Jenny felt devastated. She bought all the papers and scoured each report for details. What a waste – a desperate waste – of Dick's life.

When she met Jim for a drink that evening, she could hardly speak. He hugged her warmly but she seemed stiff and remote. More like an acquaintance than a close friend. For a moment he was consumed by jealousy. Had she cared so much for Sewell? More than she cared for him?

He felt ashamed of himself.

Jenny finally spoke. 'After I get the documents back from my aunt, we can't take any risks. They've already cost one life – and could cost more. So, no open chats on the phone. No careless behaviour.'

Then, as if she was reading his mind, she looked directly at him for the first time, and gently touched his hand. 'I'm sorry, Jim. I'm an emotional wreck right now. I just want to do justice to Dick.'

Jim nodded, putting aside his own feelings. He did

understand – of course he did. Dick Sewell's memory haunted him too.

Then he sighed – he had news of his own. Another foreign trip. The last thing he needed, but he had no choice.

He showed Jenny the letter he'd just received. He was to present his team's research at a university conference in a couple of weeks' time.

In Zimbabwe.

Next day Jenny stopped off at a phone kiosk on the way to work.

'Jenny! How nice to hear from you!' her aunt exclaimed.

When the phone rang, Ruth Brown had been catching some early morning sun on the patio of her cottage in the Dorset village of Burton Bradstock.

The two women had been close since Jenny's teenage years, when she'd chosen to spend weekends and the occasional holiday with her aunt. They would discuss politics well into the night – and during long walks over the gentle hillsides and coastal paths of nearby Thomas Hardy country. Much of Jenny's political education had been gleaned from Ruth.

'Can I pop down for a visit? It's ages since we saw each other. I got back from China a week ago. I've lots to tell you.'

'Lovely!' said Ruth. 'I was hoping you'd call. There's a special present waiting for you.'

Jenny smiled in relief – and at her aunt's discretion over the open line.

'Can I come this weekend? There's a train to Dorchester which gets in at eight o'clock on Friday evening.'

'Fine – I'll pick you up there.'

Makuyana bought an evening paper outside his hotel in Johannesburg.

The law had been altered to allow visitors like him to stay in such hotels if the owners agreed. 'Honorary whites' they were called, by sceptical local blacks – and equally sceptical whites.

He flicked through the *Star*, his attention caught by a round-up of recent attacks against the apartheid state. An explosion outside a military building in the city. Another, targeting a police station. Skirmishes with the army in the Kruger National Park, along the border with Mozambique.

Makuyana felt quietly elated. The Afrikaner regime was no longer impregnable. And now he was inside: raising two fingers as it crumbled.

Early next morning he would travel to Pretoria, to the address given to him by Oliver Magano – the ANC's Lusaka man. What would he find there? Vital new information? Or a trap?

If he walked into a trap in the capital of Afrikanerdom, there would be no way out.

The Leader stood erect on the podium surveying the million-strong mass before him, filling Beijing's Square of Heavenly Peace where Chairman Mao had proclaimed the birth of the People's Republic nearly 40 years before.

The crowd was hushed. Expectant. He knew he had to rise to the occasion. Months of work and planning had gone into assembling majorities in the Party for the next great leap forward – and orchestrating media coverage to prepare the public for the new line.

As he sat in his special seat, waiting for *his* moment, the Leader wondered what Mao would have made of it all.

Close to the Great Helmsman's mausoleum at the other end of the Square, stood a symbol of the changing times: a Kentucky Fried Chicken restaurant. Outside, there was a queue of young people in fashionably bright clothes – so different from the sombre blue or grey uniforms that filled the square in Mao's day.

The Leader knew that Mao's dictums still commanded loyalty among the old guard on the Central Committee. He also knew they would not hesitate to consign him to the role of a non-person should his reforms falter. Beneath the surface of this vast, mysterious country, were rumblings of unease which could turn into mighty waves of discontent if he did not get a grip on the current economic crisis.

He spoke for a long time – over two hours. But if the masses below felt restless, they did not show it. No coughs or shuffles of feet: just obedient attention.

The Leader explained how he would tackle inflation. Enterprise would be encouraged. Egalitarianism would be 'eliminated' so that underpaid professionals – particularly doctors, teachers, scientists – could get special pay rises. The crowd broke into cheers and respectful clapping.

The Leader also reminded them about his achievements. A third of Chinese households now had a colour television and one in eight a washing machine.

Then he turned to the most sensitive part of his speech: the many problems facing the nation. Corruption amongst Party officials; the rise in serious crime; a surge in prostitution and sexually-transmitted diseases; the return of malnutrition – for the first time since Liberation.

The crowd fell silent again. But these problems were the problems of change, the Leader insisted. They were like the flies that entered a room when a window was opened.

'We can put up with the flies, but we cannot do without fresh air,' he thundered.

The Old Man sat on the podium, listening to the speech and clapping politely at key moments. He had good reason to feel content.

The trouble-maker Sewell had been eliminated, and Wang's contacts in British intelligence had proved helpful in monitoring Evans and the girl. Nothing too serious: just discreet surveillance of their contacts and communications. A wise precaution.

The Leader was now concluding his performance with a ringing oration.

The Old Man had to admit that the speech had been skilfully constructed. It took a certain courage to acknowledge publicly how the reform programme had failed: clearly, a calculated risk.

At the reception for the Party bigwigs later, the Old Man circulated suavely – testing his most trusted supporters, making sure he spent time with the generals. What had *they* felt about the speech?

The overall consensus? That the Leader might have pulled it off for now, but was still in deep trouble.

The time was approaching for the Old Man to reveal his hand.

Aunt Ruth drove Jenny through Dorchester, passing the courthouse where the Tolpuddle Martyrs had been tried in 1834 and deported to Australia.

When Jenny was a teenager, the two had attended many annual trade union marches commemorating the Martyrs' courage.

The journey to Burton Bradstock took about half an hour. It was a bright summer's evening, and signposts to quaintly named villages flashed by: Toller Porcorum, Toller Fratrum, Puncknowle, Littlebredy. Jenny had always loved the charm of these Dorset names.

As they drove, she poured out the whole China story to her aunt – who promised it would go no further. They talked animatedly, hardly pausing when they stopped off at a favourite pub, or later when they enjoyed a home-cooked meal and the bottle of red wine Jenny had brought.

It was past midnight before they turned in. Jenny felt more relaxed than she had for weeks. Although a city girl, she loved the gentle pace of village life: the way it absorbed her anxieties and spirited them away.

She had another reason to feel relieved. Dick's documents

had arrived safely and were tucked underneath her mattress. She would make more photocopies, leave one set with her aunt, and enjoy the rest of the weekend. Back in London, the story would break in the media, and Dick's death would be avenged.

Ruth – the veteran campaigner – had advice on that front too. As she kissed Jenny goodbye at the station on Sunday evening, she warned: 'Be careful, darling. Above all, keep your names out of the media!'

The RENAMO man was recovering slowly and could soon be moved to the hospital, the doctor told Florence.

Although it was risky, she had to force a confrontation with Mngadi's three aides. Given his fragility, *they* would have to come to him. She knew it could be tantamount to murder, but time wasn't on her side. The traitor had to be exposed. There was no other option: she only hoped her boss would agree.

Leaning back in Makuyana's office chair, she ran her fingers through her hair – a habit of hers when she was under stress. She noticed a couple of spots on her face. On her last visit home, her mother had chided: 'My child, you do not look after yourself properly. Always working and eating on the move. Not enough nourishing food!'

Florence was buried in such deep thought, she hardly noticed a secretary bringing a cup of coffee. They were fully behind her, the junior women in the unit. She had made it. She could lead the way for others.

Oliver Magano, the ANC's Lusaka man, had recovered from the attack at the farm, and was being discharged later in the day. What a relief. One less target in hospital.

Now she must be decisive.

Nobody must know that Makuyana was out of the country, and *she* had to stay under the radar too. So, she instructed an assistant to do the groundwork – to call Selby Mngadi, and set up a meeting with his three aides: Petersen, Bhajee and Msimang.

They'd be told that the RENAMO man had survived, but nothing more. Then, each of the three would be monitored. Depending on what happened, they would be invited to interrogate the RENAMO man in hospital.

Swanepoel was doing some desultory gardening by the gate to keep up appearances, when a white woman with a youngster walked along the pavement towards him.

As she drew level, she spoke firmly, still looking straight ahead as if she was talking to her child. 'NOSLEN is threatened. Follow me so we can talk.'

Anybody watching would not have noticed that the two had communicated. But nobody was watching. Nobody saw Swanepoel stretch up from his weeding, walk inside his house, wash his hands and then re-emerge, carefully surveying the road. Satisfied, he headed off and found the woman playing with her little boy on a piece of waste land beyond the rows of houses with their wide gardens.

The child was tottering about, laughing as he chased a brightly coloured rubber ball. It rolled over towards Swanepoel. He stooped, grabbed it and returned it to the boy.

'Sorry!' the mother called, feigning embarrassment at bothering a stranger.

But as she walked towards them, her eyes were steely – checking for any surveillance. Then she rapidly addressed Swanepoel in Afrikaans, while pretending to speak to her son.

'They caught a RENAMO man at the farm. He's badly injured – we think he's in the city hospital. Problem is, he can maybe identify our NOSLEN source in the ANC. It's too risky for our guy to get rid of him, so you'll have to do it. But *maak gou*! No time to waste.'

The she bent down to the child, grinned affectionately, and said in English: 'Come, sweetie – let's go home.'

They turned, and made their way back to the road.

Swanepoel walked on. When he found a phone booth he dialled the direct number of a businessman in a plush city office.

Jonathan Fletcher sat waiting in Green Planet headquarters, off Islington Green in North London.

When Jenny had rung the day before, he had wondered if she was just another nutter or well-intentioned obsessive. He'd seen plenty.

Some refused to give their names but complained their mail was being intercepted, or said they were being followed. Most wanted to talk urgently, then didn't turn up for appointments. One person claimed the state was sending messages directly into his brain by electronic pulses.

Fletcher was a patient man. He dealt with public information and enquiries, filtering communications on behalf of the organisation's hard-pressed and under-resourced campaign managers. He felt his role was to be respectful: to give Green Planet a friendly face.

But he was also a veteran radical, who had experienced Special Branch surveillance and forceful policing of demonstrations. So he was not intrinsically sceptical of tales of harassment or pleas for secrecy. And there was something about *this* caller that rang true. Jenny Stuart claimed to have important information about nuclear waste. She needed to meet in person, and soon.

A call from reception. Ms Stuart was on her way up.

He met her at the top of the stairs, and ushered her in to his austere office. No power dynamics in this organisation: everyone mucked in together.

They shook hands. She was an attractive young woman, Fletcher noted. Not fussy about her appearance, but imbued with energy. Or tension.

'Thanks for seeing me at such short notice,' she said.

'No problem,' his voice was cool, though not hostile.

'Look,' she sounded embarrassed, 'I hope you don't mind, but I'd prefer to talk somewhere else. Can we go to a pub?'

If Fletcher was irritated, he hid it. Actually, he was curious. 'If you like,' he replied, his tone neutral. 'There's one just round the corner, should be quite empty this time of day.'

As soon as they were outside, she got straight to the point – much to his surprise.

'I came to talk about Dick Sewell.'

'What about him?'

'I was with him in China.'

'Oh?' Fletcher's tone was still reserved. Who was she? A girlfriend Dick hadn't mentioned?

'We were there separately, but our paths crossed.'

By now they'd reached the pub. It was rather scruffy, geared to local drinkers. Jenny insisted on buying the drinks, ignoring the men at the bar who stared at her.

Fletcher chose a table out of earshot in the corner, next to a tired-sounding jukebox playing the Beatles' *Yesterday*. Jenny put down the glasses of orange juice, pulled up a chair, and told her story.

Dick had been Fletcher's close friend. His death was a taboo subject in the office. Nobody believed it was a random knife attack, but they couldn't risk the organisation's security by revealing the truth about his mission.

It had been so hard, especially for Fletcher. And now – out of the blue – here was this woman, confirming his worst fears.

'What happened to the documents?' He almost didn't dare ask.

Jenny smiled, feeling a burden lift from her shoulders. Finally, she could do justice to Dick's courage.

'I have copies. I'll give them to you in the office. But there are some conditions. When you go to the media, you can't mention my name – or Jim's. He's already survived two assassination attempts. And don't tell anyone else in Green Planet either. Will you promise me?'

Fletcher sipped his juice. 'This is too big for me to handle on my own, Jenny. The credibility of Green Planet is at stake, so I'll have to tell my senior colleagues — but they don't need to know your names. As for the press, that won't be a problem.'

If the press believe us, he thought. If not, he might have to break the pledge he'd just given. He prided himself on his integrity, but the cause was always bigger than the individual.

Wang Bi Nan circulated amongst the defence attachés and procurement agents at the Asiandex Arms Expo in Beijing.

Staged for the first time in China, it reflected the country's growing role as an arms dealer. Even the old hands were impressed, as interpreters introduced English and Arab-speaking visitors to a variety of Chinese-made missiles, tanks and armaments.

The Silkworm missile was prominently displayed amidst a range of brightly coloured projectiles in the main hall. The C802 anti-ship weapon created a buzz of interest: Beijing's answer to the French Exocet.

In the parking lot, a mobile launcher whined through a simulated exercise, aiming a missile skywards. And apparently the Arabs were interested in the M-9: a medium range missile capable of hitting targets at 600 kilometres.

Although some of the weapons were outdated, China's ability to produce cheap systems had turned it into the world's fifth-biggest arms exporter, after the US, Soviet Union, France and Britain. The official brochure proudly announced expanding sales in Africa, the development of a new generation of fighter planes, and the sale of old Soviet aircraft modernised with Western electronics at attractive prices for poorer countries.

Wang used the opportunity to cultivate contacts and finalise a special deal: for the vital missing piece in the Old Man's plans.

*

As instructed, Venter and Coetzee cut short their holiday in Germany and flew to Harare on Balkan Airways.

They survived the bumpy flight – and hours of irritating Bulgarian folk songs – and were waved through airport formalities without a hitch, posing as archaeology students.

They had a plan. Lie low for several weeks and play as much tennis as possible, in between boring but necessary field trips to archaeological sites. Plenty of time to enjoy a few beers and suss out the local talent.

Meanwhile, they prepared for the operation. It had to go like clockwork. They were steely-minded assassins who would come from nowhere, deliver the coup de grâce and disappear.

But suddenly everything changed.

Some poor bastard had been caught by the opposition, and had to be eliminated before he spilled his guts. Now *they* had to do the eliminating: with hardly any time to plan. In and out, hoping to hell nothing went wrong.

They argued somebody else should do it. It would safeguard their anonymity: keep them nice and sharp for the big one. But Captain Mauritz Swanepoel was not a man to cross. He insisted.

Venter and Coetzee were an uncomplicated pair. Just guys who liked girls, beers and rugby. They were fanatical Springbok fans, furious with those *fokken betogers* from UK, Australia and New Zealand, whose protests had deprived their Boks of international competition.

They'd like to get hold of that bunch of long-haired drug-taking commies, but first things first.

Makuyana left his car in the underground car park in downtown Pretoria as instructed. Now he was waiting to see Jimmy Wentzel, posing as another client seeking urgent advice from the busy advocate.

Wentzel's receptionist had politely reproached him for not

making an appointment, but Makuyana's quiet authority won her over.

After a while, she popped her head around the door of the waiting room and summoned him.

'Mr Nkala' – he'd given her his alias – 'Mr Wentzel will see you now.'

The advocate's room was lined with books. Jimmy Wentzel was standing behind his large desk, a broad smile on his face.

A chubby man of Afrikaner-Jewish heritage, he had an infectious guffaw and an air of purposeful untidiness. He was one of the most tenacious lawyers in the country: a man who would take on a political trial and fight to the end – regardless of threats to his family and attacks on his professional integrity.

'Mr Nkala. Welcome. Sorry to have kept you waiting.' He pointed to a chair. 'Make yourself comfortable.'

Then his genial manner changed. 'Now, this problem of yours. The relatives are proving troublesome, I gather. I'm not surprised. Badly drafted wills have a habit of creating problems.'

He leant forward suddenly, and pushed a piece of paper across the desk, continuing to chat.

Makuyana read the hastily scrawled note: 'Not safe here. Pretend to be my client. Give me your car keys. We'll go somewhere secure.'

Wentzel's voice droned on, covering the intricacies of property rights, while Makuyana played along, responding with an occasional 'yes' or 'no'.

After about twenty minutes, Wentzel wrapped up the conversation, put his fingers to his lips to urge caution, and led him to the door. He checked to see that his staff had gone home for the night and beckoned Makuyana to follow.

Wentzel pulled a chauffeur's cap out of his briefcase and handed it to him – along with a set of car keys. Then he pointed to the lift. Together they descended to the underground car park. Wentzel's car was a two-litre Audi, its body aerodynamically designed and shaped to exert minimum wind resistance. Makuyana had a soft spot for luxury cars, and was thrilled at the prospect of driving it. He put on the chauffeur's cap.

They pulled away from the city centre, quieter now the workers had departed. Following instructions, Makuyana accelerated up Church Street, heading east. The car, unfamiliar at first, responded to his touch. Suburbs swished by and soon they were in open country, the city lights dimming behind them.

Wentzel suddenly tapped him on the shoulder. 'Bugger it! A puncture. Stop over there.' He pointed to a lay-by. Makuyana, confused, pulled in. They jacked up the car and rolled the spare tyre round to the front. Makuyana squatted down, as Wentzel pretended to direct operations.

'Sorry about this charade,' the lawyer whispered, his grin shining in the headlights. 'My office is definitely bugged. And I've never been absolutely certain about the car. Had it swept, but last week it was impounded by traffic wardens. Allegedly for illegal parking, but actually I'd left it in a metered space all paid-up.'

Makuyana pretended to fiddle with the wheel brace while Wentzel quietly briefed him.

'We've got a guy in military intelligence. He doesn't come up with the goods very often, but when he does it's pure gold. He says they've been developing battlefield nuclear weapons – shells for tanks or ground attack aircraft, that sort of thing – and they're planning to take out suspected ANC bases in Zimbabwe.'

'But we don't *allow* any official ANC bases,' Makuyana retorted, looking up from the wheel.

'Yes, I know. But the ANC still has a presence, and Pretoria's getting frustrated. It wants to teach everyone a big lesson.'

Makuyana frowned. 'I didn't realise they had the capability to use specialist nuclear hardware.'

'Well, prepare yourself for a shock,' Wentzel replied. 'Seems the apartheid regime is collaborating with China!'

He looked at Makuyana quizzically. 'You're not surprised? I certainly was! Pretoria and Beijing? Surely an unlikely alliance?'

Makuyana shook his head. 'We've had a sniff of that – but only a sniff.'

Wentzel shrugged. 'Something else. I have to direct you to another contact. Seems he may have important information about ANC officials in Harare. Don't know what.'

He stopped talking, as another car pulled up in front of them. Makuyana tensed – then realised it was his own hire car. A man got out and slipped into the Audi's driving seat. Wentzel took back the chauffeur's cap from Makuyana and handed it to the new arrival, smiling mischievously.

'All in a day's work! Now, drive to the next lay-by. Your contact will be waiting. Good luck. And be careful. You're really on your own now: one slip and they'll have you.'

The two shook hands, and the Audi disappeared into the night, leaving Makuyana alone and apprehensive.

Where would they strike first? It was 24 hours since Florence had leaked news of the RENAMO man's survival. He was still safe in the medical centre.

Deep in thought, she walked down the bleak corridor to Makuyana's office, oblivious to the buzzing conversation and clattering typewriters.

What would *she* do in their position? There weren't many options ...

Suddenly she froze. Of course! It had to be *here*! The security centre. They would want to cause maximum panic, so they'd target the top man: Makuyana. They wouldn't know he was away.

Two white men walked past carrying briefcases, nodding politely. She grunted in response, then paused: white men? Strange – she'd never seen them before. Who the hell were they?

She turned, but remembered she wasn't armed. They might be.

She rushed towards her office. She must phone the guards to get the men intercepted. Then it hit her. She now occupied *Makuyana's* office.

The men in the corridor were walking past the door. What if they'd been inside?

Cautiously she entered. Slowly looked around. Searched the desk and the steel filing cabinet. Everything seemed to be as she'd left it.

She shook herself. Stop wasting time! She must get through to the guards. She reached for her telephone – but stopped.

That could be it. A familiar South African technique. When the phone receiver was lifted it would activate a signal from a small transmitter. It would trigger a bomb, hidden elsewhere in the room. The work of a moment – for professionals.

Florence rushed to another office to raise the alarm. They had to be stopped.

Venter and Coetzee knew they were in trouble as soon as the alarm started ringing, reverberating harshly off the bare walls.

The plan had seemed foolproof. Enter the security centre through the underground car park used by field agents. Exit through the main entrance.

Now, the reception area was just ahead. But the guard in the glass cubicle was on his feet. And he was reaching for something.

Venter and Coetzee responded like automatons, pulling on their masks. Venter threw a CS gas canister at the cubicle, while Coetzee swept the area with his Z88 hand pistol: made in South Africa to beat the international arms boycott. As people started rushing towards them, he peppered the area with gunshots, stopping them in their tracks.

The assassins made their escape, leaving the coughing security man writhing on the floor, scratching frantically at his eyes as the vicious gas swirled. Alerted by the alarm, their driver was already pulling away as they bundled into the back of the old Ford transit.

They just made it. But at what cost? Was their cover blown? So bloody stupid! Venter smashed his fist on the floor of the van in frustration. Coetzee knew how he felt.

A little later, explosives experts safely defused the bomb in Makuyana's office. It was hidden under the desk – as Florence had suspected – and it would have blown her to smithereens when she lifted the phone.

For the second time in a fortnight she had smelt death. First on the farm, now in Makuyana's office. Their enemies were getting closer – and they were certainly well informed.

Makuyana's instinct had been correct. Something big was in the air. She knew it too, now.

As expected, a Nissan Bluebird was parked in the lay-by, not far from where Makuyana had left Wentzel. Its parking lights were on.

On the other side of the road, the ground sloped gently up to a line of *kopjes*, shadowy in the darkness. Alongside the lay-by, fields fell away to clumps of trees.

Not much cover for two cars, but nobody could approach without being spotted.

Makuyana had been shaken by the lawyer's final warning. His nerves tingled as he pulled into the lay-by, flashing his lights three times and keeping his engine running, as instructed.

The driver of the other vehicle got out of his car. A young white kid – perhaps in his early twenties. Casually dressed, a beret pulled sideways on his head. He loped over and they exchanged greetings. There'd been no time to arrange passwords. His name was Jannie Craven, which reminded Makuyana incongruously of the more famous Danie: South Africa's 'Mr Rugby'.

'Haven't got much time.' Jannie spoke with a strong Afrikaans accent. His eyes darted around, and he was clearly agitated.

'We checked out Bhajee, Petersen and Msimang. Nothing dodgy in their backgrounds. But George Petersen's family weren't very chatty. Our people said they seemed scared. Also, they're much better off than their neighbours – his wife has a new car. Nothing too flashy, but still unusual for that part of town.'

'Thank you, my friend.'

'I gotta go. You must turn round and head straight back for Joburg. Take the main road left to bypass the city centre. Watch your back, hey?'

They shook hands.

Suddenly two shots broke the silence. A volley of bullets hit the offside tyres of the Nissan. Jannie – shocked – wheeled round, peering towards the trees. Makuyana put his Fiat into reverse, thanking his lucky stars he'd kept the engine running.

Another shot rang out, glancing off one of Makuyana's hub caps. Jannie ran towards him and hurled himself into the car, screaming: 'Put your foot down!'

His mind racing, Makuyana spun the car round and they screeched off, back the way he'd come. Two more shots – but thank Christ – they missed the Fiat altogether.

'Shit! We're in dead trouble, man,' Jannie sounded terrified. He was holding a pistol now, staring back into the distance.

'Can they trace the Nissan to you?' Makuyana asked.

'Fortunately not. I stole it in the city an hour ago. I'm more worried that others are maybe waiting up ahead. Keep your eyes peeled. And don't drive too fast, we can't get busted for speeding.'

Makuyana slowed obediently. Did they have the number of his rented Fiat? If so, it could only be a matter of time before they hunted him down.

He'd better head for the airport and catch the first flight north.

8

The front page story in Monday's edition of the *Guardian* was headlined NUCLEAR WASTE LEAK IN CHINA, and straplined 'Exclusive: Green Planet exposes radiation crisis'

It detailed the waste leakages and environmental threat, but did not explain how the documents were obtained: simply stating they had been 'smuggled out' to Green Planet. The Chinese Embassy refused to comment, but the paper's Sino expert confirmed the documents were genuine, based on her own independent sources.

Inside the paper, an editorial called for international action to tackle such incidents, reminding readers that at least 48 nuclear warheads and nuclear reactors were still lying on the ocean floor.

'Chernobyl made us understand that ecological catastrophe recognises no frontiers,' the editorial said, 'and these incidents are potentially just as lethal. Simply because we cannot observe the effects as easily as radioactive fallout, we should not imagine that poisoning our waters is less serious.'

At Green Planet HQ the telephones rang ceaselessly as other news outlets caught up with the story.

Jonathan Fletcher fielded most of the calls and did several media interviews. As he had anticipated, many reporters wanted copies of the documents, which he was happy to provide.

The calls were generally positive. Most journalists were alive to the news value of green issues, even if their own proprietors were engaged in business ventures which showed scant regard for the environment.

Fletcher didn't mind the pressure. He was on a high. Green Planet had come up trumps again.

Six miles across the city, in a flat behind Victoria Street, Harold Williams was in a more sober mood.

The *Guardian* wasn't his paper – he preferred the *Telegraph* – but he'd gone out to buy a copy after listening to *Today*: the BBC's morning radio programme.

He read the Green Planet story, thought for a while, then dialled an unlisted number. The intelligence officer who answered was accessible only to a select few. Their conversation lasted nearly fifteen minutes.

Williams then phoned the home of a Conservative MP known for his keen interest in security matters. Next, he called a journalist from the *Daily Express*. Another home number: the man rarely went into the office. He didn't need to. A well-known author who had recently been given a knighthood, he wrote books about intelligence – often breaching the Official Secrets Act but never incurring official wrath. He could get an important story into the *Express* whenever he chose.

The final call was brief, almost curt. Williams arranged to meet his contact at their usual place. Neither named it over the open line.

By early afternoon Jonathan Fletcher was receiving very different calls from the media.

It began when a young reporter from the *Express* pushed him to identify the source of the documents. Earlier, Fletcher had successfully parried such enquiries by insisting on the need to protect his source – but the *Express* journalist was persistent to the point of aggression.

He also let slip that the Foreign Office was playing down the *Guardian* report. A billion-pound contract was being concluded for the supply of British equipment to Beijing, and London was anxious not to jeopardise the deal.

Meanwhile a backbench Tory MP had suggested to the Press Association that the documents might not be authentic, and attacked Green Planet for hoodwinking the public with 'over-dramatic' allegations.

'So, unless you tell us how you got the documents, we'll have to question the credibility of the story,' the *Express* reporter threatened.

Fletcher was in a quandary. Late afternoon deadlines for the morning's first editions were approaching. Follow-up calls from other journalists were starting to reflect the *Express* line. Radio news began carrying the MP's statement, and reporting the Foreign Office's caution.

The story was taking on a new shape.

He had given Jenny Stuart a promise – but he also knew he had no option but to name Dick Sewell if Green Planet revealed how the documents were obtained. His colleagues were unanimous: Green Planet's credibility was at stake. Sewell would have to be named. If necessary, Jenny and Jim too.

Fletcher tried to call Jenny at her workplace: Southwark Council's social services department. But she was out on home visits and they didn't know when she would be back. He left a message for her, and another on her home answerphone.

As the afternoon wore on, he felt increasingly dispirited. Green Planet's agenda had been hijacked: partly because of political pressures, and partly because of the media's insatiable thirst for a 'fresh' angle to spice up the evening broadcast bulletins and next day's newspapers. The identity of the source was now the main focus – at the expense of the more important environmental issue.

Jenny had still not returned his call. He phoned her office

again, this time giving his direct line and home number. Then he decided to act. After consulting with his colleagues, he sent out a media alert. Green Planet would hold a press conference at 10 a.m. the following day to share 'important new information'. Several journalists pressed him for more details but he just replied that the source was 'rock solid', and the press conference would confirm it.

He worked into the night to prepare a fact sheet on Dick Sewell, explaining his personal background and the nature of his mission. He just hoped to God he could keep the young woman and her colleague out of it.

It was weird driving back to Joburg with Jannie Craven, Makuyana thought. There were no signs of pursuit or surveillance, so perhaps he should just return to his hotel and continue with his 'business trip'.

If he skipped the country in a hurry, it would inevitably make the authorities suspicious. And perhaps the security services weren't behind the shooting, anyway. But if not them, who? Had the whole thing been staged? If so, was Jannie Craven a friend or a foe?

Makuyana decided to find out.

'How did you get involved in all this?' he asked.

The young man was silent for a few moments. Then he said, slowly: 'Military service changed my life.'

Makuyana nodded, encouraging him to continue.

'My family is quite well-off, so life was comfortable for me, growing up. Rugby, girlfriends – the usual. But then I got conscripted into the army. Got sent to South West. You probably call it Namibia.

'We were there to fight the SWAPO guerrillas, and my job was to liaise with *Koevoet*: the counter-insurgency branch of the South West African Police. Maybe you've heard of it? It means "crowbar".'

Makuyana nodded again. *Koevoet* had a brutal reputation for torture, rape and murder.

'At first, it seemed like a really soft option. But as soon as I went out with them on patrol ... Jeez. They were something else, those guys.

'For me the army was a job, a duty. I was there to do my time and get back home in one piece. But they were *bosbefok*. Pumped up on adrenaline, addicted to hunting down "terrs" – terrorists – and killing them.'

Jannie paused, then took a deep breath.

'One evening I went with them into an operational area to look for SWAPO. The sun was setting. I remember the mud *rondavels*, so dark against that orange sky. Kids came out to watch, half curious, half terrified. The *Koevoet* guys went crazy. Kicking over pots of food, tearing clothes off women, poking machine guns between their thighs pretending to search them. Then a couple of guys started shouting: "*Ons vat hom*: we caught him!"'

Makuyana flinched. Jannie's story was stirring up his own painful memories.

'One of our soldiers dragged a black man out of a hut. He was in combat gear. Our guy shot at him three times, deliberately missing. Then he fired at both his legs. I thought that would be it. I thought the SWAPO man would be taken off for interrogation. But then our guy started laughing hysterically. He called out to his mates to gather round.

'He took aim again. This time he fired directly into the man's face. There was this explosion of blood and bone and flesh. They all just kept laughing and slapping each other on the back. I went behind a tree and vomited my guts out.'

The car was filled with silence.

'*That* is what changed me,' Jannie said simply.

Makuyana nodded. He drove on, as the lights of Joburg appeared ahead.

*

Florence took elaborate precautions to protect the RENAMO man. After surgery, he was put in a private room isolated from the main wards, with two guards outside his door. She wouldn't be able to bring in Mngadi's aides for at least 36 hours.

Now it was nearly midnight. Florence longed for bed, but she knew she wouldn't be able to sleep. Instead, she drove to the hospital – just to check that all was well.

The hospital had a calm fluorescent glow in the darkness, in contrast to its daytime hustle and bustle.

She showed her card at reception, and waited for a guard to collect her. She started wondering how the traitor – Msimang, Petersen or Bhajee – would plan to eliminate the RENAMO man.

She was escorted into a lift and down a corridor. Ahead, a nurse pushed a trolley of medicine, and two white doctors walked by, nodding to the guard. Florence glanced up.

White doctors. They seemed vaguely familiar. *Why?* She turned to see them step into the lift.

Suddenly she froze. Two white doctors. Not unusual in Harare's main hospital. But *those* two? Where had she seen them before.

Jesus!

She rushed to the room of the RENAMO man, followed by two startled guards. He was asleep, breathing fitfully, the monitor showing a regular heartbeat. Everything seemed okay.

'Who were they?' she barked at the guards, gesticulating down the corridor.

'Doctors, madam.' They looked at each other, confused.

'Yes – but *who*?'

'They look after your patient. Part of the team. They came to do a routine check-up when the shift changed an hour ago.'

'How did you know they were genuine?'

'We got a phone call as usual – to say they were coming up.' The guards looked sullen. Was the woman cracking up?

They'd heard about yesterday's attack on headquarters, her near-miss.

'What are their names?'

One of the guards picked up a sheet of paper. 'Doctors David Lewin and John McKay.'

'Right, get them back here immediately. I want to see them.'

Maybe she was overreacting. The patient seemed comfortable. All the security procedures were being followed. But she still had that nagging sense of recognition. She could have sworn they were the same two men she'd seen walking away from Makuyana's office the day before.

One of the guards looked up from the phone. 'They can't locate the doctors. They're not responding to their bleepers.'

'Find out where their office is. And get a nurse and another doctor up here right away. Tell them it's an emergency.'

'Their office is room 110. Three floors down.'

Florence pulled a pistol out of her handbag and slipped it into her jacket pocket. She was no longer tired. Her adrenaline was pumping.

'You two stay here,' she called to the guards.

The corridor leading to room 110 was deserted. She put her ear to the door, gun in hand. Quiet. She opened the door carefully, easing inside. The room seemed empty. She felt for the main light switch and turned it on. The sudden glare dazzled her. There were a couple of open briefcases on the desk with stethoscopes tossed on top, and two white coats on a hook. Nothing strange.

But wasn't there something odd about the *smell* of the room? Not the usual hospital odour of disinfectant, something else . . .

Her stomach felt taut, her heart was thudding — if the men were impostors, the real doctors might still be here somewhere.

She noticed a door marked 'bathroom' and gingerly opened it. The stench of chloroform almost choked her. Holding her nose, she switched on the light. Two men were lying on the floor, apparently unconscious. The *real* doctors.

Florence raced to the phone to summon help. Then she took the lift again to check on the RENAMO man.

But she was too late.

A telltale syringe mark on his arm told of the poison winding its way through his system. Within minutes he was dead.

Florence was engulfed by a wave of emotions. Frustration at coming so close to catching them, and anger at being outwitted again. But above all: determination.

Next time she would get them.

Jim knew there was something wrong the moment he walked through the door of his small, terraced house in Islington.

He'd stopped off from work to change into casual clothes and collect his China photos, before heading to a pub in Covent Garden to meet Jenny.

The place was a shambles. Drawers open, cupboards emptied, books pulled off shelves, papers strewn everywhere.

Burglars, he thought bitterly. What bad timing! It was just after six. He had no way of contacting Jenny, and it would take ages for the police to come.

He quickly checked to see what they had taken. How odd: his video recorder, TV, stereo were still there. Ditto his passport, driving licence and cheque book. He checked the rest of the house, but nothing seemed to be missing. It didn't make sense.

Grabbing some clothes from under a pile on the floor, he changed quickly. Then he went to the kitchen to collect his photos. They had been taken out of their folder and spread all over the table. Weird. He stuffed them back in, pulled on a jacket and locked the door behind him.

As he turned the key, he realised here was no sign of forced entry.

Jim shivered. He thought he'd left all that behind in China – but clearly not.

*

The main Pretoria-Joburg highway was still quiet, but Makuyana remained on the alert.

Jannie kept watching the road, ahead and behind. 'Let's stop and take stock,' he muttered.

Makuyana nodded, and found a suitable place to pull off. Nearly nine o'clock now. Another hour and he could be in his hotel bed – or walking into a trap, possibly even led into one. Could he really trust Jannie?

He switched off the engine. 'What now?'

'For starters, you better sit in the back seat and I'll drive. Then we won't attract attention. I could be your *baas*, taking you back to the township.' Jannie gave a taut smile. 'Best we keep heading for Joburg, but we must check your hotel carefully.'

Makuyana nodded slowly. He might really need Jannie Craven.

If the man was genuine.

Jenny arrived early at the pub, found a payphone, and dialled her office to see if she had any messages.

She hadn't been able to check for a while. Most of her clients lived in cramped flats on decaying housing estates, and few had phones.

She was given Fletcher's numbers and called him on his direct office line. It was nearly seven o'clock and she wondered if he'd still be there.

He picked up after the first ring.

Her heart sank as he explained his quandary. He was apologetic but firm.

'Look Jenny, I really want to keep you and Jim out of it. But to be honest, there are no guarantees. If the press start digging, we'll tell them that a fellow tourist smuggled out the documents. That might not be enough to satisfy them, though.'

Jenny's anger flared, but she understood Fletcher's problem. She took a deep breath and coolly weighed up the situation.

'Okay, but please don't mention Jim's name. He's got a professional reputation to protect – and that's less of a problem for me. Also, he was nearly killed out there, you know. Twice.'

'What?' Fletcher was shocked.

'Long story. But powerful interests are at play. They're determined to keep the lid on the nuclear connection in China.'

'Perhaps that's why the Green Planet story suddenly shifted today,' Fletcher mused. 'There could well be people here who want to keep the lid on it too.'

As Jenny put down the phone, she saw Jim. He glanced around and spotted her. She had looked forward to their evening, realising how much she'd missed him. But he seemed on edge, distracted. They hugged almost absent-mindedly.

Jim found himself staring at each person in the pub, and tried to suppress his paranoia. 'A quick pint before we eat?'

She nodded, feeling uneasy. The pub was full of chat and laughter: crowded with people on their way home from work, or meeting before the theatre. Girls sipping Campari, blokes drinking beers. Normal people. Not like them.

Jim came back with two pints of real ale. 'That should cheer you up.'

'Do I look as if I need cheering up?' she asked, smiling weakly. She saw again how tense he was.

'Yes, you do, actually. What sort of day have you had?'

She told him about Fletcher, expecting him to react strongly. But he was surprisingly philosophical.

'Sure, I *am* worried about my academic position: to work in this area you have to be trusted by officialdom. And it's true that I'm not comfortable in the public spotlight. But Dick mustn't have died for nothing. We have to make sure of that.'

She reached across the table and touched his hand. He took it tentatively, and squeezed gently. 'And what about the impact on you?' he asked.

Not for the first time, she noticed how he deflected the

conversation away from himself. An engaging trait – but frustrating, perhaps, if you wanted to get close to him.

'Well, I also feel okay about it,' she replied. 'I know it has to be done – I'm just worried you might be targeted again.'

'Perhaps I already have been.'

'What do you mean?'

He told her about the break-in.

'What do I say to the police? That somebody broke in without force and stole nothing? The cops are so stretched they don't even respond to *normal* burglaries.'

Jenny was silent for a moment. 'Let's go eat,' she said.

They found a small vegetarian restaurant, and sat at a secluded table, lit by a soft candle. The food was good – and the wine. They were drawn closer together again. Over coffee, Jim produced his folder of photos and they relived favourite memories.

There was a group shot of everyone at the Great Wall, and a good one that Jenny had taken of him on his own.

But hadn't there been another? The one that accidentally captured Wang in the background? Jenny clearly remembered taking it, and Jim remembered seeing it. The image of Wang had been so clear . . .

'Check the negatives,' said Jenny.

He opened up the folder. The negatives were missing too.

Captain Mauritz Swanepoel was pleased with his boys. They had redeemed themselves after the botched security HQ job.

The death of the RENAMO man hadn't featured in the news, which didn't surprise him. It would have been hushed up.

Venter and Coetzee were now lying low for a couple of weeks. They had driven 300 kilometres south to Lake Mutirikwi, close to Great Zimbabwe: the ancient ruins of a once-flourishing African kingdom which traded in gold between the thirteenth and fifteenth centuries.

The two assassins weren't impressed by ancient ruins. Instead, they spent their days fishing and drinking beer.

But one thing worried Swanepoel. Where the hell was Makuyana? The phone-activated bomb intended for him had nearly taken out his deputy instead – and Makuyana hadn't been spotted at the hospital.

His deputy was some woman. Dube, that was her name. A woman! Christ, the Zimbabweans must be getting desperate. No way *he'd* take orders from a female.

Still, he would check Dube out – and request that Makuyana's whereabouts be traced. That bugger had always worried him. A formidable adversary for whom he had a grudging respect.

He was probably up to no bloody good.

As planned, Jannie Craven had gone to the hotel, while Makuyana waited round the corner in the car – slumped down, as if asleep.

Jannie would hang out for a while in the foyer, to make sure there was no danger. Then he would take the lift to Makuyana's room and knock on the door. If nobody answered, he would return to the reception area and ask for 'Mr Nkala' – who, of course, would be out.

Jannie would tell Makuyana when the coast was clear, but would stay close at hand, just in case.

It all made sense, but Makuyana suddenly felt uneasy. He decided on another course of action. Once Jannie was out of sight, he slipped into the hotel via the service entrance. He knew he was taking a chance – but he was a sitting target in the car.

He headed for the black staff quarters which he'd sussed out a few days earlier. Nobody was about. In a cupboard, he found some dark grey overalls which he pulled over his suit. He grabbed a trolley of cleaning materials, and took the lift up to the first-floor balcony from where he could survey the foyer.

Jannie was hunched over a newspaper on one of the settees,

not attracting any attention. After a while, he got up and strolled towards the bar. The youngster was good, Makuyana thought. He moved confidently and blended into his surroundings: key attributes when one was undercover.

Then, very casually, Jannie entered the lift as planned.

Several minutes later, he reappeared and spoke to the woman at reception. She made a phone call, and then shook her head. Jannie returned to the settee and his paper.

Makuyana started pushing his trolley quickly back to the staff quarters, passing a white waiter with a tray of drinks. Fortunately, the waiter took no notice of him. He replaced the overalls and the trolley, leaving the hotel via the service entrance again. He circled the car until he was satisfied it wasn't under surveillance, then climbed inside and slumped down.

A little while later Jannie returned. 'Everything seems okay,' he said.

'But what does that mean? Was it one of *your* people, not Special Branch who fired at us?'

'Could be,' Jannie shrugged. 'I must say it's bit of a mystery.'

He handed Makuyana a phone number. 'I'll be holed up for the next few days with a friend. Ring if you have any problems.'

They shook hands, and he was off. Makuyana drove round to the hotel's underground car park. Then he walked back to the street, found a public call box and rang the hotel.

'Ah, Mr Nkala. A friend came to see you. He didn't leave a name but said he'd return tomorrow.'

'Thanks, but I'd like to check out now. My plans have changed. Please send my luggage down to reception. I'll be along shortly to settle the bill.'

'Certainly sir. You realise you'll have to pay for tonight, though?'

'Yes, of course.'

Forty-five minutes later, he was at Jan Smuts airport. The

first flight north was bound for Nairobi, and it was boarding soon. Pity to take such a long detour home, but he had no choice.

Steeling himself, he walked as calmly as possible towards passport control. The official gave him only a cursory glance and waved him through.

But as the plane taxied out, two men in plain clothes arrived at his hotel and asked for him.

They seemed surprised to discover he had gone.

'Dick was one of our most trusted activists.'

Fletcher sat under the TV camera lights and coolly briefed the media about Sewell's death in Hong Kong, ten days before.

There was a buzz of questions which he fielded easily. To his relief, the tone was no longer hostile. Indeed, most journalists seemed shocked by the British activist's murder.

Then the *Daily Mail* man stuck up his hand. 'Who brought out the documents?'

'Sewell gave a copy to a fellow tourist who passed them to us,' replied Fletcher evenly.

'Name?'

'She would rather remain anonymous.'

There was a murmur of dissatisfaction.

'We need her name – otherwise there's no story!' a journalist retorted.

Fletcher paused. Took a breath.

'Okay. Her name is Jennifer Stuart. She's *not* a Green Planet activist, and she knew nothing of Sewell's mission. We're grateful to her for helping alert the world to a potentially catastrophic environmental disaster. But I must emphasise: she was just a courier.'

'Where can she be reached?' the *Mail* man persisted.

'Ms Stuart is not available today. Any more questions? No? Well, thank you for coming.'

Fletcher had advised Jenny to lie low for 24 hours. Perhaps this would encourage the media to focus on the content of the documents, and Dick Sewell's role.

But they soon tracked Jenny down, and her office was deluged with calls. Thanks to Fletcher's advice, she was prepared. She had briefed her boss, and he made sure she had a full day's programme of case visits.

She was grateful, but knew it was the calm before the storm.

That evening, in the privacy of a colleague's home, she watched the TV news. A picture of Sewell flashed up, and then her own name was mentioned. Just a passing reference – but it unsettled her. All the bulletins led with the story, quoting demands from backbench Labour MPs for a full-scale government inquiry and statement to parliament. At long last, Sewell was gaining the recognition he deserved.

Afterwards, Jenny called Jim and they arranged to meet at the weekend.

'By the way,' he added slowly, 'the only other thing stolen from my flat was my notebook from the Chinese trip.'

'What, the one with the missing page?'

'Yes.'

She could tell he was worried.

Next day Harold Williams monitored media coverage of the Green Planet exposé, carefully cutting out clippings from the papers.

When he listened to *World at One* on Radio 4, he realised that his earlier strategy had not been successful. The focus was now on Sewell's murder, and he had to concede that Green Planet had cleverly regained control of the news agenda.

But he was intrigued by the revelation of Jenny Stuart's involvement. She had not sparked any suspicion during the trip – though he did recall the impressive lecture she gave to the English-speaking students, and how powerfully she expressed her left-wing views. She was certainly the most politically vocal member of the delegation. Much more so than Evans.

There must be some dirt in her activist background. Maybe she and Evans had become lovers? Time to up the ante again. He would make some phone calls: to his friend in British intelligence; the backbench Conservative MP; contacts on the *Sun*, the *Mail*, the *Express* and the *Telegraph*.

He also called an official at the Chinese Embassy and arranged a private meeting in a Kensington coffee bar where the man's superiors would not monitor them.

It was after 10 p.m. when Jenny emerged from her local underground station. Her ground floor flat, in a Victorian terraced house, was just a couple of kilometres away.

Although there was a constant hum of traffic, the pavements were almost deserted. A man walked a dog on the other side of the road; teenagers spilled out of a pub on the corner, giggling and larking about.

It was dark, the moon hidden behind dense cloud.

She never enjoyed walking home at night. Rapes and violent attacks on women had steadily increased in recent years. She'd raised the issue with her local Labour and trade union branches, but nothing had been done.

Now she was on the alert for anybody lurking in a front garden. Or in a dark area where there were no street lights. She grasped her door key firmly – sharp end pointing outwards – in case she needed a makeshift weapon.

Nearly home. Relief.

But then she froze. Two men were loitering on the path by the front door she shared with the upstairs tenants.

One raised a camera. Before she realised what was happening, flashbulbs popped.

'Jenny Stuart?' The other man was wearing a light coat, collar turned up casually.

'Er...'

'We're from the *Sun*. Wanted a word about your part in the Dick Sewell story.' The camera was still flashing.

Jenny recovered her composure.

'Green Planet gave you all the details.'

'Is it true you were part of the plot?'

'What plot?'

'To discredit the nuclear power programme?'

Her temper flared. So, this was what it was like to be hounded by the media. 'I don't know what you mean. I was simply part of a delegation organised by the Chinese government. Mr Sewell asked me to take a copy of his documents to Green Planet. That's all I did.'

'So he was worried he might be killed, was he?'

'No. He was just being careful.'

'What sort of person was he?'

'Very brave. Very dedicated.' She wasn't going to let them tarnish his memory.

'How close were you?'

'We only got to know each other out there.'

'Were you lovers?'

'Piss off! I'm not answering any more of your questions! Don't you care that a British citizen was murdered? Don't you care about the danger of nuclear leakages in the sea?'

She pushed past the men and unlocked her front door. As she slammed it shut, she heard the reporter shout: 'We know all about your political background!'

Shaking, she entered her flat. Her phone was ringing.

'Jenny Stuart?'

'Yes.'

'*Daily Mail* here – we've a few questions about your role in the China documents story.'

The calls didn't stop till midnight, and her answerphone was full of messages too. Finally, she slumped onto the sofa – exhausted.

Only then did she notice.

Her desk was a chaotic mess: papers jumbled; drawers open. Her books had been thrown onto the floor, her cupboards emptied.

Someone had given the flat a right going-over.

Jenny hardly slept that night. Jim had offered to come round, but she declined, cautioning him to lie low.

By early morning she was up, listening to herself being quoted on radio. Almost immediately her phone started to ring: BBC, ITN and independent media, all wanting interviews.

Her doorbell buzzed. She peered out of her front window to see a dozen photographers. Paparazzi. She knew they moved around in a pack – attracting reporters and TV cameras.

She grabbed breakfast, showered and collected her thoughts. She couldn't stay trapped in her flat. They might hang around for days, as if awaiting the birth of a royal baby. She had to get to work.

At 7.30 a.m. she took a deep breath and opened the door to a cacophony of clicking cameras. As she stepped forward, a forest of microphones was thrust into her face. But, unlike last night, this lot seemed friendly. Some even apologised for disturbing her – although they were probably just sizing her up.

There was no point being uncooperative. She might as well explain her side of the story and, more importantly, try to shift their focus back to the threat of nuclear contamination. At the moment they seemed more obsessed with 'Red Jen', as the *Sun* had nicknamed her. Even Radio 4's early morning newspaper review had picked up the reference.

For nearly half an hour she answered questions and gave interviews: some to journalists in outside broadcast vans parked in the street, which relayed her comments live to breakfast radio and TV.

One of the TV stations wanted to chat to her in their studio. She agreed, in exchange for a lift to her office afterwards.

By the time Jenny got to work, she was worn out. It wasn't much fun being a celebrity – even a minor one.

On the flight to Nairobi, Makuyana was browsing through the Johannesburg *Star* when a story caught his eye. South African and Israeli engineers had joined forces to develop the 'Cheetah': a deadly new jet, with the capacity to strike deep into the Frontline States and withdraw swiftly.

The story claimed that two squadrons of Cheetahs were housed at Louis Trichardt airbase, close to the border with Zimbabwe. The new plane was similar to Israel's Kfir fighter jet, with a powerful Snecma engine, modified from the original French design. The Cheetah had sufficient range to hit ANC guerrilla bases as far north as Dar es Salaam in Tanzania.

Might this relate to the nuclear connection, Makuyana wondered?

When he reached Nairobi, he booked the first available flight to Harare and made two calls.

First, to Florence. He asked her to keep special tabs on 'our friend George': a veiled reference to Mngadi's aide, George Petersen. Florence had news for him, too. The 'hostage' had been eliminated. Makuyana was horrified, but couldn't press her for more details on an unsecured phone line.

Next, he called the Johannesburg hotel, and asked if 'Mr Nkala' had received any messages. There was a pause. Some clicks. Then a different voice: 'Mr Nkala, you're speaking to the manager. Some people were trying to reach you, just after you left. Can you give us a contact number?'

Makuyana thought fast. They might be trying to trace his call. With the right equipment it would take less than thirty seconds.

'I'm between appointments in Pretoria. But I'll call back later.'

Before the manager could respond, Makuyana hung up. He had several hours to kill, so he found a café in the transit area.

The UK papers had just arrived on a flight from London. The front page of the *Sun* was dominated by a picture of an attractive young woman. The headline intrigued him: 'Red Jen's Chinese Puzzle'.

He bought a copy of the paper and eagerly read the story. Two tantalising words jumped out at him: 'China' and 'nuclear'.

The Beijing connection ... again.

But what did it all mean? The tip from the President's office; the farmhouse briefing from the ANC's Oliver Magano; the information from Wentzel in Pretoria. Now this. He couldn't just dismiss it as coincidence.

Meanwhile, there were more pressing problems. Number one: the killing of the RENAMO man. So few leads, but maybe their surveillance of George Petersen would uncover something.

Problem two: how could he verify the information Jannie Craven had given him in the lay-by outside Pretoria? If Jannie was genuine, it would surely confirm Petersen as the ANC traitor. On the other hand, if Jannie *wasn't* who he seemed, Petersen might be a pawn in a bigger chess game: part of a strategy to destabilise the ANC in exile.

And there was something else he had to do. What was it?

Yes: check security arrangements for the forthcoming Chinese government visit. China again! He had hoped his staff could deal with it, but now he realised he'd better take a more personal interest.

Everything was being done to discredit the Green Planet story, Wang assured the Old Man, but it was simply not possible to eliminate the girl.

To do so would guarantee that the story would become even bigger. Better just to destroy her reputation.

It was a tense meeting. Wang had never seen the Old Man

so tetchy, the veins on his forehead bulging, as he drummed tensely on his large desk.

Then he started to rant, almost as if he was addressing a crowd. Wang was clearly not expected to respond, only to nod in agreement.

'Have you noticed the appearance of our young recently? The government is encouraging them to follow fashion and consumerism as if it were their patriotic duty!' He spat out the words.

'Nearly a thousand privately owned beauty parlours in Beijing alone! In the old days we banned cosmetics – and brassieres too. We insisted our women wore standard clothes, that their hair was cut short or plaited into pigtails. Now they look and behave like Westerners. They scream and swoon at rock concerts. They hanker after designer clothes. Disgusting!'

Wang nodded. He didn't have much choice, though he found the Old Man's obsession boring. The gap between young and old was indeed growing, but it was a fact of life.

The older generation continued to dress simply. Office workers in grey suits with clean white shirts; peasants in cotton jackets and trousers; grannies wore dark trousers and loose blue or grey jackets – and a few still hobbled painfully on bound feet.

But some women students wore high heels, denim jeans, bright blouses and jumpers. Young men might even use moisturiser, aftershave and lip balm.

The Old Man had worked himself up into quite a state. Wang wondered if he was losing his marbles, but couldn't permit himself such revisionist thoughts.

Suddenly, the Old Man swung round, and was hidden by the high back of his chair. The usual long silence ensued. Wang might as well have been alone.

Minutes passed. Then – equally abruptly – the chair swung back, its occupant cool and collected once more.

'Now, about our Zimbabwe visit. We leave for Africa next week. Once we have finished in Nairobi you will be going on ahead to Harare. Everything must be double checked. No hitches.'

'No hitches, sir,' Wang nodded, relieved to be excused at last. Now he could get on with his own preparations. He'd managed to carve out a free-wheeling role for himself, in spite of the bureaucracy which normally stifled any such independence.

Because he was one of the Old Man's protégés he was treated with deference, even by immediate superiors. Consequently, there was no problem about making international phone calls on his secure line or maintaining contacts outside the normal channels.

But his most recent call to London was hard to assess. He'd been briefed on the aftermath of the Green Planet press conference, the demolition job on the woman's credibility, and results of the surveillance on her and Evans. Nothing remarkable there.

But there was one other thing.

Evans was apparently attending some sort of conference in Zimbabwe at the same time as the visit of the Chinese delegation.

A coincidence? No reason to suppose otherwise, according to his contacts in British intelligence. But Evans was a paradox. Ostensibly a political innocent, with no record of activism, he had nevertheless been up to no good during his time in China. Then there was his association with the problem woman...

They would have to keep an eye on Evans. Wang was conscious that he had slipped up before, and could not afford to do so again.

Certainly not this time.

9

The hardware arrived in a van ostensibly delivering garden furniture. Two rifles – R1s, manufactured in South Africa, the equivalent of Belgian FNs, with plenty of spare ammunition – as well as stun grenades, tear gas canisters and a couple of nine-millimetre Z88 pistols.

Swanepoel ensured all was in good working order, then carefully repacked everything so as not to excite interest. Some items were wrapped in blankets; others stuffed into carrier bags on the back seat of his car.

It was a sunny winter's day, and he drove around in no particular direction for half an hour, assiduously watching his rear-view mirror. Nothing. He headed to the safe house in an eastern Harare suburb.

But as he turned right into the main road, a bicycle nearly collided with his offside, veering off to crash into the pavement. *Bliksem!* He'd been so busy looking for vehicles that he hadn't even spotted it. He pulled across immediately and stopped.

He was tempted to drive on, but it was too risky. Somebody might have taken his number. He prayed to God the cyclist was okay. Everything had gone so smoothly – and now this! All he needed was some nosy policeman poking about.

The cyclist was seething with anger, but unhurt, save for a grazed knee. The bike was scratched, front mudguard bent. Swanepoel calmed the cyclist with an abject apology, taking him completely by surprise by pulling a handful of Zimbabwe dollars out of his pocket. 'Can't afford another endorsement on my licence,' he explained.

Reaching the safe house, he drove up the spacious front drive and opened the garage, parking the car inside. He unlocked a connecting door into the kitchen and stacked the equipment neatly. Everything was ready for the boys when they returned from their fishing trip. He probably wouldn't hear from them until they'd accomplished their mission.

His boys. He felt wistful. He'd been like them once: lean and fit, keen as hell. Comforting to know such youngsters still existed.

Professionals. Willing to die for the cause.

Jenny and Jim were enjoying their day together in Richmond Park, strolling amongst the royal deer. The young animals pranced about, while the older males majestically paraded. It was warm and sunny for a change.

They sat down to catch their breath on a hill to the south-west, overlooking Kingston. The Thames was just visible as it wound its way back through Richmond.

The right-wing press had gone to town on Jenny, dredging up her past as a student activist. Much of it was based on truth, but negatively slanted to portray her as radical firebrand. In reality she'd never been a leader, preferring to work at grassroots level within the women's movement and Labour Party.

She was particularly angry about the 'Red Jen' story in the *Sun*. The reporter had cunningly twisted and juxtaposed her interview responses so that she came across as a left-wing troublemaker – a feckless social worker who'd abandoned her clients to enjoy a foreign jaunt. The story also implied that she was Sewell's lover and co-conspirator. They had even dredged up a backbench Tory MP, known in the trade as 'Rent-a-quote Rod', who chastised her 'irresponsibility for 'allowing' her friend to be killed.

But now, relaxing in the sunshine with Jim, Jenny felt the burden of the past week lifting. She liked being with this shy, diffident man – though she sensed that it would be up to *her* to take the initiative if their relationship was to develop physically.

And that's what she wanted.

They walked back to the car and drove down to the riverside. It was now early afternoon, and people were lazing on grass banks above the towpath. They made their way to a pub by the water, and managed to find some seats in its crowded garden. Jenny went to order two pints of real ale.

Jim checked out the food: it was always difficult to choose for Jenny because of her diet. She avoided meat, dairy products and gluten. But she ate fish, loved salads and vegetables, and drank huge quantities of herbal tea.

Alcohol was her only weakness: just as well, since they seemed to be spending a lot of their time in pubs.

When Jim returned, she was sitting, head tilted back, eyes closed, soaking up the sun, her hair falling back over the chair. He was still surprised she was happy to spend so much time with him.

'There you are – some of your funny food!' he joked, handing over a mixture of salad and broccoli. 'I'm afraid nothing else was suitable.'

'That's fine,' she said, peering at him. 'What rubbish are you eating, then?'

'Ham, egg and chips.'

'Don't you realise that's really bad for you?'

He'd never heard her criticise the food choices of others. Sure, in China she had been clear about her own preferences – but she hadn't commented on anyone else's.

As if reading his thoughts, she continued: 'I don't normally have a go at other people's diets.'

'Why start now then?'

'Because I care for you,' she said simply, leaning over to kiss him.

Quietness, as they savoured each other's company. Jim craved it: the afternoon passing quickly, always something to talk about, an animated buzz as they discussed upbringings, jobs, Jenny's activism.

In the evening, they went back to his house, armed with a bottle of wine and some food which she had supervised buying. They cooked it together, and then sat on the sofa listening to music.

'Lovely day,' Jenny said, 'thanks for looking after me. I completely forgot about the past week.'

'My pleasure.' He looked at his watch. 'God, eleven already. I'd better run you home.'

'Oh,' she looked disappointed. 'Can't I stay?'

Across the road from the house two men aimed their long range bugging equipment at Jim's bedroom window.

Eavesdropping provided some small compensation for a wasted evening, they joked, as they listened to sounds that were not remotely connected to their investigation.

General KJ van der Walt, the powerful head of the apartheid security services, sat in the garden of his spacious new bungalow which nestled halfway up the *kopje* on the outskirts of the Golden City, overlooking the bush below.

Sunday afternoon and he was enjoying a whisky, his wife asleep after a good lunch.

For him, this was what it was all about: what he had fought so hard to protect for so many years. The right to sit in your garden listening to the birds while the boy looked after the flowers, the shrubs and the fruit trees.

The right to enjoy a sunny winter's afternoon under a clear blue Johannesburg sky. After he had topped up his glass a few more times, he would cat nap in his chair until he was woken by the cold creeping in, as it did when the sun disappeared. A perfect Sunday.

And yet he was worried. His wife had sensed it, but decided not to comment. She would choose her moment carefully.

Difficult times. Independence for Namibia had been conceded, and the South African army was facing serious resistance from the Cubans in Angola. But the ANC had been forced to close its training camps there, and that was some consolation. Also, Pretoria was still supporting UNITA – the guerrilla force at loggerheads with Angola's ruling party – just as they had continued their clandestine backing for RENAMO in Mozambique.

Nevertheless, South Africa was now surrounded by independent black- ruled countries, and hostile ones at that. The Frontline States were no longer as compliant as they had been.

There were other worries too. The economy was in poor shape after low growth, international pressure was rising, and so was government expenditure: particularly on defence, and the financing of home-produced substitutes for goods cut off by sanctions. Gold was no longer the pivotal reserve currency of old; its global price and demand were falling.

International debt was also a problem, as the rand had depreciated markedly and interest rates were soaring. The budget deficit was historically high and still rising – and there was galloping inflation. Not surprisingly, the *volk* were getting restless. For the first time in generations, whites had no automatic expectation of prosperity, and class divisions had sharpened.

The yuppies – a phenomenon imported from Europe and the USA – were doing nicely, thank you. But you couldn't build a strong nation on yuppies. KJ knew that only too well.

That's why so much depended on Operation NOSLEN, and a new flexible nuclear capability. Nothing must stand in the way of the vital operation planned for Zimbabwe in the next fortnight. All information leaks must be plugged; enemies hunted down and crushed.

KJ felt security had been breached far too often recently. Old dependable Mauritz would have to be given fresh instructions.

When KJ dozed off in the chair, his black maid came and tucked a blanket around him.

As she leaned over his sleeping body, she felt a sudden sense of power. Here he was: the feared head of the country's security forces. So strong, but now so vulnerable.

The mastermind behind the police state and its apparatus of torture, repression and killings. She had his life in her hands.

For one wild moment she imagined using the blanket to suffocate him.

Down below the house, where the garden sloped away to a clump of trees, white security guards constantly patrolled the perimeter fence. They glanced up only briefly as they saw her perform the usual Sunday routine.

They would never know her thoughts.

Florence Dube was at Arrivals, waiting to meet the flight from Nairobi. She felt depressed. There was still no sign of the two white men she'd spotted in the hospital – they had disappeared into thin air, and none of her informants had any information.

She hated messing up while Makuyana was away, and wondered how he'd really felt when she told him about the RENAMO man's death.

Nevertheless, her spell as deputy had been exhilarating. She'd enjoyed the responsibility: the planning and thinking; being able to get others to do the routine tasks.

But what had Makuyana been up to? She'd been worried stiff about the unofficial nature of his mission. If it went wrong, all hell would break loose. She felt such relief when he called her from Nairobi.

She knew he travelled light, so it wouldn't be long now before he appeared.

But did she *really* know Keith Makuyana? It was one thing to work closely with him, quite another to *get* close. She admired him – and fancied him too. Probably more than she cared to admit. But how could that ever come to anything? After the South Africans murdered his family, he had built a Berlin Wall around his heart.

Yet, she could sense deep emotions under that cold exterior...

There he was! Walking past the families waiting expectantly for their loved ones.

For once, no menacing dark glasses. Instead, she saw a handsome man with gentle eyes, wearing a smart suit and tie. He looked so different.

She didn't move. She would let him take the lead. She wasn't sure how he wanted to play the homecoming, but best to keep it casual. Would 'Mr Nkala' still be under surveillance?

He spotted her, and their eyes met. But then he looked away and frowned, taking out a notepad. Florence strolled over to a shop, and started browsing the front page of the *Herald*. Out of the corner of her eye, she saw him approach. He searched the magazine rack, and feigned a cough, covering his mouth with his hand.

'Think I'm being watched,' he muttered. 'Leave your car keys somewhere here and catch a taxi to the office. We'll meet there. Did you bring your Nissan?'

She nodded imperceptibly, moving over to the souvenir shelf full of junk. She picked up a copper mug and slipped her key inside, aware that he was watching. Then she replaced the mug and walked off.

From her vantage point, she saw him buy the mug and leave. What she *couldn't* see was the man tailing him at a distance across the arrivals hall.

Swanepoel's man followed Mr Nkala out to the car park,

where his colleague was waiting, ready to move. They had to find out who Nkala really was: none of their sources had been able to confirm his identity.

Nkala's Nissan pulled away and headed towards the city centre, his pursuers following at a discreet distance. But at the crossroads after the army barracks, the Nissan shot straight on: not taking the usual right turn at Coke Corner. Accelerating sharply, the pursuers kept their quarry in sight. They nearly overshot, as the Nissan stopped unexpectedly at the first line of shops under the railway bridge. Nkala got out and went into a food store, emerging minutes later with a carrier bag.

He drove off, and moved into the outer lane, flashing his right indicator as he approached a set of traffic lights. The men followed, with one car between them and the Nissan. But just as the lights began to change, the Nissan suddenly screamed off and made a sharp left turn, its rear tyres spinning furiously, leaving black marks on the tarmac.

The pursuers were trapped behind another vehicle, speechless with frustration.

Jim and Jenny stood in the entrance of the Foreign and Commonwealth Office, just round the corner from 10 Downing Street. It was pouring with rain, and they could see the protestors were wet through.

Their banners were sodden, their leaflets damp and crumpled. But still they kept up their chants – perhaps more to raise their own spirits than to influence the evening rush-hour pedestrians hurrying by, heads down.

The 24-hour permanent picket had become such an institution that it was mentioned in tourist guides. Organised by the Apartheid Resistance Committee (ARC), it had been running more than three years. The organisers pledged to continue until Margaret Thatcher's government implemented comprehensive mandatory sanctions against apartheid South Africa.

Since its inception, there had always been at least half a dozen pickets: mainly young students. At first, the police had tried to move them on, making frequent arrests. But magistrates were reluctant to convict for obstruction, so the picketers persisted – attracting widespread admiration for their selfless tenacity.

Jim had been reluctant to engage with them, but Jenny insisted. She had to get through to the ANC somehow – to alert them about the possible nuclear deal between China and the apartheid regime. This seemed the best strategy.

Their leader was John Howells: tall and thin, a woolly hat covering his closely cropped hair. Jenny had heard he was almost always at the picket, working at night as a computer programmer to scrape a living.

He agreed to talk, but asked her and Jim to wait for him at the Red Lion pub, across Whitehall towards the Houses of Parliament.

When he joined them a little later, a puddle forming around his chair, Jenny told him about the China trip – how the South Africa connection kept coming up. Howells listened, scribbling notes, but said nothing.

'I hope we're not wasting your time,' Jenny concluded.

'Not at all, this is very important,' Howells replied, sombrely. 'But you will be discreet, won't you?'

'Of course,' Jenny replied. 'And the same goes for you. Jim was nearly killed because of all this.'

Howells shrugged. 'Just don't talk to anyone else. The ANC high command in Dar es Salaam will have to act before Pretoria finds out.'

'Not exactly a bundle of fun, that guy,' Evans muttered, after Howells walked back into the rain to rejoin his comrades.

'No,' agreed Jenny, 'but at least it's off my chest.'

The Old Man was in high spirits, as he slowly ascended the steps of the state-owned airline, Air China.

News had just reached him of the successful launch of yet another satellite from the special base hidden away at Yichang, in the mountains of Sichuan province.

Another milestone in the development of China's own Star Wars technology. Now, he could bring forward the 2010 plans for the Chinese space station: not a bad achievement for a country considered to be fifteen years behind American and European space programmes. His pleasure was heightened because they had also managed to undercut American rocket companies by 50 per cent.

His work and his vision had put China in prime position, but the Leader was only grasping this now – so late in the day, when all the decades of planning and investment had begun to pay off.

The Old Man looked on contemptuously while the Leader and his imperious wife were ceremoniously ushered to their seats. Then he glanced behind, where Wang and the others were congregated. *His* team, on the last leg together now, the country's destiny in their hands.

At the right moment he would call the generals in Beijing on their direct lines. They would be ready to move. They knew what they had to do. But it was vital to call everyone personally, for the less committed would be swayed only by his unique authority.

Makuyana had shaken off his followers easily enough, noting down the car's registration number in the process.

At the office, he immediately had it traced. It turned out to be a pool car for a company in the city centre. At first, they couldn't explain the car's presence at the airport. Then a manager came on the line to say it had gone missing – must have been stolen overnight.

Although the explanation seemed straightforward, Makuyana asked Florence to investigate the company and senior staff.

He also asked her to check again on the man called Herson:

their only connection – however tenuous – to the Robert Temba murder. A lot had happened since, an awful lot, but sometimes it was worth going back over old ground when there was nothing else.

Next on his agenda was the Chinese visit. He asked for the file and called in the security team. Two hours later, he officially requested a meeting with the President's security chief: ostensibly to go over details of the visit; in reality to report what he'd learnt about the China connection, however vague it might seem.

Night was falling before he turned to his final task: George Petersen. He drummed his fingers on the desk, then looked up a special number.

Time to make contact again with MK commander Selby Mngadi.

Jim Evans got a kick from writing under pressure. Researching, then organising the material, and finally pulling it all together.

Sometimes he would begin making notes with just the haziest concept in mind, gradually working out a logical structure. Only when he started writing did a coherent analysis emerge. On other occasions he sat down at the computer with fragments of notes and half-formed ideas, then – as he started to tap out the words – they took on a life of their own.

But now he was racing to meet a deadline for a scientific paper on plutonium proliferation. One of the London organisers of the Harare conference had phoned to ask a favour. A Scottish expert on radiation had been forced to pull out at the last moment: could Evans take his place? He wouldn't have to deliver a full paper: an informal overview would do.

'It's your field, you could probably do it half pissed,' the organiser joked.

Jim had reluctantly agreed. Speaking off the cuff wasn't his style. He always prepared carefully for lectures: perhaps too much. Sometimes he got so lost in theoretical possibilities that he missed the wood for the trees.

But now he had no alternative. He'd have to pull together some of his existing work, and plan his talk around a series of headings. He could fine tune it on the flight from London.

He was too busy to see Jenny until the eve of his departure, when she came round for a meal. But his mind was on his lecture, and for the first time since they'd met, he found himself doing all the talking. Especially about the constant leakage of radioactivity into the air, water and soil, which – according to his research – the government was trying to conceal rather than stop.

'It's in food too,' Jenny added, opening a second bottle of wine.

Jim smiled. She was back on her pet subject. 'Yes. Lots of supermarket food has been irradiated – mainly for preservation.'

Jenny nodded.

'And scientists are also to blame,' Jim continued. 'They use things called "radioisotopes" to monitor the progress of pesticides and fertilisers through plants and soils – but these contaminate food. Radioisotope gauges are even used to check if beer cans are filled to the correct levels.'

He rocked back in his chair, happily replete. 'I could rattle off facts and figures for hours. But it's late ...'

'Time for me to go then?' Jenny asked, her mischievous grin signalling she would do nothing of the sort.

Makuyana was briefing Selby Mngadi about the information he'd gleaned from Pretoria: the likely traitor was George Petersen.

The two men were sitting in a van in a city centre car park. Mngadi looked subdued, and shook his head morosely. 'Such a good comrade over the years,' he insisted, 'this is very hard to swallow.'

'But you know you are penetrated.'

'Yes. But what if *this* is disinformation? What if Pretoria is deliberately drawing attention away from the real culprit? George has a good reputation, especially amongst our younger cadres – and you know we've had some problems with them. They're impatient. Getting more radical, more militant. Many of them question Oliver Tambo's strategy of combining guerrilla action with sophisticated diplomacy. They're thirsty for action. George understands that. He responds to it. If you move against him, you risk destabilising the organisation: at least in Lusaka and Harare. And that is precisely what Pretoria wants.'

'But if we *don't* move against him?' Makuyana left the question hanging.

After the excitement of the past few weeks in charge, Florence was back to her routine duties: investigating, checking and re-checking.

Her family and friends were convinced that her work was full of drama: secret agent stuff. They never believed her when she told them how boring it really was: waiting for surveillance results, checking lists, checking names. Computers had lessened some of the drudgery – but there was still an awful lot left.

Florence was thorough and conscientious. That's why she had risen so rapidly through the ranks. Now she focused on the tasks Makuyana had given her: firstly, to uncover the truth about Vitel Systems Zimbabwe – the company which owned the car that had tailed Makuyana from the airport.

Vitel marketed computer software and telecommunications systems. Its managing director was Eugene Fraser. He had good relations with the government, and was known to make donations to the ruling Party. Vitel also supplied material to South Africa, but that wasn't unusual.

Then, Florence turned her attention to Mr Paul Herson. The print-out of his phone calls suggested he didn't have many friends, and the record of his movements – as monitored by the bleeper on his car – just showed a confusing blur of trips around the city.

There was a knock on her door. An assistant appeared with a mug of coffee – and a photocopy of subscriber names linked to Herson's phone record. Several shops in the city and some names that didn't register any alarm bells. But right at the bottom of the list there was an ex-directory number belonging to an EA Fraser.

Florence felt her stomach tighten. Surely this was no coincidence? She asked for a check on Fraser's address.

When she returned to her office after lunch, she found a message: EA Fraser was indeed *the* Eugene Fraser of Vitel. The number was his direct office line. She decided to put an active tap on his phone and Herson's. Her assistant was to monitor them continuously, and keep her closely informed.

She also assigned a watcher to keep tabs on Herson. Later, she would have his house searched. But for now, any surveillance had to be discreet.

They picked up Jannie Craven easily enough. As he opened the door of his Sunnyside flat near Pretoria's city centre, two burly special branch men bundled him inside.

They sized him up from the outset. No need for violence. They just wore him down over many hours of conversation. One man played hard; the other was softer. They claimed to understand him. They were even sympathetic. Told him he was as much a victim of the system as they were. They were simply doing their job. Surely he could understand that?

After the first day, Jannie was disorientated by their friendliness: especially by their concern for his family, their explanation of how his behaviour would affect his parents.

Having drawn him in, they showed him pictures. ANC atrocities, so they said. Burnt babies, bodies mutilated by bombs.

They forced him to justify his involvement – and, before the second day was out, he was beginning to confess. He couldn't help himself. He hadn't been trained to resist.

Well-brought-up boys like him were naturally polite. They automatically answered apparently harmless questions, then found themselves trapped in an incriminating web. Jannie knew nothing about anti-interrogation techniques. He didn't know how to remain silent, or how to stare at the wall to avoid eye contact with his interrogators.

He just felt so guilty – especially about deceiving his family. His parents would be so ashamed and humiliated: so angry at the loss of their good name.

Then came the coup de grâce. His captors made him an offer. They didn't really need to charge him, didn't need to tell his friends and relatives. After all, he hadn't personally committed terrorism, or any atrocity, had he? Why should they put a good Afrikaner boy like him in the dock? Why play into the hands of the enemy and ruin his family's reputation?

In short, if he helped them, he could help himself.

It turned out that Jannie didn't have much to confess. All his contacts had been made via dead letter drops or anonymous messages. Sure, there were some people from his university days, but most had long since gone underground – or been imprisoned or killed.

But, there was one name that excited them: George Petersen. Jannie knew this because one of the men left the room almost as soon as he mentioned it.

10

It was a chance encounter.

Jenny had gone to one of her Labour activist meetings – this time about Northern Ireland. Suddenly, a familiar voice exclaimed: 'Jenny!'

'Lesley? Haven't seen you for ages!'

'Yeah – and now you're a star, I see!'

'Hopefully not for much longer.' Jenny blushed as they hugged.

She'd always looked up to Lesley Stapleton. They'd become close friends at university, and later worked on political campaigns together. Lesley was more politically sophisticated, always ready with a quote from a progressive thinker or a feminist writer. Her breadth of knowledge was intimidating.

'Look,' she said hesitantly, 'I was thinking ... how long were you planning to stay at the meeting, Jen?'

'To the end, I suppose. But I'm easy. Only really came to hear Sue.'

'Me too. Let's disappear afterwards. The rest will be really boring.'

'Fine with me!'

Sue McBride, a backbench Labour MP, was unusual in

combining an enthusiastic following amongst Party activists with a growing reputation in Parliament. Some pundits were tipping her for a top job: perhaps *the* top job.

As she rose to her feet, there was a burst of warm, spontaneous clapping. Clearly, she was the main draw for most of the audience.

Jenny was impressed. Not only by what Sue said, but how she said it. She spoke with passion, logic and calm – making her controversial stance seem reasonable and moderate. She didn't hector the meeting: she talked *to* people, rather than *at* them.

'We are now in the third decade of failed government policies over Northern Ireland. The violence continues. The bitterness continues. The sectarianism too. When will it all end?

'I'll tell you when. The day Britain admits it is a part of the problem. The day we create conditions in which the people of Northern Ireland together with the Irish Republic can themselves determine their own democratic structures and their own destiny. The day Britain becomes a genuine honest broker rather than a partisan one, and understands where republicans are coming from as well as unionists.

'That day is when we can get a breakthrough. It won't be easy. There are risks. Risks of violence. Risks that political obstinacy and sectarian prejudice will hi-jack negotiations. But there are no easy solutions to the crisis – only least worst ones. We should have the courage to make a fresh start. Otherwise . . .' she paused – holding the audience in the palm of her hand – 'otherwise the conflict will go on forever.'

The audience rose to its feet. While the applause was dying down, Jenny and Lesley escaped to a nearby wine bar.

Pouring them each a glass from a bottle of house red, Lesley explained that she had recently given up her job as a probation officer to work fulltime for the Anti-Apartheid movement, in their Mandela Street headquarters.

'By the way,' she added, 'I thought you weathered all those

awful media attacks really well. "Red Jen" indeed! Quite a smear job. But ... tell me about the Green Planet business.'

It took Jenny half an hour to explain it all.

'If only I'd known you were working for Anti-Apartheid HQ, I'd have contacted you,' she finished.

'Why?'

Jenny sipped her wine, thoughtfully.

'Well, it's another long story – and I'm not sure what it adds up to. But it seems that Beijing and Pretoria might be cooperating over nuclear weapons.'

'What? But that's astounding!'

Lesley paused, her shock turning into concern.

'Who else have you told?'

'Just one other person. He seems reliable – and safe. He promised to take the information to the ANC.'

'Good.' Lesley sounded relieved.

Then she frowned. 'Who did you contact?'

'John Howells, from the ARC. You know, the Apartheid Resistance Committee.'

'*Howells*! From the ARC! Fucking hell, Jenny you must be bonkers! What are you, a political virgin or something?'

Lesley's uncharacteristic ferocity rocked Jenny back in her chair. Her face reddened. 'W-what do you mean?' she stammered.

Her friend reached out and touched her hand. 'I'm sorry. Just that I've had a bellyful of the ARC. They're such a headache: their London events are always clashing with ours – and they support stupid little Trotskyist sects within the liberation movement. It's a real problem. They're damaging our public image: just when the ANC is trying to get accepted into the political mainstream.'

'But they seem so dedicated,' countered Jenny. 'Those 24-hour pickets ... I've never seen such motivated young activists!'

'That's not the whole story, though.'

Lesley paused, considering her words carefully. 'Do you know much about the CIA?'

'Of course, but what's the CIA got to do with it?'

'A great deal. Listen, we all know about the CIA's dirty tricks: supporting the Contras in Nicaragua, Savimbi's murderous gang in Angola, shadowy right-wing organisations, and so on. But that's only part of the picture. Basically, the CIA just want a foothold in the corridors of power. They don't care which political party is in control: they just want to safeguard American business and military interests.

'So, in a situation like South Africa, where nobody yet knows who's going to come out on top, they'll back a whole lot of groups – sometimes competing ones. In other words – they hedge their bets.'

Jenny nodded, listening intently. 'Doesn't surprise me.'

'According to our information, they're now funding the ARC. It's their way of undermining the Anti-Apartheid movement. Of course, we can't prove it – but we've been tipped off by reliable foreign intelligence sources. People who are sympathetic to us.

'John Howells may be on their payroll. Or he might be an undercover officer for British Special Branch. Who knows with these guys? As for the rest of the ARC, they're mostly genuine, committed anti-apartheid campaigners. But they're also young and radical – especially the students.

They want direct action, and that's what the ARC offers them.

'To be honest – although few of my colleagues acknowledge this – the Anti-Apartheid movement *can* seem overly bureaucratic and cautious.'

Jenny looked forlorn, as she cupped her wine glass in both hands. 'So, by telling John Howells, I've basically told the CIA,' she said. 'You'd better introduce me to a proper ANC person, then.'

'That's not the problem. I'm much more worried about Howells.'

'But the CIA won't want to upset the Beijing government, will they?' Jenny's question was rhetorical. She continued: 'China seems pretty popular with the West at the moment – opening up trade, lifting the bamboo curtain . . .'

'Maybe, but they *will* be worried about the nuclear connection, and we have to assume they've told British intelligence. Or Howells has. And if the rightist faction in MI5 hasn't passed it on to the South African security services, the CIA might have done so themselves. Remember, the CIA shopped Nelson Mandela when he was on the run in 1962. They got him arrested by apartheid police officers – and they still have close links with Pretoria's agents.

'Also, we're under siege here. Our offices and our meetings are bugged, and the ANC's London office was firebombed. British security services are doing nothing about this. But Mrs Thatcher called Mandela "a terrorist", so it's hardly surprising that apartheid agents in Britain have a free hand.'

She paused.

'And you know what all of this says to me, Jen? That you and your friend are still in real danger.'

As Jim Evans' Air Zimbabwe DC-10 took off from Gatwick, a man with a special airport security pass discreetly called MI5's London headquarters.

Two hours later, as the plane was approaching the Mediterranean coast of Africa, the phone rang in Swanepoel's Harare house. Someone left a cryptic message to say the fertiliser for his garden had been despatched as expected.

Swanepoel received the information noncommittally, having already resigned himself to an additional task. But he wasn't happy.

He had quite enough on his plate as it was.

*

Two days before Jim's departure, Wang Bi Nan and his advance party booked into their suites at Harare's Sheraton Hotel. Only then did Wang receive the important information from London.

He didn't blame anyone for the delay. The material was highly sensitive. His people in Beijing had to wait till he got to Zimbabwe, where communications were more secure than elsewhere on the African trip.

As far as he could tell, the information came from London itself: probably via British intelligence. Harold Williams might be involved, or maybe the CIA. He didn't know, and didn't really care. What mattered was Evans.

The man was an infernal nuisance.

Of course, he already knew the Englishman would be in Harare at the same time as the Chinese delegation, and he'd resolved to put him under routine surveillance. But at that stage there was no reason to suspect Evans' visit was anything other than a professional commitment.

Now there was a real danger the whole operation could be blown. If Evans made contact with the ANC in Harare there was no telling what the consequences might be.

He would have to be dealt with. Properly, this time.

Makuyana arrived for his appointment with the President's security chief, feeling tense.

A large lugubrious figure, Stan Moyo was the President's enforcer. Known colloquially as 'the Hippo', after the most dangerous wild animal in Africa, he had a reputation for ruthlessly crushing opponents.

Nowhere more than in Matabeleland – the home region of Makuyana's late wife – where Moyo had been instrumental in the massacre of thousands of Ndebele civilians. Under the guise of quelling 'political dissidents', and emboldened by presidential enthusiasm, he had sent in the North Korean-trained Fifth

Brigade. They were zealously callous, and adept at torture. Those who survived were too fearful to tell their stories.

Moyo and Makuyana loathed the sight of each other. They worked together because they had to, both aware that the Hippo could crush the intelligence chief at any time. Makuyana only survived because he was so good at his job.

Moyo's sullen secretary directed him to the Hippo's imposing office, where he was greeted stiffly. Moyo was clearly a man with a lot on his mind.

'I don't like the smell of this,' he said. 'Not one little bit. China is an old ally. Without her help, who knows whether ZANU would have triumphed? Without China, Nkomo and ZAPU would have won the war – and Moscow would have been happy. So, I find it difficult to accept there's any link between Beijing and Pretoria.

'In a few days we receive the Chinese leader's delegation. A very important visit – perhaps the most important since independence. Our economy needs Beijing's help. It is a critical time: I don't want anything going wrong.'

Makuyana briefed him fully. Afterwards, he was given a letter bearing the Presidential stamp authorising him to take extra powers and commandeer extra resources where necessary.

He left behind a grim-looking Moyo who waved aside complaints from his personal staff that the meeting had overrun its scheduled time, and that his subsequent appointments would cascade into each other. To hell with the other appointments. What did they matter at a time like this?

Makuyana had better deliver – or he would be chopped by the Hippo.

Alone, Jenny walked the six kilometres back to her flat, her mind in turmoil. She felt so bitter with herself. Such incompetence! She couldn't have made a bigger mess if she'd tried.

The rain had stopped. She loved the cool, fresh smell of the city: washed clean, glistening in the dark. Streets resounding to the swish of tyres, pavements deserted, light reflecting from puddles into the night.

It was late and she shouldn't really be out on her own. But she had to clear her mind. She felt beaten. Adrenaline had kept her going during the Green Planet affair, but now it had drained away. Of course, the wine hadn't helped either. She shouldn't have drunk so much without eating.

Nobody took any interest as she trudged across Waterloo Bridge.

St Paul's loomed gracefully to her left, and Parliament twinkled to her right. London could be spectacular at night, especially along the Thames. Unless of course you were homeless – in which case it was cold and desolate. She glanced towards the concrete arches alongside the Royal Festival Hall, where people lined up in their cardboard boxes sleeping off another weary day of begging.

Jenny walked on, through Vauxhall, towards Clapham and her flat in Balham. Slowly, her mind cleared. She would ring Jim when she got home. He had to be warned. They might try to kill him again.

She shuddered, remembering what had happened in China. Jim was once more threatened by unseen forces – and now he was far away in Africa, where he knew nobody. She wanted to be with him. Sure, she was a mere amateur at this sort of thing, but maybe she could provide *some* protection.

As she walked alongside Clapham Common, shadows licking at her feet, she was consumed by guilt. It was all her fault: she'd put him in danger. How could she forgive herself?

When she reached her flat, she went straight to the phone and called international inquiries, who produced the number of the Sheraton Hotel in Harare with astonishing speed. But the woman on reception refused to put her through to Jim's room. None of the conference delegates were to be disturbed. They were tired after their long flights. She was welcome to leave a message.

But what to say? Phone me back? How pathetic.

It was now long after midnight, but Jenny gathered up her spare change and walked down the road to the public call box. Better not to take any chances: her own phone might be bugged.

She rang 24-hour airline bookings, and discovered there was a seat on the next Air Zimbabwe flight from Gatwick to Harare. Without hesitating, she reserved it and paid with her credit card.

She didn't know if she could afford it – or how her boss would take her request for immediate leave. But at least she would be *doing* something: not idly waiting here, in the relative safety of London, nearly 8,000 kilometres away.

Early next morning, having been granted compassionate leave, Jenny made two more calls from the public phone box. First, she tried the Sheraton again: still no luck. Jim wasn't in his room. She decided not to leave a message to say she was coming. It might alert their enemies.

Their *enemies*... already she'd been swept back into a twilight world of suspicion and fear.

Her second call was to Aunt Ruth, who nipped next door to call her back from a neighbour's house. They had arranged this precautionary measure during her visit to Burton Bradstock.

Their conversation was brief. Jenny told Ruth where she was going and why. Somebody had to know in case anything went wrong, and who better than her trusted aunt? Her parents certainly wouldn't understand.

Then she packed hurriedly and set off for Gatwick Airport.

As the plane soared over Sussex and the English Channel, she suddenly realised what she was doing. It was now irrevocable: perhaps also foolhardy and futile. Certainly expensive. She was on her way to a strange country on an even stranger mission – without anywhere to stay.

Was she doing this for love or from guilt? A bit of both, probably.

But maybe love had the upper hand.

Venter and Coetzee returned to Harare, bronzed and relaxed after their fishing trip – but no wiser about Zimbabwe's archaeological heritage.

They caught a cab to the rented safe house, unlocked the front door, and cautiously entered. It was fully furnished, and a grandfather clock ticked away in the hall. In the silence, it sounded like a timer.

The countdown had begun.

Across the city, Swanepoel was driving down his home street. Suddenly his nerves jangled. He was on full alert, but why? No apparent reason.

People talked about having a 'sixth sense'. He didn't pretend to understand such fancy theories – all he knew was that *his* sixth sense had saved his skin time after time.

At this moment, he could feel he was being watched. But if anybody had said 'prove it', he wouldn't have been able to. That familiar tingling up his spine was quite sufficient.

Were they onto him? He was nearly home. What should he do? Get the hell out, or just act normal?

He pulled into his drive and parked. There was a car in the driveway of a house opposite with its bonnet up. A man was working on the engine. To anyone else it would have looked perfectly innocent; to Swanepoel it signalled danger.

As soon as he'd moved in, he had planned for such an eventuality. He'd made sure there was nothing incriminating in his house – though he wouldn't trust his luck if they brought in sniffer dogs. The weapons and explosives he'd stored there were long gone, but the dogs might still pick up the scent.

He looked out the window. The man was still fixing his car; nobody else was in sight. His house had not been searched, but he quickly grabbed a few personal belongings. He had made up his mind.

He phoned the direct number of an office in the city centre. The man at the other end listened to his innocuous query about share prices, and immediately understood.

Swanepoel was moving out – and not coming back.

The man bending over his car engine didn't rush to follow the target. That was the beauty of a homing device: you could follow at a distance. Not so great in a chase, but ideal in these circumstances.

Half an hour later, Mr Herson's car stopped outside a house on the other side of the city. The agent radioed Florence, who carefully noted the address.

She felt edgy. Something was about to break, but what? It was high time she took over the surveillance herself.

Makuyana's phone rang. It was Selby Mngadi.

'Some news. George Petersen has skipped.'

'What!'

'Yes. Done a bunk. Yesterday. We can't locate him.'

'Christ, that's a real blow.' Makuyana didn't attempt to hide his disappointment. Petersen could have led them straight to the enemy – if they'd managed to get to him in time.

So, Jannie Craven had been genuine after all. He felt guilty for doubting him. What had happened to the young Afrikaner? And how had they discovered that Petersen's cover was blown?

Swanepoel was confident he hadn't been followed. He had taken the usual precautions to shake off any tail, and had been at the game too long to make a mistake.

But *how* had he been rumbled? And what about his controller in the city? Zimbabwe security might have tapped his phone as well.

The new safe house was fine: more spacious than his bungalow. Just as well, because now he had a lodger. The informant Petersen was to be transferred into his care. What a pain. One thing to have a coloured guy on your side; quite another to have to look after the bugger. Was he expected to treat him like a buddy?

He could do without yet another distraction: first Evans, now Petersen. How was he supposed to focus on the *main* task? Just as well Venter and Coetzee were such professionals – otherwise he'd have been in real trouble.

Evans. Why couldn't British intelligence take him out? After all, *they'd* tipped him off about Evans' visit to Harare. But no: that would be too risky for the Brits. Even he had to admit that.

Evans would be giving a paper at the conference tomorrow. Swanepoel had a ticket. He'd deal with the guy.

After that? Well, his days in Harare were numbered. That was a relief, whatever KJ said.

He was getting too old for this caper. It was time to go home.

Wang's meeting with Venter and Coetzee was strained. He didn't care for racists; his alliance with apartheid South Africa was purely for business.

They were an arrogant pair. Not rude, exactly. But sure of their physical prowess, and no doubt their racial superiority.

For two hours they checked and re-checked the plan: clarifying and re-clarifying. Nothing must be left to chance.

But as Wang made his way back to the Sheraton, he felt oddly deflated. So many months of intrigue, pressure and strain – he couldn't do anything more now.

Just wait and hope.

The official cavalcade wound through the streets of Harare, to the accompaniment of cheering crowds. The Old Man sat back in his limousine, enjoying the colourful, African scene.

Zimbabwe's top brass – led by President Mugabe himself – had all been lined up at the airport to greet them, as the Leader disembarked from the Air China Boeing.

The Old Man smiled to think what lay ahead in the next 72 hours.

If all went according to plan, he would make a few phone calls: to the army leadership in Beijing, and key Party bosses in the cities of Shanghai, Chengdu and Nanjing.

The calls to the generals would be the most important. The Beijing garrison would move fast to surround strategic buildings and arrest most members of the Politburo. At least one of the generals was known to be reluctant, so the Old Man had to ensure the others moved first, producing a fait accompli.

A period of unrest and uncertainty was inevitable. Party officials and middle ranking army officers would wait to see which way the wind was blowing before they committed themselves.

That's why the Old Man would cut short his visit and fly home to take personal command. A pity he could not be on the spot when it happened – but maybe this way was better. He would be above suspicion. He would return to Beijing as a saviour for his country at a time of crisis.

Evans was sitting in the conference hall of the luxury 5 star Sheraton hotel, waiting to give his lecture.

His brief forays into Harare's city centre had been like leafing through a history book. Up Julius Nyerere Way and left down Stanley Avenue, along Kenneth Kaunda Avenue and into Park Lane: a nice juxtaposition of modern Africa and its colonial antecedents.

But now he needed to concentrate on the lecture. His international audience were mostly fellow academics – along with a few government scientists. He felt quite at home. Evans admired charismatic speakers – like Jenny – but knew this wasn't his style. Objective, scientific inquiry was his passion. He couldn't afford to toy with value-ridden speculation.

'By the turn of the century,' he began, 'a total of 2,000 tonnes of plutonium will have been produced by the world's civil nuclear reactors and production will be running at around 160 tonnes a year.'

He paused, letting his facts sink in.

'To give you a comparison, today the world contains about 700 tonnes of civilian plutonium and production is running at nearly 80 tonnes a year. In under ten years, output will have more than doubled.

'The danger is this. Just a tiny 35 kilograms of plutonium oxide is sufficient to generate a nuclear explosive. And, if the plutonium oxide is converted to plutonium metal – a fairly straightforward chemical process – even less is needed for a nuclear explosion: just ten kilograms.

'This poses an enormous and, I would suggest, impossible security problem. We do not have – and we're unlikely ever to develop – the kind of sophisticated technology that can detect the *theft* of such tiny quantities of plutonium, when thousands of kilograms are separated each year. And I'm afraid the risks of such theft are very high.'

Evans continued talking for 45 minutes: covering each angle, backing up each fact by referring to the appropriate sources. He sat down to appreciative applause. As he listened to the vote of thanks, he wished Jenny had been in the audience.

He couldn't get her out of his mind. He thought about her so frequently and intensely. It was almost distracting him from his work – until now the entire focus of his adult life.

He was finding out things about himself he'd never known.

Although Makuyana had put out an alert to trace the ANC defector, he shared Mngadi's pessimism. Petersen was probably out of the country already.

Now his priority was the Chinese leader's visit. So far so good. Everything had gone like clockwork: the official welcome, the first of a series of meetings – and this evening's state reception.

Makuyana didn't enjoy such occasions.

Wearing a collar and tie was bad enough, but making small talk got him down. He wasn't the only one. Many of the other guests appeared to be similarly on edge: especially the wives, dutifully following behind their very important husbands.

But he did have the honour of being introduced to the Chinese leader and his ministers. They were hard to assess, as they shook hands, bowing politely. The epitome of courteous inscrutability.

The leader himself was a small bespectacled man shaped like a cone, with narrow head and broad body. Very different from his two senior ministers. The trade minister was young and at ease in the cosmopolitan gathering – a man of the new reformist era, Makuyana guessed. The other was much older with an imperious air. Must be one of the old guard.

Makuyana's staff reported a good working relationship with their Chinese counterparts. That was a relief. Foreign and domestic security teams often strayed onto each other's patches, which could cause tension.

Florence had checked through the list of ministerial aides. They were all staying at the Chinese Embassy – except a few who had arrived early, and were based at the Sheraton. Wherever the delegation went, an advance party of police and security agents would sweep the route, checking on buildings, monitoring surroundings. Nothing special: it was the usual protocol for state visits.

But Makuyana had been over the details again and again – to the point where his staff had become resentful. He was on edge, though he didn't know why.

'Stay on your toes,' he instructed Florence, who wondered what the hell else she could possibly do.

*

Jim mingled with fellow delegates over coffee, chatting about his lecture.

Some probed the detail of his argument; others wanted to chat socially. His lecture seemed to have gone down well – a good omen for the talk on radiation that he would deliver in two days' time.

Then he noticed a woman, who had been hovering at the edge of the conversation, notebook in hand. She introduced herself: a local reporter, eager to quiz him further. Had any of this material been published before? How *new* was the story? He told her that much of the evidence had been published in scientific journals, but – as far as he knew – nobody else had actually pulled it all together to reveal the true extent of the threat.

'My news editor will love this ... I must write it up before deadline!' She thanked him and rushed off.

Jim turned, almost bumping into an elderly man: 'Sorry! I didn't see you there.'

'No problem, sir,' the man spoke with a guttural accent. 'Can you do me a favour?' He didn't wait for Jim's response. 'I'm the official photographer. Can I get a picture of you outside, in front of the conference centre?'

Jim looked at his watch. 'Only five minutes before the next session. Will this take long?'

'Just a couple of minutes. While the light is good.'

They hurried out, Jim blinking in the bright sunlight. What was the man's accent? It was somehow thicker than that of other white Zimbabweans he had met.

'Just over there,' the man pointed to a van parked by the kerbside. 'My camera is in the back. We'll get a nice shot with the Sheraton behind you.'

Jim obligingly followed. The man opened the back door and reached inside. The van's engine was running. Odd, surely?

The man suddenly turned sharply; his face grim. He was holding a gun.

'Get in!'

Jim was pushed into the back of the van as it screamed off: doors slamming, his head banging against the offside wheel arch.

He felt dazed ... couldn't think straight. It was all a blur.

What was *happening*?

Jenny's taxi sped towards the Sheraton.

She had changed some money at Harare airport to supplement the hundred pounds she'd hastily drawn from an ATM at Gatwick. No time to get any local currency before she left. No idea if her credit card would work in Zimbabwe. She just had to get to Jim as soon as possible. She was sure he was in danger.

The cab stopped in front of the hotel and she fumbled for the fare, unfamiliar with the new currency. Grabbing her case, she rushed in and asked where the science conference was being held.

'The World Academy of Environmental Physics?', asked the receptionist.

'Yes – I suppose so.'

'Down there: Hall 3.'

'Thank you. Can I leave my baggage, please?'

'Are you staying here?'

'Yes,' she replied involuntarily.

'Your name, please.'

Jenny thought quickly.

'Evans, Jennifer Evans. My husband is Professor Jim Evans. He's already booked in.'

Mrs Evans! Jenny smiled inwardly, in spite of the knot in her stomach. She had vowed never to give up her maiden name – if she ever married.

The receptionist checked a list, frowning. 'I'm sorry, Mrs Evans. We don't have a record of your booking. Just your husband's.'

'Must be a mistake. I'll go and find him. Can you look after my bag?'

Christ! All this trivia. She had to get to Jim. She half ran along the plush corridors to the conference hall, aware of people watching her: a desperate figure in such sedate surroundings.

There was a desk outside the entrance to the hall. 'Good afternoon. Are you registered?' The woman behind the desk looked at her curiously.

'No, but my husband is Professor Evans. He's giving a lecture – and I need to talk to him urgently.'

'Ah, yes, Professor Evans,' the woman glanced down at her schedule. 'He gave his lecture earlier. They're about to end the final session now. Do you want to wait for him? It shouldn't be more than ten minutes.'

'Please, it's an emergency! Can't I go in and find him?'

The woman frowned.

'Well, if you insist. I'm not supposed to admit anyone without a pass, but maybe you can slip in quietly and see if you can spot him.'

Jenny pushed the wooden door, which opened with a creak. Several heads turned. So much for being quiet. She stood at the back, scanning the rows of seats. No sign of Jim. Hadn't he heard the door open? He was probably concentrating too deeply on matters scientific. Bloody typical . . .

Some delegate was droning on monotonously. To hell with Jim. Where *was* he? She found a seat in the back row, and tried to be inconspicuous.

Eventually the session ended.

She made her way to the stage and approached the chairperson: a grey-haired man with a bow tie.

'Where can I find Professor Evans, please?'

The man scanned the hall, his brow creasing. 'Can't see him, my dear. Hang on, I'll make an announcement.' He leant towards the microphone. 'Will Professor Evans please come to the front?'

The delegates looked up briefly, then returned to their conversations.

'That's odd,' said the chairperson. 'He *was* here. Gave the lecture after lunch. Bit rude of him to disappear. Try asking at reception.'

Jenny hurried back along the corridor to the main entrance of the hotel.

Jim's key was at the desk, so he wasn't in his room. Then a porter appeared, carrying a familiar, battered briefcase: 'This was left in Hall 3.'

Jenny froze: 'That's my husband's!'

'Are you sure?' The receptionist looked suspicious.

'Yes, absolutely.'

She was in despair. Jim wouldn't duck out of a conference. And even if he'd gone out for some fresh air, he would never leave his briefcase lying around. He didn't even lock it up in his car when they went out together after work. It stuck to him like a leech.

'I want to speak to the security services,' she said, her voice shaking.

Agents Venter and Coetzee were ready for the job. For once, they had somebody on the inside, feeding them all the necessary information. They could plan their operation with absolute precision.

In the last couple of days they did two dry runs. They'd even practised diving into the getaway car and timing the dash to the airport for the flight to Paris. The timing was fine-tuned: enough leeway to allow for traffic problems, but no hanging around at the boarding gate.

They had checked their equipment again and again. Stun grenades for the decoy; guns for the assassination. Pity they had to be so visible. Never comfortable operating in the open – but that's how it had to be.

For now, they had to lie low: relax, play some cards, watch lots of videos.

Just two more days.

Florence was keeping watch outside the house where Herson was now living.

Suddenly a Ford transit van drove out of his garage. The driver seemed to be alone: she couldn't tell if anybody was in the back.

She radioed HQ to get the registration checked. A pity they didn't have more resources so she could tail the van while someone else kept watch on the house, but they were badly stretched with the Chinese visit.

A few hours later the van returned and backed into the garage. Forty minutes afterwards a minicab arrived and dropped off a man who looked like an Asian. He might be local, might be foreign – she couldn't tell.

Everything went quiet again. It was dark by now. Hard to see what was happening.

Swanepoel knew he was taking a chance, but had no alternative. He phoned his man in the city centre, and uttered a curt message: 'NOSLEN One Exit.'

Back at home they would know he was leaving in a hurry. They'd be waiting for him near the border.

It was now too risky to stay in Harare – especially with Evans on board. What was the point anyway? His boys were all set; he couldn't do anything more.

His instructions were to get Evans and Petersen out as quickly as possible: the former for interrogation; the latter for de-briefing. He would have killed both of them himself, but they had to be questioned.

Not more aggro – surely not? Makuyana couldn't believe that something else was being dumped on his lap.

A visiting English professor had disappeared after giving a lecture at the Sheraton, and now his wife was making all sorts of allegations. She was insisting on talking to the security services rather than the police.

Makuyana decided to see her briefly, and then delegate responsibility to a subordinate. He couldn't head up a missing persons' bureau on top of everything else.

A knock on the door. 'Here is Mrs Evans, sir.'

Makuyana looked up slowly, without any enthusiasm. Then he frowned. Her face was vaguely familiar.

Who was she? Where had he seen her before?

Yes! Nairobi airport. The woman on the front page of the British newspaper: the one involved in the Green Planet episode. Something about China and nuclear waste.

What was she called . . . 'Red Jen'?

But what the hell was she doing *here*?

Jenny entered Makuyana's office feeling emotionally bruised and drained. It had been a battle to get a meeting with the security boss, but she'd insisted.

She expected another brush-off, but was surprised to see his expression change from neutral indifference to startled interest.

He gestured for her to sit.

'Your husband has disappeared, I understand. But how can I help? Surely, this is a police matter?'

His tone was sympathetic, and he had a striking face: thoughtful and strong. But the dark glasses were intimidating, somehow at odds with his manner.

'To begin with, Professor Evans is not my husband – just a good friend.' How embarrassing to trot out that old cliché.

'I don't really know where to start.' Jenny couldn't find the words. She'd come all the way from London, and now she couldn't get her act together. Her confidence had failed her when she needed it most.

But Makuyana surprised her again.

'It's okay. You're the one they call "Red Jen", aren't you?'

'How on earth do you know that?' She was dumbfounded.

'I happened to see an English newspaper story about you – and it mentioned a subject close to my heart.'

'Green Planet?'

'No. The nuclear connection with China.'

Jenny's mind suddenly cleared. How uncanny. It was as if this man had suddenly unlocked a door and switched on the light. At last she had someone to talk to: someone who might understand, and had the power to act.

She was almost tearful with relief.

'It's part of a much bigger story,' Makuyana was saying. 'Basically, I think the security of our own country might be threatened. But tell me why you are here. What do you think has happened to Professor Evans?'

Jenny took a deep breath and told him everything. The visit to China, the meeting with Dick Sewell, her mistake in passing on information about the Pretoria connection to an untrustworthy source, and her reason for coming to Harare.

As soon as she mentioned Pretoria, Makuyana reached for the phone and instructed his assistant to get hold of a woman called Florence.

No, it wasn't really happening. It couldn't be. The events of the last few hours were blurring into each other.

First, the abduction from his academic ivory tower to the brutal world he had briefly entered back in China. Then Wang's unexpected appearance. *Wang*? What the hell was *he* doing out here?

The man was his familiar self: arrogant, accusatory, nasty. He kept demanding to know what Jim was *really* doing in Harare. Jim kept telling him he was attending a bona fide academic conference.

'Lying again!' Wang screamed. 'Lying again as you did in China! We should have finished you off then.'

He disappeared and Jim could hear him talking in muffled tones in the next room. A guard watched over him but didn't say anything: a tubby man of mixed race. He didn't seem hostile, more the brooding type.

The sound of a door shutting. Receding steps. Jim's kidnapper returned, gestured to the guard, and both left the room. He was on his own again.

He looked out of the window: nobody in sight. Just a garden and a back fence. He had never felt more isolated.

Was this how Dick Sewell had felt in Hong Kong?

Would he suffer a similar fate?

Makuyana pored over every detail of Jenny's story.

The English professor had been seen talking to an elderly man just before he disappeared from the Sheraton: a man who fitted the description of the Robert Temba murder suspect. And Herson fitted both descriptions. What was the connection?

His phone rang.

'Yes, what is it?' He sounded impatient, then realised it was Florence.

'Boss, sorry to interrupt – but this is really important. We've got something from a phone conversation we monitored between Herson and that businessman. It's the word NOSLEN.'

'NOSLEN?' Makuyana was concentrating fully now.

'Yes. The exact message was "NOSLEN One Exit".'

NOSLEN! The codeword the ANC had discovered. Events must be moving fast. Somebody, or something, was getting the hell out of Harare.

Makuyana called border surveillance. No, he couldn't tell them what to expect. Just maintain extra vigilance – and report on anything unusual: like someone trying to cross into South Africa illegally.

And if a certain Mr Herson tried to cross *legally*, he must be detained at all costs.

They had sedated Jim and he was dead to the world.

Swanepoel had decided to use his own car instead of the van, which might have been identified earlier at the Sheraton. They propped up Jim next to Petersen on the back seat, and another agent drove so that Swanepoel could get some rest. He settled into the passenger seat as the car sped off into the evening.

As they left the house, Florence radioed HQ with the news. Then she switched on her monitor. To her relief the bleeper was strong, but she'd have to stay close until they hit the open road.

The light was bad, so she hadn't been able to see exactly who was in the car. She just had an impression the driver was not alone. For the last few hours, she had felt lethargic, repeatedly catching herself dozing off.

Now she was on full alert.

11

The Nimrod cruised comfortably at an altitude of 24,000 feet, watching and listening to the world below, its sophisticated surveillance system missing little.

Back and forth it flew, along the Zimbabwe-South Africa border, from Mozambique on the east to Rhodes Drift on the west – and sometimes north-west along the Botswana border to the Caprivi strip, which also connected Angola, Zambia and Namibia.

Captain André Geffen was now familiar with the aircraft. The Zimbabwean government had bought it from Britain six months earlier: a surprising concession on the part of the Brits – but maybe London was hedging its bets after decades of covert support for Pretoria.

Geffen and his crew had received intensive training in the UK, but it was another story when you were on your own, especially in such different terrain: wide open spaces covering thousands of square kilometres with nothing much happening – then sudden, concentrated bursts of movement on both sides of the border.

Apart from radar, the plane's photographic equipment was based on satellite technology, producing crystal clear pictures which were relayed back to base. The crew was learning how to distinguish between the routine and the unusual: between a small herd of wildebeest and a convoy of military vehicles.

They maintained a particular watch on the airbase at Louis Trichardt. That would be the hotspot for any serious aerial threat from South Africa – especially from their deadly new Cheetah jets.

For now, nothing much was happening. The Nimrod was cruising on two of its four engines, as night closed in quickly. Geffen had just taken over from his co-pilot, after a couple of hours of very welcome kip.

Then a message from control: someone high-up in security was placing them on full alert. An illicit border crossing was expected, somewhere around the main road south. Absolute priority. If Geffen spotted anything he was to contact Major Keith Makuyana directly.

Geffen knew Makuyana by repute. He was tough and honest: a man who didn't mess about. A man after his own heart – even though they'd once fought on different sides during the Bush War. Now, old adversaries had become buddies in the struggle to protect the land of their birth.

It hadn't always been like this. In 1980, when ZANU had eclipsed white minority rule under the leadership of Robert Mugabe – the so-called 'black Hitler' – Geffen's cosy world had been turned upside down. Such a reversal of roles: he'd lost track of his own identity for a while.

But no longer. Although blacks were in power, his children still attended the same exclusive schools, his wife continued to work as a senior nurse, and his standard of living had been maintained. Above all, he was the same military professional he'd always been.

There was a job to be done, and he would do it well.

The screen on the dashboard flickered in the gloom, as Florence kept a close eye on the flashing dot. The car was just a couple of kilometres ahead of her on the open road.

If only she had a colleague with her: it hadn't been easy driving out of town in the rush-hour traffic while monitoring the screen, as she anxiously followed the driver's left and right turns.

At least she was on the main road now, and Herson's vehicle showed no sign of deviating from the long drive south. Makuyana had just come on the radio to brief her about the English woman, and the information she had shared. The missing professor might well be in the car ahead.

Makuyana's men had raided both of Herson's safe houses. Nothing to report, except that sniffer dogs had located a cupboard in the first house where explosives and ammunition had been stored. Forensics were checking it out now. There was one other lead: the blue Ford transit parked outside the second house had been spotted at the conference centre about the same time as Evans' disappearance.

Her instructions were to keep tailing the car so they didn't risk compromising the mission by having to rely on Bulawyo police.

The destination might be another safe house, in which case Makuyana wanted the address. He had a helicopter standing by with extra operatives. If things got lively, he'd join her as soon as possible.

Meanwhile, everything was down to her. Florence knew all too well that if she messed up, she would not be forgiven.

The tension was starting to get to the Old Man. Nothing to do with the seminar for top military strategists he was leading. No: it was the knowledge that within 24 hours a series of carefully planned events would reach their tumultuous climax.

He forced his attention back to the task in hand: thirty senior military men sitting in a half circle before him, waiting to hear about the modernisation of the People's Liberation Army.

His notes had been prepared by the Leader's office which insisted on a common, modernising and reformist slant to the public or semi-public pronouncements of each delegation member visiting Zimbabwe.

So typical of the new regime, the Old Man snorted to himself. Public relations before ideology. As a Politburo member, he had supported the reforms – but he hadn't agreed with them. Yet, he had to sound enthusiastic, espousing the Leader's line with no hint of deviation.

He began with the famous quotation from Chairman Mao: 'Political power grows out of the barrel of a gun.'

During Mao's leadership of the Party, the People's Liberation Army had played a central political role, the Old Man explained. 'However, in the last decade or so the PLA has changed dramatically. It has ceased to play such a major role in political and Party life. Many features of Western armies have been adopted. We have restored the ranking system abolished in 1965 during the Cultural Revolution.'

He didn't add – though would have liked to – that the old egalitarian spirit of the PLA had been extinguished, and its former status as a revered institution in Chinese society had plummeted. The strict enforcement of retirement age limits meant the ideological veterans of Liberation were being supplanted by younger technocrats.

The Old Man spoke English fluently, so he didn't need an interpreter during question time. Several Zimbabwe officers wanted to know how the old peasant army of liberation had been transformed into an instrument of the state. Any disciplinary problems? Any resistance by the former guerrillas to surrendering their arms? Zimbabwe had gone through a similar process and it had been fraught with problems, with marauding bands creating havoc in some rural areas because they did not want to relinquish power.

'The Party ensured our transition was smooth. The Party must *always* be strong.'

The Old Man's audience was struck by the steely edge in his

voice. Little did they know his mind was focusing on the next momentous day.

The screen blip stopped abruptly, startling Florence out of the soporific warmth of her heated car. She pressed her foot down on the accelerator.

She crested the brow of a hill – and there was a filling station. Just as well: like Herson, she was running low on petrol.

She eased into the garage forecourt, pulling up behind his vehicle. A bit risky, but she had to see who was inside. There were three of them, plus another who was speaking to the petrol attendant. She couldn't see their faces properly, but one person seemed to be slumped over – maybe asleep – in the back.

As her tank was topped up, the driver returned and the car sped off. She didn't recognise him, but Herson was probably the large guy in the front passenger seat.

They had travelled 160 kilometres already but were still another four hundred from the border – more than three hours' drive, at the speed they had been going. Florence used the stop for a welcome visit to the toilet, and then drove off the forecourt to the edge of the road, where she could radio Makuyana more easily.

'Boss,' she said urgently, 'There are four of them, including Herson and a guy who seems to be asleep in the back. They'll hit the border in about three and half hours. Maybe four. I think you should come down now with reinforcements. And alert security ahead, please.'

There was a lengthy pause before the line crackled.

'Okay,' Makuyana responded. 'I haven't been able to get away yet. Too tied up with the bloody Chinese visit. But I'll board the chopper in about fifteen minutes. Should be with you before they reach Beitbridge. Can't get too close – but they mustn't cross the border. Are they armed?'

'I couldn't see.'

'We have to assume they are. Stay in contact – and for Chrissake don't do anything dangerous.'

Jenny was aching with exhaustion. Makuyana had agreed to let her stay in his office, so she could follow what was happening. But she felt frustrated at her inability to assist in any practical way.

She hadn't slept properly for ages. They had offered her a bed but she wanted to stick closely to Makuyana: when he went to rescue Jim, she was determined to go with him. Meanwhile, it was reassuring to observe the security chief at work. He was such an authoritative figure, in whom she had a growing confidence.

Jenny tried to doze off in her uncomfortable chair, but her mind was racing. She snatched yet another glance at her wristwatch. God, didn't time drag when you wanted it to go quickly.

A secretary brought in a tray of food. Nothing she would usually eat, but she consumed it all: partly out of politeness, partly out of sheer hunger and anxiety.

Makuyana's phone rang. She heard him talking to his deputy who was tailing a car southward. Why this game of cat and mouse? Why couldn't they just stop the car and rescue Jim? From what they'd told her she felt certain he was on board.

She understood Makuyana's reasoning. No point in a premature interception when the car might lead to bigger fish. But that wasn't much consolation – she simply wanted Jim back in one piece.

Makuyana was instructing them to prepare the helicopter and get his car.

Now was the moment. Jenny leapt to her feet, her voice urgent: 'I want to come with you, please.'

He swivelled round in his chair. 'Sorry. Not possible.' A final statement. No argument.

But Jenny was insistent. 'I *have* to come. It's the whole reason

I travelled out from London. I put him in this mess!' She paused, then added almost as an afterthought: 'Anyway, you don't know what he looks like. You might shoot the wrong person. I'm the only one who can identify him.'

Makuyana glanced at his watch, then back at the young woman in front of him. 'Red Jen': not some idealistic hothead, but a person of substance.

She might even be useful.

It was against all the rules, but what the hell.

'Alright. But on one condition. You do *exactly* what you're told.'

The Nimrod's gaze had spotted something suspicious, but Captain Geffen couldn't make sense of the pictures and signals. Something was happening in the direction of Louis Trichardt air base, 100 kilometres across the border.

An unidentified aircraft was flying towards Zimbabwe – very low, under the radar. Too slow for a fighter: probably a light civilian-type plane or helicopter. It was on track to cross the Limpopo in ten to fifteen minutes.

Geffen put in a call to Makuyana's helicopter and gave details of the flight path.

Makuyana paused as he quickly translated the coordinates.

Yes! The chopper was on course to intersect with the main road on which Herson's vehicle was travelling. It would probably airlift them out of the country.

'Any more details needed?' Geffen's voice crackled in his headset.

'Not for now, thanks. Please keep us posted.'

Makuyana needed time to think. The South African chopper would be armed to the teeth, for sure. So there were two options. Either confront them when they landed – and spark a potentially bloody clash – or play a waiting game and allow the party to be lifted out before engaging with them. The second option was just as risky: the party might be taken too deep into Northern Transvaal to be rescued.

Alternatively, could the car be intercepted? No. It was too far away and the South African chopper might still pursue them.

He called Geffen back. 'If their chopper crosses the border, do you think they will land at Trichardt?'

'Hard to say. Depends how open they want to be. If it's a covert operation, they're unlikely to return to the airbase because they know we monitor it closely. But if they aren't worried about international flak, they'll head straight back there.'

Makuyana weighed the options. The South Africans were kidnapping a British subject. Not even they could get away with that. They had to keep it hush-hush. So, maybe he should take the risk? For the sake of uncovering the truth about the nuclear connection.

'Okay. We're going to let their chopper cross the border. We'll hang back for a while. Monitor its flight and tell me where it lands,' he told Geffen.

I bloody hope I've made the right choice, Makuyana said to himself.

Swanepoel spotted the track just in time: a right turn off the main Beitbridge road. They bumped along it, towards the moonlit silhouette of a farmhouse.

It was a little early for their rendezvous, but better than being late. The car stopped next to a shed, and he climbed out to urinate in the bushes.

Everyone was tired and irritable after the long journey — except for Evans, who was still out cold.

Swanepoel was glad to be going home. It would be good to be back in the Transvaal again, where cheeky blacks were dealt with properly instead of being permitted to run the bloody country.

His time in Harare had been a struggle. He resented having to be polite to blacks, having to treat them as equals – occasionally even taking orders from them. All part of his cover, but that didn't mean he had to like it.

Swanepoel looked at his watch. The helicopter should be landing in the clearing alongside the farmhouse in about ten minutes. They had timed it to a T, and everything was working out just fine.

He lit a cigarette and began to relax.

Florence noticed a sudden deviation in the dot on the screen, and radioed Makuyana.

'Target has done a sudden right. Can't tell where to.' She gave the approximate location and slowed down, straining to see a signpost in the dark. Then she shut off her lights. Where had they gone?

The moon was high and visibility good. The flashing screen indicated that the vehicle had pushed ahead quite a distance off the main road – suggesting nobody was lying in wait. A signpost loomed up: 'Baobab Farm'. That could be it. She turned slowly to the right, and bumped along a rutted track.

The bleeper signal was getting stronger now. She cut the engine, and coasted to a halt, winding down her window.

No sign of human activity – just the monotonous vibration of crickets, and the distant howl of a hyena.

Florence sat absolutely still: listening, thinking. Then she grabbed her Kalashnikov and walked stealthily down the track, her eyes scanning the bush ahead.

Suddenly in the distance there was a throbbing sound which became ever louder. A helicopter was hovering just a few hundred meters away: its spotlights piercing the darkness like a UFO. It hung, as if suspended, then dipped out of sight.

Florence ran forward. The chopper, guns glinting with menace, had landed in a clearing next to a farmhouse. Three people ran over and climbed on board. One was carrying a fourth person: apparently unconscious.

So near, yet so far ...

With a bit of luck, she could have gunned down the chopper – but that was against her orders. If she opened fire and missed, the gunship would blast her to oblivion. On the other hand, if she scored a direct hit, she would have killed Evans.

As the chopper lifted off, Florence sprinted back to her car and updated Makuyana, giving him her exact position.

Then she walked back, towards the deserted farm. She quickly searched Herson's car. It was clean, save for a few sweet wrappers and empty beer bottles. The key had been left in the ignition. She carefully removed it, and bagged it for fingerprinting later.

Then she waited, gun slung over her shoulder.

The Nimrod watched as the helicopter lifted off and headed back across the border towards Louis Trichardt. It skidded across treetops, terrifying the wildlife, and villagers sleeping in shacks and mud huts below.

Then suddenly it veered to the left and, about fifteen kilometres south of the Limpopo, disappeared. Geffen peered at the satellite images – no movement. Nothing.

He'd just been thinking how surveillance aircraft like his Nimrod had made undercover work almost impossible. Secret agents could no longer operate so freely. Gone were the days of James Bond figures, vulnerable only to the skill and cunning of their opponents. Now you could observe a single human being from kilometres above the earth. Soon, spying would be conducted by people sitting in front of computer screens, relying on fibre optic cables and cameras in space.

But there was always some element that could evade technology. Like now. The chopper had landed just across the border north of the Magato hills, but he couldn't tell what was happening around it.

He spoke tersely into his microphone, relaying the position of the landing. It was all up to Makuyana now.

Jim blocked his ears against the deafening sound of the twirling rotor blades. He felt nauseous, half conscious. Helpless. Couldn't stop them lifting him out of the car and into the back of the helicopter.

Dumped unceremoniously on the metal floor, he battled against the numbing sedative. Then the engine revved, and the great bird lifted off. Every bone in his body jangled, and his brains shook in the cavern of his head.

How long he had been travelling? Where were they taking him? He closed his eyes again, trying to shut out the misery.

It wasn't long before the gunship sank gently to earth. A couple of figures ran towards it from some low buildings. The whirring rotor blades whipped up a dust storm, as Swanepoel shouted that Evans should be lifted out and taken away.

The voices of Swanepoel's men were drowned in the din. Even inside the building they could hardly hear themselves talk. Then, abruptly, the chopper revved and ascended again. Soon, the noise abated, leaving only windswept grass and clouds of dust.

Swanepoel rubbed his hands in the cold. The plan had been executed perfectly. Everything at the deserted farmhouse was as expected: plenty of provisions – thank God, because he could eat a horse – along with beds, and even some liquor. Cars too, for later. His people had prepared well.

Meanwhile, the chopper had scuttled back to the airbase, leaving no evidence that this had been anything but a routine border patrol. If necessary, the incursion into Zimbabwe could be passed off as an error.

It was midnight. Soon Swanepoel would get some sleep, but first they would interrogate Evans. Best to go for the jugular while your target was disorientated. He beckoned to Jan Viljoen, the agent sent from Pretoria earlier. Young and lean where Swanepoel was old and paunchy, Viljoen was the perfect foil.

Together they had broken many tough men. This one would be a piece of cake.

Makuyana's helicopter landed in the clearing marked by Florence with her car headlights.

As a qualified pilot, she had flown choppers herself. She was in awe of their flexibility: how had people ever coped without them?

Makuyana ran towards her, wasting no time in greetings.

'They landed just across the border. We're going in after them.'

'What? Will the President sanction that?' Florence was astonished.

Makuyana frowned. 'The kidnapping and Herson's letter bomb give us justification. Come!'

They settled into the cockpit, as the chopper lifted off and swung round towards the Limpopo.

Jenny was hunched on the bare metal floor, braving the relentless noise and cold. She was surrounded by six armed men, AK-47 assault rifles glinting, grenades clipped to their combat jackets. No place for small talk. You had to shout to be heard.

She could see Makuyana upfront with the pilot, headphones on. After a while, the woman they'd just picked up – his deputy, apparently – made her way to the back of the chopper.

'I'm Florence Dube. Good to meet you!' she shouted.

Florence was munching a sandwich. 'Haven't eaten since lunchtime! Let me know if you want one, yes?'

Jenny smiled, and shook her head. How nice to have another woman around – especially now that Makuyana was so aloof. Perhaps he regretted his decision to bring her on such a dangerous mission.

Florence was about her own age, but that's where the similarity ended. With a Kalashnikov casually slung across her shoulder, she reminded Jenny of the women combatants who featured in posters she'd collected at university.

For a moment, Jenny was transported back in time. She recalled the intense debates about feminism at her local collective. Some had argued that feminism was intrinsically non-violent: that there would be fewer wars if women were in charge. But Jenny had always insisted that patriarchy was more powerful than maleness. In a world devoid of sexism, she believed women could act as violently as men.

How would Florence respond to the heat of battle?

Jenny shivered.

She would find out. Probably sooner, rather than later.

Evans wasn't such a pushover after all, Swanepoel realised.

He didn't exactly *resist* the interrogation: he just seemed genuinely confused – repeatedly denying any ulterior motive for his visit to Harare; insisting he was a professor, not a political activist.

When they returned to the bare room and switched on the light, he looked pathetic: near breaking point, huddled on the floor. But still no confession. There was a puzzling innocence about him.

They pummelled him with questions again. Viljoen played the hard man; with Swanepoel sometimes behaving as a 'friend', almost apologising for Viljoen's aggression.

When Evans eventually collapsed, Swanepoel decided to let him rot for a while with the light on, while they caught some much-needed sleep. By the time they came back, the remnants of his inner defences would have crumbled, and he would sing like a canary.

And when they'd broken him, they would debrief Petersen – who was sullenly keeping himself to himself. He'd been such a good source inside the ANC, but he seemed uncomfortable now. As Swanepoel dozed off, he made a mental note to keep an eye on the man.

The Zimbabwe military chopper touched down in the darkness on South African soil.

As they disembarked, ducking to avoid the downdraught, Jenny stayed close to Florence. The chopper immediately headed back across the border, where it would wait for their signal.

Makuyana had instructed Jenny to leave also, but she'd fiercely resisted. Eventually he relented, perhaps realising she could be useful after all.

'Look after this . . .' – he handed her a walkie talkie – 'and as soon as you hear shooting, press the red button. It will send a signal to the helicopter to come for us. Don't wait too long – we may need to get out fast.'

Makuyana reckoned it would take them about three hours on foot to reach the spot where Herson's party was now based. That meant they would arrive at daybreak. Total darkness would have been preferable, but he couldn't risk landing any closer – and at least the map showed unbroken terrain.

Two of the soldiers had remained in the chopper. The other four fanned out, with Makuyana in the lead and the women in the middle. It was bitterly cold.

Walking along under the vast African sky with its low moon, Jenny felt terrified as the enormity of their mission engulfed her. Just a few days ago she'd been living a normal life in London. Now she was in enemy territory, heading towards a violent confrontation. Should she have stayed behind after all? Maybe she'd just hinder the others.

Only the thought of Jim kept her going.

They marched briskly, stopping sometimes to listen and observe, checking they could proceed safely. The lowveld was alive with nocturnal sounds: the high-pitched squeal of bats; the rustle of rodents and small mammals.

Jenny found this unnerving. She remembered long walks through the rolling Dorset countryside with Aunt Ruth – hours of gentle tranquillity, a world away from this rugged, unfamiliar country.

At last, dawn peeked hesitantly over the horizon. Florence tapped her on the shoulder. Makuyana, who had gone ahead, was now turning back, motioning them to stand still.

'Nearly there,' he said, in a low voice. 'They're inside a farmhouse at the bottom of a small dip. Only two guards, as far as I can tell. There's a light in one room. Everything else is dark.'

Florence took Jenny's hand. 'We won't shoot anybody who is unarmed. That should protect your man. Stay here, out of sight. Remember the red button.'

She gave her a quick hug. 'Take this too. I hope you won't have to use it – but just in case. It's loaded, and the safety catch is off, so be careful! All you have to do is point and pull the trigger.'

Before she could reply, Jenny found an automatic pistol nestling in her hand, ominously heavy and cold.

It was just after 4 a.m. at Louis Trichardt airbase, and the night supervisor was routinely checking the surveillance log.

Sometime after midnight, helicopter activity had been detected on the border: not far from where their own chopper had carried out a hush-hush security mission several hours before.

Earlier, they had logged another helicopter journey south from Harare. He'd seen the report when he came on duty.

He consulted a large map which hung above the screens in the control room. Interesting: the flight of the Zimbabwean chopper ended in the vicinity of the reported border activity.

He stared at the map, frustrated by his ignorance of their own security mission. Then he made a decision. It was time to deploy a Cheetah to take a closer look.

Better to be safe than sorry.

*

Outside, the cold cruel wind had howled unremittingly all night across the lowveld, penetrating everything.

Finally, a sliver of sun peeked over the horizon, seemed to think better of it, and settled back.

A *dassie* surfaced, sniffed, twitched, then scampered down its burrow.

An owl, beacon-like eyes swivelling, watched and waited, knowing its hunting time would soon be over when darkness ended.

But inside, Jim had lost all sense of night and day.

The relentless bright light had seen to that. Whichever way he turned, or however tightly he closed his eyes, the glare pierced through, blurring him into semiconsciousness.

'We'll leave the light on to keep you company – so you don't get lonely.' Viljoen's thick Afrikaner accent made the sneer more biting, the mirthless laughter more sinister.

They had gone with a promise to 'come and talk again', the door banging shut, then firmly bolted.

Jim was enveloped by utter loneliness – and numbing fear.

Fear of being forced again to stand at an angle to the wall, his feet a metre from it, fingers resting against its whitewashed surface taking his bodyweight. Simple yet devastating. Any slump, and a strategic kick sent him back into position.

At first, he needed complete concentration just to stop screaming. Later, his senses were so deadened he could barely produce a grunt in answer to the endless questions – eventually sliding down the wall, collapsing on the concrete floor, too exhausted even to groan.

As their voices died away, Jim tried to get a grip. The room was bare, save for some old sacks in a corner. The bitter cold disorientated him. Surely this was supposed to be a warm country? Well, not this time of year. Not at night anyway. Not here in this remote building.

Painful memories returned. Feeling groggy on the car's back

seat, being lifted into a helicopter, half conscious, aware only of the deafening noise.

Minutes later, bundled out again and deliberately allowed to glimpse the total isolation: no chance of help. He knew he was across the border – but only because they had told him so.

Ever since his abduction from outside the Sheraton he had implored them to explain. What did they want? Where were they going? Who *were* they? But they ignored his pleas, pounding him with a barrage of their own questions and accusations. What did he know about the China operation? Who was he *really* working for? This nonsense about an academic visit – who the bloody hell did he think he was kidding?

They seemed to know an awful lot – in fact most of what Jenny had told Howells, the anti-apartheid activist leader in London. How was that possible? And what did it have to do with Zimbabwe?

He could only repeat: 'You're making a terrible mistake. Don't know what you are talking about. Don't know anything. Anything ...'

Even now, hours later, denials bounced round his aching head, seeming to echo away into the cold – only to be thrown back by the dazzle of light.

Then, through the silence broken only by the unfamiliar, penetrating screech of a hadeda, came a sudden, even more bewildering, thought.

They wouldn't go to all this trouble for nothing.

Perhaps I *am* guilty after all?

If only they would tell me what on earth I'm supposed to have *done*.

Jenny peered over the dip, as the soldiers circled below. Two other figures – Florence and Makuyana? – crept across the yard and slid up against a whitewashed wall. The outline of the buildings sharpened as dawn broke.

It seemed like a farm, but clearly wasn't. Everything was unnaturally clean and tidy: no sign of animals, the fences were in good order, the bush had been cut back.

Jenny's toes, ears, fingers were frozen. She could feel her heart pounding. When would the action start? It was like being in a movie – but a lot messier. And where was Jim? Was he even still alive? Maybe she'd been crazy to come here ...

Suddenly, all hell broke loose. A deafening crash, followed by gunfire and screams. Whose?

Jenny was numb with fear. But she remembered what she had to do: press the red button on her handset.

Now!

Makuyana had already spotted the guard at the front door, cigarette glowing as he stamped his feet in the cold. Another guard persistently circled the building: he should be taken out first.

Three cars were parked in the courtyard. Probably a group of twelve people – a few more than their own, but at least they had the advantage of surprise.

He and Florence took up position. He waited for the guard to come round the corner; she would deal with the one at the front door.

Makuyana suddenly remembered Robert Temba and Ed Mugadza: their valuable lives blown to smithereens. It was time to settle scores and avenge their murders.

A shadowy figure emerged around the corner, and stopped. Makuyana could hear the man breathing and shuffling. Then he peered into the darkness, saw Makuyana, and raised his gun. In a split second Makuyana was upon him, his stainless steel knife slashing viciously at the man's Adam's apple. The guard's gun clattered onto the hard ground, and his eyes glazed as he collapsed.

At that precise moment, Florence pumped two shots into the

other guard. One bullet exploded in his brain, turning it into a tangle of useless matter; the second drilled through his heart. She rushed to the door and wrenched it open.

A man was sitting on a chair, in what must have been the main living room: a fire glowed in the hearth. Not a white guy – unlike the others – and he was pointing a submachine gun right at her.

She started to raise her Kalash, but knew there was no point. The man would splatter her against the doorframe before she had time to fire. She had recognised him at once – though that was no consolation.

It was the traitor, Petersen.

Swanepoel was jerked awake by the gunfire. Jesus! Had Evans escaped? Not possible! But what the hell was going on?

As he switched on the bedside lamp and lunged for his pistol, the window shattered and a figure tumbled into the room, rolling across the bed, half on top of him, involuntarily knocking his gun to the floor. The momentum threw his attacker against the far wall, but he recovered quickly and dragged himself back onto his feet.

Swanepoel saw a tall black man, who was reaching into his pocket for a pair of tinted dark glasses.

He knew him!

It was the man they had photographed at Harare airport. The one they'd never been able to identify – come back to haunt him again.

Gunfire ... screams. Chaos and commotion.

Jim could tell something was happening – but what?

Suddenly the door was flung open and Viljoen burst in, pulling him roughly to his feet.

'*Kom*, professor ... you my ticket to safety.' His rasping accent cut through his captor's confusion. Jim received the message loud and clear, as he was dragged, stumbling, into the darkened corridor.

Transfixed, Jenny saw two Zimbabwean soldiers approach the building. Then a window suddenly swung open and a vicious rattle of machine gun fire cut them down.

Writhing simultaneously in agony, they shuddered and lay still on the ground. She gasped: the two had died in front of her, no more than 50 metres away.

Then she spotted a third Zimbabwean edging against the wall towards the open window. He crouched low, lobbed something inside, and darted away. A thunderous explosion: the inside of the room seemed to spill right out.

On the other side of the building, more firing. A figure fell from a tree and hit the ground with a dreadful thud. A burst of fire was returned from elsewhere. From the corner of her eye, she spotted another figure running fast.

More shots. A deathly silence.

Were they all killing each other? Would she be left on her own?

It was the longest, most terrifying moment of her life. But Florence finally understood. Petersen wasn't firing at her – nor would he.

His gun was real enough, his advantage unquestionable – but he seemed unable to move. Slowly, he lowered his gun.

'Shoot me if you want,' he blurted, falling into an armchair – the gun slipping from his hands. 'I can't kill you.'

Florence was stunned, but swiftly recovered herself.

'Where is Evans?'

'In the cell next door.'

'Take me there.' She stared at Petersen's drawn, troubled face.

More gunfire erupted, followed by an almighty explosion which shook the whole house.

'How many South Africans are here?' Florence demanded.

'Four inside, two outside.'

They headed out of the room, Petersen leading the way: his posture and her machine gun implying he was a prisoner. Perhaps he wanted that, in case they bumped into anyone. Florence didn't care as long as they kept moving.

Time was of the essence – as never before.

Their recognition was mutual, but Makuyana didn't pull the trigger – yet.

'Mr Herson. Not your real name, I suppose.'

'Mr Nkala. Not *your* real name, I suppose.'

Mauritz Swanepoel kept his composure. It wasn't the first time he had faced death, or been in a jam. But how in hell had the Zimbabweans tracked them down?

'I am Captain Swanepoel of the South African security services,' he said, evenly. He wanted the other man to know who he was dealing with: whose patch he was trespassing upon.

Makuyana seemed not to hear.

'Where is Evans?' he asked.

'Who is Evans?' Swanepoel shrugged nonchalantly.

No time to waste. Makuyana hit him in the teeth with the barrel of his Kalash, drawing a spurt of blood.

'Don't piss me about, you bastard! You killed Robert Temba – and many others. Now it's your turn to die: unless you cooperate.'

Swanepoel felt curiously detached. He no longer cared. He was at the end of his career, in the twilight of his life. He could read the situation calmly. He knew this black man didn't have time for a proper interrogation.

'*Fok jou*,' he sneered.

Makuyana smashed the butt of his gun into Swanepoel's jaw. Then he kicked him deliberately in the groin, provoking a scream of pain. He didn't enjoy the violence. He felt no emotion at all. It was as if someone else was doing what had to be done: coldly and methodically.

'Where is Evans?'

'*Fok jou!*'

Makuyana kept his temper. He'd heard the gunfire. It was time to move. This one would be too hard to crack in the time available.

He picked up Swanepoel's pistol, and shot him in both knees. Then he quickly searched the room to ensure there were no other weapons. He left Swanepoel writhing in agony – in a spreading pool of his own blood and mangled flesh.

Job done.

Jim found himself being pushed outside, into the fresh sharpness of the dawn – a revolver dug into his ribs. Viljoen constantly shifted his position, to ensure that Jim would shield him from any gunfire.

In the clear morning, Jim was able to take in his surroundings for the first time. The terrain was flattish and dry, scattered with patchy bushes and flat-topped trees. It was all so unfamiliar – physically and emotionally. He couldn't make sense of anything. He could only submit.

Viljoen had been heading towards one of the parked cars, but they were too far away. And as he edged closer, he spotted someone there: crouched down, with his gun poking out. Viljoen knew he was right up to his neck in shit. No safe exit. No idea how many of his team were still alive.

He tightened his grasp on Jim, and the two shuffled awkwardly up a path, then ducked behind some bushes.

'You so much as fart, you're toast,' Viljoen grunted.

The limbs and body parts of two dead South Africans were splattered around the room where the bomb had exploded. Makuyana grabbed their guns and headed off to recce the rest of the single-storey farmhouse. Minimal furniture: the place felt unlived-in.

Then he spotted Florence and Petersen, emerging from one of the rooms.

'Boss!' hissed Florence.

Her eyes met his. Relief that each was still alive.

'Evans has disappeared,' said Florence. She gestured towards the empty room, rounding on Petersen: 'Are you sure that's where he was kept?'

Petersen nodded.

Makuyana stared at him. Petersen was unarmed. What had happened, and why was he cooperating? But the ANC traitor wouldn't return his gaze, keeping his eyes fixed to the ground.

Makuyana turned to his deputy: 'Florence, check out the other outhouse. We must find Evans.'

Then he jerked his head towards Petersen. 'What's he playing at?'

'He could have killed me, but he didn't. Says he wants to help.' Florence shrugged: let the boss make sense of this – if he could.

Makuyana couldn't disguise his contempt for Petersen: 'What the hell's going on?' he barked.

'They didn't tell me much. Swanepoel was their main field agent in Harare. Responsible for most of the explosions and killings.'

'What about Evans? Why did they kidnap him?'

'Don't know. Except . . .' Petersen hesitated.

'Yes? Come on man! We haven't got much time.'

'Something to do with the Chinese. Swanepoel kept hinting about a big operation. Their people are in place, so it must be very soon.'

'Is that all you bloody have to tell me?' Makuyana's spine tingled – but he kept his voice steady. He mustn't let the traitor see his excitement.

'They were playing it close to their chest. Wouldn't tell me much. After Evans was taken to their safe house, a Chinese guy appeared. He had a go at Evans, then left.'

'What did he look like?'

'Horn-rimmed spectacles. Not old, not young. Nothing distinctive.'

'Why should I believe a man like you? A traitor to your own people!'

Petersen was startled by harshness of Makuyana's tone.

'I had no choice.'

'No choice?' Makuyana spat out the words. 'What about all those who died because of you? What choice did *they* have?'

'The security police were after my wife and kids in the Cape. They'd have killed them if I hadn't cooperated.' Petersen's voice was now confident, no longer defensive or diffident. 'You can't understand! I should never have left them behind – I should have brought my family into exile with me.'

Makuyana kept his expression neutral. But he felt Petersen's anguish keenly.

'Come with me.'

They must check on Swanepoel again.

Florence was desperate. Where the hell was Evans? The carnage was dreadful. Only one Zimbabwean soldier had survived. Most of the South Africans were dead or captured. As far as she could tell, just one was unaccounted for – and he could be anywhere.

She searched for movement. Nothing. What about further up, towards the open terrain? She ducked involuntarily as a South African Air Force jet shot low overhead. Shit! Where was their chopper? Had Jenny summoned it yet?

They *had* to find Evans – then get out before it was too late.

The Cheetah's pilot spotted the Zimbabwean helicopter flying low over the Limpopo. Illuminated by the early morning sunshine, its shadow skimmed the bush. He radioed HQ, then dived straight towards it.

The chopper was a couple of kilometres into South African airspace when its pilot recognised the threat. He immediately banked away, then turned quickly, and raced back: dodging about to avoid becoming a clear target.

Meanwhile, at the farmhouse, Viljoen looked up in relief as he heard the distinctive whine of the Cheetah's Snecma engines. Were they sending help? He had to get to safety, but Evans was a pain in the arse. He'd gone limp – seemed in a complete daze. Was he really hurt that bad, or was he faking?

Viljoen banged his gun into the Englishman's back. No reaction, so he let him sink to the ground. Better to make a run for it on his own. Not much cover up here: he must circle back, get to the car park before he was seen, and creep up on the guy guarding the vehicles.

Viljoen began to creep through the long grass on the ridge. He was concentrating so hard on the buildings below that he almost stepped upon the girl.

Jenny heard a rustle in the dry grass, but had no time to investigate. The sound was suddenly drowned out by the deafening roar of a jet. No wonder she was caught completely off guard when a man almost fell on top of her.

She toppled over, and her pistol dropped to the ground. What would she have done with it anyway? The man straightened up, levelling his machine gun at her. She was no longer a spectator: she was about to die. She felt empty and numb.

'Who are you?'

His harsh South African accent identified him as one of *them*.

'J-Jenny Stuart,' she stammered, 'from London.'

Christ, she sounded pathetic.

'*Bitch!*'

Instead of squeezing the trigger, he turned the gun upside

down – butt raised high – to smash it against her head. She screamed. Then, as he prepared to put his whole weight behind the blow, the world exploded.

The man was lifted bodily into the air. His head had become a grotesque cavern. His gun clattered down, grazing her shoulder.

Then, the sound of running feet. Florence! Kalash at the ready, her eyes darting.

'Are you okay?'

'Yeah ... thank you ...' Jenny's voice trailed off, feebly.

She was in awe of this woman: one moment a clinical killer, the next a supportive sister giving her a reassuring hug.

Florence grabbed Jenny's handset to talk to the chopper.

'Come on, come on – what's the hold up?'

Jenny couldn't hear the reply, just a crackle of sound.

'Going back? What the hell do you mean you're *going back?*'

Florence stared into the distance. Took a breath. Then she spoke firmly: 'Okay. Retreat. But get back here in twenty minutes and hover just across the river. We'll drive towards you. Pick us up this side if possible.'

'Come on,' she urged Jenny. 'We must find Jim. The South African jet is tracking our chopper. There's not much time.'

Makuyana wasn't messing about. 'Answer my questions and I'll leave you here to be rescued. Say nothing and I'll kill you.'

Swanepoel knew he had no choice. They'd kill him anyway. It would be a relief: the pain was unbearable. He'd never walk again. That black bastard could go fok himself.

'What is the China operation? We know there's a plan. What is it?'

Swanepoel ignored him, eyes closed. Almost passing out, he grasped his legs, as warm piss dribbled down inside his pants.

'Tell me your plan. We know it will happen soon. We're prepared.'

Makuyana was bluffing, and he knew Swanepoel wasn't fooled. If only he had more time – he could have broken the old man.

Makuyana kicked one of Swanepoel's shattered legs. The man screeched in agony. 'One last chance. Answer!' Makuyana barked.

'I don't understand your question.' Swanepoel was grinning, despite his excruciating pain.

Makuyana knew it was time. As he raised his Kalash, he saw the slaughtered bodies of his pregnant wife and son. He fired into Swanepoel's heart. The explosion echoed round the room, almost piercing his eardrums.

Someone was trying to drag him to his feet again. Jim wasn't having it. Going limp was the only way to resist.

Then he heard a voice: 'Jim! Jim, wake up!'

No guttural accent. This voice was different. Somehow ... familiar.

He jerked himself awake.

Could it really be ...?

'Jenny!' He began to tremble uncontrollably. What on earth was *she* doing here?

Nothing made sense anymore.

Makuyana was unaware that the Cheetah had radioed back to Trichardt for a support gunship. He just knew there wasn't much time.

The six of them piled into two cars: the only surviving Zimbabwean soldier with Petersen; the others together. Florence drove, so Makuyana could talk to Jim. The man was clearly in shock. They had to be gentle.

'Jim, I'm sorry – but I have to ask you some questions. Something terrible is about to happen,' said Makuyana.

Jim nodded.

'Who was the Chinese man who questioned you at the house in Harare?'

'How do you know about that?' Jim looked even more confused.

'Petersen told me.'

'Petersen?'

'The coloured guy in the other car. He was with you in the house. Said a Chinese man tried to interrogate you. Who was he?'

Jim looked at Jenny. She'd turned round to watch them from the front passenger seat.

'Wang Bi Nan,' he replied.

'*Wang?*' she gasped. 'In Harare?'

'Who is he?' Makuyana realised this was important.

'The man behind the attempts on Jim's life in China,' Jenny answered. 'If *he's* here, we're in trouble.'

'What sort of trouble?'

'Who knows,' she replied wearily. 'But he's got good connections – even with British intelligence.'

'The photo,' Jim murmured.

'Photo?'

'Yeah,' said Jenny. 'I accidentally snapped Wang on the Great Wall.'

Makuyana frowned, trying not to lose his patience.

'Jim's home was searched when the Green Planet story first broke. Nothing was taken. Just *that* picture: one of dozens.'

So, Wang is important, Makuyana thought. But why is he in Harare?

Florence was sure the car's suspension had gone. The steering wheel jarred her shoulders as she bumped down the dusty track, little more than a cattle path.

Although the sun shone brightly, it was still cold and would remain so until midmorning. They were just a couple of kilometres from the river, she judged. Not long now, though the going was painfully slow.

She was trying to listen to the conversation between the other three, but it was difficult because the driving needed such concentration. How did she manage to keep going, she wondered? By refusing to think about the killing, the danger, how desperately tired she was.

Suddenly they came to the end of the rutted farm track. But there was no gate – just a deep ditch which their cars couldn't cross.

'We'll have to make a run for it!' Florence called urgently.

They jumped out and started crossing the ditch into the field.

But Petersen tapped Makuyana on the shoulder. 'I'm not coming,' he said simply.

'What do you mean? We have to *move!*' Makuyana, angry at the delay, gestured to the others to keep going.

But Petersen sat down on the ground. 'There's no future for me back in Harare. You'll have to try me for espionage – if the ANC don't execute me first. I don't want the humiliation. My family will never recover. The township comrades would kill my relatives. I am not coming.'

Makuyana could see it was pointless to dissuade him. 'What will you do?'

'Get away, maybe start a new life. Can you leave me those spare guns and ammunition from the dead soldiers? If there's any problem getting across the river, I'll try to cover you.'

Makuyana pondered. The guy might pump bullets into their backs, but he didn't think so.

He hoped to hell he was right.

'Okay,' he shrugged.

'*Amandla!*' Petersen called. Makuyana heard the ANC's 'power to the people' rallying call as he hurried away, but couldn't bring himself to return it.

Petersen didn't mind. For the first time in years, he was at peace with himself.

The throbbing sound of gunship engines pierced the morning stillness. Sadly, not one of theirs, Makuyana realised. By now, the others were halfway across the field leading to the Limpopo, and he hurried to catch up with them.

The South African pilot was sweeping the area for any sign of activity. First, he spotted some people running, then two parked vehicles: familiar unmarked security service cars.

A man was standing by the cars, trying to wave him down. The pilot considered his options: he might *just* have time to drop a rope ladder, haul the man up, and still catch the others before they reached the border.

Problem was, he didn't know who was on their side. He'd been ordered merely to 'go and take a look'. But he could see that the farmhouse was deserted – and that there had been a bloody battle. He decided to drop the rope ladder.

As it tumbled down to the man below, his crew started yelling in alarm. The pilot pulled sideways and the chopper sharply lifted. The man was still lying on the ground – but he was pointing a machine gun right at them.

Shots crashed into the cockpit, gashing the pilot's leg and drilling a neat hole in the gunner's head. Gritting his teeth, the pilot pulled desperately at the controls, trying to bank the gunship so they could gun the bastard down.

'Chopper ahead! Chopper ahead!' The voice of his navigator burst through the intercom. The pilot saw another helicopter hovering over the running figures near the river, no more than two hundred metres away.

His crew were still firing at the man on the ground, but they couldn't get a decent sight – the gunship had to keep twisting to avoid the bullets assailing them from below. Ignoring the searing pain in his legs, the pilot continued to climb, then threw the gunship round to face the enemy chopper. He fired off a rocket but had no time to steady it, so the missile sailed harmlessly overhead.

But then the enemy chopper settled on the ground. Yes! The pilot began to accelerate towards it.

Another bullet from below crashed into the cockpit, hitting him in the stomach. He jerked, frantically grappling with the controls.

'Got the bastard sir!' one of the crew shouted. Too bloody late, he thought bitterly.

Maybe not ...

He had a clear sight of the enemy chopper in the middle of his viewfinder. There could be no mistake this time. He fired some tracer bullets which tore into its fuselage.

Pain was flaming through him, blood bursting from his shattered body – yet somehow the pilot was able to position his index finger to trigger another rocket. But the gunship fell sharply to one side. He had lost control, and the rocket was sweeping away into the distance.

His 'Sparks' just had time to put out a distress signal before they crashed in a sheet of raging orange, setting the field ablaze.

What a beautiful sight ...

That was Petersen's last thought, as his bullet-riddled body slumped down onto the veld.

12

Harare was still sleeping, but the Leader had been hard at work for more than an hour, finalising the speech he would give to Parliament that evening.

A rare privilege for a visiting head of state to be given this honour. It reflected the importance Zimbabwe placed on its links with China, and the debt it owed Beijing for consistent support during ZANU's liberation struggle.

The special gathering would take place in the old parliament building erected by Cecil Rhodes, which had been dominated by whites until Independence in 1980.

The Leader wanted to mark the occasion with a major speech about the need to adapt communist principles for the modern age. Gorbachev was doing it in the Soviet Union, and the Leader was taking a similarly reformist stance.

The Communist bloc was in a state of flux, and China was being pulled in all directions. Centralised economic planning of all production, distribution and exchange hadn't worked. Therefore, to secure the massive growth his country needed, he was throwing the door wide open to private capital – even from the West.

But it was still important to plan, because market economy

was wasteful and inefficient. Besides, it created huge injustices and inequalities. Ownership had to be spread – not concentrated in the hands of either the state or a privileged few.

He knew the old guard were vehemently opposed to this, and wanted the state to maintain total ownership. They claimed that Chinese culture had never had a strong localised or privatised tradition, but this was untrue. Private enterprise should be allowed to grow – albeit only under the Party's ever-watchful eye.

It would be a watershed speech. The world's media were already briefed, and there'd be saturation coverage at home. One of the advantages of state control, as he knew full well.

Venter and Coetzee were also early risers. They showered and ate a light breakfast, relieved that after weeks of waiting and detailed planning, their big day had arrived.

Fit and fresh, their tanned muscles honed to perfection, they felt completely confident. Nothing was left to chance – they would pick up the special van at midday, load it, then drive to the chosen position. They would place bollards at the parking spot which had been officially cleared for their use. Then they would return to their rented house to rest for a while.

At the appointed hour, Venter and Coetzee would drive back to the city centre. All being well, they would fly out of Zimbabwe two hours later.

KJ didn't wake early by choice – his emergency phone jerked him out of a deep sleep.

As he listened to the news, his mood changed abruptly from half-awake irritation to pure, concentrated anger.

The debacle at the border was an absolute disaster! How the hell had it been allowed to happen? There was no explanation. Some of his best people wiped out on their own patch, a chopper shot down, and two crucial detainees snatched back.

Who was behind it? The ANC or the Zimbabweans? Nobody

was able to say. But a Zimbabwean helicopter had been detected crossing the border hours earlier, so it sounded suspiciously like a Harare-sanctioned operation.

How had a wily bird like Mauritz allowed it?

Ah ... Mauritz. Memories of his old friend flooded back. They'd enjoyed such great times together – when to be a white security policeman was to be immortal. Nobody could touch you, certainly no black. Now it was different: you had to fight for your very existence. And sometimes you lost.

The old counter-measures were no longer sufficient. Neither were tit-for-tat killings, bumping off ANC sympathisers, harassing the opposition, or letting your boys loose in the townships.

The enemy must be taught a *real* lesson before things got completely out of hand.

Yes. They had to be nuked.

Not by a big one. A short range weapon would do nicely: something that could be fixed to the chassis of an armoured vehicle.

They already had nuclear shells for their tanks, but these had severe limitations. Something like NATO's Lance missile would be good. But the Pentagon's new Multiple Launch Rocket System would be even better: more accurate, with a longer range than the Lance's 120 kilometres.

It would shake the very foundations of Zimbabwe – and put an end to ANC activity within its borders!

Of course, battlefield nuclear weapons had their dangers: you might wipe out some of your own forces, and fallout could drift back into your own territory. But so what? A small price to pay for the bigger prize: security for the *volk*, and a guarantee that God-given rights for the white man would be entrenched.

Just one problem. South Africa still lacked the necessary technology – and that's where Beijing came in.

*

Jenny grasped Jim's hand tightly as the helicopter swept up and over the hills, racing northward across the border in the bright sunshine.

Jim still felt numb. Shocked by the brutal killings; disorientated by all the noise. He kept seeing the South African chopper exploding into flames: it could so easily have been *them*. He mumbled a few tender words to Jenny, but mostly stared ahead, his eyes closed – trying to escape the terror.

Jenny was his rock, but her sudden appearance at the farm had only added to his confusion. Like a classic heroine, right on cue, she had saved him.

Now he wanted to comfort her, but somehow he couldn't. He had nothing to give. The trauma had left its mark. He felt remote and detached.

In time he would try to make it up to her. But he couldn't imagine when that might be.

From the helicopter, Makuyana radioed HQ. Then he contacted the President's security chief – who did not sound thrilled when he heard the news.

Makuyana could imagine him assessing the diplomatic and military consequences of invading South African territory. 'Invading': that was the word Pretoria would use.

Ever since independence, Zimbabwe had lived with the nightmare of a border incident – or an ANC incursion – that might provoke open warfare. And today's operation could easily be portrayed as an act of aggression, even though the intention had been to rescue a kidnapped civilian. The bloody bodies left behind – including those of Zimbabweans – would be hard to explain.

But Makuyana had a bigger concern: the visit of the Chinese head of state. What were the South Africans planning to do? He'd gathered enough evidence – albeit scraps – to suggest an imminent climax. But *what*?

The main breakthrough was Jim's identification of the Chinese aide, Wang. Makuyana had asked HQ to pinpoint the man's whereabouts and put him under covert surveillance.

They'd come tantalisingly close to cracking the whole business, but another door had slammed shut with Swanepoel's capture and death. Makuyana had felt angry when he shot him: not with Swanepoel, but because he'd been forced to blow away another vital source – perhaps the most vital one of all.

He glanced over at the English couple. They looked absolutely shattered, especially the man. He didn't want to disturb them, but he had to ensure that no detail was missed.

For the next hour, the three huddled together uncomfortably on metal seats, trying to talk above the din of the rotors.

All night and into the dawn, the Nimrod monitored much to-ing and fro-ing in the airspace around the border. Now the situation was back to normal, Captain Geffen told Makuyana's people.

But suddenly the Nimrod's screens went into meltdown: blips, flashes, darting flickers. The world below had erupted into a frenzy of activity.

Inside South Africa the airspace around Trichardt was abuzz. Fighters were taking off, transport planes were approaching from the south, and ground vehicles were moving toward the Zimbabwean border. Some of them were fast – probably trucks and jeeps. Some were slower – maybe Casspir APCs. Others crawled along – probably tanks.

Grim-faced, Geffen alerted Makuyana and Harare HQ. Zimbabwe was about to be invaded.

Wang was on his way to breakfast when there was a knock at his door: one of the Sheraton's porters, delivering a sealed envelope. It contained an instruction for him to call a certain number immediately.

When he heard the news, he gripped the phone until his knuckles whitened. Disaster at the border. Evans on the loose. That probably meant his *own* cover had been blown. Not for the first time, he cursed the English professor.

Wang grabbed some essentials and left the hotel. If Evans had identified him he would claim diplomatic immunity. Meanwhile he had important things to do. The Old Man had to be warned. And later he was to meet a South African undercover agent downtown.

He was so engrossed in his plans that he failed to notice the unmarked car following his cab at a discreet distance.

Amazing how adrenaline could keep you going. Makuyana hadn't slept for 24 hours, and had survived a vicious gun battle in enemy territory – but after a quick wash and shave, he felt fine. Brittle, but fine.

It would hit him later, he knew. Meanwhile, there was work to be done. Florence was in a similar state, and had looked surprisingly cheery after her shower and change of clothes. Again, he was in awe of her stamina and guts. She'd acted with such brutal efficiency at the farmhouse – he knew he could always count on her, no matter what.

He'd sent the English couple back to the Sheraton, with strict instructions to rest. Wang was under surveillance and had just entered the Chinese Embassy. They'd have to pick him up soon, but first needed to see what he was up to – so Florence was despatched to keep watch outside the embassy, along with another colleague.

The Nimrod's report of South African military movements was disturbing, but he couldn't do anything about that. Better to focus on the Chinese delegation. Who were the key players? How did Wang fit in?

Systematically, Makuyana sifted through his notes – including the new information from Evans and Jenny. So much intrigue and complexity, but it all boiled down to one thing: a faction within the Chinese ruling elite was apparently cooperating with Pretoria over nuclear weaponry.

But why had the action shifted to Zimbabwe?

Makuyana stared at the ceiling, noticing a spider's web in one of the corners.

A faction in Beijing's ruling elite ...

China's top brass – the leaders – were right here in Harare! Were members of the faction here too? What were they planning? And who *exactly* was Wang's boss?

He ordered an aide to bring him the names of the full delegation, including back-up staff and the people for whom they worked. He could get the names in a couple of minutes. But the relationship between the leaders and staff would have to be checked: either with the President's office, or the Chinese Embassy itself.

General Gert Strijdom, head of South Africa's armed forces, wasn't a fan of consultation.

Ever since President PW Botha had taken over the leadership in 1978 – initially as prime minister – the military had become increasingly powerful, supplanting the security services. The General had been waiting for the right moment to show what South Africa's armed forces could do.

As soon as the hotline buzzed at his bedside, he was ready for action. In the morning light, his muscular naked body was as taut as a coiled spring – but he listened impassively to the briefing, giving no hint of his true emotions.

This was exactly the opportunity he needed!

Thinking quickly, he called the Army Chief and then his counterpart in the Air Force. Both had anticipated his instructions and assured him that troops and aircraft were fully prepared.

But they were shocked when he gave them an additional

order: to replace conventional shells and bombs with nuclear warheads in selected Olifant tanks and Cheetah aircraft.

Was there Presidential authority for this, they asked?

Yes, Strijdom told them. He was lying of course, but he would get the necessary clearance later.

Meanwhile, the first tank regiments should cross the border in about five hours.

News of Zimbabwe's successful attack in the Northern Transvaal spread like wildfire through unofficial networks in South Africa's bleak black townships.

Pupils heard about it in the mid-morning break, and surged from their school yards into the streets. Young comrades led spontaneous demonstrations all over the country.

ANC cadres in *uMkhonto weSizwe* began to activate plans which had lain dormant for years. Arms and ammunition were gradually retrieved from ingenious secret stores. Guns and bombs were moved around in old cars and dustcarts; grenades and pistols were hidden in the nappies of babies on their mothers' backs.

By midday KJ's informers were reporting the biggest black mobilisation for armed struggle ever imagined.

As news leaked of troop movements towards the border, there was panic selling of shares on Johannesburg's stock exchange and the rand took a sharp tumble internationally.

White mothers looked anxiously at their black maids – who continued to iron and clean, obediently performing their duties. In solemn tones, white head teachers briefed ranks of white children at emergency assemblies, while parents jammed nursery school switchboards to say they were coming to collect their little ones.

In affluent white suburbs, the chatter at coffee mornings and on bowling greens was about nothing else. Office canteens buzzed with feverish speculation.

By early afternoon wildcat strikes were erupting across the country. Thousands of black miners walked out. Car mechanics too. Construction workers downed tools and left building sites.

The Chamber of Commerce issued an urgent statement: if the strikes continued, production would grind to a halt within a day.

In Harare, the atmosphere was almost as febrile.

The armed forces were put on standby, but there was to be no aggression. Pretoria was by far superior in strength and firepower: direct confrontation was not an option. The Zimbabweans could do no more than block the South Africans at strategic points and force them either to retreat or attack.

The President was to make a live broadcast that evening, after the state ceremony for the Chinese leader. Despite everything, the ceremony would go ahead. Pretoria must not be allowed to disrupt such an important diplomatic and economic milestone.

Meanwhile, Makuyana uncovered more details about Wang. He was attached to the staff of Mr Hua Zhi Yang – a veteran minister in the Chinese politburo – and he'd arrived a few days before the main party.

Interesting: had it given Wang more time to plan and prepare? But if so, for what? Makuyana kept coming back to the central questions: *what* and *when*?

His political intelligence team gave him a quick briefing on the politics of the Chinese ruling group. Then he called an aide: 'I want an appointment with the Chinese leader. Urgently. I have the President's authorisation.'

Nobody took much notice when Eugene Fraser arrived at the Chinese Embassy for an appointment. It was normal for local business people to meet visiting delegations. One way or another, diplomacy was usually a lubricant for trade.

But Florence Dube was *very* interested to see Mr Fraser. For some time she had been watching the embassy from a surveillance vehicle parked outside – and she immediately called Makuyana.

Fraser disappeared into the building. He was ushered into a small room occupied by two men: the elder was diminutive and formal (he must be the minister, thought Fraser); and his younger colleague wore horn-rimmed glasses (that must be Wang).

No need for an interpreter – they both spoke fluent English. They got down to the discussion right away, much of which was technical: the delivery of more warheads, and a timeframe for testing the new weapons. An hour later, Fraser departed, climbing into his white Porsche.

As he sped back to his office, an unmarked car swept through the embassy gates. Major Keith Makuyana – wearing a smart dark suit – gave his credentials to the receptionist, explaining that he had come for a pre-arranged audience with the Leader. He also casually inquired about the previous visitor, and asked whom he'd met.

The receptionist smiled at the courteous, tall man in front of her. 'Mr Hua,' she replied, unaware that she had added a vital piece to his jigsaw puzzle.

The meeting with the Leader didn't take long. Makuyana decided not to tell him about his suspicions of Hua and Wang. He didn't want to risk alerting the pair – or raise any suspicion with the delegation.

Instead, he simply informed the Leader of the likelihood of an assassination attempt. The timing was uncertain, but he would be most vulnerable that evening: when he appeared in public to address Parliament.

The Leader absorbed the information calmly. He was a cool customer, Makuyana thought.

Did the Zimbabweans suspect who the assassins might be?

No, the security chief replied truthfully, thankful not to be challenged about the source of his information. In return, he asked the Leader if *he* had any thoughts on the matter. No, none.

Makuyana had two requests. First, that the Leader should tell only his personal security team and not the rest of the delegation. That did provoke a raised eyebrow, but the Leader agreed.

The second request was immediately approved: that Makuyana should travel with the Leader in his armour-plated car when he left the embassy, and would stay with him at all times.

As Makuyana departed, he noted that the Leader looked very thoughtful – and rather subdued.

The two had dozed through the morning and into the early afternoon, lying back-to-back in Jim's bed. Makuyana had insisted there was nothing more they could do, and had posted a guard outside their hotel door.

Despite their exhaustion, they slept fitfully. Jenny was troubled by Jim's remoteness: both emotional and physical. It made her feel lost, miserable.

Eventually she got up and rang room service for sandwiches and salad. Jim still lay in bed with his face to the wall, barely acknowledging her suggestion of food.

She turned on the radio – just to break the silence. Then she jerked to attention. A sombre newscaster was reporting the threat of an invasion after a border clash. There were no other details, but Jenny knew it was the battle at the farmhouse.

'Jim . . .' – she shook his shoulders, urgently – 'listen to this!'

He turned slowly, emerging from under the bedsheets. Then, as if a mask had been pulled from his face, he was suddenly alert as they both digested the news.

Wang made his first mistake just after lunch.

He had been procrastinating all morning. No operation had

ever been as crucial: nor had he ever been so dependent on people outside his direct control. But ... should he risk contacting the two South Africans for a final check?

He couldn't phone from the embassy, and there were few public callboxes in the city, so he decided to go to a nearby hotel. There, he dialled a number, let it ring twice, and replaced the receiver. He repeated the action, and rang again.

The voice at the other end was curt, but Wang wasn't deterred. He just wanted to confirm that all was well, and the itinerary was unchanged.

What they hell was *that* about, Venter wondered? The man must be jittery, but why? The two Afrikaners hadn't listened to the news, and knew nothing about developments at the border.

Wang was walking out of the hotel, lost in thought, when he almost bumped into a young woman. He apologised, and tried to step out of the way – but she blocked him.

'Mr Wang Bi Nan?'

'Yes.'

'You're under arrest.' She took him by the arm, keeping her other hand in her jacket pocket.

He cursed his stupidity. He'd been caught off guard because she was a mere woman.

'There must be a mistake! Who are you?' he demanded. Then he pulled back, frightened. The woman was much stronger than he thought.

'No mistake, Mr Wang. You're wanted by the security police.'

'I claim diplomatic immunity! I am a Chinese citizen and my embassy is nearby.' He pointed in its direction: 'I am returning there now.'

'No, you are not,' the woman replied firmly.

He realised there was no point in arguing. She had pulled a gun on him.

*

The United Nations Security Council was unanimous in its condemnation, but this fell on deaf ears – as did cool diplomatic pressure from Washington and London.

South Africa was a pariah, yet the ruling white elite found this perversely reassuring. Deep down, they'd always known they were on their own: like the Old Testament patriarch Jacob in Egypt. In the final battle for survival, fair weather friends would desert them, but white supremacy would prevail.

So, the military advance northward gathered momentum: led by the engineer corps. They carried portable steel bridges – specially designed a decade earlier – which could drop into position across the Limpopo.

Just across the border in Zimbabwe, so-called 'sleepers' were activated: white farmers, businessmen and pensioners, who had long been awaiting the call. Their task was to provide the South African army with intelligence – so far, they had little to report.

Harare was on full alert, but there was no mass mobilisation. A few signs of military activity, but no apparent push south. The Zimbabweans were playing a waiting game.

Meanwhile, the first Olifant tank clattered across the Limpopo on a portable bridge. It strained up the other side of the bank, and onto the plain. There, it stopped: its turret sweeping slowly round in an arc, as its long barrel menaced the landscape. A grazing herd of zebra galloped away.

Otherwise, nothing.

The tank crawled forward cautiously. Still nothing. Soon, other military vehicles followed.

Four hundred metres away, hidden behind some rocks on the slope of a small *kopje*, a young soldier passed his binoculars to a colleague and reached for his transmitter.

He was the first to confirm the rumours. The invasion had begun.

*

They made love as they showered together, washing away the anguish and confusion of the last 24 hours. Afterwards, still breathless, they let the water flow over their bodies for a few minutes more.

Jenny felt exhilarated by the power she had roused in Jim – and relieved that he had come back to her. He was no longer cold and distant, but imbued with a new drive and sense of purpose.

But, as they dressed, Jim found his own thoughts returning to Wang and his insistent questioning the previous day. What was the man doing in Harare? Why was he so obsessed with Jim's presence?

He opened the door of their hotel room and asked the bored-looking guard in the corridor where he could find Makuyana. Impossible, he was told. The boss could not be contacted today: he was in charge of security arrangements for the Chinese leader's state visit.

It was the first Jim had heard of any such visit. The Beijing connection yet again. Something bad was about to happen: he could feel it. But *what*?

He went back inside to Jenny, rigid with tension.

Wang wasn't giving anything away. This was a breach of diplomatic protocol, he protested vehemently. But they ignored him, bundling him into the back of a vehicle, and forcing a bag over his head.

He was taken to an interrogation room, where he refused to say a word – either to Florence or Makuyana. The Englishman Evans must have informed them of his presence in Harare, because they clearly knew about his undercover movements. But it seemed they were still unaware of his actual plan.

Except that Makuyana kept mentioning the Leader. Did Wang support the Leader? Did his boss Hua support him? These questions were uncomfortably prescient.

Say nothing: that was the mantra that had been instilled into him. Once you start talking, you can't stop. It was too risky for them to use torture, so he just had to remain silent for the next four hours. After that, the Old Man would secure his release.

For by then, the Old Man would be in power.

Makuyana and Florence were frustrated by Wang's obduracy. They needed time to break the Chinese man – but that was exactly what they didn't have. They were so near, yet still so far. It was the Swanepoel situation all over again.

The sense of crisis was heightened by reports of South African convoys crossing the border. To what lengths was Pretoria prepared to go? Was the 'invasion' just a tit-for-tat response to the farmhouse clash?

Usually the South Africans reacted to an ANC incursion by hitting a village or attacking ANC officials. But this was something bigger.

Much bigger.

Strijdom paced around the control room, pausing periodically to peer at the huge electronic screen which continuously mapped the steady advance of his forces.

The President was unhappy. He felt his hand had been forced. But Strijdom had politely reminded him of the contingency plans which the President himself had authorised two years before.

In any case, it was now a fait accompli. The President could rest assured that he would be consulted before the war cabinet convened under his chairmanship.

But something was puzzling: the lack of any obvious military response from Harare. The Zimbabweans seemed to be holding back – almost egging him on.

Maddening. Strijdom needed a confrontation: he needed them to attack – even just to get in the way – so his forces could justify a military clash. As soon as there was a real battle, he could produce his ace.

For all its ruthlessness, not even apartheid South Africa could deploy a tactical nuclear weapon without some sort of excuse.

An excuse – that was all Strijdom needed.

Predictably, the trouble started in Soweto.

Angry school pupils burnt down the home of a black councillor, denouncing him as a collaborator. Within minutes, police opened fire: tear gas, then live ammunition. The crowd scattered, carrying their dead and wounded. But surprisingly, they regrouped, their mood defiant. The police saw a new and terrifying determination in their faces. Cars were overturned and set ablaze. Smoke billowed.

Then, the police heard something astounding: a sniper was firing back at them! Streams of bullets whipped into their lines. But where was the firing coming from? Somebody in the crowd? Crouched in their Casspirs, they couldn't tell.

The protestors roared their approval, surging forward: frenzied young faces at the fore, not caring about their fate.

A grenade burst under one of the police Land Rovers, disabling it. The chief called for reinforcements, but another unit was under attack a couple of kilometres away. And the army was fully focused on the invasion.

The police chief yelled into his radio: didn't they understand? He'd already lost a dozen men, and many more were wounded. White lives were being lost right now! This had never happened before ...

It was true. He had policed Soweto for five years, but had never witnessed such murderous fury. And the well-organised sniping was without precedent. There was no alternative but to retreat.

With excited shouts, the people surged forward triumphantly. They were winning. For the first time, they had beaten the police.

The snipers melted away into dark alleys, seeking refuge in the small brick hovels that passed as homes.

And the township comrades went on the rampage.

Rows of people lined the approach to Zimbabwe's parliament building, straining to catch a glimpse of the President as he waited to welcome the Chinese leader.

Jim was there with Jenny: not really to see the spectacle, but because of a gut feeling that he *ought* to be there. Florence had shared the reassuring news of Wang's detention, but he still felt uneasy. Anyway, he was curious to see what the Chinese leader looked like.

Florence scanned the street systematically. The most dangerous moment for the Leader would be when he emerged from his limousine and walked the short distance to the entrance of parliament. They had cordoned off the crowd, ensuring that everyone was kept well back from the parking place.

Everything seemed in order. Nearby buildings had been searched for snipers: police were everywhere.

Despite the invasion, the mood was jolly. Why was the President playing it so cool? She longed to discuss it with Makuyana, but there had been no opportunity.

Florence walked away from the parliament building, having surveyed the approach. By now, she was beyond exhaustion: operating on automatic pilot.

A telecom van was parked across the road, in a spot cordoned off by cones. A white police officer was checking the van, watched by the driver who stood by the vehicle with his back to her.

The driver got back into the van, and the officer remained nearby, checking the crowd. Florence glanced at her watch.

The official cavalcade would now be leaving the embassy, and should arrive in about five minutes. Everything was under control.

*

The Old Man was worried. Where was Wang? And why was the Zimbabwe security chief now part of the official entourage?

Makuyana pressed into the back seat alongside the Leader and his assistant, apologising for the squeeze. As the cars swept out of the embassy gate, he cradled his pistol in his lap. The Leader seemed nervous and grumpy.

Nothing was said during the journey. Makuyana kept his eyes fixed ahead. If anything was going to happen it would probably be out in front. Side roads had been closed off so traffic could not intercept the procession. But he wouldn't be able to relax until everyone was safely inside the building.

No traffic, no red lights. Outrider sirens screaming, the cavalcade swept past bystanders hoping to glimpse the famous Chinese head of state.

Gun in hand, safety catch off, Makuyana leant forward.

Florence was crossing the road again to check the other side, when a murmur went through the crowd. She turned and saw the official cavalcade: about 400 metres away.

Then, much closer, she heard an engine starting up.

It was the telecom van.

She started to walk towards it. The police officer – probably an inspector – was still standing by the vehicle. He looked unconcerned.

Reassured by his presence, Florence approached.

As she did so, she felt oddly uneasy. There was something familiar about the officer's posture ... something that didn't feel right.

The cavalcade was just a hundred metres away, headed by police motorbikes. As they swept past, the van suddenly roared into life and accelerated out into the road – right in front of the Leader's limousine.

His chauffeur hit the brakes but couldn't prevent the limo from sliding into the side of the van and shuddering to a halt.

The police officer ran over to the car, and the van driver climbed out. He was also familiar: tall, young, white. Yes: the killer! The guy she'd seen in her office and at the hospital.

Sprinting forward, she saw him lob a stun grenade into the crowd to clear a path.

As she ran, the police inspector rattled on the limo's passenger door. The chauffeur, relieved that there was hardly any damage, leaned across to wind down the window.

Makuyana had been jerked forwards by the emergency stop, but quickly recovered himself. He saw the policeman peering in. Christ! He had seen this man before! And now he was levelling a pistol straight at the Leader ...

In a split second Makuyana aimed his own revolver at the policeman and squeezed the trigger. There was a deafening roar, and the man rocked back: a neat hole drilled in his forehead; his face twisted in astonished agony.

'Get us out of here! Might be others!' Makuyana shouted at the shocked chauffeur. Then he turned around to check on the Leader. He looked emotionless – but unhurt.

Jenny and Jim hadn't been standing far from the parked telecom van, so the explosions were shatteringly loud.

Jim saw a man burst through the crowd, followed by the sprinting figure of Florence. The man was tall and strong: she was losing him.

Without thinking, he left Jenny and joined the pursuit.

Florence was 100 metres behind the man. Jim saw her stop and fire, seeming to hit him in the shoulder. The man stumbled, but ran on, disappearing round a corner.

Jim caught up with Florence. Panting with exhaustion, she was startled by his sudden appearance.

'Chase him!' she gasped. 'I'll follow. But be careful!'

Buoyed up by adrenaline, Jim sprinted off in pursuit – any residual weariness forgotten.

The man came into view again. He was heading down a side road lined by offices. His injury seemed to be slowing him down.

Jim slowed too – what would he do if he caught him? He had no idea, but couldn't give up now.

Coetzee was staggering from the pain. The bitch! She'd hurt him badly. He was losing blood fast – from his right shoulder. How would he hold his gun?

But where was Venter? He'd heard the gunshot and assumed his friend would follow him, as planned. The unlocked getaway car was parked just ahead, with their hand luggage in the boot. But he couldn't wait much longer. Some bastard was following him. Blood was soaking through his overalls, and he felt dizzy ...

Would they let him board the plane in such a state?

Jim could see his quarry clearly now. He had stopped by a Fiat Tipo, and was opening the door.

Looking back, he could see Florence running towards him – staggering with exhaustion. Then she slipped. Her gun clattered onto the road, and slid towards him. Automatically, he picked it up. It was strangely heavy, making him feel lopsided. Florence was still not back on her feet.

He lifted the gun, holding it with both hands as he remembered seeing on TV. He pointed it at the man and squeezed the trigger. The gun jerked upwards, jolting his body. A bullet hit the back window, just as the car was pulling out of the parking space.

Jim pointed and fired again. The second bullet went straight through the driver's window, shattering the windscreen.

Fragments of glass splintered into Coetzee's face, half blinding him. He pushed his foot onto the accelerator, and the Tipo lurched across the road, mounted a pavement and smashed into the front of a building.

Jim was transfixed by the chaos that had erupted from his clumsy shots. Then fear struck him. If the man was still alive, he could turn and shoot him. He shrank into a nearby doorway, and peered out.

'Well done!' Florence startled him with a clap on the shoulder. Wordlessly, he handed back her gun.

She crept towards the car, poised to shoot. But there was no need. Coetzee was slumped unconscious on the steering wheel, blood streaming down his face.

Despite a fifty-minute delay, the Leader's address went ahead as planned. He sounded a little shaky at first, still in shock after the near-assassination.

His audience responded warmly – from relief and politeness. They were less enthusiastic about the contents of his speech. For the ZANU stalwarts, it marked a revisionist departure from Marxist principles.

The Old Man would have agreed, but he hadn't heard a word. His mind was in turmoil. The plot had failed: no point in alerting the generals back home. All those years of planning were in vain, and his own future was now in question.

He felt utterly defeated.

With the Chinese delegation safely back at the embassy, Makuyana confronted the badly injured Coetzee.

The man was in no state to resist. He knew very little: was just carrying out orders.

But Makuyana kept him slumped in a chair, blood still trickling from his shoulder. Then he had Wang brought in. The Chinese man immediately lost his insolent manner, realising the plot had failed.

Makuyana put it to him bluntly: either he talked, and would be allowed to return home, or he would be detained and prosecuted.

Wang had nothing to lose, so he talked. He explained how the South Africans had acquired battlefield nuclear weapons but needed to upgrade their equipment to deploy them effectively. Under Makuyana's merciless probing, the whole story spilled out. The pieces of the jigsaw finally fitted together.

Makuyana was shaken by the full enormity of the plot, and found himself shivering. He had to get hold of Stan Moyo: the President's security chief. There was no time to waste.

The President was about make a television address to the nation about the South African invasion. His speech had to be rewritten – and quickly.

Strijdom's nerves were rattled. Why were the Zimbabweans not fighting back? His forces had seized all border posts, and arrested the guards and officials without a shot being fired. Now they were well over a hundred kilometers inside foreign territory.

According to intelligence reports, the Zimbabwean army was retreating. That meant his troops could take Bulawayo before the night was out. But did they *want* to? The intention was to teach Zimbabwe a lesson: not to occupy the sodding country.

Meanwhile, Cabinet was growing restless. Shares continued to plummet, and business leaders – who had profited greatly from apartheid – were up in arms. Foreign companies and financiers were threatening to pull out, and the International Monetary Fund was demanding instant settlement of the country's debt. Gold was at a record low, and dealings were suspended.

At the same time, the townships were in uproar. The police could no longer contain the violence without military assistance.

Strijdom deliberated for a long while. Then he picked up the phone and spoke to the top brass.

The military advance was to be halted.

*

The staff lounge at security headquarters in Harare was crowded and silent. Jim and Jenny squeezed together on a sofa with Florence, as everyone stared at the television.

A solemn President appeared on the screen, his glasses reflecting awkwardly under the harsh lighting, a sheaf of notes before him. The media had received embargoed copies of the text an hour before, but at the last minute rumours had spread of substantial changes.

Across town in State House, Makuyana was also staring at the TV. He loved his country, but hated the President's growing despotism. Yet, at this moment, only he could save Zimbabwe.

The President had begun to speak.

'Comrades and friends,' he began, 'I had prepared to address you about the South African invasion of our country. But I have just received disturbing new information which makes the crisis even more serious than we had assumed.'

He paused, letting his words sink in. Then he took a breath, and continued.

'It seems that our very existence as a people is now threatened.'

Another pause.

'Some of you have heard of the attempted assassination of the leader of China, whom we have been honoured to receive as a guest. Fortunately, our security services were alert and saved his life. We caught the assassins. I have to tell you that they were South African agents.'

The President allowed his audience to absorb this.

'Today, the apartheid regime took over a great stretch of our country – *and* committed an act of terrorism, right here in our capital. We will not give in to such barbarism. We will fight if necessary.'

He rocked back slightly in his chair.

'You may be asking: why have we not done so already? Let me assure you, it is not because we are weak. No! We are ready to fight the oppressor until our beloved Zimbabwe is free again. But we must be strategic.

'My brothers and sisters ...' – Makuyana flinched at the phrase – 'I have confirmed today what we suspected for some time. Pretoria wants to provoke us. They need an excuse to unleash the terror of nuclear war upon our people and our beautiful land. Some of their aircraft and tanks are carrying nuclear warheads.'

Another long pause. The President cleared his throat.

'I do not need to tell you what a nuclear attack would mean. The devastation that would be caused by radioactive fallout. It does not seem to bother the South Africans that *they* would be affected too! That their people will also die, and *their* land will be contaminated when prevailing winds carry the radiation back across the border.

'I appeal to the people of the world, including white South Africans, to prevent such a catastrophe. I say to Pretoria: you have nothing to fear from Zimbabwe. I reject the assertion that last night's clash on South African territory could possibly justify lethal military mobilisation on the scale we now see. Zimbabwean forces were indeed involved, and I regret that. However, the truth about the clash has not yet been told.'

The President consulted his notes. Then he looked unwaveringly into the camera.

'Yesterday, a brave group of Zimbabwean soldiers and agents briefly crossed the border to rescue a British citizen who had been kidnapped in Harare by the South African National Intelligence Service. In the ensuing clash, there were casualties on both sides. Afterwards, our people retreated immediately.

'I have this to say to the South African government: if your forces continue to advance into Zimbabwe, we will defend ourselves. However, I urge you to withdraw before catastrophe strikes. Above all, I appeal to you to instruct your armed forces *not* to deploy their nuclear weapons. The horrific consequences of such action will disfigure our part of Africa for generations.'

Makuyana left State House with mixed feelings.

He was proud to have done his duty, but felt angry that the President – who was responsible for so many human rights atrocities – had now reinvented himself as a man of peace.

Makuyana wondered what his own future would hold. The President's security chief, Stan Moyo, was clearly jealous of his success, and would be gunning for him. How long could he survive?

Suddenly, he was overwhelmed by loneliness. There was only one person he needed at this moment. He plucked up his courage, and drove to HQ to find Florence.

Would she join him for a celebratory drink? Just the two of them? He sounded flustered.

Florence was astonished – and thrilled.

The general in charge of the Beijing garrison had been waiting three hours for his special phone to ring. Finally it did.

He answered: half enthusiastic, half apprehensive.

The familiar boom of the Leader's voice caught him completely off guard. He could barely concentrate as the Leader calmly informed him about the assassination attempt.

Everything was now under control: no need to worry. He was to convey this message down the line, to reassure the People's Liberation Army in the event of unsubstantiated rumours and fears.

At the end of the call, the Leader added casually – almost as an afterthought – that he had some additional news about their trusted colleague Hua.

Sadly, age had finally caught up with him, and his retirement would be announced immediately after the delegation returned.

What a fine man: a dedicated servant of the people, the last of the Long March veterans. Irreplaceable.

Such a pity.

Pretoria's public response to the Zimbabwean President's dramatic broadcast was a denunciation of his 'wild allegations' – and a flat denial that South Africa had ever contemplated using nuclear weapons.

Their troops had merely been sent over the border as a warning: that any further transgressions by Zimbabwe into South African territory would not be tolerated. They had never intended to advance further, a government spokesman lied, but they would stay until Pretoria was satisfied that no 'further aggression' was likely.

But in reality, the broadcast had rocked the government and the population. Its accuracy had stunned the few cabinet ministers and military leaders in the know. The clamour for a convincing rebuttal suggested that even whites loyal to the government believed there was something in what Mugabe had said.

As the implications of deploying even tactical nuclear weapons sank in, pressure mounted on the State President. A meeting of the ruling national parliamentary caucus was demanded by hitherto compliant MPs, who had virtually been on the leadership's payroll. There were even rumours of an unprecedented motion of no confidence in the President.

The Washington-based Gold Institute, representing bullion dealers and refiners, issued a 'member alert', warning of an imminent freeze on dealing in South African gold.

From Geneva, the World Gold Council, a public relations agency for the South African mining industry, expressed alarm that unspecified 'recent developments' could knock the bottom out of the country's market in gold exports. Prominent figures in the Italian jewellery business, which for decades had bought hundreds of tonnes of gold from South Africa, announced they were investigating alternative sources of supply.

There was just one dissenting voice: a backbench British Conservative MP, known colloquially as 'the Member for Pretoria'. He said he fully backed the military intervention. 'You can only answer force with force,' he insisted in an interview on *Today*: the BBC radio programme.

The incredulous interviewer omitted to ask if the Honourable Member's opinion might have been influenced by his many free trips to South Africa: most recently two luxurious weeks in the famed Kruger National Park, in the company of a glamorous woman half his age.

Quietly, unobtrusively, the retreat began. First, supply vehicles slipped back over the border, followed by troop carriers, then tanks.

No announcement, no admission. But the invasion ended two days after it had begun, as the military turned to more urgent matters at home.

In an unprecedented gesture of defiance, the green, yellow and black flag of the ANC was draped over the statue of Paul Kruger – the old Afrikaner hero – in Pretoria's main Church Square. It had been illegal to display the flag for decades.

KJ spoke darkly about a 'nationwide conspiracy mounted by the ANC', and his forces moved to suppress it. Privately he wondered if the white state still possessed the will to fight: he was tired, they were all tired.

But not everyone.

On Robben Island, across the freezing waters from Cape Town, another old man sat in the garden of his prison compound tending his tomatoes: growing plants from seeds as 'a small taste of freedom'.

He sensed his time was coming. He had prepared long and hard: the careful diet and daily keep-fit sessions. He had even learned the language of the ruling Afrikaners: studying their history and culture, while making tentative contact with their secret emissaries.

They had locked him up for two decades, but they had not broken him. He was stronger. They would need him to save the beloved country.

It was his destiny.

The world's media were waiting for Jim and Jenny outside the Sheraton.

Amidst a barrage of clicking cameras and jostling journalists, the BBC's Southern Africa correspondent thrust forward his microphone: 'Professor Evans, do you have any knowledge of nuclear weapons deployed by the South African army?'

The question was cleverly worded. Jim could not give a flat denial – but it didn't matter. At last, he could have *his* say. At last, he could pay some debts: to Hu and Hu's father, to the brave students in Beijing, to Dick Sewell, to the Zimbabweans ... and to Jenny.

He took a deep breath.

'The South Africans have battlefield nuclear warheads, developed in co-operation with several other countries: notably China. Pretoria must come clean, and Beijing must deal with the faction responsible for trading nuclear know-how and weapons with South Africa.'

The journalist did not interrupt. He already had a perfect clip for that evening's news bulletins.

The questioning went on for another twenty minutes. Jenny was pressed for an eye-witness account of the battle at the farmhouse – she could imagine a resurgence of 'Red Jen' stories in the London tabloids.

They had another question for her, too. Why had she come to Zimbabwe so soon after the Green Planet story had broken in London? She told them everything: her CIA suspicions and her fears about the duplicitous role of British Intelligence. Sceptically, she wondered how much of *that* would be printed.

As she talked, Jenny glanced towards Jim. He was surrounded by another camera crew, and someone was fixing a microphone to his shirt. They wanted his views on the dangers of nuclear radiation.

Would he ever be able to leave the world of activism behind, he asked himself? Could he return to his quiet, anonymous academic life?

Jim caught Jenny's eye, and smiled. He probably didn't want to.

Not now.

EPILOGUE

The kicks of her first baby sent a tremor through Florence's belly.

She excitedly called to the father: 'Come and feel!'

He placed his powerful hand tenderly upon her, remembering another beloved baby and mother – the family he'd once had, eviscerated by apartheid fighter jets.

So many years ago: now it was time to build a new life. He was no longer Major Keith Makuyana. He'd resigned, filled with foreboding about the autocratic and corrupt leadership of the President.

The security services had been compromised. They no longer served the nation, just the President's coterie. They didn't protect the people, just the ruling Party.

Although he hadn't asked her, Florence had followed. She too felt uncomfortable: an Ndebele woman in a Shona-dominated, male environment, under the command of an increasingly sectarian President.

They easily found jobs in the country's burgeoning private security sector – and soon became husband and wife.

Makuyana felt the baby stir. What sort of life would their child have in this young democracy? This beautiful land, for which he had sacrificed so much, whose future was now so precarious.

Still wondering, he stepped outside onto the veranda. He gazed up at the wide African sky, heard the music of birds and rasping cicadas. It was late afternoon and the lowveld was shimmering.

GLOSSARY

Amandla! – Power!
Awethu! – To the people!
betogers – Afrikaans for demonstrators
biltong – dried salty meat
bliksem! – Afrikaans slang for shock or annoyance
dassie – small rodent
lowveld – subtropical, low-lying region along the border with north-east South Africa and south-east Zimbabwe.
ouma – grandmother
oumie – granny
oupa – grandfather
rondavels – circular mud homes
stoep – veranda
uMkhonto weSizwe – ANC's paramilitary wing, or 'MK'
Unjani – Ndebele greeting: 'How are you?'

ACKNOWLEDGEMENTS

In September 1980 I was invited to join a quaintly-named 'Noted Persons Delegation' to visit China for three weeks, organised by the Society for Anglo-Chinese Understanding.

A fascinating time, shortly after the ignominious fall of the Gang of Four who had malevolently wielded power after the death of Mao Zedong four years earlier. The country I observed seemed poised between a communist past and a quasi-capitalist future.

I took detailed notes which formed the background to the novel I began writing in 1983, then paused before resuming in 1987. It was finally published by Lawrence & Wishart with a small print run in 1995 as *The Peking Connection.*

Set in the 1980s *Fallout* has been rewritten from that initial version. My thanks to my publishers Sarah and Kate Beal and Fiona Brownlee of Muswell Press – all a joy to work with – also to excellent line editor Fiona Lloyd.

I am grateful to our family friend and former apartheid political prisoner, the late Hugh Lewin for his guidance on Zimbabwe where he lived until democracy superseded apartheid; as well as to another friend and writer the late Roger Williams. Thanks also to my close friend and comrade André

Odendaal for his prescient advice, and – as always – to my marvellous wife Elizabeth Haywood who meticulously read and corrected a draft.

As a footnote, I returned to China as a British Labour cabinet minister in 2004, to find Beijing was no longer a cyclist-dominated, foreigner-curious city but a car-choked, polluted, modern metropolis.

The charming Forbidden City I'd first witnessed was much tattier and overrun by mass tourism. Visitors to the majestic Great Wall were perpetually harassed into purchasing unwanted merchandise or trinkets.

Progress and prosperity, certainly – but gone forever the enchanting place and people I had witnessed a quarter of a century earlier.